LionHearts

The Willowbend Beast

Sigfried A. Kneier

Book Cover & Chapter Heading by Sigfried A. Kneier

Map Design by Isaac T. Kneier

Edited by Isaac T. Kneier

ISBN: 979-8-218-65430-6

First Edition Paperback 2025

For my beloved partner in life and beyond, who convinced me that this novel was even worth finishing.

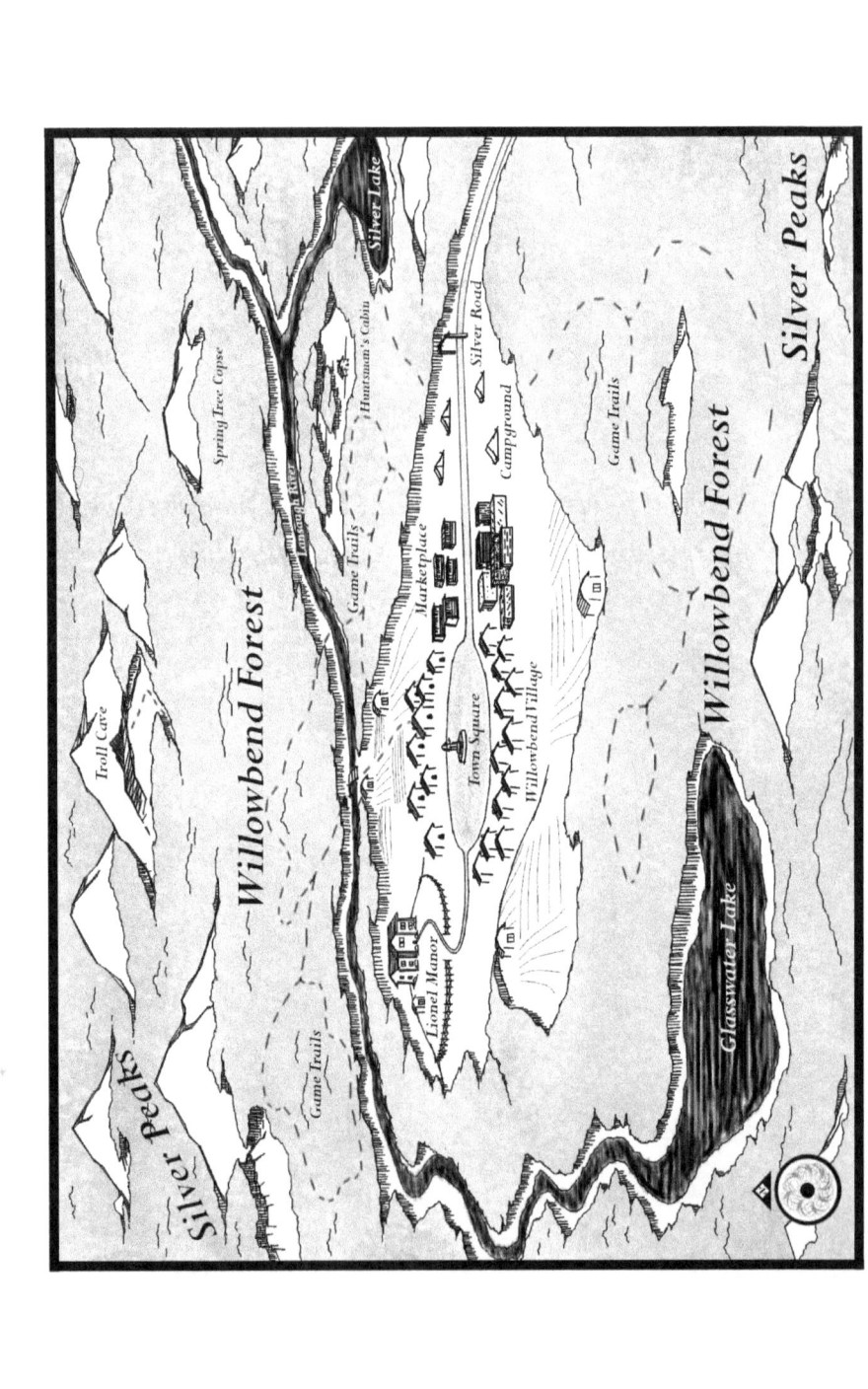

Chapter 1

Deep within the Willowbend Woods, high up in an alpine ridge, laid a profound cave. From the yawning maw of stone echoed a distinct noise, one that drove the birds to silence. A sound that would send a mortal man into a fit of anxiety. The sound of obsidian scoring across rock.

Ebony talons dragged along the ground, force dictated by a massive body. Bear-like in shape, the heft of its feathered arms forced each step into a thunderous plod. Its long, lion-like tail thrashed, struggling to maintain balance as it staggered. Tooth-like bones jutting out wildly like a pox from its hardened flesh bit into the walls as it fell to its side. The creature whimpered, holding up a human-like hand to touch the side of its mangled, weary face. A bony, beak-like muzzle filled with sharp fangs gasped as it forced itself to its limbs once more. Fleshy membranes flared within the beast's hole of a nose with each frustrated breath, leaking as if ill. As the creature approached a wall, the glowing blue rings inside its

1

black eyes narrowed. The damp, smooth surface was marred with various scratchings, like the attempts of a child learning to write.

The beast cried out, a sharp pang of agony racing against its skull. It lifted its body into a kneeling position, holding its head with its elongated forelimbs. A symbol. He had to write these symbols. One of those shaking talons pulled away from long, greasy black hair and began to write.

A....D....R...I.....A....N

The pain subsided as he wrote this, staggering away from the wall to examine the strange carvings. What did they mean? He had these pains before, usually after he woke up in cold, oily sweats. It was perplexing to say the least. Beasts like him shouldn't suffer with such night terrors, especially not with his mountain troll blood. While yes, he looked and acted a bit odd compared to the rest of his kind, surely he wasn't *that* bizarre. The troll shook his head. He stalked away from the wall and its torturous carvings to fish through the pile of bones at the other side of his cave. He stuck his beak into the pit, shifting the ossified carrion aside until he found a particularly delectable morsel. His neck ruff shivered as he pulled out the bone, a deer pelvis, and began to gnaw at it. It only took three hardy chomps before the pelvis cracked, releasing the wonderful aroma of bone marrow within. A long, sharp blackened tongue peeled away from his slavering maw, lapping at the nutritious meal eagerly. Those pains were dull now, only occasionally biting at his head. Like all things, it was temporary. When he sucked up the last of the marrow, he chewed up the bone and swallowed it, pulling out another piece to continue his meal.

The mountain troll crawled out of his cave and into the light, stretching like a cat in the morning sun. It was peaceful out here, hardly any other fae to speak of other than the Green Man, a forest troll that lived deeper in the woods. With no territories to fight for and no trespassers, the creature had little reason to pull away from his damp, warm den at all. Even so, a little walk or two never ceased to amuse him. He reared up, resting his weight on his back legs as he rose to his full twelve-foot tall height. His heavy feathers made it difficult to stand long-term, but something about it always felt right. Like this was how he was supposed to stand. The beast tilted his head up towards the sky, letting his hair catch the breeze and flutter behind him.

Slowly and deliberately, he began to hike down the slope of the ridge, taking care to stop and regain his balance. The bracken below crunched harmlessly against the hardened pads of his feet, catching in his tail fur, and scattered with each lash of the tip. The uninhibited sun gave way to a dull emerald dappling glow as he reached the bottom, finally falling to his forelimbs to begin stalking through the forest.

The birds and mammals scattered at the sight of him, a heralding of his status as a predator. He wandered along for a mile, stopping every so often to stare at a particular flower or flash of feathers that darted past. Beautiful bird songs caught his ear, making him tilt his head and serenely close his eyes as he walked. The troll would stop by a river, dipping his head down to lap at the clean water. His ghastly features reflected upon the glassy surface. Too alien for a troll. That fact prickled at his spine, making him snarl and pull back when he was finished. Blasted mirror... wait... what was a mirror?

Standing in front of glass. His reflection. He reached out with a claw. A human hand.

The troll hissed, shaking the distraction free. He gazed down at his claws below him. Perfectly normal. Beautiful talons and lumpy deep green skin. Some attractive spots of grey as well. The sight soothed his mind as he continued on, past the river and deeper into the woods. He could hear the distant striking of a hammer against steel, something his head leaned towards. He strained his ears, picking up a distant conversation.

"Corzan! Get the bloody tongs!" An older man... in his fifties? Must be Farin. He was the blacksmith of Willowbend Village.

"Yes sir!" A smaller, nervous voice. Corzan was very young, maybe fourteen years old by the troll's estimate. This was his first year as an apprentice, nervousness was to be expected. "Got them, sir!"

"About time, lad. Could you grab a fresh can of oil from the shed?"

"Yes sir!"

The conversation was already disappearing as he walked away, stalking towards a ravine. His talons dragged in the loose dirt as he slid down, his tail thrashing to catch his balance. When his feet had finally rested upon the flat stones below, he began to follow the dried river bed back towards his den. No need to hunt for food today. Surely the other carcasses he harvested the day prior were ready to be eaten. He stopped near a gradual slope that led into more woodland, taking a moment to judge his options. He chose to abandon the riverbed for the slope, climbing to the top and slinking deeper in the undergrowth.

The troll was trudging along, thinking about the symbols from earlier when he stopped, feeling something deep in his intestines. His heart beat loudly in his chest. His breathing quickened. A throbbing, painful desire. The desire to hold something, to take something into himself, to be one with something. A lace of pain pulled at his temple and he reared back, crying out.

A face. A woman's face. She was smiling at him.

He wailed, slamming his head against the dirt. The strike did not dislodge the memory. The throbbing filled his pelvis, forcing him to his knees. He held his stomach as if his organs would come spilling out at any moment.

A soft body. His hands gently caressing her sides.

The beast attempted to crawl away, trying to escape an invisible enemy. His hand clasped at his forehead, claws digging into his flesh. Yellow ichor dripped down his face as he fought against the tears. Why was he so sad? He wanted the foreign desire to go away. He wanted her face to stop hurting him. He flipped onto his back and pulled himself against an ancient oak. Shaking talons reached down, taking the hunger and soothing it. With a quiet gasp, the pain and desire disappeared, and he was overwhelmed with joy.

Her face was so close. Her hand was touching his cheek. He never felt so happy.

Yellow tears stained the troll's face as he was once again alone with his thoughts. His mouth opened in quiet sobs, pulling into himself to lay on his side. After a long moment of this, that horrible sorrow disappeared. Shaking limbs pulled his body back into a quadruped position, with his mind still spinning from the memory. Why did this happen? This wasn't the first time the strange desire and the human woman had overwhelmed him. He had been dealing with these feelings ever since he first woke up. As far as he knew, no other troll had desires like him, let alone mountain trolls. He was far too sentimental and passive, not even trying to chase off other lesser fae. No, he spent his days taking quiet walks, hunting only when he needed to, enjoying the company of the nearby village, and staring out over the landscape. None of which were proper activities for a mountain troll. He was supposed to kill, devour, sow chaos upon mortals, and annihilate any other fae that crossed him. Strange thoughts shouldn't bother him. He shouldn't be so weak. And he most certainly was not to touch his own body the way he did. His instincts told him as much. But those were always a tiny whisper, a minuscule buzzing that barely held any ground in his psyche. And the memories. They were getting worse. Ever since two years ago...

What was wrong with him?

"....Adrian?" a voice creaked like dry wood. Blue rings darted up to see a familiar face. He was covered in a dense mossy cloak, one that covered most of his bark-like skin. Leaves and lichen fell from the top of his head and down to his shoulders like hair. Delicate antlers decorated his brow, gnarled with thick bark and scattered leaves. Dewy spider webs laced between the crown, a halo of glittering thread that hung high over his shrouded face. He had black eyes, with small cherry blossom pinpricks that were his pupils. Above his jagged, wrinkled lips was the long hooked nose of his kin, something the mountain troll himself lacked. The Green Man. The hunched forest troll shuffled out of the bracken towards him tentatively. "Are you... alright? I heard your cries... from a few tree-lengths out..." he spoke slowly.

Adrian. My name.

6

The troll nodded, steadying his nerves before rearing up onto his hind legs. His arms sagged under the oppressive weight of his feathers, forcing them to his sides. The forest troll dared not to get any closer, instead inspecting him from afar. "I see... Are you sure.. ?" he asked, pink pinpricks gazing at him with worry. Adrian nodded his head. He was fine.

"Very well then... Do take care..." The Green Man bowed his head. Adrian did as well. As he trudged past the forest guardian he heard its body creak. "That human boy..." his voice cracked. The mountain troll turned. "He has wandered into the woods again... If you see him, take him home..." The beast grunted in response, nodding before turning away towards the mountain. He needed to rest.

His hands felt heavy as they stamped against the dusty ground. Adrian's head was sagging, the tip of his beak practically grinding against the pine brush. Today was just a bad day. That was all. He would be able to go home, lay down, and forget all about it. Just like he always did. After all, what was the point in chasing something that hurt him? Something in his gut twisted and his mouth opened in a growl. Yes. He killed his progenitor. No more pain. No more suffering. Something twitched at the corner of his vision. The blue rings turned, spotting a lone figure in the bushes.

It was a tall, shadowed, sullen creature. It wasn't fae... but he wasn't certain it was human either. The face was grey, stained with patches of sickly green. Sagging black skin rotted under its piercing blue eyes. A mangled cage of mismatched and random teeth gnashed silently as it breathed, the nose nothing more than a useless skeletal gash in its face. Inky hair cascaded down their shoulders and framed the hellish visage. The rest of the body below the sagging, fleshy neck

7

was coated in sharp, angular ebony armor engraved with scarlet and gold accents. Its head and back were arched back, held with the pride of a noble warrior. It was... staring at him. The troll stopped in its tracks. "W...HAT....WA..NT?" the beast hissed, glaring at the creature. His feathers flared with rage, making him appear gigantic, even more so than before. The figure did not back away, continuing to watch from the shadows with that unblinking stare. It didn't move when the troll reared up and snarled. Saliva was dripping from the beast's maw, an acidic ooze that bleached the leaf litter white. "WH...AT?!" he roared. Those piercing blue eyes merely turned as the figure began to move towards the brush, as if disinterested or... disappointed? The audacity! The troll was sent into a fury, throwing his body at the intruder. How dare he look at him with pity! He was prey! How dare he?! How-

Adrian felt a bolt of pain race up his muzzle as he crashed into the thick trunk of a weathered oak. Against all odds, the forest giant remained upright, albeit at an awkward angle and with a massive gouge in its gnarled bark. Leaves scattered around him in a soft rain as the troll fell back, holding his beak in pain. Blood poured from his nose cavity, weaving between his fingers in golden rivulets. His enraged eyes snapped open, searching for the man. The beast's tail thrashed against the undergrowth, his talons raking across the foliage, hoping to strike flesh. Nothing. The wraith was gone. Adrian growled, feeling foolish for chasing a ghost.

Probably a filthy fairy playing tricks on him.

He was fed up with the forest for the day. With a sharp crack of his whip-like tail, he slashed the undergrowth clean, leaving nothing but shredded debris. He knew the Green Man would be frustrated with him for such unwarranted destruction, but what did it matter? He was a mountain troll, he could just as well kill him too.

That thought caught in his mind. ...He couldn't... He didn't want to harm him. It was thanks to the Green Man that he learned what he was and how to find his place in the forest. He helped him secure the cave and taught him how to avoid mortals. He protected his escapes with bramble and bracken when a curious hunter got too close. He always made sure he had a place here in Willowbend. He told him his name. No, he was a friend. Adrian could never kill his only friend.

Chapter 2

The troll dug its claws into the cliffside before launching himself up the rock face with ease. As he finally reached the top and crawled up to the entrance of his cave, he froze. There was something echoing within the darkness. Prey? He instinctively lowered his body to the ground, letting his rocky skin blend with the surrounding stone. He pulled his feathers tight between his legs, hiding their bright colors and leaving only black and bone. His mouth watered. Perhaps fresh meat was what he needed. The noises within stopped, seemingly hearing the scraping of his talons against the gravel. He cursed his eagerness, pulling his massive frame off to the side of the yawning entrance. He had to fight the torrent of saliva attempting to fall between his exposed fangs, lapping it up as quietly as he could. The noises began once more, coughing. Gagging. Odd. They sounded human. What was a human doing all the way up here?

He has wandered into the woods again... If you see him, take him home.

The human boy? Stars and bones. Adrian growled and pulled himself back onto his forelimbs, striding into the cave with an irritated lash of his tail. The human spotted him before he did. He heard the rapid tappings of small feet to his left. With a sudden flourish of his crimson wing arm, he slammed it down in front of the sounds with a confident snort. Watching the shadowed human falling on its hindquarters with a yelp made a smile curl at his fangs. He turned his glowing blue eyes towards the sound, a dull cerulean light falling upon the terrified form of a human child. The boy couldn't have been more than twelve years old at this point, his tiny frame and awkward proportions indicative of what Adrian had seen of other young humans.

"Wha- wait!" the boy cried out, shielding his face as the troll's other talon reached out. The beast stopped, almost in amusement. "I- I'm warning you! I-I'm not very g-good eatings!!" the small voice whimpered, backing away fearfully.

"OH???" Adrian's thunderous voice echoed through the caverns, his fangs glimmering in the dull light. He stepped forward, blocking the rest of the entrance with his tail.

"Y-yes!! Trust me! W-Wren says I have a terrible diet! I would surely sit like a rock in your stomach!" He pointed his scrawny hands towards his own body.

"SOU....NDS... YU..MMY...." the troll hissed, lapping at his fangs as he lowered his menacing skull. Ah, scaring children was so terribly fun. The boy's frown comically deepened as he scrambled to reach for something at his belt. The troll looked on in amusement,

11

watching the boy pull out a laughably small knife and point it at his beak. He felt a thunderous spasm in his chest as he stifled his laugh.

"F-fine then, rock eater! I'll h-have you know my father slayed beasts like you!!" the boy's voice cracked. The child staggered to his feet.

"OH??? IS....TH..AT....SSSSO?" Adrian hissed, stalking forward. His eyes were deadly slits, glowing with restrained savagery.

"Y-yes! And I'm s-s-sure I got some of that power in me too!!!" he yelped, backing against the cave wall.

He couldn't take it anymore. The beast threw his head back and a horrifying caw exited his throat. It was a rattling sound that shook the cave walls and made the trembling boy clutch at his ears. The troll had to rest his weight on a forearm to keep his balance. What a funny little creature. After wiping the tears from his eyes, the troll effortlessly plucked the little human up by the back of his shirt, pulling it close to his face as he breathed a rotten breath.

"FI...NE.... LITT...LE...SLA...YER... HAV..E...AT...ME..." he sneered, making sure that puny knife was within range. The boy did what he expected; cry. What he didn't expect was the blade being driven directly into his nose. The troll's eyes widened as the boy gripped at his face with an animalistic fury and began stabbing, over and over again. His claws released their grip on the shirt, but the child held firm, jamming the knife deep into his bleeding flesh. He tried to gingerly remove the stinging gnat from his muzzle with a talon, only to get slashed there too. He pulled his finger away with an irritated shake, glaring at the creature attached to his nose. As annoyed as Adrian was... he couldn't help but be impressed. All he would have to do was yank him into his maw with a little lash of his tongue, one motion and the boy would be dead. But here he was, fighting for dear life.

Something about that felt familiar. The beast sighed, letting the lad go mad with his stabbings as he turned his frame back towards the entrance of the cave. He walked out with the screaming mass of metal and child still attached before setting his muzzle down on the flat rocks outside. At the touch of rough stone against his boots, the boy stopped, looking at the creature in confusion. "I... HA..VE... BEE...N... SLAY....ED... CAN... YO..U... GO... NO..W...?" he sighed.

"Wha... what?" The lad stepped back and away from the bleeding bone. "You're... just letting me go?" The troll nodded, rubbing at his face with an irritated talon. He rested on his belly, making no hostile motions. "Why? Aren't you gonna eat me?"

The troll raised a brow. "ARE...N'T... YOU... AF...RAID...?"

"Well, yeah! But... you're a troll, right?" The boy's green eyes scanned the beast's curious form. Adrian nodded. "You eat people, don't you?"

He shrugged. He lowered his voice to a more acceptable level. "You...sa..id...you... ta...ste... bad..." Another comical expression decorated the blood-soaked child: pure dumbfounded confusion.

"Y-yeah but you said-!" The boy shook the bloody knife at him, scattering golden droplets all around the stone. The troll just licked at its wounded finger as he plucked the boy by the back of the collar with his other hand and turned him around, facing the trail to Willowbend Village.

13

"Go..." he sniffed, lapping at his mangled face. Blasted iron. It would take a while for this to heal.

"What? Hey, answer my questions!" the dark-haired lad snapped. There was another familiar expression: indignation.

"GO..." he snarled, flicking him in the back with a claw. The boy yelped and staggered away, pointing the weapon at him again.

"You will answer me! B-" his bravado quickly melted against the troll's withering gaze. "-Uuttt I guess I better go now! This isn't our last meeting, troll!" The lad shook a fist before running off into the brush.

Something in his mind told him that he should have come along to make sure he arrived safely, but Adrian couldn't find the energy or care. Instead, he turned back towards his den and gazed down at his nest. Piles of stolen hay, bones, and parchment littered the pressed nest, weathered under the years he spent laying here. He loved the smell of fresh paper, so much so that he couldn't help but steal some from the village in the night, maybe even grab one of those book-things they adored. He was always careful with them, as they were so delicate and bizarre. Those interesting piles of scribblings always rested by the nest, ready to be plucked and examined. He settled his massive body into the bedding, curling his tail in as he grabbed one of those books. A small violet tome with embossed patterns on the front. His favorite. He couldn't read the writings, but he knew there was a story somewhere inside. And this one... it had a beautiful smell. A smell that made him feel happy. He stole this one from the largest house by the forest, the place he first tried to hide in. He didn't know why he wanted to hide there, the doorways could barely fit his frame and a woman lived there... but that's where he found this book. He rubbed the leather cover with a talon, gingerly prying it open to gaze at the scribblings. He sensed a reason with these symbols, shaped much like the ones his mind forced him to scrawl. The troll had to resist the urge to touch the page with his claws. The last time he did, he had shredded the paper, though thankfully not from this book. So instead he just stared, trying to make sense out of the symbols. How did humans come up with stories? It seemed so senseless. Making up something not real. He tried to scrunch his sore muzzle to force an idea to the forefront but nothing came to mind. Instead, the symbols remained. Alien, yet familiar.

He set the book down, turning to lay on his stomach. The sunlight barely reached this far back in the cave, leaving Adrian in darkness. He sighed, the pain in his face making it hard to shut his thoughts away. This truly was an abysmal day... perhaps hunting later in the night would brighten his spirits. He could only hope as he nestled into his ruff of feathers and shut his eyes.

Chapter 3

He was running past the wailing screams of fire. Glowing, lashing tongues reached out to lick at his tender skin. He was in incredible pain. His flesh ached, his bones creaked, his muscles burned. But he kept running. He had to help them. He had to make that beast see that only he was a worthy enemy.

Blue eyes opened. Unlike some of his other dreams, this one did not frighten him too much. It was odd. Fire was the ultimate enemy of troll-kind... yet in that dream... he was fearless. Adrian was almost envious. The troll heaved his heavy skull out from his curled arms, picking at the gouges still in the bony muzzle. He turned, peering over a stalagmite that shielded his nest from encroaching light. It was dark, with only the cheerful chirps of crickets reaching his pointed ears. The troll sat up, taking a moment to stretch out his back like a forest cat before trudging outside. Adrian's head tilted towards the sky, staring up at the thousands of sparkling lights in the inky blackness. Stars whose light shone down upon him without fail every night. He smiled at this fact, closing his eyes to let a cool evening breeze caress his ruff.

Her hand ran down his calloused neck with the tenderness of touching glass.

Adrian shuddered, shaking his head. None of that. It was time for him to start acting like a proper troll. The beast started down the slope and disappeared noiselessly into the woods.

Like most of his kin, if he wanted to go unseen, he could. It was something he enjoyed as a troll, allowing him to hunt for prey and watch the mortals in peace. Humans were certainly curious little creatures, what with their smooth flesh and tiny frames. Why, they didn't even have claws or sharp teeth. How could they have possibly survived as long as they did? That was a question Adrian pondered frequently.

Before he knew it, he caught the scent of deer musk. A male was rutting, marking territory and generally making a fool of itself. His talons pressed into the cool dirt methodically, sniffing the soiled leaves as he passed by a bush. His eyes flicked over towards the south, the location of the village. Figures. The deer loved the lichen that grew along the wooden fences of the northern pass, with no prevalence quite like the village border. He followed the scent, stopping only to sniff the air again. His tail was relaxed, sliding along the undergrowth like a snake, avoiding the loud brackens and twigs with a fluid motion. This was his element. This is where he belonged.

Before long, he found his quarry, a two-year old buck that quietly stalked a clearing as the females feasted upon some rotted fences. The few fawns were staying close to their mothers, a nostalgic eagerness wafting from them. But his eyes were on the buck. Their bones were particularly delectable, protein-rich and full of flavor. He could already imagine the warm ichor dripping down his tongue, making him salivate. The troll was about twenty yards from the prey. He could wait.

For several minutes, he was motionless. Moments that felt agonizing for his empty stomach. Closer... Closer... the buck was fifteen yards out. Just five more yards. Five more and he could leap for it. He could already taste it. The savory iron aroma. Smooth flesh oozing down his throat. The cracking of bones. The melting of fur. The popping of organs in his jaws. His muscles bunched, his eyes narrowed in on the prey. Four... three... two...

One.

An arrow shot out of the dark, striking the buck in its thigh. It let out an alarmed shriek as it reared up. The does and fawns fled past the shocked troll before he gathered his bearings. The buck began to dart into the woods towards Adrian's right as he gave chase. A foolish hunter tried to steal his prey! He wouldn't let it win. He launched his body forward, smashing through the brush to catch up to the terrified animal. He wasn't quite as fast as his dinner but he was persistent. An injury on its thigh would inevitably tear at the muscles, making it slow enough to catch. He just needed to give it a reason to tear.

He could hear the hunter far behind, trying to chase the quarry as well. No matter. Adrian could easily dispatch and hide the carcass long before those weak legs ever did. He smirked, the thrill of the hunt filling him with a primal joy. The deer was six paces away now. It was starting to flag. The muscles in his legs bunched. Like a bolt of lightning, the troll catapulted into the air, claws outstretched.

He knew his feathers would slow him down, but by then it would be too late. Victory was within his grasp-

An arc of pain raced up his leg, the beast gasping in agony. His claws reflexively clenched and failed to catch the animal in time as it darted to the left and he slammed into the earth. A howl of rage exited his maw, dragging his shaking leg behind him. It felt as if it was lit on fire. Adrian whipped his head around, spotting an arrow lodged into his calf. He hissed, snatching the shaft and yanking it out with a talon. A glint of cold iron flashed against his glittering eyes. A shape disappeared into the brush.

How dare he?!

Golden saliva frothed from the edges of his jaw, his body shaking. The burning remained, long after the metal was gone. How dare a human injure him?! Before rage could drive him to madness, he heard another bellow from his prey. His snarl deepened as he rushed ahead, albeit with a painful limp. The hunter would be there. He could just kill him and have two bodies to eat. A feral grin grew on his face as the smell of blood intensified. The arrowhead must have shredded an artery on the deer's flank. Even now he could see and smell the sweet blood on the edges of leaves.

Only a little longer... and both prizes are mine.

Just as the troll reached the clearing leading to the fallen animal, he ducked down, waiting for the hunter to arrive. The dense, dark leaves of the vines and bushes hid his large body well, weaving like they wound against any other rock. Adrian shut his jaws tight, determined to not let his pungent breath give him away this time. He watched as the moonlit buck brayed weakly, trying to stagger to its feet. The injured leg hung limply, tangled in the dark vines reaching out from the forest floor. It fought against the foliage, driving its antlers into the plant and trying to wrench itself free. It wouldn't be enough, however, as the vine was far stronger and older than the young antlers could handle. The scent of blood hung heavy in the air and made the troll impatient. He was so hungry.

Thankfully, he didn't have to wait long. A bramble bush shuddered and shook before a hooded human figure pulled itself free, waltzing into the clearing. The small hunter was covered in leaf litter and a leather coat slightly too large for their person. They had a bow held to their back, a quiver of crudely-crafted arrows bumping against the weapon. They held a knife in their hand, cautiously approaching the animal. He was so close. Adrian readied himself. He would make the human regret ever hurting him. His jaws parted when the person struggled to get near the thrashing animal, holding his hands up with a gasp every time those sharp antlers got close.

The troll sprung, landing on top of the deer hard, snapping its neck cleanly with a small splatter of blood. The hunter fell back, trying to crawl away. The beast's talons lashed out, snatching the human before it could get to its feet.

"FIN...AL...LY..." Adrian sighed, pulling the struggling creature close to his face. It fought against his grasp, but with their arms bound to their sides, there was nowhere to go, no way to fight. The beast couldn't help but relish this moment, this joy. This was what it meant to be a troll. These were his lands and this creature was nothing to him. Just more prey... he hesitated.

No.

He jolted, shaking his head. A voice?

I don't eat humans.

That's... right. He never ate a human before. He would never harm a villager. He could never hurt them. The beast snarled in frustration, dropping the human unceremoniously to the ground. He had his food, no reason to cause further trouble. Adrian already turned and plucked the carcass into his jaws when he heard the human speak.

"Again?! You're letting me go again?" the voice cracked with inexperience.

Adrian's blue eyes turned. He recognized that voice. "Y..OU..." the troll growled. He shifted his massive head to see the figure standing, bow aimed at his head. With their hood down, he could see the shoulder-length black hair shining in the night. Those bright green eyes glaring at him. The boy.

"Why did you let me go again?" he asked, trying to hide his fear under a level tone. But the bow and string were shaking, and his voice was too small, too weak.

"I... DO..N'T... KILL... HU...MANS..." he stated plainly, the rumbling of his voice failing to make him sound passive.

"But I struck you, w-which was an accident I should say, but aren't you angry?!" the boy's voice quaked. He tensed up when the troll fully turned and approached him, rearing up to his full height. The quivering child barely held onto the weapon, the looming figure blocking the moonlight and casting him in an eerie shadow. Only those piercing blue eyes shone against the black.

"OF... COU...RSE... BU...T... I... WI...LL.. N..OT... HU..RT..VIL...LAGE..." the troll gasped, fighting with his memory of words. They were coming in waves.

"Y-you promise?" the boy pressed.

The troll blinked. What a nonsensical question. He said he wouldn't, did he not? With a solemn sigh, he snorted, "I... PROM...ISE..."

Tentatively, the lad lowered his weapon, pulling the arrow away to rest his arms limply at his sides. The child let out a breath that they seemed to have been holding for quite some time. "If you're not gonna eat me, then why were you out here?" he finally asked.

"HUN...TIN...G..." the beast growled, nodding towards the deer.

"Y-yeah?" The child paused to glance at the deer. Their expression morphed. "Well, I shot it first so it's finder's keepers!" he sniffed, putting his hands on his hips.

What on earth did 'finder's keepers' mean? He blinked, shaking his head. "I... KIL..LED... IT... MI...NE..."

"Nuh uh! I shot it! My arrow was gonna kill it before your fat butt sat on it!" the boy yelled, almost forgetting he was arguing with a troll.

"FAT?!" the beast snarled. The child leapt back. "YO...UR... AR..ROW... WA..S... MAK...ING SUF...FUR...ING... NO... KILL...!" the creature snarled, circling him. The boy instinctively pulled out his knife, the one that hurt the beast earlier.

"I was going to hit its head till you jumped in the way of the arrow, you bloody vulture!" he argued.

Vulture.

Something about that word made Adrian lurch back, clutching his head. A burning in his brain like a hot iron. He cried out, falling backwards from the child and dragging himself away. The boy stood dumbfounded. "...huh?" When he saw the creature whimpering and trying to crawl away, he glanced at his weapon and dropped it, rushing over to his side. "H-hey! What's wrong?!"

You're not a vulture! A vulture wouldn't save me! They just take what they want and leave! You didn't do that!

A woman's voice howled in his mind, filling it with images of crimson and flashes of metal. His whimpers continued. "ST...OP..."

"S-stop what? What did I do?" In a panic, the child threw his remaining weapons away, like they were somehow hurting the creature.

Vulture... I don't like that word. Is that what I am? Am I...

The beast stopped. His exhales became ragged. He blinked, almost in confusion. The troll heaved itself onto its hind legs, staggering when they couldn't hold the weight of his arms. He blinked again, like trying to scatter a dream. He looked at his arms. Feathers. So many feathers.

Vulture! Vulture! Vulture!

He yowled in fear, flinching away from his own outstretched limbs. The boy jumped away from the thrashing beast, pressing himself against a tree in alarm. The creature fell back against a rock. Tears ran down his face as a claw reached out and started pulling. Agony laced his bones as a wad of feathers were yanked free, bleeding all over his chest and legs. The troll tried again, pulling more feathers.

Get them off! Get them off!

"S-stop it!" a voice cried as hands grabbed at his tail. Adrian kept pulling. "You're hurting yourself! Whatever I did, I'm sorry!!! Please stop! Stop!"

Adrian's eyes snapped open. He felt pain all over his arms. He lifted them, seeing patches of feathers missing, some still attached to his quivering claws. What just happened? He blinked, staring at the blood flowing from his arms and staining his body. His eyes moved from that image to the sight of the boy crying and holding onto his tail. Stars and bones, did he hurt him? One of his claws reached out and when the boy saw it he flinched. Adrian pulled away reflexively. "A...RE...Yo..u... al...rig..ht?" the troll whispered.

"Y-yeah, just scared my soul right out of my body!" the child wheezed, finally letting go and stepping back.

"hu...rt?"

"N-no. Just freaked out. I know I was... Well, I didn't like you... But I didn't want to give you a panic attack..." The boy's eyes flicked towards the ground, rubbing his shoulder.

The troll gazed at his bloodied arms. New pin feathers were already growing in. "pan...ic... at...tack...?" He tilted his head in confusion.

"Yeah, they're like, terrifying moments that make you wanna cry and run away. Sometimes you hurt yourself. Wren gets those sometimes..." the child mumbled, looking nervous. Wren. The woman living at the large house in the village. He had seen her before. He liked her voice.

"I...se..e..." he nodded. Panic attack... that doesn't sound like something a mountain troll should have... and yet... The beast continued to ponder this, even while he began to lick at his wounds.

"Are you ok?" the boy suddenly asked, looking up with conflicted worry.

Adrian nodded. "I... he..al... fa..st..."

"Oh. Yeah. Troll..." The child sat down, watching the creature nervously. The clearing was silent for some time, just the sounds of a wet tongue lashing against the troll's skin and the crickets chirping. "Um. You might be a monster and all..." the boy began. Blue rings glanced up to meet his face. "But... I don't think my dad would kill you. You seem like a fairly nice troll..." The beast blinked in confusion. "Well, you didn't kill me, that's the first thing. And the second thing is that," the boy explained, pointing at Adrian's head. The beast's brow furrowed, trying to feel his face. There was wet against his cheek. Tears.

"Trolls can't cry. Not the bad ones. But you can. Maybe that means you're not an evil monster after all," the child explained.

"I... am... moun...tain... tr..oll..." he pointed to himself.

"Maybe, but those guys eat humans and terrorize villages and stuff. From what I've seen, you don't. Cause I've been here for awhile and I haven't seen or heard of any troll attacks," the boy shrugged, flicking a leaf off of his trousers.

"If... no..t... tr..ol.l... wha...t... am... I?" Adrian growled. Of course he was a troll. The Green Man told him. His own mind told him. He was a troll.

"I don't know," the kid shrugged again. "Maybe you're just a person..."

A thunderous cawing sound erupted from the troll's mouth, the explosive noise making the child jump. He was laughing at the boy. "F...ool... I... am... no... hu...man..."

The child's face scrunched and he crossed his arms. "I never said that! I didn't say 'human', I said 'person'. You don't need to be human to be one!" he snapped.

The troll stopped laughing to ponder this for a moment. Was he a 'person'? If 'person' wasn't the same as human, what did it mean? He wouldn't bother trying to get a good answer from a child. No, he would ask the Green Man. He was far older than any creature that lived in the village or himself. He lowered his massive head to stare at the lad. "F...ine... am... per...son... now... wh..at?"

The boy's emerald eyes blinked. "Uh, I don't know. Persons like to chat and stuff. Make friends. Play games. Do jobs. Tell each other their names."

"Na....mes? Na..me... ha..ve... po..wer..." the troll grunted. As if he would tell him his name.

"Yeah? Well, mine's Vantis Lionel. One of the most powerful names in the world!" Vantis boasted, puffing out his chest.

"Oh... re..al..ly?" The beast smirked.

"Of course! I come from a long line of monster slayers! And when I become a full-grown man, I'ma be one too!" Those eyes glittered with an eager light.

The troll snorted. A monster would find this child a fitting toothpick, not a slayer. He sighed. "Fo...ol... don..t.. tell... fae... na...me..."

"I'd like to see you try to do something about it," the kid smirked. What an idiot. "Tell me yours, Mr. Not-evil-troll-person, it's only fair!"

"I... ne..ver... ag..re..ed... to... sa..y... na...me..." Adrian scowled, his head pulling back towards his ruff.

"Aww, come on, please!! I can't call you Not-evil-troll-person forever!" Vantis whined. "Please???"

The beast sighed, rubbing his temple with a talon. "Fi...ne... ca..ll.. me..." he started, pausing when he realized he couldn't find a decent name. At least one he wouldn't be embarrassed about having this child say. He thought long and hard, wishing the wait would make the child lose interest. But there he was, starlight sparkling off of those eager eyes. Once again the troll sighed. "Ca..ll... me... Li...on..."

"Lion?" Vantis echoed, perplexed.

Adrian nodded. "I... at..e... a..ll... moun...tain... li..ons... I... ta..ke... pla..ce... no..w..."

The boy blinked. "That's... SO AMAZING!" The loud sound made the troll cringe. "You know, my last name is Lionel! And they say my ancestor rode a massive lion! And you ATE all the ones here?! That's so awesome! It's like fate or something!!" The child grandly gestured towards the sky. Adrian already regretted his decision. "Maybe that means we can be friends or something!"

Stars and bones...

The troll stood up onto all-fours, starting to make his way toward the carcass. "Ye...s... we...ll... hun...gry..."

Vantis blinked. "Y-yeah! Sure! Friends give each other gifts! And here," he ran up to the animal and slapped its flank. "Is my gift to you!"

The troll gave him a mixed expression of horror and annoyance. "Ye..s... acc...ept...ed... go... ho..me... now..." he grumbled, snatching up the carcass and dragging it away into the woods.

"Of course! I'll see you later then! Bye, Lion!"

Chapter 4

Adrian enjoyed his meal quietly, mulling over what was said. A person. He needed to know what that word meant. Could a troll be a person? Maybe that's why he saw that horrible man. Did other trolls who were persons have the same problem? The fact that he had these foreign human desires was terrible enough. Was he cursed then? His mind darted from question to question until his head was full of buzzing noise. It was the snap of a bone that jolted his attention towards the present. Warm marrow poured down his throat and soothed his stomach. Adrian sighed. It was meaningless to dwell on such things now. He dragged the carcass away towards the side of the cave entrance, having his fill of meat. The flies could have the rest, he would simply pick the bones later. He lumbered back over to the rocky entrance and sat down, crossing his legs as his feathers draped over his frame like a cape.

Adrian lifted his gaze up to the stars. They were so simple, shining up there. They shone so diligently, so proudly. They never interacted with anything. They just were. Sometimes he wished he was a star. Maybe then he could live in peace. Maybe then the nightmares would stop. Maybe then he wouldn't be so worried about being a terrible example of a troll. Could fae make wishes? Humans made wishes all the time, praying upon idols and dark powers for all their desires. Can a creature like him make a wish? Did he deserve a wish? Adrian seemed to realize how ridiculous of a thought process it was. Trolls don't make wishes or care about such things.

Then what does that say about me?

He blinked. He looked down at his claws. They were well-worn, scarred from years of walking upon his palms. The lumpy green flesh creased as a finger twitched. He reached out and rubbed one of his palms with his other hand, an expression of sorrow on his features. These claws were his, these feathers were his, this body was his.

So why was he unhappy?

The Green Man would know. He told Adrian everything thus far, this would be no different. He ran his fangs down the newly unfurled feathers, meticulously preening the oily wings. He had to shake his hair away every time it draped over his eyes, making him grunt.

Wasn't there a way to stop that?

He thought about this for a moment before making his way into the cave, stopping by his pile of trinkets to pull out a long spool of red ribbon. He collected this shiny thing from a traveling merchant, so enamored by its color and texture that he had to have it. He did try to trade the man how he saw the humans do. So he gave him a chunk of silver ore he found within his cave, setting it in the wagon before the troll was seen. Humans seemed to like metal and Adrian's cave had it in abundance. What purpose would he have for rocks anyhow?

The creature took its prize and flopped down onto his hindquarters with a soft thud. He adjusted his wing arms so that the feathers draped away from his lap, giving the beast an adequate workspace. He unwound the ribbon, gazing at it with the intensity of a flame. Humans tied knots all the time, how difficult could it be? His clumsy hands messed with the ribbon for a while, growling every time the knot failed and fell apart. At first, one of his talons snagged against the line. Next, his finger was stuck in a loop and he had to shake it out. Then he was too gentle and the arrangement fell away in his hands like slow-cooked meat. One problem after another, more confusion after every minute action. "MU...ST... B..E... TI..N..Y... HA...N..DS..." he grunted with an irritated flick of his tail. Adrian thought he was being clever, using a knot to tie his hair back. He sighed, letting the line rest in his lap as he lowered his head.

A shift in the shadows made him jolt. Blue rings snapped up beneath the curtain of hair to spy an eerie figure. The man was watching him from the inky blackness of the cave's interior, just between two stalagmites. The troll's breath stilled, watching the intruder with alarm. Where did he come from? How did he get here? Without a sound, the man lifted his arms, revealing a string between them. One hand was human enough, but the other was more... troll-like than anything. Thick, lumpy green flesh dotted with various tooth-like bony protrusions, with an elongated hand sporting long black talons on each tip. It was frighteningly familiar. The beast blinked at the string before growling at the man. Wordlessly, with those piercing eyes still staring into his soul, the man lifted the string and held the two ends. He moved them across each other and wound them together. It was the beginning of a knot. The troll glanced down at his ribbon, hesitating before picking it up and mimicking the shadowy man. After a few attempts, he had what the man made. The ghastly figure continued, showing the troll the next few steps before stopping, waiting for his student to catch up. Before long, the troll was effortlessly mirroring the man, even when the teacher had put the string to his hair and refused to turn around. The beast did the same with the ribbon, continuing until the knot was securely holding his oily locks. The creature, realizing what he did, reached up to feel the ribbon in his hair, reflexively turning as if to see it. When he turned to face the man once more to say something, the noise caught in his throat.

The apparition was gone.

Adrian looked around, sniffing the air, and straining his ears. There was no one there. He shook his head, getting up on all fours before padding over to the entrance once more to continue preening. After an hour of work, his feathers looked immaculate. The beast rested on his haunches, extending his wing arms to let the heavy feathers breathe in the night air. He couldn't fly, but his feathers were sharp, deadly. They made him feel beautiful, albeit bizarre as a troll. The new ivory tips clashed heavily against the stained red ones. This would not do. The troll got up, climbed up to the side of the cave mouth, and wound through the boulders until he found a small pool of reddish liquid. A spring flowed from the ice-capped mountains, bringing water and this odd red clay with it. He was certain it was made of iron, as drinking large amounts made him sick. But applying it to his feathers had no ill effects; if anything, they made the wings far more enchanting to look at. He reached in with a claw and rubbed the thick fluid on his feathers, slowly staining them crimson. Dried blood, the more reasonable option to his carnivorous habits, always looked terrible on his wings, more of a fetid brown than anything. This red, however, matched him quite nicely. He gave the wings a flourish, letting the clay and water fall away. Finally, back to normal.

The beast proudly arched out his neck, puffing out his ruff. He almost wished he had white on those feathers to dye them too. His beak twisted into a ghastly grin as he made his way back down the slope. A part of him wished that there were other mountain trolls nearby. Then he could have a regular territorial fight every now and then. He could show off his feathers and his intelligence. He wouldn't have to be afraid of spilling some blood. And he would have less of a reason to worry about stupid thoughts and feelings that had no place in a fae's life.

Adrian jolted as he felt the slap of oily locks against his back as he dropped down a small cliff. He still had his hair tied. The creature halted on the slope, reaching up tentatively to touch the ribbon. It felt so... normal. He never tied his hair back before... but this felt so familiar. The troll almost liked it. He sat up, looking at the loose ends of the ribbon drifting against his ruff. A talon picked one up, examining it. How strange... How can someone feel nostalgic for something they never saw before?

Perhaps it was another weird side-effect of this whole 'person' thing. If that was the case, it would be best to remove it. He deftly pulled at the end, untying it in one fluid motion and sending the rest of the ribbon drifting to the floor. He plucked it from the ground, carefully dusting it off before continuing his walk with it firmly held in his jaws. He leapt off the top of the cave entrance, landing with a soft thud.

Adrian padded inside, rewound the ribbon around the spool, and placed it gingerly in the pile. Other objects rested here; scrolls, non-iron tools, rocks he liked, bird feathers, a jar of ink with a pretty wax seal, some furs, bones that were too interesting to eat, and some worn human clothes somebody left behind that he used as a napkin... all of these things were his treasures. He would not part with a single one. He gazed upon them with a possessive fondness before flopping into his nest. The beast craned his neck to look at his leg. The hole was still burnt into his calf, throbbing after all the movement in the night. A snarl escaped his throat, taking a scrap of cloth laying on a rock and wrapping it around his leg. He grunted at the tightness, yet knew it was necessary. He may be resistant to illness, but not immune. With his wound sufficiently covered, he laid down on his stomach, breathing in the comforting scent of parchment. Soon enough, his mind drifted off with the smell and landed deep in his dreams.

'Momma?'

'Yes, sweetheart?' Her voice was a soft blanket. Warmth and love.

'Why don't you get outta bed? I wanna play outside with you!' He was sad. Confused.

'...oh darling, I'm sick.' Her eyes were clouded with sorrow. Her hair was a funeral shroud.

'When will you get better?'

'I'm not quite sure...'

'Will you be able to write your story?'

She enveloped him with her arms. She was so warm. Her eyes were so wonderful. He wanted to cry. 'Yes, I believe I can. I promise you'll be able to read it when I'm done...'

Blue rings opened slowly, fighting against the crust of tears that coated them. Adrian was holding something in his right hand delicately. His fingers pried themselves away, revealing a weathered book. His favorite. He stared at it for a while. "Mo.. ther..." he whispered, pulling the book into his lumpy chest. He was certain trolls didn't have parents, only progenitors.

According to the Green Man, Adrian had killed his own when he was created. But this person, the woman... he genuinely felt he knew her and... missed her. Mother. Was this book hers? The talons gingerly pulled away and opened the front cover. He desperately wanted to know what it said. He wanted to touch the pages. He wanted...

Adrian roared, leaping away. For a moment, there was a human hand, *his* hand, reaching out towards the book. The tome flopped harmlessly onto the floor. The troll's vision darted down to his arms. Normal. With a swift motion, he plucked the book off the floor, dusted it off, and set it back on top of the others. "J..ust... a... dr...ea..m... no... fam..il..y..." he wheezed, rubbing his head. Sunlight was filtering through the caverns, striking the plates of bone on his shoulders and making them glitter like fangs.

Adrian sighed, padding his way out of the cave and beginning his search. Unfortunately, saying names was out of the question for him. He struggled to say the most basic of phases, let alone muster the power to summon a powerful name. He would have to look for the Green Man naturally, with only his eyes and nose to guide him. He snuffled and chuffed along the undergrowth, more like a bear than a fae. He lumbered throughout the woods until he finally caught the scent of old magic in the air. It drifted through the morning breeze like a loose filament of thread, weaving and twisting in his mind's eye. The beast followed the scent, feeling the magic caress his face and pass through his body. It made him shiver. Even though he was fae, he couldn't use magic. Unlike the Green Man, he couldn't make a flower bloom or the vines dance. Even so, magic seemed drawn to him, dragging itself into his flesh where it would stay, lodged in his body. Usually the threads of energy would linger for only a moment, but over the past year they were beginning to stay with greater frequency. The build up was starting to burn in his gut. Adrian shook his head. It was a worthy pain. He needed answers, even if it made the magic burrow deeper. It was a long journey through that dense forest, underbrush and detritus catching in his talons and hooking onto his hard, lumpy flesh. The dappled light overhead cast him in an emerald glow, making him almost appear a forest troll himself.

His beak parted, sucking in another breath. More magic weaved into his throat. He fought the urge to cough. He was close. Visually speaking, there was no difference in the surrounding foliage. No broken branches, footsteps in the dirt, or disturbances in the wildlife. Forest trolls were practically one with the woods they lived in. Caretakers, really. And as one would expect a caretaker to do, Adrian found him kneeling over a sick fern, gingerly holding the sagging fronds in his large hands. He whispered some quiet words, almost encouraging the plant as patches of black dissolved away. The Green Man quaked, a small dose of magic leaving him and filling the plant with new life. Before long, the fronds lifted free from his claws and bounced happily in the wind, good as new. Adrian watched, always curious how the troll had managed such feats. A part of him couldn't help but be in awe, such actions beyond his reach and scope of vision. The Green Man was the wisest being he knew, he could help him.

After the lichen and moss-cloaked creature stood from the dirt, Adrian cleared his throat. Pin-pricks the color of cherry blossoms met his gaze. His mouth opened, shards of bark-like teeth finally visible. "...Ah, Adrian... You are looking well..." The Green Man gave him a small smile.

The huge mountain troll bowed before the smaller kindred, a sight most comical to those unaware of their history. "I... ne...ed...h..e..lp..." the beast wheezed.

A mild look of concern creased the forest troll's wrinkled skin, making him look impossibly old. "...I see. What... do you need?"

Adrian hesitated, unsure of how to phrase the question. After a moment, he began, "I.. f..ou..nd.. ch...ild... i..n... w...oods... W..as... in... d..en..." The expression on his friend's face deepened. "Ch...ased... o..ut... b..ut... n..ow... sa..y... fr...ien...ds..." The Green Man's shoulders sagged a little, like they were releasing an uneasy tension. "He... sa...id... som...eth..ing... o..dd... he... sa...id... I... w..as... per...son... Wh...at... me..an?" Adrian gave him a pleading look, his head low between his shoulders. He appeared so small like that.

The Green Man thought for a moment before slowly stating, "Well... as for the concern with the child... you should do well to steer clear of the lad... you could... hurt him." Adrian's claws clenched in the dirt at this. A spark of fear raced up his spine as he gazed down at those talons. He wouldn't want to hurt him. But the Green Man was right, he was a monster after all. One wrong twitch of a claw and the child could be lying upon the dirt, in a puddle of his own blood. His fingers pulled into a fist. It was only when the forest troll spoke again that his bristling feathers fell. "...but... As for your question... 'person' is... a term humans are fond of to refer to beings who have an emotional intelligence in... equivalence to themselves..."

"I..s... it... a... dis..ea...se?" Adrian asked, his rumbling voice barely hiding his concern.

The forest troll's eyes blinked, perplexed more than anything. "...No... It is merely a... state of being..." Adrian lowered his gaze, frustrated. "...albeit... one they force upon others..."

"C..an... it... be... re...mov..ed...?"

Concern laced the wizen caretaker's face again. "No... not exactly... they are just... qualities humans see in themselves... Why the concern?"

The beast flopped onto its hindquarters, scattering loose leaves and twigs around him. A conflicted expression settled on his features. "Th...e... mem...or...ies... ge..t..ting.... w..or..se..."

The Green Man sucked in a breath, taking some pollen with it. "...I see... Are you... worried?"

Adrian held up his claws, looking at his scarred palms. "I..m... no..t... do..ing... tr...oll... th...in..gs... ri..ght..."

The forest troll stepped forward tentatively. "...Like what?"

"I... h.a...ve.. dr..ea..ms... of... tho..se... I... ha..ve... ne..ver... m...et..." he paused, remembering the mother's face. "I... c...ry... I... ha...ve... mem..or..ies... th..at.. ma..ke... n..o... s..en..se... I... ha..ve... emo...tion...al... mo..men...ts.." he was rubbing his claws together, a nervous gesture that made his friend more worried.

"...I see. You are... having mortal thoughts then..." he rested a finger against his bark chin. There was an odd light in those eyes. Hope? "This... could be a good thing..." the Green Man reasoned.

"H..ow...?" Adrian held out his claws. He looked between them, watching his shaking fingers. "Ho..w.. ca..n... be... g...ood...? I.. am... tr...oll... Y..ou... sa..id... mor..tal... th..ou..ghts..."

"I did. Just because you are something... does not mean you don't have the power to change it... Or witness a new perspective..." the Green Man smiled.

"W...hy... wo..ul..d... I.. wa..nt... to..?" the beast asked, concern creasing his beak.

The forest troll thought about this for a long time. Only the cheerful trill of the songbirds above filled the silence left in his wake. "Because... it may show you who you are... better than you could know now... You... had a life when you sprung forth from your progenitor... Don't you see this as a chance to know where you came from...? And even if not that... maybe... it could give you a better understanding of humans and their actions..." The hunched creature shuffled over to Adrian, gingerly taking one of his hands and putting it into his own. The caretaker rested a claw on top of them. "It may seem like a curse... but you could make it a boon..."

The beast gazed into that confusing expression on his old friend's face. He couldn't understand it. He closed his eyes, slowly pulling away. "I... ne..ed... ti...me... to... th..in..k..."

"Of course, Adrian... you have plenty of time... please... just don't discredit all you see and hear... there is a whisper of truth there... Only if you are willing to listen..." The Green Man pulled his hands into his mossy cloak. He gazed up at the sky. "Ah... the sun rot has plagued us heavily this year... There are more plants to tend to..."

The mountain troll bowed his head. "Of... co..ur...se... I... wi..ll... ke..ep... yo..u... no... lon..ger... than...k... y..ou..."

The older fae bowed his head in turn. "Of course, my friend... Do take care..." The ethereal being turned slowly, trudging through the undergrowth that parted in his wake, until it fell back into place and obscured him from view.

Chapter 5

Adrian thought hard about what he heard as he lumbered through the coming days. Over a meal of bones, through a walk in the woods, sitting in his nest... he mulled over the quandary. The child made sure to periodically interrupt him, approaching his cave with a nonchalance that irritated him to no end. Of course, he humored the runt, letting him prattle on as he quietly rested. He let the child explore, at least then he would stop asking so many stupid questions. The boy had seen his things and was promptly warned to never touch them. For once, he listened. The pain in his stomach became a dull throb, one that made it difficult to sleep. It was annoying for sure, but as all things did, it would pass.

Adrian carried on like this for several days, struggling with his thoughts, until he found himself upon a stroll through the eastern woodland. He hardly traveled this far out, as a man had made a cabin here. He knew how to steer clear and further still made sure the route wasn't as common as his others.

His tail lashed in irritation, flicking away leaves and twigs alike that strayed too close. His brow furrowed and the flesh on his beak wrinkled. He began another round of thought. How could having human thoughts be good for a troll? How could any of this be a gift when it just continued to torture him? If it wasn't a disease causing it, then what did this? His progenitor? Was he malformed? He glanced at his wings as he considered this and snarled. Of course he is. He was *born* defective. Not a single mountain troll looked remotely like him.

None struggled with words like he did. None were as passive as he was. None were as sentimental as he was. None were plagued with this curse.

Fine. He would see where this led. If he was unhappy with the path, all he would need to do is step off of it. He held his neck up proudly. He could choose not to follow those stupid desires whenever he wanted. It changed nothing. He was a troll.

The crashing of branches and grunts of pain towards the left caught his attention. He saw a small hand wave in the air. "Lion! Hey!"

Stars and bones... How did he find him? Adrian moved a little quicker, hoping that the undergrowth would slow the little brat down. The rustling continued getting closer and closer. "Lion!" The child flopped onto the dirt path behind him.

Sigh. No dice.

The troll turned his head, glaring at the boy. There were leaves and burrs stuck in his long jet black hair and scratches littering his exposed skin. Dirt coated parts of his fine clothes, making him look more of a wild child than ever. "He...llo... Van...tis..." the beast sighed.

"You said my name!" Vantis gasped, scampering up to his front. "I tried to tell Wren about you! But she said she was 'busy'," he added with air quotes and a growl on the final word. Adrian lifted a hairless brow. "Ugh. She's *always* busy! Trade this, money that, 'I'm doing important things, Lionel!' It's like she never has time!" The troll's eyes followed the boy's flailing arms. "Ugh, that's fine. Maybe she doesn't *deserve* to know about my friends!" Vantis crossed his arms, comically upset.

The troll sighed. "It... ma...y... be... a... bl..es...sing... f..or... me..."

Vantis gave him a quizzical look. "Why?"

His fangs curled into a sneer. "Hu...man..s... do..n't... wa..nt... ch..il..dren... ne..ar... tr..olls..."

"Well, I was *gonna* tell her you were a good troll!" the boy snorted, looking away.

"Y..ou... hon..est...ly... th..in..k... th..at's... mu..ch... bet..ter...?" He tilted his head with a smile.

"Well-! I- um... ugh! Doesn't matter anyways 'cause she never listens to me!" Vantis threw up his hands, which Adrian dutifully followed with his gaze. "My uncle listens to me, he never tells me he's too busy..." he grumbled.

"I... s..ee..." the beast nodded. His face scrunched. "Un...cle...?"

"Oh, yeah! My uncle is my father's brother. He says not literally... It's like... found family or something. Either way, he's a really cool guy!" Vantis explained.

"I... se...e..." the creature growled, moving along. If the runt wanted to talk he could walk. The child did indeed follow, his shoes echoing across the forest floor.

"He's a hunter, y'know. Used to be in the military with my father. He was a knight!" The excitement in the child's voice implied that the troll was meant to be impressed.

"Oh... re..al..ly...?" he sneered. Knights. Yes, he was aware of them. Braggards and fools, the lot of 'em. Knights tried to slay creatures like him, back when the fae were more prevalent. Now, they were the glorified dogs of human kings, dressed in fanciful armor that could just as easily be peeled away with his talons.

Not that he would.

Vantis continued on, unaware of the sarcasm oozing from his monstrous companion. "Yeah! My father, Wren, and him were knights! They all used to fight together, killing monsters and evil Golossians!"

Golossia. Another name he was aware of. A kingdom of men that used dark magics and enslaved fae to rend asunder the lands of the kingdom he resided in. What did the humans call it? ...ah, Solania. While Solanians offered little threat, Golossians were prey. Prey not fit to be eaten even if he did have a taste for human flesh.

No, he felt an intense hatred for them, although he wasn't sure why. He let the boy go on.

"My father was a monster slayer!" he squeaked.

"Y...ou... men...tion...ed... th..is... al..rea..dy..." Adrian growled.

"I know! It's just *that* important! He saved the kingdom *sooo* many times, he was given a special plaque and a replica of his armor was placed in the royal halls! How awesome is that?!" Vantis was running ahead of him at this point, drifting towards a direction unknown. The troll figured he should keep an eye on him, at least so the wolves didn't eat him. Adrian gave him a disinterested *mhmm*. A thought crossed his mind. He decided to let it out.

"Wh...at... ab...out... mo...ther...?" he rumbled.

The boy was silent, stopping in the middle of a clearing of trees. "She's... well, I haven't seen her really. According to the letters Wren gives me, she's off trying to provide for us at the capital. She says she misses me and loves me a lot but she's worried that someone would hurt me there, since father had enemies..." his voice was a whisper. "...I've... never even seen her face before..."

A shiver raced up the troll's spine, a flash of an image. That woman. Mother. Instead of shaking it away, he held it in his mind, trying to commit it to his active memory. He didn't realize his talons were clenched.

A shift in Vantis's position jolted him back to reality. "Do you have a mother, Lion?"

The beast hesitated. He opened his mouth to shoot down such a ridiculous question but it began to move a different way. "Y..es... I... be..lie...ve... I... di..d... Sh..es... g...on..e... no..w..."

Vantis frowned. "I'm sorry." The troll cocked his head. What was there to be sorry about? "I'm sorry I brought it up. It had to have been hard. Losing her. The truth is... I don't really know a single thing about my family... I only know what they did and what they sacrificed... but I didn't *know* them. They were gone before I had the chance to make memories with them," the child retreated into himself, falling against a tree with his arms crossed on his knees. His chin rested upon them, a sorrowful expression on his face.

The troll sighed. What a sorry whelp this creature turned out to be. Regardless of his feelings, he found himself laying down next to the boy on his side. He tucked in his feathers so as to not strike the child. He just sat there and listened. "Honestly, I wish I could see them just once. Hear their voices. I don't know, maybe get a hug? Something. Because right now one is just a picture on the wall and the other is a letter in my room."

Adrian was silent for a moment. "B...ut... y..ou... ha..ve... yo..ur... un...cle.. and... W..wren... ri...ght?" He struggled to say that name for a moment. Something about it made him want to scream out.

A soft smile flashed on the boy's face for a moment. He wiped his eyes. "Yeah, I do. I guess... at least I'm not alone." He looked over at the lounging beast beside him. "And I got you. A fantastic troll friend."

Adrian's eye twitched. He wanted to recoil in disgust at the sentimental child. Yet he remained, just resting his head on his hands. The two sat there quietly, the boy braiding some blades of grass while the beast gazed out into the woods. How odd. Resting near a human should make him want to flee but he found that he didn't mind it much, especially after a week of visits. The little creature was interesting, as pathetic as it was. He would continue to indulge its fantasies of friendship with fae a little longer. Just as his eyes closed, he heard a motion next to him. The boy was standing, holding his arm as he gazed out into the forest. His eyes were distant, betraying little in terms of his thoughts. "Wonder what my uncle is doing right now..." the child muttered.

"Y...ou... ca...n... go... f..in...d.. h..i..m... I... mi...gh..t... mo...ve... ba...ck... h..om...e..." the troll growled, getting to his feet.

"Hmm," Vantis pulled away from the tree, starting to look up at the sky. "We are.... east of your den, right?" Adrian was impressed. He figured all humans were clueless once they ventured from their homes. The troll nodded. "His cabin should be along the way, could I tag along?" the child asked, giving him an exaggerated pleading look. The beast sighed.

"F...in...e..."

Chapter 6

It was the second time he had to fix this bloody thing. The second time the blasted squirrels somehow managed to trip the trap and wriggle free. A gloved hand lifted the line as he scowled. "Fucking rope," the man hissed, tossing it away. He might have tried to stretch its lifespan a little longer than he should. The hunter reached into his pack beside him, producing a new line. He began to reset the snare, this time with a new rope before he heard a familiar loud noise.

Heavenly father, it's Vantis.

Figures, the child would come floundering around his neck of the woods, terrifying everything in a half mile radius.

Oh well, he thought as he continued his work. *At least I won't have to worry about scaring anything myself. I can take my time.*

The hunter worked at the trap until it was finally set, barely held down with a small rock. All it would take is one tug and the prey would be caught.

Harris swiped a hand across his forehead, pulling himself up to stand. He had a tired, weathered visage, the face of an aged outdoorsman. His dark brown eyes were shaped like a predatory beast's, with eyebrows sharp as fangs. His nose was angled and narrow, pinching the features in. The nature of his face gave him the air and power of a bird of prey. His brown hair was medium length, loosely brushed and ready to be cut back again. Stubble attempting to make a mustache and beard patched along his face, marred by ancient battle scars. And while his body was normal for a lithe outdoorsman, his legs were most curious indeed. With his pants cut to his knees, thick black fur grew over exposed digitigrade calves and feet, two of his mutated toes vaguely in the shape of a deer's hoof. His remaining three toes were higher up on his extended arch, nothing more than dew claws with excessively hard to trim nails. Delicate and dainty as these bizarre legs were, he moved expertly and gracefully, a harsh contrast with his rugged appearance.

He dusted his hands off on his patchwork of a leather coat, still hearing the boy. He was getting closer and presumably wielding a big stick with all the racket he was making. Harris sighed and leaned past the underbrush to see what the brat was up to. He saw the boy, prancing around as expected. What he didn't expect was the pile of feathers and green flesh next to him. The man hadn't the best rest the night prior, and blinked curiously. "Wonderful, Vantis found a troll..." he muttered. He was about to lean down to grab his things when the realization struck him. "Oh fuck, Vantis found a troll!"

~~~~~~

49

Adrian heard the rushing of footsteps. They didn't sound like human boots. No, these were... hooves? Instinctively, his feathers and hair bristled as a low growl filled his throat. "Huh?" Vantis stopped, peering over a berry bush. "Oh hey, it's my uncle! Hmm, he's running pretty fast..."

The monster was confused but shook his head. The snarl deepened. "I...m... a... tr..o..ll... y..ou... fo..ol... o..f... c..our....se... he... is... ru..nn..ing..." The beast's back arched, thin skin pulling taut against his visible spine. His tail whipped in towards his body, his wing feathers pulling up towards his arms.

"Uh, I don't think you are helping our case, Li-" The boy was tackled to the ground by the man, pulling him away from the monster with a knife in his hand. The middle-aged man was breathing heavily, sweat at his brow as those hawkish eyes bore holes at the beast. There was conflict in his expression.

Adrian calmed as soon as he recognized him. It was the deer-legged hunter he saw with relative frequency. The same man who built the cabin in the woods. The hunter would sometimes encounter the beast and look as if to say something before rushing away into the brush. He would not hurt him or the child. Adrian's hackles lowered and his neck arched up proudly. He sat like a guardian hound, looking down upon him.

Vantis pulled his gaze up from the forearm wrapped around his chest with a smile. "Hi, uncle! You got here fast!"

The older gentleman was still breathing heavily, shakily readjusting his grip on the knife. "Hey, kid. Now, uh, what the hell are you doing?!" The man's face creased into a concerned snarl.

"Oh, I'm just taking a walk with my friend Lion here!" the child explained, effortlessly slipping out of the hunter's grasp. Much to the man's chagrin, Vantis danced away from his open hand before he could pull him back in. "Uncle, meet Lion. Lion, meet uncle!" The lad went over to the troll and patted his left arm with a hand. The troll gave the child a scowl, pulling away his wing to tuck it against the other. Vantis was so small against the colossal monster. "Don't worry! He's a good troll!"

The hunter's eye twitched. "Great hells, you are such a fool..." the man's voice was barely above a growl.

"Un...cle..." the beast hissed. Harris's lip quivered for a moment. *He could... he could speak,* his mind whispered, a quaking dread slithering up his spine. The creature bowed its head, greasy hair scattering to the ground as its beak almost touched the earth. The hunter felt compelled to do the same. "Sor...ry... f..or... fri...ght...en..ing... yo..u..." the creature wheezed.

Why was he apologizing? Adrian owed this man no honor. If anything, this human should bow before him. But there he was, holding the position for a moment before pulling his head back to its original height.

The man had to gather his bearings for a moment before turning to the bouncing lad. "I need to speak with you, Vantis... alone, if you don't mind."

The boy shrugged, shifting his gaze to Adrian. "Is it alright if I go with him for a moment?"

Stars and bones, why would he ask him?!

The beast sighed, nodding his head. He would remain here, at least until he was certain the boy would follow his uncle home. He laid down, beginning to preen. The two stepped several yards away, where a normal human couldn't listen in. Of course, the troll's ears could still hear quite clearly.

"Vantis, what the hells are you doing out here, alone with a troll no less?" the man hissed.

"Just wandering about. I *did* tell you that I had a new friend," the boy smirked. Adrian could imagine him crossing his arms.

"Yes, well, I assumed that when you said *friend* you meant a kid in the village. Not the only bloody mountain troll in this whole valley!"

"Who cares? I told you he's nice!"

"And that's lovely and all but at the end of the day... he's... it's..." there was agony in the final word. "It could hurt you."

"He wouldn't! He said he wouldn't!"

"And have you not considered it a little odd to believe that?"

"No! He's a fae! He can't lie!"

"They can still twist the truth, Vantis. They don't need to lie if they can just change definitions..."

Adrian's eye twitched. As if he would do something so low. He said he wouldn't harm the boy. That was that. No other definitions. Before his better judgment could stop him, the beast stepped through the bushes behind the man. The only way Harris noticed the silent creature was the deep shadow cast over him. His umber eyes darted up to meet blue looming over. He couldn't help but step away from the monster, keeping Vantis behind him. The troll could smell his fear. He had to stifle the shiver of joy running down his spine. The beak opened with a snap. "I... do...n..ot... ea...t... hu...ma..ns..."

The man spoke with a glare, "That may be the case, but that tells me nothing of your intentions. You don't need to eat someone to harm them."

"I... wi...l..l... n..ot... hu..rt... vi..ll..ag..ers..." the beast growled.

This made the hunter's eyes narrow. "And what if you're attacked, what then?"

The beast's head arched up towards the sky, thinking for a moment. "Th...en... I... ru...n... Le..ave... Fi...nd... n...ew... h..om...e..."

Harris closed his eyes, almost expecting this. "Fine then, let me ask you this, *Lion*, what's with the name? Ironic that you are friendly with a *Lionel* of all things."

"Oh, oh! I know this one!" Vantis jumped up, raising a hand. Both the troll and man gave him a quizzical look. "That's 'cause he ate all the mountain lions in the valley! And when he did, he decided to take their place! Isn't that amazing!?"

The hunter snorted, crossing his arms. "That's... a bit of an exaggeration, although I suppose I have not seen any on this side of

53

the pass. And I have noticed little change in the deer populations, so I suppose that holds up..."

"Yeah! And it's amazing 'cause father was said to have a troll friend! And now I do too! It's like... *destiny!*" the boy added with a flourish. His audience all gave him a dubious expression. "I'm already so much like him, right?"

Harris gave him a sad smile. "More than you know. But, there was one thing your father had over you..." The middle-aged man put his hands on his hips, leaning over with a sly smile. Vantis moved in eagerly, ready to hear this secret. The boy was just inches away from his uncle's face, the smell of dried meat on his breath. "He did his schoolwork," the hunter smirked.

Vantis's face fell as he pulled back with an exaggerated huff. "Aww, come on! It's super *boring*! It's economics! It's literally the *worst*!" the boy groaned. He was still turning towards home, though. Adrian had to give the brat credit, at least he still followed orders when he whined.

"Yes, well, an educated warrior is a living one. Run along. Get it done. If you finish before sunset, I can teach you more on how to hunt," he added with a smile.

"Really?! Fuck yeah!" The lad leapt up and began to run.

"Language!" Harris snapped, albeit playfully.

"Sorry! I'll go right now! I'll get it so done and so good you'll have to teach me everything!" The child ran through the woods, slamming into the underbrush and causing a racket loud enough to scare a flock of songbirds.

The two watched the child disappear into the brush, leaving them with the sounds of the wilds. Harris glanced over at the hunched beast. The older man's mouth moved before he could stop it. "You still there?"

The troll cocked his head. "Of.. co..ur...se... I... ne...ver... le...ft..." The man's eyes welled with hope before the troll spoke again. "I...m... no...t... th...at... qui...et..."

"Ah, heh, I see. Nevermind then." The hunter turned away. His tone shifted to something more soft, delicate, "How have you been fairing lately?"

"I'v..e... be...en... st...rug...gl...ing... bu..t.. I... ha...ve... ha..d.. go...od... ki..lls..." The creature bowed his head.

The ghost of a smile tugged at the man's lip. "That's good. That's very good." It was quiet again for a moment. "How did you meet Vantis?"

"Br...at.... wan..der..ed... in..to... m...y... ca..ve... Fo...ol... wa...s.. tr..yin..g... to... fi..nd... a.. tr...oll..." The beast's fangs curled into a sneer.

"You're kidding me... He really is too much like his father..." the man sighed.

"Tr...ied... to... sc..a...re... hi..m.. o...ff... he... st...abb...ed... me... fif...tee..n... t...im...es... in... fa..ce... wi...th... kn...ife..." The creature licked his muzzle, still feeling the dents in the bone.

Harris glanced over. "Hmph. You look like you're healing up well. Not a stab over seven..."

"Bu...t.. I... wa...s... hi..t.... fif...tee...n... ti..mes..." The creature cocked its head.

The hunter shook his head with a chuckle. "It was a joke."

"Ah... no..t.. go..od... wi..th... tho...se..." Adrian sighed.

"Heh, that's fine. At least I know the lad wouldn't go down without a fight," he smiled. "Wren taught him well in that regard."

"No..t.. ba...d... hu...nter.... Need... bet..ter... ai..m... Br..at... sh...ot... m...e..." Adrian growled.

"On purpose?" The man raised his eyebrow.

The beast shook his head. "Sa...id... acc...id...ent..."

"The kid can't lie to save his life so I believe that," he breathed, his eyes following the path of decimation left by the child.

"I... can...no..t... li..e... ei...th..er..."

Harris thought about this for a moment before sadly smiling, "Yes. That's true."

Adrian wanted to end the conversation there. He was already unnerved by how calm the human was around him. But then he noticed a smell. A smell he recognized. He gave a deep sniff. "I... sm..ell... s...alt..."

"Ah, yes, that might be my meal," the man pulled out a piece of parchment. Within it was a slab of dried meat. He set it back into his bag.

"N...o... it..s... yo..ur... fa..ce..." the creature shook his head, pointing at the man's dewy eyes with a claw. Harris promptly wiped them.

"My apologies," he said with a chuckle.

"N...o... I... ge...t.. th..em... to..o... I.. ha..ve.. be..en... a.. ter...rib...le... tr...oll... lat..ely..." Adrian sighed. Why was he telling a human this?

"How... How do you mean?" The man turned to fully face the beast.

"Dre...ams... me...m...ori..es... se...nt...ime...ntal... th...ou...ght...s... pan...ic... a..tta...ck..s..." the beast sighed, trying to distract himself by cleaning his feathers. The man seemed to mull this over.

"... Have you ever heard of the kin?" Harris asked.

"Y...es... ha...lf...bre...eds... Fa..e...an..d... mor..tal..." he nodded. The troll was honestly impressed that this man knew about them at all.

"Have you ever considered you might be one of them?" The hunter stared, looking way too deep into the monster's eyes.

The beast gave a cawing laugh. "No... I... a...m... a... tr...oll... No... ha...lf... br..eed..."

"Can you say that with certainty?" the man pressed, clenching his gloved hands against his folded arms.

The beast went silent, remembering the images of mother. And the beautiful woman's soft smile. He shook his head a little faster. "Y..es... I... a...m.. tr..oll..." Harris's shoulders sagged as he let his arms go. The man turned away and pulled out the jerky, nibbling at it. He pulled a slab apart, holding it out to the beast. Without much consideration, the beast took the gift, snapping it up with one bird-like clack of his toothy beak. The beast stood, shaking its feathers. "I... mu..st... g..o... n..ow..."

"I understand, it was... good to finally speak with you," the man nodded. His face was hidden away, but Adrian could still smell his tears.

"D...o... ta...ke... c..ar..e..." the troll nodded before sliding into the greenery, leaving the man alone with his thoughts. Now that the beast had gone, Harris's lip began to quake. He staggered against a tree, slid to the ground, and sobbed.

Chapter 7

Vantis thrust open the door with more gusto than expected, slamming it against the outside wall. He heard a person cuss inside as he catapulted up the stairs. "Vantis, you great lummox, you scared the shit out of me!" an irritated voice called from down the stairs. The boy rushed to the banister from the top landing, looking down upon his caretaker. She was grumbling and wiping something off her clothes. It appeared to be ink.

Wren's eyes were a softer brown than Harris's, with a tired yet sharp look. Her long, dusty auburn hair was tied in a messy bun, loose strands decorating her neck and soft cheeks. Scars littered her arms and delicate face, making her appear far more weathered than she actually was. Her muscles bulged even under her dress shirt and pants, revealing a staggering strength to her beauty. Wren was clearly a warrior, even after taking over the company. That feral spark would never leave her. It was something Vantis found comforting.

"Sorry, Wren! Uncle said that if I finished my homework before sunset he is gonna teach me more about hunting!" he squeaked.

"Of course he did. Well, try to remember that you have to do it *right* as well as fast. Don't half-ass it or I'll collect you myself!" she smirked.

"Yes, ma'am!" the boy saluted and went straight to work. This work was particularly tedious, with plenty of new vocabulary words and descriptions of materials, all entwined with copious amounts of math. His family was fortunate enough to afford a private tutor, something that many couldn't. Vantis learned as much as he could... and yet he was only twelve. His caretakers seemed to forget that far more than he did. No matter. Once he was finished with this horrible mess he could go and learn with uncle Harris. The boy wanted to give Lion a special treat for being his friend, and he couldn't do so if he couldn't even fell a deer.

Soon enough, as the last hour dragged on, he finished the work, slamming the books shut with a giddy smile. The boy threw the report on top of his other papers upon the desk and snatched his coat. He paused by a chair, spotting a strip of grey cloth with golden accents resting over the back. The piece of his father's cloak. He couldn't forget it. Vantis quickly wrapped the band of cloth around his waist before throwing himself out of the door. As soon as he reached the main hallway he paused, realizing how undignified he looked.

Succeed with grace, it's what Lord Lionel did.

Smoothly, he dusted himself off and strode ahead, puffing out his chest. Surely Wren and Harris would be proud of his work. He could go hunt with his uncle all night! And from the sounds he heard downstairs, his uncle seemed to already be here. He quietly made his way down, not willing to bother the two. They seemed to be very serious with whatever they were talking about. He could wait in the foyer. Vantis set himself down on a plush bench, pulling out his boots to get ready. It was the angry voice of his caretaker that caught his interest.

"Absolutely not!" Wren hissed.

The boy jumped, pulling away from the bench in curiosity. He pressed his back against the wall, near the archway leading to the study. He could hear her tending to the fireplace in the reading room, the crackling of the flames accenting the conversation. From the harsh sounds of scraping wood, she was clearly agitated. "... I know, Wren. But he *is* getting better!" Harris sounded hopeful, his hooves clicking against the wooden floor.

"Is *he* even there?" Wren's voice cut in the hall.

"He's... buried deep. But I know he's there. Wren, I'm telling you, the boy could bring him back to his senses!" Harris pleaded.

The sound of heels clicking on the floorboards echoed over the foyer. Someone was walking away. "Have you ever seen someone in a coma, Harris?"

The silence was burning like fire. "...Yes. I have."

"Then you know I don't want to talk to a sleeping body. That is not my leader. That is... not my friend." There was a dagger of agony in her words. Vantis was so confused. Who were they talking about? He fought against every impulse that told him to reveal himself from his hiding spot.

"Adrian Lionel is *dead*, Harris. That... fucking *thing* is not him! Instead of trying to focus on the dead body, we should be trying to keep the one living part we have left!" Wren argued, spitting the words between her teeth.

"Vantis..." His voice was tired. Pained.

"Yes! And we can't do that by letting him go gallivanting into the woods with the corpse of his father!" A sharp clang echoed as she threw the fire poker in its rest.

Father... wait... was she saying that Lion was...

The boy cupped his hands over his mouth, sliding to the ground. His body shook uncontrollably.

"I've been trying to raise him how he would have wanted... trying to let him have a chance to live in peace... make his own choices... but..." She went silent. Tears were rolling down Vantis's face.

There was no way. Father killed trolls! He didn't become one! He died protecting his family. That's what Wren said! What could she possibly mean?

He wouldn't listen any longer. He needed to get out. In a rushed panic, he forgot his coat, barging out the front door roughly before throwing himself into the woods.

~~~~~~

Adrian was happily gnawing on a femur he had been saving, excited to finally gain access to the delicious marrow. His fangs gnashed and chomped, fragments of bone falling off of his face and littering the cave floor. His fluffy tail tip would periodically swipe the stone clean. He learned this trick relatively quickly after several fangs jammed into the arch of his foot when he first claimed this cave. The beast lounged as he enjoyed his extravagant meal, sucking out the coagulated fluid with a growling purr. Just as he finished, he began crushing the bone into shards, letting his powerful stomach acid dissolve the nutrients caged within. He licked at his talons with a long black tongue, relishing his meal. While he had been dealing with the odd stomach ache, he finally felt well enough to get a delicious dinner. The beast sighed, laying his head down upon his claws with a lazy grin set upon his ghastly features. It was the tell-tale tappings of human feet that turned that smile into a scowl. Stars and bones, again?!

"LION!" Vantis's voice yelled into the cave. The harsh resonance made the troll cringe. He almost wished he could jam some straw in his ears. The beast threw up his head in an exaggerated fashion, ready to scold the boy. Instead, before he could even let out a word, the child threw himself into his ruff. The troll froze, his eyes wide. He had to punch down the instinct to bite the human's head off, only a twitch present on his back fangs. He slowly closed his eyes and willed his clenched claws to release the floor.

I will not harm a villager. I will not hurt a child.

His muscles relaxed and the creature sighed. "W..ha..t.. is.. i..t... r...un..t...?"

A whisper. "...Lion... are you my father?"

The beast was dumbstruck. Honestly, a little offended. "W...h...at...? W...hy... as..k... a... foo..l..ish.. qu...es..t...ion... li..ke... th..at...?"

"Wren and uncle Harris said you were... they said you were my father's corpse..." The boy looked up with a horrified expression.

The beast chuckled, plucking the child away from his feathers. "N..o... I... th...in..k.. y...ou...r... ca...re..ta..k...er..s... a...re.. mis....tak...en..."

The lad struggled in the claws as the troll set him down. "But why would they lie?!" he cried. "If it is you, please tell me! I won't be mad or anything, I promise! Please, tell me the truth!"

The beast blinked, absolutely confused. "I... ne..ve.r... sa..id... li..e... I... sa..id... mi..s..tak...en..."

The boy glared up at the monster. "What's the difference?! They still said it!"

"I..t... w..a.s...n't....mal...ic..ious..." he began, curling in his tail. "Ma...ny... vil....lag...er...s... sa..y... I... am... a... spir..it... o..f... som..e.... lo...rd... Th...ey... ar..e... ju...st... des....per...ate... ho..pes..." the creature explained, scratching under his chin. "Hu...man..s... a...scri...b.e... me...an..ing... t..o... un..rea...lat..ed... th...ing..s... a...ll... th..e... ti..me..."

The boy seemed to listen to this, falling against the wall before sliding to the floor. Those tear-soaked eyes darted around in thought. "So... they are just making things up to feel better?"

The troll shrugged. "Hu...man...s... ta...ke... th...eir... fa...tes... har...der... th..an.. mo...st... Ca...n't... acc..ept.... rea..lit..y..."

"I see..." The child retreated into himself. "You... promise you are not my father?"

"I... do..n't... re...me..mber... su..ch... a... th..ing..." the beast yawned. That ball of pain in his gut made him shift position.

"Okay... okay then..." Vantis sighed in relief. "That just means that they need help. They can't take out father's death on you, that's unfair. You didn't kill him. I didn't think they would be hurting so much they would make up lies in their heads..." The creature picked at his teeth, becoming agitated with the pain in his stomach and the current location. The beast stood up, walking towards the entrance. Vantis followed him, scampering beside his massive claws. "Gods... they must be hurting so bad... I didn't even bother to think about that... poor Wren... poor uncle..."

A pang of something struck that ball in his guts, making the troll stop near the edge of the cliffside. He considered taking the boy on a walk, at least to help him get those ridiculous thoughts out of his head. The weight in his belly said otherwise. Instead, he laid down, lounging like a cat. He gestured for the child to sit down beside him. The boy seemed to ignore his invitation, instead choosing to stand. Vantis gazed out over the forest. "It's... very pretty here..."

"Y...es..." the troll nodded.

"I guess I never considered why you made your home here. You have the best view in the world..." the boy breathed, spotting his house's roof just beyond the trees.

Adrian felt a smile tug at his jaw. "I...t... is... bea...ut..if...ul... is...n't... it...? Ha...d... to... ch..as.e... t...he... li....ons... ou..t... to... h...a..ve... i...t..."

The boy gave him that starry-eyed look. "That sounds like a lot of work to get a house..."

"He..h... ye..s.. b...ut..." he paused, letting the wind brush his hair away from his face. "T...he.. p..ain... w..as... wo...rth... i...t..."

The boy stepped closer to the edge, as if lost in a trance. An unknown emotion jabbed at the beast. "Do you think... mother and father believe I'm worth it?"

"...Van...tis..." he sighed. A force made his mouth move. "Yo..u... a..re... al...ive... Th...at... wi..ll... al..ways... b.e... wo..rth... it..." The boy stopped moving, his shoulders shaking. His fists were clenched. A drop of water struck the ground. "Wh..ere... ev..er... yo...ur... par...ent..s... a...re... I... be..lie...ve... th..ey.. c..are... f..or... yo..u..." the troll continued, looking over the edge.

His mother cared for him. She died for him.

"Y...ou.. a...re... no... tr...oll... Yo...u.. ar...e... hu...man... Hu...mans... ar..e.. sel...fish... Mo...stly... fo...r.. th.e... th...ing...s... th..ey... lo...ve..."

There was someone he cared for too. If only he could see her face...

The boy started to collapse. He was too close. Talons lashed out, snatching the child away and pulling him closer to his body.

Adrian breathed a sigh of relief. "Stu...pid... bo...y... Do..n't... sta...nd... s..o... cl...ose... t..o.. th..e... ed..ge..." he snarled, his gaze hard with worry.

"Thank you..." Vantis whispered. The troll gazed down at the shaking child. His face was hidden under his quivering hair. "Thank you..." The child's arms wrapped around his ruff, pulling himself in for a hug. Stars and bones... What was he going to do with him? The troll's hands moved on their own, enveloping the boy in feathers and claws. "I... needed to hear that..."

"Y.. ou... wi..ll... b...e... fi...ne..." he patted the delicate boy with a talon. What was he doing?

Caring.

He sighed, turning his gaze out over the woods. That house was always in his view, his first den. His first home. He smiled. "I..t... sou...nds... to... me... th..a.t... yo...u... alr..eady.... ha...ve... a... go...od.. vi..ew... to...o..."

"Yeah," Vantis laughed, wiping his face. He turned towards the treetops. "I guess it's not that bad. I can see the whole village from the hill!"

"Oh...? Co...ul...d... yo..u.. te...ll.. me... abo...ut... yo...ur... vil...lag...e...?" Adrian asked, genuinely curious about the place.

"Yeah! Well, my favorite place to go is by the marketplace. There's a nice lady there that always lets me sweep. She says I'm the best sweeper in the whole world! The library is fantastic, they named it after my father, Lord Lionel!" he began, pointing out over the trees to the tiny buildings in the distance. The troll followed along, asking questions about the townsfolk. By the time the first rays of gold struck the horizon, the boy was grinning and laughing again, resting in Adrian's wing. The troll smiled, actually enjoying himself for once. He prodded at the child after a statement of foul language and Vantis giggled, trying to roll away from his claw. As the boy flipped over onto the stone, he finally saw the sky.

"Oh no! It's sunset! Wren and uncle must be terribly worried about me!" He leapt to his feet. Adrian moved to stand, but a stab of fire forced his body to the ground. He kept his composure, not willing to let the child see. "I have to go, Lion! They're probably gonna bring out torches if I don't get back!"

"V...er..y... w...e..ll... do... ta...ke... c...ar..e... Va..nt...is..." The beast bowed his head.

The child started to run off before stopping at the beginning of the trail. "Hey, Lion?"

Adrian's muzzle perked up. "Y...es...?"

"I think you would make a good dad!" Vantis smiled.

The ball in his stomach raged. It took all his willpower to not cry out. But in that moment, a smile crept upon his face. "Th...ank... yo..u.. Van...tis..."

Those dewy eyes squinted with joy before rushing down the path, back home.

Chapter 8

Yellow sweat beaded at his brow. The sitting rock in his stomach was burning. He struggled his way over to the cave, falling to his side with every snap of agony. The ball was getting heavier. He managed to make his way inside after fifteen minutes of desperate struggle. Adrian clutched at his organs, seemingly afraid that they would burst into flame. The energy pulsed, throwing the beast towards the floor. He roared in pain, curling in on his side as he desperately tried to keep his mind clear.

What is happening?!

Another throb of electricity bolted up Adrian's spine, making the troll seize in agony. He was howling. It felt like he was going to burn up, like his body was a lantern that couldn't contain its flame. The creature desperately dragged itself to its nest, seeking any comfort in this mindless pain. The next bolt sent his head back, slamming into the ground. The world was swallowed by blackness.

The troll was alone in the dark, his body quivering. He could still feel the echoes of pain lacing and coiling around him, even with his dulled senses. The beast shook his head, rising to his hind legs to see out into the void.

Stars and bones, was he dying?

No. A voice stated emotionlessly. The troll growled, trying to locate the source, until he gazed directly below him. It was that mutated man that stalked his every step. The beast lurched back, snarling in outrage as he dropped to all fours, bristling.

"WH...AT... WA..N..T..?!" Adrian snarled.

That question is meant for you. The figure stared, its contorted maw of sharp teeth not moving as the words flooded the creature's brain.

"W...HA..T...?"

What do you desire? What is your wish?

The troll staggered back, tail thrashing. What a bizarre question. He had no wishes.

That's not true. You have a wish. A desire that burns at your very being.

Adrian growled, unease prickling up his spine. He didn't like that this... whatever it was... could read his thoughts.

What is your wish?

After some hesitation, the troll thought about this. His first answer was to tell the entity to go away... but another desire bubbled up from his heart. "M...y... w..is...h... i..s... to... kn...ow... wh...o... yo..u... ar...e..."

Are you certain? Even if it causes you pain? Even if you suffer for all eternity for the answer?

The creature pondered this. "Y...es..."

The man nodded slowly, approaching the cornered animal. Adrian tried to pull away but it felt as if his back struck a wall. He snarled at the man as his hands reached out, gently holding the sides of the beast's face.

I am....

This time, the pain ripped into him like a jagged iron blade, sending the beast into a fit of hellish agony. He screamed. He cried. He begged for it to stop. It would not... until it burst, pouring out over his body in a wave. Soon, all he felt was a hazy numbness that lulled him into a deep sleep.

He began to stir a few hours later. Adrian opened his eyes, still in his den, still in the nest. The void and the man were gone, leaving him soaked in his own sweat. The troll groaned, trying to lift his body out of the straw. He felt so drained. He uselessly flopped back into his bed, trying to gather his bearings. The nest was... bigger than he was expecting. Yes, it actually felt huge around him. The beast tried to heave himself up yet again. This time, his arms succeeded, shifting him up into a sitting position. He glanced around, and as he did, he felt the curtain of his own hair tickle his collar bone. That's odd. It had never done that before as his ruff was usually in the way. Now, it felt as though there was nothing there. He glanced down in confusion before letting out a terrified shriek.

His higher-pitched voice rang out as he fell away, his now dust-covered, smooth, tanned chest rising and falling with each panicked breath. He saw a lock of hair, jet black as he expected... but lacking the greasy texture he was fond of. He ran his claws through his scalp, feeling the soft hair and pulling it to look. The tips faded to white, much like his feathers. And his hands... they were still claws, but much more tiny, delicate even. The nails couldn't have been much longer than an inch. His skin was taut and smooth to the touch, still stained the green of his troll skin. That color faded to tan flesh at the middle of his forearms, covered in more of that dust. There were no bone fragments and... there were no feathers. He cried out, seeing those lithe human arms, feeling naked. He was bald everywhere else and he didn't even have a tail.

The man staggered to his feet and furiously wiped himself off, feeling the pounding in his head continue. Adrian rushed to his pile of trinkets, hearing his weak human feet tap softly along the stone floor. He rummaged through before pulling out a small mirror he had collected. It was too tiny for him to find any use before, just another shiny surface. But now, his smaller hands were able to grip the frame firmly and look inside.

His eyes were the same glowing rings that illuminated the pane... but everything else was wrong. First, his beak was gone, replaced with an elegant human nose and soft lips. His skin was tanned here too, his defined cheeks and smooth features giving him a regal beauty. His ears were still sharp, the tips stained with green as the rest melted into human flesh. He opened his mouth, spotting a row of sharp fangs glittering in the dark, much smaller than normal.

The beast whimpered, dropping the mirror as he staggered back from the pile.

Clear tears rolled down his cheeks, soft gasps exiting that beautiful face. His voice was wrong, so terribly so. It was so much weaker, smaller than the proud growls of a mighty predator. It was too delicate and soft, befitting a human merchant or nobleman, not him. The man's soft back touched the wall, the snapping cold making him rip away in shock. He had never felt this cold before, his thick skin and fur always keeping him warm. He was holding himself now, looking about frantically.

"Wh...at... happened... to me?" the man whispered. His face and voice seemed much more comfortable with these words, his mind flooded with new painful vocabulary every time he blinked. He cried out again, holding his head as he fell to his knees. His legs burned from the rocks digging into his thin, weak flesh.

"Help... I need help..." Adrian muttered, trying to shakily get to his feet again. He felt... naked... ashamed...His eyes darted over to the pile. Quietly, he dug through, searching for the human clothes he had collected. He plucked a pair of sandals that were tangled in the filaments of a torn pant leg, shakily pulling them over his vulnerable human feet. He fought to pull on the tattered pants and ragged shirt that had been shredded by his own claws when he first collected them, shivering at the texture against his skin. It was so alien... yet familiar. He saw some leather gloves in the pile with three of the five fingers torn off, archer's gloves by the looks of it. He pulled them on as well, needing to force them up and over that disgustingly smooth flesh to drive his talons through the material. They poked out freely, the only normal part of him he could see. He snatched one of the furs he had stuffed into the pile, dragging out one that could cover his shoulders and hide most of his hideous body. He tugged it up and over the shoulders, taking a shard of bone to spear it together in place. If anyone saw him, they would find him no different than a normal hunter or fur trader, although his ethereal face would probably draw an eye or two.

Adrian was about to leave until he felt that creeping sense of vulnerability. His eyes drifted towards a glittering shape in the dark. The femur he ate earlier. He never finished it. He needed something at least larger than his claws to defend himself. He pulled the shattered bone out, tucking it between his belt and pants.

The terrified man stepped tentatively out of the relative safety of his cave and into the dark forest. This was supposed to be his home, but as he gazed into the shadowed trees... all he could feel was fear. Fear of being too small, too weak to fight against what hid in the bushes. At this size, he wouldn't be able to stand up to a bear or even a mountain lion. Adrian squashed the rising panic. "The Green Man... he will help me. He can fix this," he muttered, reaching the edge of the cliffside. He gazed down, nauseated by the long drop below. A drop he had taken countless times before with ease. But like this... He shuddered, staggering away. No, he would take the path.

The man flinched at every noise, his head whipping around at each howl and snapping branch. He clutched his cloak tight to his sides and held his head down low, determined not to make a sound. The troll had never been so terrified, never felt this small. Anything could kill him, even a well-placed kick from a deer.

My prey could kill me...

Adrian shook his head, his pace quickening. If he found his mentor in time, he wouldn't need to worry. He would help him fix this, and everything would be alright. Everything would be alright.

A snarl behind him caught his attention. Just as he whipped around to defend himself, Adrian saw the shadow of a beast lunge, biting into his raised arm. The man cried out in pain, falling onto his back. A wolf pinned him as it began to tear into his flesh. Red blood spilled onto Adrian's face and, with a panicked shriek, he snatched the bone from his belt and drove it into the animal's neck. The wolf fell away with a gurgling yelp, still twitching on the floor as the man shakily leapt to his feet. Wide eyes darted around to see at least six pairs of glittering orbs in the darkness, all with fangs bared. Instinctively, his lips curled back in a growl before attempting to roar at them, but all that came forth was a pitifully human howl that did little to dissuade the bestial might of the pack. They took a step closer.

"B-back away..." the man whispered, wrenching his weapon free of the corpse in front of him with both hands. "This... this is my forest..." Doubt crept into his voice, the pain in his left arm throbbing. He could feel the sinew starting to snap back into place, bones crunching and pulling against torn flesh. It hurt, but it would heal. At least there was some troll left in him. The animals drew closer, their mouths slavering. Amidst his primal terror, something in his mind crept forward, something he never felt before. Adrian felt his foot move back, grinding against the dirt. His grip shifted, moving in a way alien to him. He extended his left arm in front of him like a shield while his right held his makeshift weapon firmly. The oozing fear turned into an oil, and that oil erupted.

"I said... this forest is mine!" The man's face twisted into a determined snarl as the beasts leapt forward. The one leading the charge jumped up and latched onto his exposed, bloodied arm. He prepared for the attack this time, managing to keep his footing as he held the wolf at bay. Gritting his teeth, Adrian shifted his position to use the animal as a shield, keeping it in between him and the other predators that snapped at him. He thrust the bone into the creature's jaw with a sickening crack before tossing it aside with a well-aimed kick. In the chaos, another wolf managed to circle behind him, leaping onto his back and biting into his shoulder. He hissed in pain, jamming the jagged weapon into the neck of his attacker. The animal yelped, a shower of blood staining both man and beast as the makeshift weapon finally shattered with a low crunch, leaving him unarmed. Even so, he whipped around, his stance low and his talons wide. Adrian's eyes were that of a wild animal, determined to survive. He would not die like this.

The remaining four wolves circled him, sniffing at the carcasses with low growls. The largest one howled, leaping into the arms of the man as they tumbled into the dirt. Fangs flashed for his throat, only to be met with his bleeding arm. The wolf's teeth shredded the muscles with ease, the thrashings scattering his blood all around them. His nails dug deep into his palms as he fought against the tearing agony. The claws of the beast ripped at his skin, drawing more of that foul crimson. He had to end this. With a sharp twist, the man wrenched the arm free with a sickening snap, taking this moment to drive his nails into the open maw. Adrian felt the claws connect with soft tissue, flooding its mouth with an iron-rich warmth. The animal's eyes went wide as the man yanked his arm free, snapping off some of the wolf's fangs in the process. The arm fell uselessly at his side as the muscles failed, slapping against the dirt in a heap of meat. The animal, still in shock, was thrown off of its prey with a strong kick, sending it crashing into its remaining packmates.

The creatures yelped and backed away, watching their companion twitch and choke on their own blood. The man stood, his long hair stained red and covering parts of his face as he staggered back to his feet. The arm still dangled loosely, dripping with viscera and falling teeth. The madness in his eyes narrowed as he roared, this time with all the force of a mighty beast. The wolves hesitated, gazing at the fallen before fleeing into the brush with mournful howls. Adrian spat on the ground, a manic curl in his lip. He wasn't helpless, even like this. He could still fight. He could still...

Before he knew it, the man sank to his knees, his vision going blurry. Before his mind could fathom what was happening, Adrian's head hit the dirt path, and the world was swallowed into the night.

Chapter 9

"Adrian..." A hand caressed his face. One of his eyes opened, a smile tugging at his fangs. She was so beautiful. His claw reached out and touched the hand. "I'm worried..." her voice sighed. He lifted his chest off the bedsheets, following her shadowed form as it pulled away. "This target... It seems too simple... staged, even..." The man's tail flicked, concern written in his body language. He gazed upon her at the other end of the tent that shielded them from the world.

"What does... it... matter...?" his voice began. He was getting so much stronger. After years of this affliction, words hardly gave him any trouble.

"I'm not sure... call me paranoid but..." her face turned towards him. "Something feels off."

He stood up, his head nearly brushing the top of the tent. Adrian felt his clawed toes scrape against the grass and dig into the *dirt. He gingerly rested his claws against her shoulders. "It will... be.. fine... After... this... let's go... home... The one... I... promised."*

She leaned her head against his mutated arm, gazing up at him. Her eyes bore into his, a flood of emotions inside those soulful pupils. "I would love that, Adrian."

"I... love... you..."

Adrian awoke, surrounded by warmth. His body felt heavy, distant. His left arm and shoulder were covered in bandages, the flesh writhing underneath as it healed. Blue rings searched the darkness. He appeared to be in a mortal's bed, covered in deer furs. There were wooden walls all around him, a human den by the looks of it. Perched upon shelves were small, neatly ordered mementos, simple things. A knife on a pedestal, a crudely carved piece of wood, a horn from some beast, neatly stacked books... A writing desk sat in the corner by a shuttered window, covered in leatherworking implements and utensils. In the back of the den was a stone fireplace, embers still smoldering. Next to the hearth was a rocking chair with a man silently sleeping within. A wave of panic rushed over the troll as he began to sit up with a strained grunt. The slumbering man awoke, standing up calmly as the fae struggled with a spinning headache. "Stay down," he ordered.

"W-what?" Adrian stammered, trying to settle the blood throbbing in his pointed ears.

"I said stay down," the man urged as he gently lowered the wounded fae back into the furs.

"I... I'm... ugh..." Adrian tried to protest, but the pain in his skull made him turn aside and hold his head. His host sighed, the sound of small hooves striking the wooden floor as he walked away.

The hunter...

The troll heard the man strike some flint, starting up a fresh fire within the seething ashes. He set some new logs into the budding flames, tending to it quietly.

Fires.... I spent so much time near fires...

No he didn't. He was afraid of fire.

The flames... remind me of her...

The man groaned again, shaking with pain. The hunter merely continued his work until the fire was large enough to heat the cabin. Then, he began to set a metal spit over the flame, hooking a kettle in the middle over the tongues of heat. Adrian could hear the sound of pouring liquid, chopping, slicing, and dragging. Soon, only the sound of boiling water echoed through the cabin.

The smell wafted over the troll's elegant nose, making his mouth water. The savory scent of meat mixed with the light, snappy smell of greens, all accented with a salty air. For some reason it felt nostalgic, soothing his mind and easing the pain of the headache. Eventually, the hunter presented the man with a bowl and spoon, waiting for Adrian to sit up. Taking the soup into his claws, he gazed down, stomach growling. Tentatively, he grasped the utensil and began to eat quietly, surprised by how good it tasted. He was used to bones and fresh sinew, not human food; but the warmth seemed to comfort him against prickling anxiety. When he finished the meal, he set the bowl on the ground next to the bed.

"You are... that hunter..." his soft voice spoke, breaking through the oppressive silence.

Those brown eyes snapped up from his own bowl as he sat in the chair once more, staring at his guest. "Yes, I am. Whatever that means."

"I... I'm sorry. I'm just confused," the man whispered, holding his injured arm with his other claws.

"Hmph. You're lucky I found you. You would've been easy pickings if I hadn't been walking by." Blue eyes darted up to meet the hunter's before quickly looking away. "I must say, however, I'm impressed. Not many people can take on a pack of wolves and survive..."

"Y-yes..." Adrian shrunk into himself, fearful of those clever eyes.

"Although, based on how quickly you're healing, I don't believe you are exactly human, are you?" the man mused, his eyes glittering dangerously in the dark. Adrian's jaw clenched. He shook his head. "I don't want to make any assumptions..." the hunter began, standing up from the chair and walking over to the bed. "But you are definitely some kind of fae. From the features, a troll."

The fae hesitated, lowering his gaze again. "To be honest... I'm not quite sure what I am anymore..."

"Then I must ask, what were you doing out so late at night?"

"I was... looking for someone," Adrian answered, nervous.

"Do you live in these woods?" The man's voice was low.

"Yes..." he nodded.

"Have you met a boy named Vantis?" The troll's claws clenched the fur. He nodded. "Are you the one he calls 'Lion'?" The wounded man nodded once more. The hunter sighed, leaning back to gaze up at the ceiling.

"I... don't know what's happening to me. I don't know why I look like this..." Adrian started, holding out his claws and staring at them.

"Could you tell me what happened?" The middle-aged man pulled the chair from the writing desk over, easing himself down.

"I was... talking to the boy... Vantis..." Adrian whispered.

"What did he say?" the hunter pressed.

"He said I might be his father, but I told him that was ridiculous. I comforted him, stayed with him until he felt better, and then he ran off. After that... I had a bad stomach ache, but at the time, I didn't consider it odd. Summer months bring disease all the time, but this... this was far worse. I tried to get back to my nest to sleep it off and then... I awoke... like this."

The hunter nodded, crossing his arms. "That checks out. We had gone out to find the boy after he ran out of the house. Ended up finding you two together by the cliffside. Didn't catch the start of the conversation, but when we saw that you weren't going to hurt Vantis we went back to the house to wait for him. I'm sorry for not announcing our presence."

"I knew you would. As soon as he came to me crying, I knew he would be followed." The troll's eyes seemed distant, as if he was still on that cliff.

"Again, I do apologize." The hunter bowed his head. The beast shrugged, rubbing at the bandages on his arm. The man spoke once more. "I'm sorry, but it would probably be best if Vantis didn't see you like this."

"If I had it my way, *no one* would see me like this," Adrian growled.

"Yes, you look too much like him," the hunter grunted.

"Like who?" Those blue rings narrowed.

Umber eyes shifted, mulling over what to say next. "What has Vantis told you about his father?"

"That he was a knight and a monster slayer," the troll said with a smirk.

"That is certainly a... basic understanding, but he is a far more complicated subject than that." The middle-aged man shook his head, standing up from the chair and starting to walk towards the fire. "To be fair, little of what is said is exaggeration."

"What? So you're telling me the child saying that a human able to 'bend the elements to his will' is real?" the beast smirked.

"No, he had no magic." The man shook his head, his hair glittering in the soft firelight. He knelt down on those odd deer legs to adjust some coals. "But what he could do was make allies. He befriended trolls, enchanted water spirits, talked to wild beast men... But unlike most people, he never feared them. They could be slain as easily as he befriended them. In many ways, it almost seemed as if they *did* bend to his will."

"Arrogance. A human cannot have that much power," the beast scoffed, baring his fangs.

"But he was no normal human... In fact, many believed he wasn't human at all."

"Oh? What makes this monster slayer of yours so special?" Adrian sneered.

He sighed. "At this point, anything I tell you will just end up hurting you. Do you still want to hear?"

"Of course," the troll snapped. How on earth could this hurt him? What, was the man going to rise from the grave to throttle him? He had to resist laughing.

"Fine, then let me tell you a story." The hunter pulled away from the fire, sitting down once more in the chair next to the bed. His eyes were distant as he began to recall, "Over thirty years ago, a child was born to an ailing mother and merchant father. He was a delicate soul and the last of an ancient bloodline. His mother loved him dearly and made sure he was well-cared for, despite her sickly nature. She died when he was still a boy."

Mother... her curtain of hair concealed her emaciated face. The troll shuddered, violently shaking his head.

"His father, stricken with grief, took it out on the boy, driving him away. While he grew to resent him, he also desperately clung to him, straining their relationship further and further. Soon, the boy became a man, and decided to join the military. He wanted to tell stories like his mother, and thought knighthood was the perfect place to find such tales." The hunter paused.

Another sight. Another memory.

A step onto the path. A breath of fresh air. Courage.

"When his father passed, that was exactly what he did. But when the man began to rise through the ranks, the empire of Golossia made its first move. In an attack that would end up starting a war, they struck the fort that young man was in. They brought a monster. A mountain troll, who killed every single human he saw. The man tried to fight back, managing to sever the troll's fingers." Adrian's left hand twitched, a shadow of pain falling over his flesh and driving him to unconsciously hold it.

"Even then, he was beaten to near death. The Golossian strike force left the fort, making way for the larger central army to move in hours later. He was a broken doll, a dead man walking. But still, he managed to make it out of the fort and towards an oncoming army with those severed fingers, proof of the monster. Thanks to him, Golossia's first attack failed. But he was on death's door. The medics figured he only had a few hours left. It was by fate then, that a mysterious doctor had arrived at that village. He gave the dying soldier a choice: die a man, or forsake his humanity for a second chance. With his rage, vengeance, and hatred... he chose to live."

Blood filled his lungs. Something looming overhead. Fury.

His claws dug into the straw mattress. Harris continued, "He always said that he didn't remember what happened; but the object that ended up saving his life were those fingers he collected."

"He made himself kin..." Adrian breathed. "But that's not possible! Humans cannot just turn others into fae!"

The man shrugged. "Either way, ever since then, his body became part troll. He had teeth and bone fragments jutting out of his skin, he became weak to fire and iron, and he was strong enough to fell monsters... In the end, he did slay that beast, and went on to become one of the strongest knights in the Solanian army."

More pain.

Banners flapped in the air. He was heavy, covered in metal. He was surrounded by others. They believed in him.

"No one knew what he was, what he was becoming. He hid himself under special armor, something that could hide his affliction from his allies and frighten his enemies. No, the only images that remain of him lie in the capital and here in Willowbend; back at his ancestral home."

"The largest house in the village..." Adrian breathed. The hunter nodded.

"He never knew he was going to be a father when it happened. When he disappeared, Vantis was left alone." He paused, gazing into the fire. "That woman and I..."

"Wren," Adrian whispered. The hunter seemed surprised, turning towards him with an appraising look.

"You remember her name. Do you remember mine?"

"I..." the man started, clutching his head as another stab burned his brain. He did know. The wound opened, revealing a name. "H-Harris..."

Harris nodded, adjusting his position in the chair. "Everyone thought he died... Officially, the commander of the Black Lion Executioners is considered missing in action. Only we knew the truth. We knew he wasn't dead. No... instead we saw him change into something. We saw him fall to his kinship. We saw him turn into a beast."

"And you... You think that's me?" Adrian growled with a sneer. It barely covered his fear, his self-doubt. "You think I'm your human friend?"

"I'm not saying that. His body may still exist, but the Adrian Lionel we knew is gone." Harris shook his head.

"...Adrian?" the troll whispered.

Harris's face twitched. "Yes, Adrian Lionel. Father of Vantis Lionel." He gave him a hard look.

"That's... my name..." The beast's legs curled in, making him look so much smaller as he held them. "...My name... Adrian Lionel..."

"Look, I'm not saying you are him. At this point, you might as well be your own person. But I am saying that you were made from his turning, and that those memories still reside in you."

"...Memories... I... I have so many of those..." the man whispered, his eyes glassy with distance.

"Of?" the hunter pressed.

"Of... two women. My mother... and another... someone I loved... My mother was kind, she wrote a book... a book I still have in my cave... I can't read it... I should be able to... I should be able to read it..."

Harris leaned forward, resting his elbows on his knees. "And what of the other woman?"

"I... cannot recall her face. She was... so beautiful though. I loved her so much. I..." Adrian stopped, clutching his forehead hard with one of his talons. He felt something warm bead from his scalp. An agony filled his stomach, an emptiness.

"You needn't say more if it makes you uncomfortable..." The softness of the man's voice pierced Adrian's pain.

"This... isn't possible... I was born thirteen years ago..." the troll's voice could barely be heard at this point.

"You *woke up* thirteen years ago," Harris corrected.

Adrian glared at the man, his lip curling into a snarl. A question howled inside his head. "Do you know the name of... that man's enemy?"

Harris faced him. His brown eyes were nothing but black holes boring into him. "The name of the troll that Adrian Lionel slayed, the one that harmed him so grievously, the one that drove him to become a fae kin, is Aladarr."

Memories of blood, screaming, and rage flooded the troll's mind, sending arcs of agony up his spine. Sickening laughs filled his ears. He felt as though his jaw was being pulled from his face, his arm tugged and snapped away from his body. Adrian cried out, clasping his head with his talons as tears ran down his face. His back arched, seizing. Harris's hand trembled for a moment before he clenched it, leaning over to help the man back into the furs.

"That's enough... Rest now, I have to go out for a moment," he said, an edge of gentleness in his voice. "But you must promise me something..." A single puffy eye cracked open, a small blue ring looking up at the face looming above him. "You will not leave this cabin while I'm gone. You will stay here until I get back." A look of terror flashed over those eyes before closing with a shaking nod.

"I... promise..." Adrian whimpered.

"I promise I won't bring any torches or pitchforks back with me. As long as you are my guest, no harm will come to you," Harris solemnly stated. All Adrian could do was nod. He held his arms close. Tears ran down his face. With that, the hunter backed away, grabbed his bow, and walked out, leaving Adrian alone with his spinning thoughts.

Adrian Lionel...

That was his name, he was certain. But all of that, that whole story... It was too much. There was no way that was him. He wasn't a filthy human, he wasn't some king's warrior pet, he was a free troll. He didn't have a child, he didn't have a wife, he didn't have a mother.

But how could that be true when he remembered so much?

The man curled in on himself in the fetal position, sobbing. If all of this was true, then how had he forgotten for so long? Why couldn't he read anymore? Why did it take so long for him to speak? He was a troll! He knew it in his bones. His body knew it, his mind knew it.

Then what did those memories mean?
Why do you have human desires?
Why did you turn into this man?
Why is his name yours?

It was too much. It was all just too much.

Chapter 10

A few hours later, he woke up. The man was still alone in the cabin, the firelight completely smothered. Adrian pulled himself up. He didn't know what to think anymore. At this point, he wished he could shut his mind down. He was both a man and a troll but... neither? He had human thoughts because he was a human and not a pure fae. He was some kind of freak amongst kin. And he was apparently a father. He gagged, the torment in his stomach making him heave.

Adrian threw the uncomfortable thoughts towards the back of his mind, instead choosing to focus on what was directly in front of him. None of this changed anything. He was still Adrian, wasn't he? The man slid the blankets away, setting his bandaged feet on the ground. He sat there for a moment, uncomfortable being in someone else's den. He gazed at his human arms. They still possessed the scars that littered his troll form, markings he had when he first woke up.

And apparently from his previous life...

Adrian shook the thought away. He began to unwrap the bandages, revealing fresh glossy skin underneath. It would take awhile to fully heal, but the skin was at least intact. He peeled all the wrappings away, letting them fall to the floor. He gripped the side of the bed, taking a deep breath. With some effort, he heaved himself up and out of the mattress, staggering to his feet. Without his tail, without his feathers, the troll was completely off balance. But he also felt light and flexible, a harsh contrast with his ridged troll flesh and heavy wing arms.

It was... exhilarating?

The man pulled away from the bed, stepping over to his cloak hanging on a rack next to the door. He pulled the fur around him and locked it in place with that bone fragment, sighing. At least he had something that smelled of home, bringing him some small semblance of peace. Finding his sandals next to the door as well, he stooped down to pluck them away. As he put them on he kept the bandages on his feet, the leather wrappings still too rough for his fresh skin. There was a comfort, being covered in his own things. It made him feel in control. It made him feel safe. "How miserable..." he muttered, pacing about. He was a mighty mountain troll, not some scared little boy! He shouldn't act so meek!

You're a terrified man... not a troll.

Adrian shuddered. He tossed the cloak behind him with an exaggerated swipe of his hand. "This is nonsense. I should just leave and go find the Green Man," he hissed, turning towards the door. The man marched over and put his hand on the handle. Instantly, a sharp jab of agony raced up his arm and into his brain, making him lurch away. His free hand grasped the shaking claw.

You made a promise. An oath.

"Bullshit!" he snapped. The word he said confused him. Where did that come from? Wasn't that a human saying?

One of my favorites.

The troll snarled, backing away from the door. Of course, he had made a promise to the hunter. Now that it was in place and agreed to, he couldn't take it back. If he did, the result would backfire, hurting his very being. That was the way of fae. He was trapped, locked in a box, and at the mercy of a man that he hardly knew.

A glare. An order. He ran away. He cried when he came back. He went ahead. He always went ahead of him. He stayed when he had to leave. He always followed orders. He always stayed by his side. He was his right hand.

The man howled, throwing himself against the floor. So many flashes burned within his head, so many images flooding his vision. The troll laid there, shaking like a leaf. Adrian's whimpers eventually faded, leaving the man exhausted. Desperately, his claws pulled under his chest and heaved his body off the ground. His legs shuddered as he stood up, resting his back against the wall with a heavy breath. "These visions... are going to be the death of me..." Adrian chuckled, wiping the sweat from his brow. He glanced at his hand. His sweat was clear, not yellow like he was expecting. He sighed.

Adrian pulled his arms underneath his shroud, scanning the room. With the window shuttered, it was as dark as night inside. The troll moved over to the sill, reaching out to grab the shutters. A searing bolt of fire raced up his fingertips. He lurched back with a hiss. "That too is in violation?! I can't even open the bloody windows?!" he roared, whipping around to face the center of the cabin.

His furious eyes drifted to the pile of ash sitting in the fireplace. He knelt down next to it, staring into the dead embers. His gaze panned over to the pair of flint stones resting on the hearth. The man picked them up, glancing at them curiously. "How did he use these again?" he muttered under his breath, holding them out over the pit. The troll tried rubbing them together to no success. He frowned. Suddenly, his hand moved on its own, striking the side of one rock with the other. The spark that leapt free made the beast yelp, dropping the stones and backing away. When his panicked breathing finally faded he scowled. "Afraid of a tiny spark... What are you, a pinecone?" he hissed. Adrian brushed the old ash away, clearing a spot in the pit. He stacked some logs in the center, making the same tent-shape he saw Harris build. He snatched some dry grass kindling from an urn next to the hearth, setting it in front of him. His claws grasped the rocks once more, taking a deep breath. "I just need some light... Don't be afraid of a bloody spark..." With a couple of smooth strikes, the kindling caught fire. His claw daintily plucked the wad and set it in the center of the pit, watching the tiny flames begin to fade. "N-no! Wait!" he breathed, pressing his chest against the hearth.

Blow on it. Gently.

He obeyed, softly exhaling on the embers. The tongues of flame reached out, licking at the logs until they too caught. After a few minutes of gentle coaxing, the fire roared to life. Adrian sat back, a wave of pride washing over him. He made this, with his own two hands, no magic. Just as the gentle tongues of heat lashed his skin, just as his pride settled, a door opened, flooding the room with light. Instinctively, the troll whipped around with a growl, still holding the two sharp flint stones, this time as weapons.

Harris blinked as he walked in. He glanced at the rocks in his hands. "Glad to see you didn't burn the cabin down."

Adrian's lip curled into a sneer. "Not that you gave me much choice. It was dark as night in this rotten place with the windows closed... Speaking of which, is the deal done; can I open the bloody window?"

Harris blinked, nodding. The troll rushed over to the sill, flipping the latch and thrusting open the shutters with way too much gusto. They slammed roughly against the cabin walls, making the hunter wince. Adrian leaned out, taking a deep breath of the forest. Oh, how he'd missed the sunlight on his skin. The hunter closed the door behind him and set a rucksack of goods on the writing desk. The troll could smell the sweet scent of meat emanating from it. The middle-aged man raised a brow. "You could've opened the shutters earlier, you know."

The beast turned towards him, the aggravation clear in his voice, "Yes, well, thanks to our little *deal* I wasn't exactly allowed to."

Harris raised a brow. "I thought that had everything to do with intention."

"Unfortunately, no," the beast hissed, dragging his nails away from the threshold. "I was told not to leave the cabin. Opening the shutters would set my hands outside said cabin walls. Therefore, I couldn't."

"I see," Harris replied, walking over to the chair by the fire. He was silent for a moment. "Why didn't you just use a stick to open it?"

Adrian glared, marching over to him. "Well, I didn't exactly think there were many suitable sticks nearby..."

Harris blinked before jabbing a thumb over to the logs. Blue rings darted over, noticing a fire poker leaning against the fireplace wall behind them. Adrian's eye twitched. The hunter smirked. "Sorry, couldn't help but point that out."

The troll glowered, the lowering of his head casting his beautiful face in ethereal shadow, "Why do I feel you being a smart-ass is a rather common occurrence...?"

The hunter shrugged. "I won't deny it." His brown eyes glanced down at the snapping flames. "Hmph. Been practicing building fires in that cave of yours?"

"No," the man turned away, covering most of his body under his fur cloak. "This is the first time."

"Guess muscle memory served you well," Harris smiled, marching past the man over to the sack. He pulled out a plucked, raw pheasant, holding it out to the fae. Tentatively, the troll accepted it and sat down in the chair next to the bed, digging into the flesh with his sharp fangs. This didn't seem to unnerve the hunter. Rather, his expression was almost nostalgic. He sat down in the rocking chair, staring into the flames.

It was silent as the beast ate his meal. Only the sounds of smacking lips, snapping muscles, and crunching bones permeated the cabin. When the troll finally finished, he sat back and sighed. "Is it true?" Adrian asked.

"Hmm?" Harris gave him a glance.

"Am I... really that boy's father...?" the troll's voice was barely above a whisper.

"Yes. In body at the very least," the hunter answered, gazing into the fire.

Adrian clenched his hands. "Does that mean... he's kin too?"

Harris sighed, rocking the chair a little. "Not sure. You were rather far in your corruption at the time, but you were still there. As far as he looks, he's pure human. But if my information is correct, kin don't start gaining fae traits until they hit puberty..."

Adrian was silent for a moment. "I... don't want that boy to suffer as I have. Stuck between worlds like this..." the troll whispered, his eyes locked onto the wooden floor.

"Even if it's the case," the hunter began, readjusting his position in the chair. "We have plans in place to protect him. He'll be fine." More silence. A smirk graced his rugged features. "In spirit, he's a lot like you. He's annoyingly impulsive."

"All hu- All boys act impulsive at that age. They have desires they don't understand, whims and wishes that drive them to acts of stupidity. And they always feel like dragging well-adjusted adults into all their bloody problems..." Adrian added, resting his elbows against his spread legs.

The hunter snorted. "What, like trying to befriend a troll against his will?"

"Yes," the fae growled, baring his fangs.

Harris shrugged. "You could've scared him away, you know."

A snarl exited between his teeth. "No, I couldn't. Remember, he stabbed me in the face."

"You could've hurt him," the hunter shrugged. "Not to kill, but enough to drive him away."

Adrian gave the man an aghast look. "I would never! I could never hurt him like that. I don't hurt villagers."

"But what if you're attacked?" Harris pressed.

"I told you! I wouldn't! I wouldn't hurt anyone! I don't want to!" the troll yelled, glaring.

Those tired umber eyes closed. "Then I will hold you to that..." The two sat in silence, illuminated by the dappled light outside. The birds chirped, insects buzzing in and out of the cabin. Leaves rustled gently in the afternoon breeze.

In that peaceful moment, Harris's expression hardened, as if certain of something. "I got everything arranged," Harris stated.

"For... what?" Adrian gave him a perplexed look.

"To get you inside the village. Wren and Vantis will be going to the market today to give the boy a hands-on lesson in economics. That will give us about an hour to explore the Lionel home," he explained, looking at the man.

"For... my mementos...?" the troll asked. The hunter nodded. "I see... maybe then I can be certain..."

Harris shrugged. "It could jog some more memories, help you get your head straight. Either way, it's worth the trip."

"I see... Will showing my face in that village give people the wrong idea?" Adrian questioned.

Those intimidating brown eyes met his. "They'll think you're back."

Adrian recoiled, holding his hands roughly. "I... don't want to do that to them. I don't want them to get their hopes up."

Harris nodded. He stood up from the chair, smothering the fire Adrian worked so hard to start. The troll couldn't help but scowl. "Well then, let's not waste time, shall we? Does that cloak of yours have a hood?" The beast blinked, reaching for the shroud and pulling it over his head. It was rough, but it would do. The hunter gave him an appraising look before nodding. "Very well then, let's go."

Chapter 11

The village was nestled in a clearing made between the two massive halves of the Willowbend Forest. A wide, 50-yard diameter circle of dirt sat in the middle of town, where carts and pack animals moved from building to building. Wooden houses and shops were pressed together, with little difference in use of space. The blacksmith and his dutiful apprentice slaved away in the forge. The weaver sat at her shop humming away as she worked. The syrup makers stirred their heated pots of product. Everyone was in a state of motion. They called out to one another, exchanging goods and words as they paused. Some took breaks, reveling in the arts of wandering bards; be that as song or dance. Young lads and ladies giggled by the open fields that formed an outer ring around the settlement. Children frolicked and scuffled in gardens, much to their parents' chagrin. The market, the busiest part of town, laid towards the eastern main road, littered with stalls and storage buildings. This was economics in action, a far cry from what the quiet little village used to be. As harsh as the outer world was, they had their peace here.

In the middle of the dirt clearing, a circular pool stood, a brief glimpse of extravagance in the humble town. At the center of that stone pool stood a statue. They were clothed in flowing fineries, with elegance in their form; positioned like a saint. In one hand, a mighty curved sword drove into the center of the pedestal. In the other, a book held out regally for the face to gaze upon. Their hair was sculpted in motion, the flow of the locks caressing the face and billowing out against the arm holding the book. The tilted face was kind, soft with its gentle smile; half-lidded eyes gazing down upon the pages. A face that looked exactly like his.

Adrian's jaw clenched, driving his gaze towards the ground. He held the cloak tightly, praying the hood never fell. Some villagers did turn their attention, nervously curious about the newcomer. But at the sight of Harris leading him on, they relaxed. They knew he could handle any trouble a stranger could give. The troll shielded his eyes, certain the black sclera surrounding his blue irises would give away his ethereal nature instantly. They walked on, past the whispers and the mumblings of the bystanders, until they approached the shadow of the Lionel Manor ahead.

Harris strode on with complete confidence, only halting at the door. He pulled out a bronze key, setting it in the lock and twisting it. With a deep thunk, the dead bolt unlatched, and Harris pushed open the heavy door. The man stepped inside the shadowed halls, leaving Adrian to stare at the threshold. He couldn't will himself to step inside, as if shackles laid at his feet. Harris spotted this, turning around to offer a hand. The troll hesitated, almost terrified of this place.

Adrian took it and was finally granted entry. Harris closed the door behind the both of them, leaving the man to wander the main foyer. The ceiling was high, hanging at least thirty feet above him, and made of carved stone columns and wooden beams. A cobweb-dressed chandelier of tarnished brass hung above, having been unlit for decades. The halls were adorned in hand-woven tapestries and crimson linen curtains, making the barren stone walls far cozier than one would expect. A staircase sat in the center of the foyer, with carved hardwood banisters shaped with the likeness of animals foreign to these lands. Glancing down, Adrian realized that his sandals were stepping upon a fur rug, something that made him step back. He watched Harris kick off the boots he used to hide his animal legs by the front door, striding deeper into the echoing halls. Adrian mimicked this, taking off his shoes to roam the interior.

Harris led him through a massive entryway to the left of the foyer, into a large room containing a fireplace. Bookcases littered with old and dusty tomes surrounded the room, only broken up by unlit lamps and drapes hung over the massive window facing the front of the property. Upon the space above and around that fireplace hung trinkets and weapons; a massive crossbow, the tusk of some imposing beast, a small tree branch, some tokens from friends and colleagues, knives held delicately by a plaque, and a huge, jagged sword mounted on the mantle. And above it all laid a massive portrait, one depicting the same face as the statue. An elegant man dressed in fineries, his hair tied back with a green ribbon as it flowed down the side of his shoulder like water. The man's tan skin was unblemished, making him look almost angelic in nature. The position of his head portrayed a regal air, more befitting of a king than a merchant of his status. His face was set in a soft smile, one that oozed benevolence and contentment. Ocean-blue eyes gazed out serenely, almost boring holes into Adrian's own as the claws of a rising headache drove themselves into his skull.

The man backed his way out into the foyer. "Could we... visit this room last?" he asked, holding his head. A fragment of worry crossed Harris's face, gazing up at the portrait before looking back at the distressed man.

"Yes, of course. Where do you want to go first?" The hunter stood beside him in the hall. Adrian gazed up the stairs, spotting a painting on the far wall.

"There," he breathed, drifting towards the steps. As soon as his gloved hands touched the banisters, a jolt of remembrance flowed into his soul, threatening to make him gasp. He pushed the feeling down, willing his body to ascend. With each creak of the floorboards, a wave of nostalgia washed over the man. After a moment, he reached the top, met with a long hallway that continued past the landing walls on either side. Pedestals of vases and other trinkets graced the sides of the room, testaments to the achievements of the merchant family. At the center of the far wall was a large family portrait.

A stern-looking man with long, wavy blonde hair stood at attention, almost glaring at the viewer. His finely-laced black suit was tailored expertly to his angular shoulders and lithe frame, with flowing cuffs and accents bringing to mind a more courtly visage. His blue eyes, remarkably similar to the person in the painting downstairs, were seas of conflict. Unlike that person, this man's face was more chiseled, more masculine. Next to him, sitting in an ornate chair, was a beautiful woman. Her ghostly pale features were soft and graceful, her tired green eyes shining with pride and joy. Her jet black hair cascaded down her shoulders, framing her head like a shroud. She was dressed in a flowing black and green gown covered in intricate golden markings, depicting vines and roses. In her delicate arms, laid a swaddled bundle. A baby. The pudgy face was sagging in a state of rest, with small tufts of black hair poking out from under the grey wrappings.

Just below this, stood a pedestal holding an urn. The troll couldn't stop the tears. "Mother... Father..." he whispered, approaching the painting. Her face was just as he remembered, kind and ghostly. His father, always the stoic one, and presumably upset by the complications of the birth of their son, always glared. He never seemed happy unless mother was near. She was his world after all. Adrian's birth began the road that would take her life, leaving the man embittered. The fae's frown deepened, hiding his face. For all his father yelled, for all the distance... Adrian never stopped loving him. Just like he never stopped loving mother. Adrian approached the urn silently, already knowing what laid within it. He set his hands upon the cold porcelain, resting his head against the surface.

Harris watched on in silence, a prickle of unwelcome excitement crawling up his spine and making his hair stand on end. He could almost see his solemn friend return. After a moment, the troll pulled away, gazing back up at the portrait. "Father never liked me, you know. He was a lot like a troll parent in that regard," he chuckled. "He blamed me for mother's death."

"I... thought she was sick," Harris stepped beside him, crossing his arms as he scanned the painting.

"She was, and it was because of my birth. Something went wrong and her strength never returned... It only took a brief spell of pneumonia to drive her away from us..." Adrian sighed, starting to make his way down the right hall.

The hunter followed, speaking up. "That's not your fault, you know."

The troll shrugged, tapping a trinket on another pedestal. "Doesn't really matter either way. She's gone. He's gone." The cloaked man shuffled along, gazing at the various rooms and paintings. At the end of the hallway, stood a closed door. He tried the handle, only to feel it jam. Adrian glanced over to Harris, who gave the troll a hardened look.

"That's your room. Wren had it locked since you left," he explained.

"Where's the key?" Adrian asked, a hint of irritation in his tone.

"Don't know. I'd assume she hid it somewhere. Or, knowing our luck, Vantis probably has it," the hunter grumbled.

The cloaked man gazed upon the door for a moment before pulling his hands back under the shroud. "Very well, then. Let's go. I don't exactly plan on destroying anything while I'm here..." he shouldered past Harris, making his way back to the landing.

Other than my own sanity.

The troll had to resist the urge to snort. He strode past the family portrait, towards the left end of the top floor, gazing into the unlocked rooms. One particular room caught his attention. It was only a little larger than the bed laying within. The remaining floor space was consumed by a nightstand and a narrow walkway. On that nightstand, laid several miscellaneous objects. A crimson brooch, a sash of black cloth with golden embroidery, a knife, and a folded piece of paper. The bed was neatly made, even in the cramped space. Before Adrian could ask, Harris already answered. "This is Wren's room."

The troll turned with a raised brow. "Of all the rooms she chose to sleep in within this massive home... and she chose the broom closet?"

"You sound disappointed," Harris grunted, resting his back against the wooden wall.

"I am! Any self-respecting troll *or* human would pick a greater room! There's no space for anything! No hoards, bones, or bloody books!" the man gestured with a scowl.

The hunter chuckled. "I don't think she has any interest in bones... There *are* plenty of books in the library... and you're already looking at her favorite possessions." He pointed to the objects on the nightstand.

Adrian's brow furrowed. He gave a frustrated grunt, marching past to continue browsing. The other rooms were nominal, as expected, the specters of memories drifting past his vision. Those sharp daggers in his mind remained, flexing arcs of pain threatening his every thought. The beast approached a set of double doors.

The master bedroom...

He thrust open the doors, his growl deepening. The gigantic window on the left side of the room cast a gleeful afternoon glow on everything within reach. An unmade king-sized bed laid at the center, surrounded by drapings of red. The floor was dotted with scattered books and scrawled papers, with the right side of the room entirely devoted to study. It was horrifyingly messy. "Of course the brat has the largest room..." his voice hissed.

"It was Wren's decision..." Harris shrugged. "Believed it was more his house than hers."

Her hands held onto the tube containing the scroll. Her way out. Her way home. Her home.

His temper boiled over. "That's bullshit! I gave her this damn house! She deserves it just as much as he does!" Adrian roared, fury burning in those blue rings.

Harris stepped back, his eyes wide with shock. The hunter almost seemed hopeful at the outburst. But the sharp growl that erupted out of the cloaked man's maw as he clutched at his skull tainted the joy. He was suffering thinking about this. The man reached out to help the troll but Adrian raised a hand. In a moment, the pain subsided, and he gingerly closed the doors. Before Harris could find any words to say, Adrian had already passed him, making his way down the stairs. Defeated, the hunter followed along, frustrated at himself more than anything.

The troll drifted over to the right of the foyer, walking into a parlor. Here, a table sat with four seats, each formed with immaculate carvings of trees and animals. Curtains hung heavy over the windows, shrouding the stone room in darkness. Adrian's eyes were better suited for the shadows, already spotting various details. Unlit lamps hung on the walls, surrounded by paintings of previous Lionels.

Included amongst these faces was the frayed and tattered painting of a younger-looking man, one that appeared eerily similar to himself. This person had a harder, more angular face, and his eyes were far more sunken into his skull than Adrian's. The face was littered with scars and his stern gaze only seemed to accent them. They were painted with an expression of terrible sorrow and torture that none of the other pampered merchants had. This was clearly the oldest painting, and Adrian had a vague sense he stared at this one often.

Who was it? He wondered. Mother never knew, and Father never cared. This painting was maintained, seemingly for over a few centuries. So it had to be important. Who was it?

He blinked away the memory, still perplexed. Whoever it was, they were forgotten. No different than the other nameless faces. He stepped past the table towards a doorway, peeking inside to see a small kitchen. Not particularly interested in a meal, he stepped away back towards the main foyer. There was only one room left to examine. The library. The room with that painting. The troll steeled his nerves, determined to get through this last challenge.

Just one more. One more and I can leave...

Adrian sucked in a breath and made his way over to the archway. His eyes refused to look at the painting, choosing to instead approach the trinkets resting on the surrounding walls. He gave them a cursory glance before turning towards Harris. The hunter was leaning against the doorway, his arms crossed. "May I?" Adrian gestured to the wall.

"Be my guest. They were yours," the hunter shrugged. "Just don't break them or you'll make Wren and Vantis upset."

The troll nodded, turning towards the knives. He plucked one from its mount, flipping it in his hand. At first, the motion was clumsy, and Harris became concerned that he would hurt himself. But before long, he'd spun it around in his grasp with the fluidity of a master, a vague expression of smugness on Adrian's face. He sighed, setting it back. His gaze fell to a worn black slate resting against a shelf, with a fragment of chalk laying beside it. His hands gripped the sides, pulling it away to gaze down upon it. What was the purpose of this? And what was the point of the chalk? He shifted his grip and grabbed the dusty white stone. He flipped it around for a second before resting it against the slate. With a soft grinding sound, an ivory mark was left behind. Adrian pulled the chalk away roughly, fearing he'd already broke something. He rested a finger against the mark and wiped it away, leaving a clear surface. The hairs on the back of his neck rose.

My voice is broken. I must find a way to be heard.

"I... could write... Then that means..." The troll frowned. He'd been puzzling over the bizarre markings he was leaving behind on the wall, the writings in his books. He used to be able to read them... but now that skill was lost to him. His brow furrowed and his lip curled.

I can't write anymore. Did I seriously lose that much intelligence?

Such a self-deprecating thought enraged him.

I am a troll! What need do I have for reading and writing?! That is a human pass-time, not for a fae of my status!

He was certain in his assertion, that was until doubt wormed its way into his thoughts.

Mother's book....

His face fell, conflict in his eyes. He carefully set the slate back up on the shelf. The man gazed over at the crossbow to the right. There was a black sash tied around the stock, similar to the one in Wren's room. The troll stepped up, pulling it off the pegs. The grip was well-worn underneath his claws, the wood dented and scratched from years of torment. He pulled the weapon up to his right eye, viewing down the sight.

Harris held his breath, clenching his fist. The look in Adrian's eye was so... nostalgic. The way his hands maneuvered around the weapon, pulling back on the crannequin, checking the string... the Black Lion was there. And in a moment, it was gone, Adrian setting the crossbow back on its mount. There was a moment of silence, enough that the huntsman could hear the floorboards creak as the troll shifted his feet. A clawed hand reached out, reaching for the final object of interest. Harris pulled away from the wall, watching intently. His heart was racing. This was it.

Fingers wrapped tight around the leather grip, heaving a large, curved sword off of the mantle. The troll seemed to expect the weight, shifting his stance slightly to lift it up with his one hand. The blade was a mess of swirling metals, each a slightly different color than the next patch. The division gave it a brittle look, but he knew that this weapon was anything but. The man backed up with the sword, trying to get to a clear location. Adrian braced the bottom of the grip with his left hand, giving the weapon a smooth swing that seemed to make the air gasp. His cloak billowed behind him elegantly, following his body and blade. Adrian was absorbed in the weapon, in its familiar power and speed. Despite the weight, it flowed through the air like a ribbon, and he was the dancer. His eyes were fire and determination incarnate. As he stopped this exercise, his mouth moved. "Terminus..."

Tears ran down Harris's face. His commander had returned. The Black Lion Executioner, Lord Adrian Lionel, stood before him, with all his pride and fury. And for all his joy, he failed to notice Wren opening the door behind him, mumbling something about Vantis being forgetful under her breath as she strode inside. It was Adrian who spotted her first. His eyes went wide as he lowered the blade.

She was covered in blood. None of it was her own. She was alone. She was scared. She was strong. She stood by his side. She was a quick learner. She had a beautiful, silly laugh. She was great at cooking, even if she told herself she wasn't. Her eyes were autumn flames. She was never alone. She was always covered in blood. Never her own.

It was as she stood up from gathering a water skin from the bench by the door that Wren's eyes met his, the two of them freezing in place like deer caught in the light of a lantern. The water skin fell to the floor with a dull thud as she staggered back, the sudden sound making Harris twist around in alarm. Trembling hands cupped her mouth as soft gasps rattled through her strong form. Adrian, seeing her mental anguish, quickly turned away. Harris tried to call out to her, but before he could say anything, she fled into the parlor at the other end of the house. A horrified expression cursed Harris's face as he blindly rushed to tend to her.

Adrian could hear her shaking sobs from where he was. He gazed down at the sword in his hand, his grip tightening. The man whipped around, slamming the weapon onto its mount. His lip was trembling as his eyes threatened him with tears. "It was a mistake to come here..." he muttered, pulling the cloak up and over his anguished face, retrieving his shoes, and rushing out the door. In a blind, sorrowful fury, the troll rushed through the woods, desperate to cause no more harm. He ran and ran and ran, until his legs tangled in a mass of roots and he fell into the leaf litter. The man just laid there, covering his face and sobbing.

It's all your fault.

It's all your fault.

Chapter 12

Adrian found himself nestled between two large maple trees, pressing against them like a frightened child. His knees were drawn up, held by his elbows as his claws frayed at a stick. The nails peeled away at the outer layers of bark before moving towards the inner flesh of the wood. Blue rings drifted up to the canopy above, gazing into the greens and golds of the leaves above. Autumn would soon be here. Even now, a cool breeze reminded him of this fact, a fact that filled him with dread. How on earth was he going to survive the winter in this state? Without his thick skin, without his fangs and talons, how was he going to weather the blizzards and hunts he needed? He couldn't rely on Harris forever, and it was clear to him that going near that house with his shattered memories would provide little comfort. Adrian didn't want to hurt Wren again. He would need to find a way to survive on his own, making sure no one saw him while he did. It was too dangerous. At least for him. The soft crunching of leaves behind his hiding spot made the man's eyes snap to his side. They were light... delicate... like deer hooves...

"Harris," he stated evenly.

"Yeah, it's me. Didn't want to scare you," his voice greeted, still coming closer.

"You're not as stealthy as you think," the troll smiled, still working away at the stick.

"Heh, only when I'm not tryin'," the man retorted. Harris paused, trying to collect the words. "Sorry about earlier, I needed to make sure Wren was alright," the hunter sighed, passing by the trees to gaze down upon him. The troll looked small. Injured.

"No... I understand. Is she... Did I hurt her?"

Those slightly wrinkled brown eyes drifted back down the valley, towards the manor. They closed solemnly; disturbingly showing his age. "She was... shaken... She didn't know how to handle seeing you..."

"I'm sorry..." Adrian whispered, drawing himself in tighter. He snapped off one of the twigs.

"No," Harris argued, a hint of frustration in his tone. "This was my idea. You had nothing to do with this. I was... I was just trying to help." The hunter paused, drawing up his face as he stopped the torrent of words threatening his quivering lips. He took a deep breath. "This wasn't supposed to happen. She wasn't supposed to come back to the house... I should have kept a better eye out, I'm sorry."

Adrian's face fell. His gaze went to his clawed hands, the nails peeling away at another layer of wood. Hands he was supposed to be proud of. Hands he was ashamed of. "I don't know why... but making her cry like that... scaring her like that... Hurt more than any wound I have ever received. I didn't mean to... I didn't want to..."

"That wasn't fear. I've seen her scared. This wasn't it. It was more like... she was seeing a ghost. She had accepted you were gone a few years ago. She said that she had moved on..." the hunter sighed. "But then you came back, looking how you did and it... It opened up a fresh wound in an old scar..."

"I'm sorry... I'm so terribly sorry..." the beast whispered, curling deeper into his hovel.

He sensed the huntsman's stance shift, hesitating before walking over. Adrian heard the crunch of his knees as the man knelt beside him. Tentatively, Harris rested a hand on his shoulder. "It will be alright. It will take some time... Perhaps one day you'll be able to meet her again. Not now... but someday. We should just focus on making sure you can survive out here till then."

The troll snarled. "I'm not a child." He dropped the stripped stick to the ground.

"No, you're an unarmed, untrained human. That means you have to fight and survive by our rules, and I'm not going to leave you to figure that out on your own," Harris explained, standing in front of him. "I don't want to have to lug your heavy backside home again," he added with a smirk.

Adrian chuckled. "What? Afraid you'll break a hip, old man?"

"More like I'm afraid of having to deal with your whiny ass on top of a sore back," Harris smirked. The two laughed, a brief spark of levity that seemed to calm Adrian's nerves. The hunter seemed to notice this, as his tone changed. "Come on, let me teach you how to make a weapon." He held out a gloved hand. The troll sighed, taking it and getting to his feet. While his guide carried on, Adrian hesitated, glancing back towards the noise of the village. In a moment, fear and doubt, but only a moment. The next, he turned his head away, following along deeper into the shadowed woodlands. The two men traveled a decent distance away before Harris spoke up. "So, what kind of weapon do you need?"

"I'm not entirely sure. Something that kills things?" The troll glanced around, trying to size up any sticks that caught his fancy.

"Wow," the hunter breathed. "That certainly narrows it down..." He ducked under a low vine.

"Well, I don't know!" The troll snapped, reaching up to the vine and pulling it apart as he came upon it, flinging the two ends behind him. "I usually just used my claws and fangs to catch my prey!"

"Yeah, well, you don't have those anymore. You can't go running around trying to get a nip at something if you can't even reach it first," the hunter sighed, leaping over a rock gracefully.

The troll followed behind him, kicking the large stone away with a hiss. "In that case, something that lets me reach prey. Something I can swing with my own two hands."

"Now that narrows it down," Harris chuckled. "You can't go swinging at everything. At this point, you run the risk of just splattering the food across the trees with that strength of yours." He expertly clambered over a cluster of fallen trees along the side of a small cliff, bounding from trunk to trunk. When he settled at the top of the plateau, Harris rested his hands on his hips and gazed down. "So a spear it is."

"Bloody spindly deer man..." Adrian spat as he extended his claws, gripping at the bark. Harris smirked, leaning over to watch him. The troll's small but thick talons dug in, scoring deep trenches into the dead wood. He braced the muscles in his shoulders before launching himself up into the air with a leap. He landed roughly on the second-to-top tree, hissing to himself as his chest roughly smashed into the bark. "Fucking thin human flesh..." he cursed, using the reach he had to climb the rest of the way up. Adrian wanted to punch the smirk off Harris's face when he caught up.

"What's wrong? I thought you were supposed to be younger than me. Where's that pep in your step?" he sneered, continuing on.

"Oh, I left it behind when you decided to take the most annoying path here, you rotten bastard," the troll retorted.

The hunter let out another laugh, one that shook his body and made Adrian jump. The troll's glare intensified. "Well, I didn't come all this way to torture you, if that's what you're thinking. Some of the youngest and healthiest trees lay here on this plateau," the man explained, gesturing out to the innumerable saplings around them.

Adrian raised a brow. "Yes, and what does this have to do with getting me a weapon?"

"Well, for starters," Harris turned sharply, sizing up his six-foot-five tall companion. "We are going to need something big, just considering your frame. Secondly, we need something strong and flexible enough to handle the sheer amount of force you put behind your jabs. These saplings got all of that."

Adrian blinked, accepting that explanation. "Very well then..."

"On a third note," Harris pulled out an axe. "There's a river nearby. Exposed flint stones there will make an excellent spearhead. The reeds will give us the cord we need." He approached one of the saplings, sizing it up. "Basically, this is our forge. It may be hard to reach, but the materials are worth it."

Adrian nodded, standing beside him as the hunter struggled with getting a good angle. He pushed him aside roughly and, before the man could retort, the troll wrapped his arms around the trunk. He wrenched the plant free from the soil, roots and all. Harris just shook his head, sighing. The two then got to work fashioning the haft of the spear out of the tree's remains, something that could be easily held in the troll's claws. Adrian was a quiet student, preferring to watch Harris demonstrate every motion before attempting it himself. After the work was finished, they made sure to leave an offering to the forest spirits, thanking them for the life of this tree. Adrian held the green-laced staff in his hands, feeling the smoothly carved wood on his scarred palms. He wasn't sure what to expect, but a glorified troll toothpick wasn't it.

Harris then led the way down to a ravine on the other side of the plateau, sliding effortlessly down the slope to land neatly on the embankment below. The troll sighed, trying to ease his way down using the exposed tree roots... That was until his weight betrayed him. With a harsh pop, the root he held onto snapped, sending

Adrian careening down the slope with a started yelp. As the troll ground to a halt in the reeds below with a cloud of dust, the hunter had to fight the all-consuming urge to laugh. The fact that Adrian held a big stick frightened him enough. After a snarl of embarrassment, the troll dusted his shoulders off, readjusting his cloak as he stopped by Harris's side. "Any more acrobatics I must engage in?"

"N-no," the hunter replied with a cough. He was already scanning the riverside. "Although, it certainly was the most graceful I've ever seen you."

"Asshole," the fae spat.

While they gathered appropriate stones for the spear, Adrian gazed out towards the river. Despite open water always unnerving the troll, there was admittedly a certain peace that came with it. A sense of cleansing. He had never seen this particular body of water before and reveled in that fact. The surface softly glimmered with sunlight, bubbling quietly across the smooth, tile-shaped stones that made the bed below. The reeds resting on the bank rustled peacefully in the easing breath of summer, the insects flittering and buzzing about like fairies. In fact, some actual flower fairies drifted around, giggling with ethereal joy as they rode the wind upon soft plant-like wings. Adrian glanced over to Harris, half-expecting him to notice the fae above them. He either didn't see them or didn't care, as he continued uninterrupted to shape the strands of reed he collected into cord. Even now, it seemed some fae could will the mortal world not to notice their presence.

Sometimes he wished he could do the same.

Harris showed him how to carefully shape the slate, using light manipulation of the stone's position in relation to gentle tapping on the rock below. The troll followed through until he held a sharp-edged rock, not too dissimilar to the arrowheads he saw the hunter make. The troll showed him his work, having created a crude tall triangle. The man nodded, offering more tips and suggestions to refine the shape further. Eventually, they switched tasks, with Adrian weaving the reeds as Harris worked on the final parts of the spearhead. After three hours, the three components were ready for final assembly. Harris walked him through the process; setting the spearhead into the notch at the top of the staff and using the twine to tie the flanged base tight to the haft. After a long day's work, Adrian had a spear.

The man held it in his grasp, bracing it against his forearm. Unconsciously, he tried swinging it like a sword before quickly realizing how stupid he looked. Shaking his head, Adrian began thrusting the spear forward, striking at the dirt and sand with quick, powerful motions as it ripped through the ground cleanly. He nodded, happy with the quality of the weapon. Harris sighed as he rose to his feet, snatching a discarded branch from the dirt. He held the stick out as he approached Adrian.

"What on earth are you doing?" the troll asked, giving him an incredulous look.

"You learn nothing from stabbing the ground, so come on. Let's test that weapon out," the hunter smirked.

"What? No! I could hurt you! I don't hurt villagers!" he spat, backing away with a snarl. But despite his protests, the hunter was already swinging the stick down, forcing Adrian to block it with a horizontal hold above him.

"Just don't go all out! This is a sparring match, not a fight to the death!" He pulled back and jabbed at the troll's ribs, making the beast's side buckle inward. Adrian cussed under his breath, holding his stinging flesh.

How did a blunt stick hurt him?!

"Anyways, so what if you give me a few cuts? Even if you break a finger, it wouldn't be the first time," Harris replied, continuing his onslaught. He went for another thrust, this time aiming under the ribs.

"You're mad, you know that?!" the troll snarled, grabbing the stick with his free hand and pushing it away from his body. His sharp nails ground into the wood.

"Good!" The hunter laughed, struggling for a second. "Never forget you have a free hand," Harris gripped the branch with his other hand and twisted, pulling the weapon inward sharply. This act forced the troll's wrist to turn painfully, making him let go with a yelp. "Just never forget that the enemy does too!" he added with a smirk.

"Rotten old fuck..." he hissed, shaking the pain in his claw.

That's it, no holding back.

The two sparred for half an hour, exchanging blow after blow. In the end, Harris did indeed break a finger and get covered in cuts... But Adrian had just as many bruises and a busted nose. They stood there for a moment, trying to catch their breaths. Harris threw his stick away before roughly flopping down in the leaf litter. He chuckled to himself. "You got me good there at the end, I have to admit!"

"Only because you went for a cheap shot at my face," the beast hissed, wiping the blood away from his nose.

"Not cheap. Opportunistic. The easiest way to fell a larger opponent outside of balance is to go for the face," Harris explained, waving his injured hand as he started to pull out some bandages.

"Feh. You always were a pain, weren't you?" The troll sat down by the stream, washing his bruised limbs in the cool water.

The hunter gave him an amused look. "That's why you insisted on referring to me as 'Captain Hardass' all those years ago..."

Adrian laughed, washing his face. "That does sound like something I would do." By now, the sun was beginning to edge its way over towards the horizon, casting the sky in a luminous golden glow. The troll dipped his head into the river, attempting to take a drink before gasping back out.

"Bloody short nose! How on earth do you creatures drink with this thing?!" he hissed.

Harris chuckled and pulled out a cup from his mess kit, dipping it into the stream. He held it out to the aggravated and soaked man. "We make things. Just like we did here. We make things and life gets easier."

The beast scoffed, taking the cup roughly. "Sounds like an excuse to over-complicate things..."

"Heh, you're not wrong there. Humans are plenty good at overcomplicating things. Suppose it gives us something to focus on when all other problems are cared for. Instead of base survival, we can cook, make art, sing songs-" Harris started to explain.

"Kill each other," Adrian chimed in with a snarl.

The hunter's eyes gazed out over the river. "That as well," he sighed. "Instead of helping each other, it seems we became awfully good at sabotage..."

"Feh. That's just human nature. They kill because they desire to be separate from nature, from their own kin. They fell in love with death," the beast growled, drinking quietly.

"That may be the case, but death isn't everything. You taught me that." Harris turned his tired eyes towards the man. Adrian had to fight the shudder of unease crawling up his spine.

The troll shook his head. "It's going to be dark soon, you should go home."

"Oh, and what of you?" The hunter cocked an eyebrow.

"I will find a place to stay here in the ravine. There are plenty of caves I can rest in," Adrian explained. "And... I'm not unarmed anymore, am I?" he added with a smirk.

"No," the middle-aged man sighed, shakily getting to his feet. His joints popped painfully as he rose, age appearing harder on his face. Adrian's smirk faltered.

He's... getting older...

The realization of the time he missed rattled him. The troll shook his head, fighting the trembling of his lip. Harris spoke, "No, you're not. Tomorrow, I'm going to show you how to build snares and set up a more permanent shelter."

The huntsman began to pick his way up the ravine, stopping at the top. Adrian gazed up at him. "Do take care, you old goat."

Harris gave him a coy smile and pulled up a middle finger. "Don't make me find your torn up carcass again, asshole." He disappeared over the ridge, leaving Adrian alone at the bank. A fairy drifted in front of him, giggling as it floated upside down.

"Funny troll! Friends with a human! So silly!" the fairy chirped.

The man snarled, snapping his fangs towards the little creature. The fae jolted away with a shriek, hiding in the reeds. He drew himself up, holding the spear firmly in his right hand. With the dance of fairy lights high overhead, the troll wandered the ravine, following the river as he began the search for a new home.

Chapter 13

Many weeks would pass. Adrian managed to locate a decent cleft in a cliffside far away from the river to use as a shelter. After the first few nights, he began work on turning the barren hole in the wall into an adequate living space. He collected moss by the riverside and dried it out, using it to make a nest that would be soft enough for his new human body. He cleaned out the nests of spiders and other insects, replacing them with walls of dry mud to discourage future settlers while he brushed out the excessive dust caked to the floor.

Pleased with the location of his new campsite, he saw it fit to settle in and build up more permanent accommodations. He collected wood and dried it within the small alcoves in the cliff wall, later digging out food stores in the dirt beside his campsite, guarded with the scent of deer urine. With all that said and done, Adrian had a rather comfortable home. It wasn't completely safe by any means, as wolves approached often. But with his new weapon and revitalized muscle memory, he fended them off with ease.

Harris came by often, teaching him new skills each time. Basket weaving, long-term meat storage, how to use a bow, traps and snares... All skills Adrian would find invaluable in the coming weeks. At one point, the hunter came by with a heavy looking sack of... something. "What's with the rock?" Adrian sneered.

"It's not a rock, it's a bloody brick of clay!" the hunter spat, dropping the burlap sack onto the ground. "Woven baskets are fine and all, but a solid container will serve you better in the long term," Harris explained.

Yet, as he attempted to teach Adrian how to make pottery, Harris quickly realized that he did not know himself. At first, the clay failed to form into anything at all, falling apart before they could bake it. Next, the first pot crumbed to dust, unable to hold itself together. Third time, they almost set the whole forest ablaze when the older man dropped a blob of clay into the makeshift furnace, jettisoning the flaming logs out into the camp. The two tried and failed multiple times to create one pot, only to end in an argument.

"You have no clue what you're doing, do you?!" the troll finally hissed, dropping his sagging wad of clay.

"I know damn well what I'm doing! I'm just trying to remember if this is step three... or step four...?" the hunter retorted, attempting to salvage the latest blobby creation.

"So you don't know what you're doing!" Adrian pressed, holding up his hands.

"I'm just a little rusty, you impatient jackass! Gimme a second!" the man snapped, resting a muddy hand on his chin, deep in thought. At being referred to in such a vulgar manner, the troll hurled his blob of wet clay right into Harris's face. The resulting tussle would end with the two of them trying to roughly shove clay down each other's throats. In hindsight, it was quite ridiculous. But in that moment, they were two mud-covered warriors still cussing each other out until the end of the day.

Their relationship got better in the coming weeks after the incident, finding themselves chatting as they checked traps and skinned their quarry. There were moments where they would just discuss simple things, such as the coming harvest, the migration of the deer, and what interesting things they saw that day. Then there were days where Adrian would find himself with particularly terrible headaches and become distant to his companion. These tense moments mixed with the good, leaving Harris with a sense of contentment he hadn't had in years. While this man certainly wasn't the same Adrian he knew over a decade ago, he was happy to have found himself a new friend. It was that sentiment that drew him towards Adrian's shelter, even when he had nothing to teach. Instead, he would just work at his own personal pet project while Adrian cut his pelts and rolled them. It had become a regular enough occurrence that Adrian eventually spoke up four weeks in. "Harris, why are you here?"

"Hmm? What are you talking about?" The hunter gave him a look as he dipped a sinew bowstring into a pot of melted wax. He ran his nails lightly down the string, removing the excess material; apparently the final piece to his current project.

"You haven't had anything to teach in awhile. So why are you here?" the troll pressed, cutting out a slab of raw meat to shove in his maw as he worked.

Harris shrugged. "Because I want to. I like talking to you. I like working near you. So I'm here."

"Feh, whatever makes you happy I suppose..." Adrian lowered another slab of juicy flesh into his mouth. "What... are you working on anyways?" he asked, talking with his mouth full.

Harris blinked, gazing down at the curled in, circle-shaped rod on top of a pelt. He sighed, setting down the string. "I'm trying to make a bow."

"That's an awful lot of curve for a bow," the troll snorted.

"Well, this ain't any average bow. It's a special kind, something I learned about while living in the mountains. I knew a guy who used to sell them to make a few extra coins... Figured I would try my hand at one now," the hunter sighed.

Adrian shifted, glancing at the weapon currently tied to Harris's back. "But you already got one, why make another?"

"'Cause I felt like it!" Harris snapped. "You don't *need* something to want to make something new. Sometimes the fun is in the process!"

"At this point," the troll sneered. "You should just be a craftsman with all your wants..."

Harris scowled. "No way in hell. I'm allowed to like something and not want it to be a job. I'm a fur trader and that's where I stay."

Adrian shrugged. "Whatever you say, o' great sage."

Harris flipped him off while Adrian stuck out his tongue. A normal juvenile interaction. They were silently going about their work before Harris piped up. "I noticed you changed your spearhead. Looking more narrow."

Adrian turned, spotting the weapon laying on the ground to his left. "Yes? And what about it?"

"Nothing," the hunter shrugged. "Just curious."

The beast sighed, finally removing the pelt from the deer carcass. He slapped the bloody flesh on a drying rack. "I did it because it was more efficient to kill things without damaging their fur."

"Oh?" The hunter raised an amused brow.

"If I recall, humans love their shiny little rocks. If I can sell these furs to a trader for a bunch of those things, I could buy myself a long-ranged weapon. When winter arrives, I won't be able to chase after prey as easily. I'll need it," the troll explained.

"Huh, if you just wanted a ranged weapon, I could have taught you how to make yourself a bow," Harris raised a brow.

"I don't want a bow," Adrian grunted. "I want a crossbow." The hunter blinked before lowering his head with an amused grin. The troll glared. "What? What's so funny?"

"Nothing, you just always preferred crossbows. Funny that remained, even now," the middle-aged man gazed at him. Adrian didn't reply, snorting before continuing his harvest. At this point, the hunter noticed the pile of furs beside his friend. Harris pulled the rolls up to his scrutinizing eye. From the looks of it... two deer, three mink, two beaver, and one raccoon. "These are... very well made! You should be able to get a decent amount towards your crossbow. How do you intend on selling them? Did you want me to do it?" he asked.

"No, that won't be necessary. I'm going to the village myself," the man replied in a matter-of-fact tone. "I have a brilliant plan."

Harris blinked. "O...kay, go on. What's this plan of yours?"

Adrian gave him a terrifyingly giddy smile, stretching over to his nest and pulling out a strip of leather. He wrapped it around his eyes, pulled up his furred hood, and put on some full-fingered gloves over his green flesh, grinning proudly at the display. "I'm going to go there as a blind man."

"...A blind man... Why?" Harris rubbed at his eyebrows, already exasperated.

"It's simple," the troll began, pulling the cloth down to his neck. "People can't see my face or they'll believe I am their lord. But! Humans identify people based on the shape of their eyes in relation to the face. So, if I cover my eyes and keep my hood up, they won't be able to tell who, or what, I am. "

The hunter chuckled. "Yes, but you'll draw attention. A blind huntsman isn't exactly a common occurrence. It will raise a few eyebrows."

"I'll just say my quarry was caught in traps, they needn't know of my spear," Adrian smirked, pulling out a bone to eat.

"...A random blind stranger selling furs from the woods..." Harris sighed, rubbing his temple. "I'm coming with you. There will be less talk if I do. I'm already a well-known trader there, my presence should raise your reputation at least a little."

The troll gave him a toothy grin. "Well, if you were truly that *desperate* to accompany me in my endeavors, all you had to do was ask," he purred.

"Heavenly father, don't make it weird. I'm just trying to make sure you don't get yourself killed," the hunter growled.

"Well," The elegant man began, "Your concern for my safety is much appreciated. Why, I'm really starting to feel my human status!" He added with a ridiculous flourish.

"Ugh. Shut the hell up, you greasy bastard," Harris snarled, almost regretting his decision to help. He stood up from his work, tying the ends of the sinew into hoops. The hunter plucked the curved ring from the ground and began to string it. To Adrian's surprise, he placed the loop on the outer edge of the ring and pulled against it, forcing the bow into a curved 'w' shape. Harris struggled against the tension; grunts escaping between his clenched teeth as the troll watched on in amusement. The hunter fought to string the other end, sweat dripping from his brow as he finally set the hoop in place. The hunter pulled up the large bow, frowning a little. "I might have gone a little overboard with the size... I believe these things are supposed to be a touch smaller..."

"Huh, never seen anything like it," the beast snorted, snapping the bone between his hands and letting the marrow pour down his throat.

"Odd, isn't it? The guy knew how to make them, but never gave them out for the others in my troupe to use... supposedly the design comes from the eastern clans for their horsemen," he gazed at his handiwork. The bow was almost four feet long, far too large for its original purpose. Only one piece was missing. The hunter glanced at the rolls of pelts next to the troll. "Adrian?"

"Hmm?" the beautiful man grunted, glancing up at the hunter.

The huntsman pointed at the small grey fur on top of the pile. "Would you be interested in selling me that raccoon pelt?"

Blue eyes blinked, picking it up. A small smile pulled at his face. "Sure, how much are you willing to part with?"

Harris set the bow against a tree, resting a finger against his chin. "Hmm, how about ten pennies? It's rather small and I'm going to have to shave the leather." Adrian considered this for a moment, almost ready to accept, until a small thought crept up his back.

That's a terrible deal. This pelt is worth way more, even without it being shaved.

"Hmm, see, that's not a lot considering the quality of the pelt. Regardless of the work you must put in, this piece has very few blemishes on the skin and is quite well-cured, " the man explained, words pouring out of his mouth before he could stop himself.

Harris blinked, not expecting that response. "Well then... how much do *you* want for it?"

"...Fifteen pennies," Adrian answered, a hard look in his eye.

Harris snorted. "Sorry, but I'm not doing anymore than twelve. At the end of the day, it's a raccoon pelt."

Adrian nodded, his eye twitching. "And yet here you are, praising the quality of my furs... fourteen."

Harris glared, realizing what he had done. This was no troll, not anymore. Adrian Lionel, the merchant of Willowbend, was awake. He sighed, his shoulders sagging in defeat. "Thirteen."

Sharp fangs glittered in the sunlight as Adrian extended a clawed hand. "Pleasure doing business with you." The two men shook hands and the goods were passed, a sly smile on the troll's lips as he set the coins into a pouch on his hip.

"Definitely no fool when it comes to trade... at least you won't get screwed over..." the hunter sighed, beginning to shave the pelt.

"Some of these memories are useful, very useful. Should make the trip short and bountiful. Gives me plenty of time to visit the cave when we return," the beast sighed, turning back to the carcass to begin dividing the remaining deer meat for storage.

Harris gave him a look. In the time since his transformation, Adrian never went back to his beloved cave in fear of Vantis spotting him. The hunter told him staying low was the best option, and at the time, the troll was inclined to agree. "Are you sure that's a good idea?"

The man set the remaining slabs of meat into a tightly-woven basket, picked it up, and walked over to his food stores. "Should be. Haven't heard news of the brat in a while. Anyways, I need to grab my books and treasures before some animal soils them during hibernation. Now is a better time than any," Adrian explained. The beast heaved the stone slab covering his food store away and set the basket inside before replacing the cover. The man plucked out a bottle of foul-smelling yellow fluid from his bag. He pulled his cloak over his nose as he unstoppered the cork, pouring some of the fluid around the covering. After setting the bottle away and ensuring the smell was thoroughly soaked into the earth, he sauntered back over to the fire and plopped down on his backside. There was a conflicted expression on Harris's face. "What?" the troll asked.

The hunter sighed, cringing as he wrapped the shaved pelt around the grip of the bow. "Well... When Vantis found out you were gone... he... well... He wanted to protect your things while you were out, so... he kind of... took everything."

Adrian's eye twitched with barely contained fury. "I... see. Where are my things, Harris?" The hunter bit his lip. The beast cleared his throat. "Where. Are. My. Things. Harris?"

The middle-aged man rubbed his temple. "They're back at the Lionel Manor... in your room. Locked up."

Adrian could barely contain the growl rising in his throat. His lip twitched, revealing his sharpened fangs. "Great. Lovely. I'm not getting them back then. Good to know." He tossed a branch into the fire, watching it crackle with a barely guided malice.

"Don't be mad at the boy. He's just trying to help," Harris explained, tenderness easing into his voice.

"Yes, and that 'help' makes it so I'll never see any of my treasures, *including* my mother's book, ever again until I miraculously find a way to cure myself of my affliction... *Which hasn't had any sign of occurring since I became a human over a month ago,*" Adrian hissed.

"...If it's of any consolation, I am working on that," the hunter pointed out, getting to his hooves.

"Oh? And what exactly are you planning?" the troll sneered.

Harris reached into his quiver, selecting an arrow with the best fletching. "I contacted an old friend of yours. A forest troll by the name of Old Dusk."

Adrian blinked, a shiver running down his spine as he heard the name. The sound conjured up an image of a terrifying figure composed of sharp thorns, jagged teeth, and piercing sunset eyes. "I see... How is that going to help?"

Harris set the nock of the arrow against the string and started to pull back. "He's one of the oldest fae we know... If anyone is going to know what's going on with you, it would be him," he explained, his voice straining as he struggled against the tension of the string.

Adrian raised a brow, a tickle of concern at the edge of his thoughts. "I see, when will he arrive?"

"Sometime... Mid-autumn..." the hunter gasped, sweat beading at his brow. The string shakily pulled back. He fired, the arrow launching with such force that it cracked and shattered against the tree trunk twenty yards away. Harris cried out in pain, clutching the forearm that held the bow. "Sonovabitch!" he snarled. Adrian leapt to his feet, rushing to his side to take a look at the injury. The troll easily pried the arm away, spotting a long dark line of blood that ran from his forearm down to the hunter's wrist. How in the hells did this happen? A simple bow couldn't have done this, right?

"This... needs to be seen by a doctor," he breathed.

"It's fine, Adrian. It's just a scratch," Harris grunted, trying to pull away.

The troll raised a brow, "A 'scratch' wouldn't make you seize up like this. Stop moving." He pulled out some cloth from his bag, still holding the arm in place.

"Heavenly fires, Adrian, I can do it myself! Gimme that!" Harris snapped, snatching the roll from the troll's hand. The man scowled but let go of the arm.

While the hunter dressed his wound, Adrian began to bind the fur rolls together with twine, putting on his cloak before hoisting the heavy furs up over his shoulder. With the rope tied as a makeshift backpack, he reached up and touched his eye covering, ensuring it was around his neck. "We're going to a doctor. At least so you don't get an infection." Harris gave him an annoyed glare, his mouth opening to give an offensive remark. The troll wouldn't let him have the chance. "Look, while I'm there I can do some trades. Spare you from ridicule for a little while."

Harris sighed, shifting his gaze from the man to his bandaged arm. Blood was already soaking through the wrappings. "Fine. Adrian, could you put this away?" He held out the weapon. A clawed hand reached out, taking the bow and holding it firm. While it was a bit too large for the hunter, it felt perfectly sized in the beast's grip. Out of curiosity, he gripped the string and pulled it back effortlessly, feeling the intense power behind the tension. It was easy for him, but for a normal man... this kind of power could make a feather slice through flesh.

The fletching must have struck the bare skin while firing.

Harris watched the man, noting the ease of which he held the string taut. The hunter reached down beside him, pulling out another arrow from his quiver and holding it out to Adrian. The troll blinked, slowly easing the string and lowering the weapon. He gripped the arrow, giving Harris a sideways glance. "Go on, you might have an easier time of it," the hunter urged as he waved him on.

Adrian nodded, nocking the arrow against the sinew and raising the weapon. He took a sharp breath, pulling back the string and aiming down the forest. His target was a tree twenty-five yards away. Instinct overrode confusion. His eyes narrowed, his back straightened, and his muscles bunched. Clawed fingers slowly slipped away from the string.

The arrow flew free, a sharp hiss of triumphant glee as it arced through the open air. Both the arrow and the bark of the tree shattered on contact; wood and stone fragments scattering in all directions. As the power left his fingertips and he lowered the weapon, a soft exhale exited his parted lips. Watching the man go into such a state was mesmerizing, like watching a master flex their expertise after years of disuse. "Looks like I may have overdone it a little," Harris's voice snapped the man to his senses.

"How do you mean?" Adrian carefully un-stringed the weapon and set the bow down in the furs of his makeshift home.

"It's just a little stronger than I was expecting," the older man chuckled, lowering his head. "Forgot how powerful the damn things are..." Adrian's eyes never left his face as he spoke, a neutral expression on his features. "It's been so long I seem to have left my wits behind... using a bow without gloves at the very least..." The hunter gave a hearty laugh as he shook his head. "How foolish indeed."

"Let's get a move on then. Before you bleed out as a fool," Adrian smirked.

The two men trekked across the untamed wilderness, passing by streams, wild brambles, and herds of placid beasts. Harris would wince every so often, both his injury and age catching up to the weathered hunter. The troll couldn't help but feel a tinge of concern, an annoying human emotion that seemed all too common these days. A stern frown creased his delicate features as he hiked beside his new friend.

On an occasion, Adrian would try to strike up a casual conversation, a nervous habit that Harris noted. The amnesiac man would seemingly only do this to drive his chaotic thoughts away, a distraction from an overwhelming tide that always seemed to quiver at his tight lips. He also had a habit of fidgeting with objects in his hands, in this case a stick he shaved with his talons, a habit the hunter knew quite well. Lord Lionel had done this fairly often with his quills and knives when something bothered him. There was a warm nostalgia to the action. It was the closest he had been with his leader in a very long time.

That alone was enough for him. Harris couldn't help but let a small smile tug at his lips as he came to that realization. No matter how far his memories slept, the Adrian he knew now was enough for him.

As they drew closer to the village, the troll pulled up his eye covering and raised his hood. At a cursory glance, he was just a normal human, at least until the beast grinned at him. Harris chuckled. "Try not to be so smug, your teeth are still sharp and out of place, enough to make the most oblivious suspicious."

Adrian frowned. "Ah, ever the dower critic, aren't you? Oh well, I suppose I could mirror your misery for a little while..." Harris couldn't help but scowl at the blind man's smirk as he swiftly walked ahead. Adrian tilted his head to the side, listening to the underbrush crunch under his steps. With each forward motion, he tested the ground with his toes before resting his weight on the striding foot, taking his time to make sure he did not trip on any roots or discarded branches. It almost appeared as if he had done this before. Harris simply sighed, walking beside him as they exited the bushes and made their way out to the central clearing.

Chapter 14

Some stared at the two before wandering off, evidently less interested in the two huntsmen than they were a few weeks ago. Then, Adrian had been a nervous, obvious outsider that stuck out like a sore thumb. Now though, he had a confidence and comradery with the experienced huntsman that made him fit right in. Before Harris left for the local apothecary, he pointed Adrian in the direction of the local fur trader. With what little directions the troll could follow without his eyes, he made his way to the market.

His ears were flooded with the voices of foreigners and locals alike. Some sold things, some bought things, some were idly chatting, while others were arguing or bartering with consumers and shop owners alike. It was a different cacophony than the central village, as that area had been full of the mundane chatter of harvesters and families. This one, however, was filled with the desires and needs from all mercantile types. Humans loved their shiny stones after all. And even if he didn't quite understand why anymore, Adrian's test with Harris had proven that he was very good at making others part with their stones. He just needed enough to get his desired weapon; the crossbow that would get him through the winter. Based on the values Harris gave him on the materials while they traveled, he should expect most if not all the money he needed.

"Be aware," he warned. "The shopkeepers are here to make a profit. Even if a pelt is worth a great deal, expect a lower amount unless you can make a damn good show of it."

Those words rang through the troll's ears, even as he zeroed in on the scent of tanned hides. His gloved hand reached out, feeling wood caress his fingertips. He halted, waiting for the shopkeeper to notice. The stall was silent, even while the world around him flew by. In the next moment, footsteps crunching on dirt and scattered gravel approached him from the front. He could smell the scent of rotting teeth and dried meat emanating from the breath. Middle-aged, based on the decay. "Can I help you?" the low voice asked, a friendly snap to his tone.

Adrian lifted his head, giving the open air a friendly smile. "Hello, I am here to sell some furs I collected."

The man shifted his weight, the low groan of the wood indicating a greater weight than average. He could almost feel his scrutinizing eyes sizing him up. "Uh, excuse me, sir. I don't mean to be rude but I don't believe I've seen you around these parts. Are you friends with Harris?"

Adrian could hear the man scratching at his scalp. The troll nodded slowly. "Yes, he found me lost in the woods here. Saved me from dire circumstances, he did!"

"I see..." The man thoughtfully nodded. He was stroking his facial hair for a moment. Stars and bones, this man fidgeted so much. "Well, a friend of Harris is a friend of mine! Whatcha' got for me?" He gave a low bellowing laugh.

Adrian set his bound goods from his back onto the wooden table in front of him. He thumbed his hands down the rope to untie the furs and take the line away. He was silent for a moment as the man picked up the pelts, seemingly drawing them up for a closer look. A mumbling could be heard under his salty breath. "... Did'jya catch these yourself?" he asked, barely hiding his disbelief.

Adrian gave him a warm smile. "Yes, caught and harvested."

"Err... Well, I am about to make a right fool of myself but... aren't you... blind, sir?" the man stumbled over his own words.

"Yes, sir," the troll answered. Thanks to his mask, his own fae laws couldn't punish him for such a lie. After all, at this very moment, he couldn't see anything. There was a thrill to this minor trickery.

He could hear the keeper nod his head slowly. "I don't mean by any offense, it's just that these look expertly done!" the man chuckled.

"None taken," Adrian nodded, hiding his budding irritation. "I'm glad my work can be appreciated."

The man seemed self-conscious as he quickly shifted the conversation over to the goods. "Based on what I'm seeing here, I'm looking at two deer, three mink, and two beavers. Hell of a catch," the man grunted. Adrian nodded. "These two deer are fine, I'll give ya... 15 pennies for each."

That's bullshit. His mind hissed. *They are at least a silver each.*

The troll set aside his prickling thoughts. "I'm sorry, sir. But you did say that these pelts were well made. That is the price for a lower quality fur. I was more considering a silver for each."

He could almost hear the frown on the man's face. "Yes, but these are deer pelts. At the end of the day, they are not hard to come by. But you are right, these are higher quality. Twenty pennies."

Five away from a silver... he mused. It wasn't much of a difference, but enough for him to drop it. There were better pelts on the line anyways. "Very well, then. Twenty pennies for each," the troll agreed, letting the man continue his appraisal.

"Alright, now these mink are mighty fine. I could take 'em off your hands for a silver-twenty!" the man reasoned. At first, Adrian became excited.

A silver-twenty was not bad... but for all or per?

"Is that for the whole lot or for each fur?" he pressed.

The keeper's stance shifted. "For the whole lot."

The blind man shook his head. The foreign words were leaving his mouth before he could stop them. "Each of these is worth at least a silver on the current market."

Frustration edged at the voice. "Yes, but that is for southern river mink, not northern."

"That's because northern river mink go for silver-ten. A lone silver each is a steal," Adrian stated smoothly. Stars and bones, how did he know this?!

There was silence. Then a sigh. "Two silver and ten pennies. That's my final offer."

The troll couldn't help but smile. "Deal." He must have been a merchant at some point in his human life. This was far too easy.

The shopkeeper sighed and scratched at his beard. "Now, these two beaver furs. I'll give you two silver for each."

That was certainly closest to the price he expected. Three silver was the standard, especially in the capital where they were the most popular. But here, two would suffice. In fact, with the combined funds he had collected from his previous deals, he should be able to get his weapon. The blind man nodded, holding out a hand. "Deal."

The salesman seemed surprised, almost expecting an argument. But the man just chuckled to himself before accepting the gesture, his meaty paw wrapping around the trapper's delicate fingers in a firm handshake. Before he could pull his hand away, the man hesitated, Adrian still firmly within his grasp. There was confusion in his voice. "You know, you look awfully familiar..." The keeper quickly let go, as if realizing how odd he was acting. "I'm sorry. Something 'bout you just kinda jostled some dusty memories."

Adrian's heart sank. He recalled the statue at the center of town. He gave a nervous chuckle. "You're not the first. I've been told as such by many others."

The man scratched at his shoulder. "Must be one of those faces then, eh? Ah, well, I'd better grab your coin." He heard the man shift behind the counter. "Oy, William! Get the bloody lockbox!" he yelled.

The sudden sound made the troll grimace, hiding his discomfort from view as the shopkeeper impatiently waited. Eventually, the sound of distant footsteps from inside a building rushed over, setting the box down on a table in the back with a labored grunt. "Sorry about that, Da. You set it under the bolts of leather again," a younger voice explained.

The merchant moved away from the counter to the back table, shaking his head. "Hells, again?! Harvest Festival has got me in a fit. Going to have to put a blot of paint on the fuckin' thing at this point..." the man mumbled, fumbling with the lock for a moment. The Harvest Festival. The celebration of not only the autumn equinox but all those born in the season.

Wren's birthseason...

The man frowned. He had felt terrible since the incident at the manor. Just the memory of Wren's horrified expression hurt him. He wanted to make it up to her. He *needed* to make it up to her. But how? Just seeing him made her upset... Adrian would have to make something, or send a gift of some sort. The troll considered his options before he was jolted to the present with the sound of a stack of coins hitting the table.

His hand reached out and found the stack, pulling it in to test each coin. The fae was nervous to reveal his fangs so he lowered his face to pluck a coin and test it between his teeth. He did this with each piece of metal. A sharp inhale sound almost made him stop before he heard a voice pipe up. "Da, don't. He can't see. This is the only way he can tell," William whispered.

The man sighed. "You're right..." the troll heard the tension in his shoulders fall. "Probably just got swindled in the past... no honor out there in the wilds..." When Adrian finished his test, he set the coins away in a pouch at his side.

"Thank you for the business," the blind man bowed. He was about to turn away when the rough voice of the merchant spoke up.

"You live near Willowbend?" the man asked.

"Y-yes..." Adrian nodded. "Why?"

"Well, if I'm gonna see your face more than once I might as well introduce myself," he laughed. "My name is Gareth. And you are?" A bead of sweat ran down his spine. What should he say? He couldn't say his name or his cover would be catastrophically torn asunder. His mind drew a blank, his mouth opening into noiseless syllables. The wood creaked as the man shifted his stance. "I'm sorry, I couldn't quite catch that."

"Ah, you see, I come from a land far from here," the troll began. Yes! His fae heritage would help here. "So pronouncing my true name would be difficult."

"I see! You must be from the north lands, then! Heard they've got quite the exotic language! Surely you got a nickname, then!" The man almost sounded excited, as if the northern tribes had the most bizarre culture.

Stars and bones, they live next to the northern clan borders! They're not that rare.

But that naive outlook would be his savior here. He smiled. "Yes, you may call me..." he began trailing off. His voice started before he could scold himself. "Lion."

"Lion? Like the Lionels here?" William piped up.

"I..." the troll began.

"Heh, hell of a coincidence!" the older man chuckled, "Sounds like a good omen to me! It's a pleasure to meet you, Lion!"

Adrian nodded, fighting the rising panic in his throat. "Y-yes, thank you for your business. Apologies for leaving in such a rush, I'm afraid I must go check on my friend now," he bowed with a stiff flourish of his arm.

Damn it, too formal!

"Ah, of course! Don't be a stranger! And give Harris my regards!" Gareth exclaimed as he left. Adrian's sandaled feet shuffled quickly through the marketplace, keeping his head down. That was way too close. At any moment he could have ruined everything. He would need to be more careful. More calculated. Next time, he would need a plan to-

Something fast slammed into his knees, almost completely bowling him over. Adrian staggered away with a vicious snarl. "Watch where you're going!" he hissed, dusting himself off.

A small voice huffed. "You should watch where you're going, mister!" An insolent brat by the sounds of it. He was so enraged that he hardly noticed how familiar the voice was.

"Wha-?! I'm blind, you little rodent!" Adrian snarled, lowering his head and clenching his fists.

"O-oh... I'm sorry, then! I didn't know!" the boy apologized, concern in his voice.

"Ah, yes, because the cloth tied around my eyes wasn't apparent enough!" he snapped. "Have more respect-"

"Vantis!" a strong female voice roared. The child made a frightened sound. Wren. The troll froze, panic rising once more to grip his throat. The two people he was desperate to avoid. He heard her stomping footsteps rush over and grab the child by the back of the shirt as he protested. "Ugh, I'm sorry, sir. I told him *not* to run off," she hissed. "But of course he never listens to me." The child made an exaggerated huff at this remark. He heard the woman's head shift, feeling her gaze bore into his soul. "Haven't seen you around, you new here?"

"I... um... y-yes. I'm new..." he stuttered, fighting against the choking feeling in his voice. He was fighting the shaking in his shoulders.

This didn't seem to convince the woman. If anything, she seemed more suspicious. "You... passing by or a new resident?"

"I-I'm just passing through!" Adrian mumbled. A burning feeling filled his skull. He wanted to run.

The troll heard her step closer. There was something in her hand. He couldn't tell what it was. A small hand gripped her loose sleeve. He could just barely hear what was said next. "Wren... he smells like a troll..." Vantis whispered.

Adrian stepped back. "Look, I'm just here to check in on a friend. I'll leave as soon as I can afterwards. I'm not looking for any trouble."

Her voice was quiet, contained. "Neither am I. Who's your friend?"

"H-Harris," he whispered, feeling the back of his foot strike against stone. He was next to the fountain. Next to that ornate statue of himself. He was shivering. She was silent. He could smell her sweet scent on the wind as it blew past him. An uneasy calm washed over him.

" ... I'm sorry for bothering you," she said suddenly as she bowed her head, grabbing the boy by his hand as they marched away.

"H-hey! Wren!" Vantis yelped as he was practically dragged away.

Adrian let out a gasp as their footsteps disappeared, falling onto the lip of the fountain. He clutched at his beating heart, desperately trying to make it calm down. He needed to find Harris.

He needed to leave. With a moment to catch his breath and take stock of his surroundings, the troll stood to his feet and followed the scent of his friend's blood to the apothecary.

Chapter 15

Wren was moving with haste, carefully weaving between concerned people as Vantis protested. When she felt they were a sufficient distance away from the 'stranger', she knelt down in front of Vantis in an alley between two buildings. "Wren, why did we leave so fast? If he smelled like a troll, maybe he knows Lion!" Vantis exclaimed.

She sighed. "Because, Vantis. He may not know *your* Lion. He could be friends with a different troll, which makes him dangerous."

"But Wren, that guy was blind. Also, he said he was friends with Harris! He's gotta know Lion!" Vantis reasoned, holding her wrist.

"Vantis, don't talk to that man, no matter who or what he may know. I can't believe I have to tell you not to talk to strangers at this age," she growled, rubbing at her temples.

Vantis lowered his head. His lip quivered. "Do you... think Lion is alright? I haven't seen him... it's been almost two months at this point..."

Wren sighed, gazing up at the sky. Why did Vantis have to make friends with the one creature he shouldn't? "Look. I know you miss him but maybe he's just out on a hunting trip," she reassured, trying to hide her suspicions.

"For two months?" Vantis pressed in a deadpan tone.

"He's fae, Vantis. They work in mysterious ways," the woman shrugged. "Anyways, if you smelled a troll that means there is one around. Please keep your guard up. Okay?" Her umber eyes pierced his. She saw the boy clench his fists in frustration.

"Yes, Wren," the child sighed. "Can I go to the market now?"

Her face creased with concern. "Sure. Will you be fine without me?"

Vantis's eyes crinkled with confusion. "Where are you going?"

"If Harris is here I need to talk to him before he goes back out. I would rather search here in town before I risk an expedition in the woods," Wren smiled, reassuring him.

The boy nodded, gripping the knife on his belt. "I'll be okay, then. Tell uncle I said hi!" Vantis smiled, starting to scamper back towards the open path.

Something twitched in her heart. "Vantis?" Wren called.

The boy's black hair shifted in light as he whipped around. That wondrous sparkle in his green eyes never faded. "What's wrong?"

She paused. "...Nothing. Stay safe."

The boy beamed, an expression that radiated the same warmth as the sunshine on his face. "Of course! I love you, Wren!"

"I love you too..." she whispered. As the woman slowly stood to her feet and heard the child's footsteps rush away, her gaze narrowed. That blind man... that was Adrian. She was certain. But what was he doing here? As Wren marched through the town, she heard news that the huntsman landed himself in the infirmary, some sort of accident. Was it the troll? Did he do this? If it wasn't, what could he possibly want?

Maybe he came back.

That thought made her stop in her tracks as she made it out onto the middle of the path. People shifted around her like river water against a rock. She fought the shaking in her limbs. Her will pushed down the maddened sobs, determined not to fall down that road again. She already did it once in front of that beast...

His eyes were so worried. He was worried about me.

Her hands quietly shifted, wrapping around her stomach like a safety blanket. Mindlessly, she continued her march towards the apothecary. She needed to know the monster's intentions. "It's not him. It's not him..." she whispered, her own words coiling like a noose around her throat. It felt like poison injected in her veins.

His masked face gave her a reassuring look. His gauntlet was resting on her shoulder. Those eyes made her stronger than ever. He believed in her. She believed in him. She would not stay her axe until he told her to. She would fight for him.

One of her hands reached up and she bit down on the finger, letting the pain ground her whirling thoughts. A small rivulet of crimson fell from the hand, her wild eyes seemingly unable to notice. Her footsteps were soft, calculated as she approached the side of that wooden abode. As if trying to evade the notice of a predator, Wren crept past a supply crate in an alley to stand next to the window, listening closely.

"So, finished making a fool of yourself?" a harmonious, strong voice said. There was an immense sense of self-satisfaction to the tone, mocking his companion in such a way he could be mistaken for hiding something. "Cry when the doctor had to stitch up your little 'scratch'?"

"Shut the hell up, you self-indulgent jackass. No stitches were needed. Just need to keep the thing bandaged and braced until it heals," an older voice snapped.

Wren heard footsteps shift in the room. At this point, she was resting her back against the wall, keeping her breathing quiet and steady. "Good, maybe then some of that famed sense of yours will come prattling back into that thick skull of yours," the snarky voice hissed. Adrian.

He was always such a smartass... even when he couldn't speak.

A soft smile tugged at Wren's lips, pleasant memories whispering in her ears. The woman shook her head in frustration. No time for that. She held her arms and continued to listen.

"Oh, come off it. I made a stupid mistake, that's all. No major harm done," the older man growled.

A snort from Adrian echoed in the room. "Ah, yes, because a braced arm is no major harm..." he was oozing sarcasm at this point.

"Bah, whatever. Did you make some money, or are you just hiding your failure by picking on an old man?" Harris sneered.

Adrian adjusted his position, the floor creaking under the shift of his weight. "I made out like a bandit," the man stated proudly.

"Oh? How much are we talking?" She could hear his hooves gently rest against the floor. She heard the other man shift from the wall and approach the huntsman. A rustling sound emanated within the room until eight distinct metallic clanking sounds fell into an open palm. There was silence in the room as the older man counted. "Eight silver... Fit for a silver tongue. That's enough to get you a decent crossbow," Harris commented, nodding in approval.

A crossbow? Why would he want-

A memory flashed before her eyes.

155

He raised his arbalest, leveled with an experience like no other. She was beside him, calling him to run. His horse was so much slower. She could take the rear. She could defend him. But he never moved, quietly aiming as a hellish howl echoed over the moorland. The sodden, emaciated horse beast was charging, even from a distance of forty yards. The monster was impossibly fast, cresting over the hill with unnatural grace. Its mouth was slavering. Adrian did not flinch. He fired, the iron bolt sailing true and striking the water horse cleanly in the eye. It reared up with a shriek, turning to flee, but Adrian was already upon it.

Wren shook her head. Adrian was a huntsman at the end of the day. He'd slain many beasts with a crossbow. He probably just needed it to hunt. Especially after what Harris had told her after the incident at the manor. She remembered what he said clearly.

"He can't turn back..." the man sighed, resting his hands on his hips.

"What... what are you talking about?" Wren breathed. Her senses were finally coming back to her. She heard the door slam and something rush out into the woods. It was him... but it wasn't at the same time.

"Something happened in the woods, something that made him adopt that human form. It's not an illusion. Not like the ones Aladarr or Old Dusk were capable of. It's real. It's real human skin," the older man explained, holding out a tissue for her to use.

Wren wiped her face roughly, rubbing her cheeks red. "What does that mean?" she asked, almost demanding.

"I... don't know... I'm going to call upon Old Dusk and see what he has to say about this... but I'm telling you, Wren. He's in there. He remembers his mother and father. He remembers this house!" Harris gestured towards the walls, his voice rising with hope. "I saw him pick up Terminus and he was back! I saw Adrian Lionel!"

Wren shook her head, scattering tresses of brown hair across her face. "I... This is too much. I can't deal with this right now. Vantis needs me. I can't be chasing after ghosts." She turned her head away, holding her arms tightly. Wren almost felt ashamed to say such a thing. The woman began to walk into the main foyer, determined to finish what she set out to do. She would give Vantis his waterskin and move on.

Harris was following her, the sound of his hoofbeats almost frantic. "Look. I'm not telling you to get over what happened. Or to tell you that... that man is him... He may be different. He might be confused. But I'm asking you... to just give him a chance. Don't shut him out. Please, Wren."

She remembered pausing by the door, her quarry in hand. She was almost crushing it. Her free hand rested on the ornate frame, a frame she imagined Adrian touching time and time again. Her gaze lowered. "I... need time," was all she could say as she stepped out into the blinding light of reality.

And now... here he was, chatting with Harris oh so casually. Wren couldn't help but clench one of her hands, pulling roughly at her skin. It was at this moment she heard the man's footsteps... dangerously close. The volume of his voice almost made her jump. "Yes, I was meaning to talk to you about that. Could you go buy one for me? Not some shoddy piece, but something that eight silver could afford," Adrian asked, his voice loud enough that she could hear the refined edge. He was inches away. She felt his back press against the wood, and in turn, herself. The warrior's jaw was set tight, her fists clenched. A grotesque nostalgic sensation crawled up her spine. She was afraid. Not of being hunted. Of just being found.

"Of course. I'm not an idiot with weaponry!" Harris chuckled.

"Yes, only an idiot with bows, it seems..." her leader snorted.

She could sense the offense in Harris. "Now you listen here, you prick. If you continue this smartass shit I won't help you with anything!"

Wren felt the presence behind her shift, almost uncomfortably. "Very well, then. I'll stop. I'll entrust that money to your capable hands. I'll just be the simple blind man following you around and listening in."

Her wide eyes glanced at a sudden motion in the window to her left. It was one of Adrian's locks of hair, ebony fading to a snowflake white, drifting softly in the breeze. She couldn't help but stare.

"What? Don't trust me?" Harris smirked, starting to stand.

"Ha! Nothing of the sort! I just don't want to be seen as a lone blind man wandering into the brush! People will ask far too many questions..." the man laughed, a loud, handsome sound compared to the caws she was used to. He was pulling away from the wall now, approaching his friend by the door. "And I could possibly make a fool of myself tripping on a rogue stick..." Adrian added with a wry grin.

"Yes, and we wouldn't want any of that, now would we?" Harris barked out a laugh, striding out of the room and heading towards the front of the building. Wren's eyes darted to the large crate beside her hiding spot, and let her legs give way, falling to her backside and holding her knees tightly to her chest. It would be alright. She could cry now.

Chapter 16

Half an hour later, Adrian held his quarry in his hands, running his claws gently down the stock. No cracks, no water damage, no rust. Excellent. His covered eyes gazed down, dragging a talon carefully across the flight groove as his imagination tried to draw up an image. The two men managed to snag a decent deal with what they had, a more decorative crossbow that could easily be fitted for more practical use. The owner almost seemed disappointed to part with the weapon, only convinced by the realization that he hadn't been able to sell the item in years. Watching the brass-gilded piece land in the hands of the seemingly simple huntsmen almost made the artist within the merchant sob, something that Adrian took mild amusement in.

Humans were so easily swayed by appearances; it was one of their greatest weaknesses after all. The man tried to get them to spend more on a quiver and some bolts, but Harris harshly rebuked him. By the time they left, they had an elegant, capital-built hunting crossbow in hand, and a frowning weapons merchant behind them. The trees had long since covered their escape, enough that Harris nudged Adrian. The younger man pulled his eye covering and hood away with a soft chuckle, finally getting a chance to see his new weapon. "My, I feel like a child on the solstice," he laughed, tapping the engravings with a sharp nail. While most trolls cared little for such frivolities, Adrian couldn't help but admire the weapon's beauty. The string would need to be changed out, the metal buffed, the components re-oiled and greased... but it was his. His first new treasure since becoming human. Gathered by the might and intelligence of his own two hands. It was enough to make the troll's lips draw up into a childish grin.

The huntsman seemed to notice the shift in his friend's demeanor. "Don't get too excited now, at the end of the day it's a decorative piece. It's gonna take some work before it's operational," Harris warned, failing to hide his own smile.

"Yes, yes, but it's work I *can* do. I'll have this up and running before the start of the first snow," the troll reassured, running the strap across his shoulder and letting the weapon lay against his back. Harris chuckled at his companion's confidence, honestly missing seeing him in such a happy state. Adrian hadn't been this excited since he-

The sound of a snapping branch jolted both of the men to attention. Adrian instinctually reached back and pulled out the crossbow, holding it at the ready even though he didn't have any bolts to fire. He instead shifted his grip and clasped the stock hard between his taloned hands, realizing he would have better luck striking an enemy with the weapon itself rather than the empty air in it. Harris pulled a knife from his side, standing as motionless as a spooked deer. The older man's eyes were wild and ready despite his injured arm. The rustling of the hillside bushes stopped as they waited with baited breath. A head poked out, staring wide-eyed at the troll. It was too late for him to pull up his hood. He was spotted.

"...Father?" Vantis peeped, staggering out of the brush. Hearing that word made the beast's jaw clench. Adrian dropped his crossbow in shock, his eyes locked in a panic. "Father!" the boy cried, rushing down the leafy slope towards him. A wave of fear washed over the troll, driving him to stagger back. Only Harris was able to throw out a hand in time to catch the child.

"Vantis, stop!" the huntsman ordered sternly. The boy slammed into his forearm, halting with a gasp.

Vantis gazed up at him, a sorrowful look in his eyes. "Uncle? What's wrong? Why can't I hug him? It's father, isn't it? He came back for mother and me!" the boy reached out, desperation in his voice. "Father! Please! It's me! It's your son! You didn't forget about me, right?"

Adrian pulled away, his limbs shaking with a barely contained terror. The man turned, the coldness of the response making the boy's arm snap back towards his chest. "Vantis Lionel! Stop it!" Harris yelled. The child gave him a hurt look as his head sagged. Those desperate eyes were still upon the troll, an action that made his father nervous.

"What...?" Vantis peeped, still gazing deep into Adrian's blue rings. They seemed so familiar...

"Look, it's complicated. But right now you're overwhelming him," the man began, kneeling down to hold the boy's shoulder with his good arm. The huntsman turned towards his companion. He spoke softly, "Hey, I'll meet up with you later at your camp, alright?"

Adrian just gave him a tiny nod, turning on his heel and marching away. "W-wait! Father!" Vantis cried, reaching out once more as his idol disappeared into the brush. Harris calmly lowered the boy's hand.

"Please, Vantis. Please stop," he sighed, completely unprepared to deal with this.

"But where is he going? Why can't he talk to me? Did I do something wrong?" the boy asked, a pleading look in his eyes.

The huntsman sighed, standing up and gazing out towards the forest. "Let me explain. It's... It's a long story." The older man thought for a moment. "Walk with me."

The hunter and the child trudged through the woods, scaling rocks and fallen trees alike. Vantis dutifully followed with some difficulty, but Harris was willing to wait for him. "Your father... is not the same man he once was. Thirteen years ago, he *was* the commander of the Black Lion Executioners, he *was* our leader. And thirteen years ago, he changed," he began, his ragged voice carrying on the wind. Vantis frowned, but before he could ask any questions his uncle continued.

"He was cursed... or blessed in some ways... after the Battle of Terminahill. He was left half dead, and likely had only hours left to live after a troll ravaged the fort," Harris sighed, holding onto a tree trunk as Vantis staggered over a nest of branches.

"I know this story... the one about Father's enemy... but I never heard about no curse," the child breathed, digging his nails into a rotten trunk as he dragged himself up and onto its flaking side.

The huntsman nodded. "He was saved by a traveling doctor, one who used dark magic to heal his body. That man melded troll flesh with Adrian's to mend his injuries... turning him into something like a troll-kin."

"What?" Vantis cocked his head. "But other than his one friend... father hated trolls!"

The man shook his head, scanning the clearing ahead. "Regardless of how he felt about them at the time, he took this second chance at life. It gave him his extraordinary strength and durability, but at a terrible cost. It mutated him and forced him to live between two worlds, between fae and mortals. And one day... the fae side took him..." The older man looked distant to the boy, pained. He saw this face every time his father's birthday rolled around.

"My dad was... but what does that have to do with this?! He looks mostly normal! Just pointy ears and scary eyes!" the boy smiled, ignoring a nagging thought tugging at his mind even as it whispered.

His eyes were so familiar...

"It doesn't matter if he was a monster anyways! I'm sure mother would love him just as much as I do now!" the boy blurted, rushing ahead to meet his uncle's gaze.

Somber brown eyes closed. "The curse first took his body... and when it fully held him in its grasp... it took his mind too. He became a mindless beast."

Vantis was silent. "What... what are you saying...?"

The huntsman stopped, spotting his cabin in the distance. "I'm saying that your father never left. He never died. He became a troll, Vantis."

The boy mulled this over, realization hitting him like a bolt of lightning. He was shaking, even as he numbly moved ahead towards the cabin. "...Lion..."

Harris made his way over to the door, grasping the handle. "Yes, Lion was your father. Just in a state where he couldn't remember- No... rather, he never knew."

Hot tears ran down the boy's face. "Father... didn't even know that I existed?"

The older man calmly led the child inside, lighting the candles with some matches nearby. His heavily-shadowed eyes glanced over. "You were conceived just before our last mission. He turned before your mother was even a month along. Neither of them knew at the time."

Vantis held a quiet glare as he sat down, pulling up his legs against his chest. "Then... What about now? He looks so normal... Does he at least remember mother?"

Harris shook his head. "His memories are still hazy, but he seems to be regaining his humanity... at least as far as I can tell," he added with a shrug.

"He... he was the blind man in the village! That's why he was so scared of Wren and me... Oh gods, I just ran into father without even knowing it!" the boy whispered, hiding his head in the shadows of his legs. A startling thought came over him, and his head jolted up

to face the huntsman, a look of sheer terror upon his visage. "If he's...
Then what does that make me? Will I become a monster too?! Will I
forget you and Wren?!"

The older man sighed. "We don't know, Vantis. We don't
know what is going to happen. But we had plans in case you
presented any symptoms of kinship. For now, you are fine." The boy
settled down, at least mostly satisfied with that answer. They would
protect him if anything happened. Everything would be okay. Harris
continued, gathering up some materials for Adrian's crossbow.
"...The one who isn't fine, however, is Adrian. He needs time to
readjust. He won't be the person you heard about in the stories. He
will be agitated, he will be rough around the edges... but please
remember, the man he once was is gone. And that's alright."

Vantis noticed him preparing. "Where are you going?"

"I'm going on a little camping trip with him to make sure
he's okay, and I need to help him with his crossbow as he fixes it up,"
he explained, grabbing some canvas to use as a tent later.

The boy thought about this for a moment, black hair
covering his eyes. His head snapped up, a determined expression on
his face. "I want to go with you. I want to meet my father," Vantis
began. "'Cause even if he isn't the same... I should still try to get to
know him now. He was Lion. He was my friend, and... well... While
Lion was awfully rude, he cared about me. That has to amount to
something, right?"

Harris was about to protest before his voice caught in his
throat. In his whirlwind of thoughts and arguments he realized
something. That this was not his choice to make. This was between
Adrian and the boy. With that decision firmly holding him, the man
turned to face the child. "We will have to discuss it with Wren... and

with your father... If they both agree, you can come camping with us this weekend," he declared.

Vantis nodded quietly, receding deeper into the harsh shadows of firelight. "Could you go ask Wren? I... I need some time alone if that's okay... I'm..."

A gloved hand rested on the lad's shoulder, an understanding smile on his uncle's face. "That's fine... I'll go talk to her. You can wait here. Take your time."

Vantis simply nodded, hardly paying him any mind as the man exited the cabin and implored him to lock it. The boy numbly did as he was told, settling upon the floorboards by the foot of the bed after all was said and done. Soon, those hooved footsteps disappeared into the forest, and all the child could hear was the cheerful chirps of birds and insects. Vantis shook violently before beginning to sob, the sound echoing through the cabin and drowning under the cacophony of the wilderness outside.

Chapter 17

Adrian was hard at work trying to make new bolts, doing his best to keep Vantis out of his mind. Even as he whittled, those malicious thoughts crept forward.

He saw you. You can't run anymore. You are trapped.

He snarled, raking his knife down along the haft of a stick he was working on. "What does it matter?" he growled, desperately attempting to reassure himself. "It doesn't change anything."

It changes everything. You are his father. You cannot go back to your cave. Not now, not ever.

Snap

His grip shifted, hard enough to shatter his work into useless fragments. The beast hissed, tossing it into the fire. "He already has parents. He will gain nothing from me other than disappointment." he mumbled.

Or... he will help you wake up.

A headache spiked across the top of his head, making the man grunt in pain. Adrian shakily reached into a small leather bag and pulled out a piece of willow bark. He inserted it into his mouth and began to chew. As the bitter juices ran down his throat he rest assured, knowing that they would soon enough soothe his mind. The troll sighed, grabbing another stick and shaving the outer layer of bark. "Not that it matters what I do... Either way, the runt will find his way to me..." he muttered to himself between chews.

After thirty minutes of tense labor, he managed to shave down two sticks to an appropriate shape and size, setting them aside on a mat of woven reeds to be used later in assembly. There were other implements here too; triangle-cut turkey feathers and stones carefully chiseled into the shape of arrowheads. This activity was the only barrier between him and the hellish maw of unruly human emotions that gnawed at the back of his skull. As long as he kept at it, Adrian would remain calm and centered. He was so absorbed by his work that he never noticed the approaching sunset, and barely heard the plodding hoofsteps of Harris. He finally spat out the wad of tree pulp into the woods, his lip curling into a sneer. "Ah, about time you came back, you old goat. And here I was thinking you left me because of one little-" The words caught in his throat the moment he noticed the small shape walking beside the hunter. Adrian's face fell. "...Oh. Great."

Vantis forced his nervous gaze towards the ground as Harris gave the man a grimace. Adrian, fed up with his own ravaging worry, merely turned away, focusing on his sticks. The huntsman sighed, stalking over towards the fire. "Adrian? I need to ask you something important," the older man began, holding a level tone.

"Is it private?" The troll cast his gaze sideways towards the distant child. The boy averted his eyes.

"No. It's about Vantis," the man explained.

Adrian set down his tools, pulling up a knee to rest his arm. "Yeah? What about him?"

"Remember that camping trip I suggested a week ago?" Harris asked, rubbing his temples. He wasn't exactly thrilled for this conversation.

"Yes?" The troll raised a brow.

"...I wanted to ask if Vantis could come with us," the hunter sighed.

The fae turned his head towards the boy. The child's jaw was set tight in a weary grimace while his clenched fists were shaking at his sides. Blue rings scanned Vantis's scrawny form for a moment before his lids slowly closed like a cat. "Sure. Whatever. It's no skin off my bones," Adrian said with a shrug. Harris solemnly nodded, honestly surprised with how well this was going.

"'Whatever?' You've been gone my whole life and all you can say is 'whatever'?!" Vantis hissed.

Annnd there it was. The huntsman couldn't help but scowl. "Vant-"

"No, let the brat speak," the troll growled, now fully shifting his body to face his bristling son. "I didn't even know you existed until recently. It matters not to me. So yes, you can stay. At the very least to get those foolish notions of past grandeur out of your skull."

Fury quickly turned to outrage. "Oh, consider them gone! 'Cause now I know you're just a self-serving jackass!" Vantis snarled.

"Heavens' gaze, shut it! Both of you! I cannot believe that you two are already fighting!" Harris spat. Vantis gave him a fiery glare while Adrian merely shrugged, turning back to his work. "You, stop antagonizing him!" He jabbed a gloved-finger towards his friend.

The troll nodded disinterestedly. "Sir, yes sir," he added with a smirk.

Harris grimaced before shifting his attention. "And you! Sit your ass down and show some respect," the man pointed towards the boy.

The dark-haired child gave him a withering look. "You told me respect had to be earned."

"Yes, and he has shown it in more ways than you'll ever know. Sit down," the older man growled, pinching the bridge of his nose. Vantis obeyed, choosing to sit next to his uncle across from his father. The child hissed and looked away, sick of his smug face already.

The middle-aged man eased himself down into the soft leaf litter with a sigh. "So much for getting to know him, huh?" he chuckled. There was no response.

The camp was quiet, save for the sounds of a knife shaving down wood. Soon, even that disappeared, as Adrian ran out of sticks. The silence was deafening at this point. Inevitably, as the depths of night washed over the camp, Harris began to set up a well-seasoned flat stone, one large enough to rest over the fire. He set some cuts of venison on top, watching the meat begin to sizzle. He gingerly seasoned it before flipping it over and spicing the other side as well. The hunter tended to the roasting meat for about twenty minutes before cutting it up into slices and plopping them onto some wooden plates set beside them. He handed them out until everyone was attended to. Then, the trio ate, the sound of Adrian's grotesque gnashing teeth enough to make his son scowl.

"Could you eat any quieter?" the boy hissed.

"Mayhaps. But I see no point to do so other than for your own comfort," the beast said with a smirk, lowering a strip into his jagged maw. Vantis watched those shearing fangs with a disgusted snarl.

"Come on, Adrian, lay off. Unless you want to clean the stone this time," Harris chuckled, jabbing a finger towards the thick shellac of grease and seasonings on the cooking stone cooling beside the fire.

Adrian gave him a horrified scowl. "Most certainly not!" he exclaimed before quietly resuming his feast.

The hunter turned towards the boy, giving him a gentle smile as he finished his meal. "So, are you excited to finally be outside the manor for a full night in the woods?"

"Yeah, I guess. It's my first time... Although I didn't expect it to be like this..." the boy admitted, dabbing at his face with a handkerchief. He gingerly set his plate down in front of his crossed legs. The huntsman plucked it free of the ashy detritus and set it on top of his own.

"I didn't exactly expect to be spending time with you either," Adrian chuckled, the firelight casting his beautiful face in a sinister glow.

"The hell is that supposed to mean?" Vantis snarled, his emerald eyes shining in the orange light.

The troll shrugged. "I suppose I didn't expect to see your face again." He handed his plate over to Harris, who took it after giving the two a concerned lap of glances.

"What? Didn't plan on trying to meet me even after finding out who I was?" the child pressed. The huntsman sighed, already sensing this was getting out of hand as he cleaned the plates.

"Trolls usually eat their own offspring before they can get the chance to scuttle away. You being my son doesn't make you all that special," Adrian gave him a dismissive shrug.

That's a lie. This man constantly fretted for the child's safety, especially when he found out there was a chance he inherited his curse. He is putting up a barrier. A defense.

The hunter knew at least that much. "Anyways, I already *did* meet you."

"That was when you were a troll! Now that you're a man again you can come back!" Vantis yelled, almost standing.

The beast gave him a vicious snarl. "I'm *still* a troll. This *form* doesn't change that."

"Bullshit!" the boy spat, almost leaning over the flames. "You're just too much of a coward to face mother and me directly!"

"Vantis!" Harris scolded, resting a hand on the child's shoulder. The huntsman took a deep breath. "Relax. This is no time for fighting."

Vantis grumbled, plopping down roughly and crossing his arms. Adrian seemed to pay the child no heed, which just seemed to piss him off further. The hunter turned his attention toward his friend, attempting a different conversation starter. "How far along are you on your bolts?"

"Eh, I still want to gather a few more sticks before I start assembling," the man sighed, resting his back against a tree. "I also need to collect some more flint from the cliffside by my cave, but it has been rainy lately. I would rather not risk a fall in this form, easy recovery or not."

"Maybe it would finally knock some sense into your fat skull," the boy hissed.

"VANTIS," the hunter roared. The boy flinched back reflexively but held his gaze. There was pure fury creasing his uncle's features. "If you have nothing nice to say, then shut it. One more snide remark, one more insult, and I'm marching you straight home... Am I understood?" His words were deathly quiet, barely containing his rage. The crackling of the fire threatened to swallow his voice while his eyes kept his intentions clear.

The boy gave him a small nod, drawing in his legs with his arms and looking away shamefully. The man sighed, turning towards Adrian. "Unless you want to clean the stone, why don't you collect some more sticks for your bolts while Vantis and I go get firewood?"

The troll gave him a dismissive shrug before getting to his feet and wandering off. When the man was mostly out of eyeshot, the huntsman turned towards the boy. "Come along, now."

Vantis quietly obeyed, getting to his feet as the older man struggled against his ailing joints. He was getting far too old to be putting up with this nonsense. The two went along, gathering appropriate dry branches while staying within sight of the flickering amber firelight. Harris gazed over towards his young ward. "What has gotten into you?" he questioned.

"Nothing," the child grunted, kicking at a loose stick. "I guess I didn't expect him to be so miserable to be around."

"Sorry to say he has always been like that. Unfortunately, being a smartass runs in the family," the older man chuckled.

"He's... absolutely nothing like the stories..." Vantis whispered, plucking a branch from the detritus and shaking the rotting matter free from the bark.

"Of course not," the hunter began. The boy gave him a confused look. "Those are just stories, after all. He never was a statuesque figure. At the end of the day he was just a man, and men are not perfect."

"No, apparently he was an asshole..." the child spat, panicking the moment the words left his mouth. His wide eyes turned, opening his quivering mouth to defend himself before Harris raised a calming hand. The hunter refrained from correcting his language, choosing to instead focus on the meaning of his words.

"Actually, you two aren't that different," Harris gave him a wry smile.

"What's that supposed to mean?!" Vantis hissed, his face creased into a snarl.

Oh, how often he saw that outraged expression...

The hunter laughed, rifling through the fallen leaves to grab another log for the fire. "It means you have a lot to learn from him... I told you he wouldn't be what you expected, and you ended up putting unfair expectations upon him anyways. Stubbornness also runs in the family, it seems."

"I...! Feh! Whatever! It doesn't stop him from being a dismissive, awful, rude, gross, terrible JACKASS!" Vantis roared.

In the distance, Adrian was rummaging through a fallen tree, snapping off twigs and testing them for flexibility and use. While amidst this act, he heard the boy's sudden outburst, forcing his hands to crush in and shatter his prospective bolt. The troll's eye twitched, dropping the remains with a frustrated growl. He stalked ahead, eager to get his work done.

Harris let out a small laugh, patting the boy's back. "Do you happen to have more colorful vocabulary you wish to share?"

Vantis gave him a serious look. "Yes, actually."

The huntsman pondered this for a moment. Better to get the outburst out now than next to a fire and the ire of a troll. He nodded, closing his brown eyes. "Very well, then. Let it out."

Adrian just found another prospective stick, this one far superior than the last two he had collected. Gingerly, he plucked it free from the dead branch and set it between his two claws. Then the yelling began. A vicious cavalcade of steaming profanity blasted over his sensitive ears, making him reflexively jump.

Snap

The wondrous twig crumbled in his talons. His jagged teeth were bared into a feral snarl. "Wretched brat..." he hissed, his glowing eyes darting over to see the child's unhinged rant. From what the beast could see, the huntsman was calmly standing with his arms crossed, almost professionally assessing the terrible tirade of hellish words as the boy flailed about. Adrian waited with an impatient glare for the noise to cease, inevitably watching the child gasp for breath. The troll smirked, aggravation giving way to mild amusement as he turned back to his work. Oh, another lovely specimen! He pulled the haft free and examined it.

"And he's a ROTTEN, PIG-FACED HORSEFUCKER!!!" the boy suddenly shrieked.

snap

Fury consumed the man as he dropped his final straw, raking his claws across the tree with an unbridled rage. He was practically drooling with madness, turning his gaze back towards the fire. His voice was barely above a whisper. "Fine, fine! I can't take it anymore." The beast stalked back to the campsite and roughly snatched a hard brush from Harris's discarded bag, almost tearing at the leather. He wrapped his talons in gloves and pulled up the cooking stone from its place beside the firepit. The man slammed his backside into the dirt with a frustrated huff and began scrubbing. He would rather do this than suffer with any more wasted materials.

Harris smiled at the wheezing child. "Got it all out? Feeling better?"

Vantis staggered to his feet, wiping the spittle dangling from his lip with a sleeve. "Y-yeah, actually. Much better."

"Good," the hunter nodded. "Now no more cursing your father or I'll take you home."

The boy lowered his head, hiding a gratified grin as his uncle patted his back. "Yes, sir." The two gathered their logs quietly, the silence broken by the sound of distant scrubbing. Harris raised a brow, spotting the hunched form of an enraged Adrian working away at the stone. He snorted.

Less unpleasant work for me, I suppose.

After both of their arms were laden with their heavy quarry, they made their way back to the guiding firelight, back to their remaining companion. Adrian had long since finished with his task, grumbling softly as he laid out the two surviving sticks for his arrows. The beast eyed the boy with a fuming glare, almost waiting for a snide remark or an uncomfortably loud noise. When nothing came, he began to cautiously whittle away at the shaft of wood. Amused, Harris set the logs beside Adrian's cave, stacking them with a quiet neatness reserved only for regimented veterans. Vantis helped the man the best he could before moving back by the comforting warmth of the flickering flames, avoiding the ire of his clearly frustrated father. After ensuring the pile was stocked and organized, the hunter joined them by the pit, taking a brief drink of water. The older man cleared his throat of drifting ash. "We will be up early tomorrow, so I suggest we get ready for bed."

"What's the plan?" the troll grunted, setting one of two finished sticks aside.

"Well, we will need to check the ten traps we set around the Silver Peaks and reset any that failed," Harris began, pulling up a hand as he listed off objectives. "Next, we will draw up some water from the mouth of the Lansaugh River, then collect some more wood, and finally prep the fire for tomorrow's breakfast-"

"That's all before breakfast?!" Vantis interrupted, slack-jawed.

The wrinkles at the edges of his eyes creased as he smiled. "But of course. Without adequate preparations we cannot begin to consider breakfast, and we are certainly not raiding your father's winter food stores. That is unless you *want* to engage with a hungry troll during the harshest months of the year..."

179

Emerald eyes snapped over towards his unearthly father, watching him produce a nasty grin. "But... but..."

"What? I thought you wanted to go on a camping trip with your father and uncle?" There was an edge of teasing malevolence in Harris's smile. "I mean, that is unless you want to go home and meet up with us later..."

"N-no!" the boy sputtered, shaking his head furiously. "I can do it!"

"Very well, then. We will see you up bright and early before the first sunrise. Adrian, you'll take the first watch," the hunter chuckled, casting a nostalgic glance over towards the beautiful man as he located an adequate place to rest. The troll met his gaze with a serene smile of his own, only turning to address his bewildered son.

"Welcome to the company," the elegant fae said warmly, his expression completely at odds with his previous behavior.

Harris couldn't help but crack a smile once more as he laid against the granite wall of the cliff. How familiar...

"All before breakfast?!" Wren asked, shocked outrage exiting her quivering mouth.

"Wel...co..me... to... th..e... com...pany..." Adrian purred, his shadowed eyes creasing into a smile. Even under his visored helm, his amusement was evident. The young woman gave him a dumbfounded expression before turning away with a frustrated glare.

She did ask for this after all.

Vantis could almost see the demon on his shoulder as his father snorted out a laugh, the troll drawing in his cloak tight around his shoulders. Black talons reached out behind him, pulling a sharp spear from the furs in his cave. Adrian set the jagged pike beside him as he gazed out into the sleeping forest. The weapon was large and intimidating, enough for Vantis to pull away.

The boy, desperate to be near at least one person who *wasn't* overtly hostile, chose to settle down next to the wall Harris leaned against. The lad unrolled a blanket the hunter gathered for him from the manor, unfurling it upon the cold ground. A small cushion flopped atop the center, wrapped within the soft fabric. He plucked it from the cloth, looking it over. It was a tiny kindness amidst the harsh situation he put himself in. Vantis couldn't help but smile as he nuzzled into the pillow, imagining Wren quickly stuffing it in the roll before handing it off to Harris.

Speaking of which, the boy turned to glance at the hunter. He was covered in a loosely draped cloth, his arms crossed underneath. His head appeared to have fallen to the side as his soft breath fogged in the cool night air. Vantis watched him for a moment, impressed by how quickly the man had fallen asleep. He always knew he was at least fifteen years older than Wren, but the boy never thought of his uncle as old. Yet at this moment, his age showed. It was enough to make his contentment sink. He shook his head and laid upon the pillow, the familiar scent of home lulling him to sleep.

Chapter 18

The night went along with little incident; Adrian switching with Harris as the watch continued. Several hours passed as the moon rose high over the western sky. By then, it was Vantis's turn. The hunter gingerly shook the boy awake by his shoulder. The young lord grumbled, sitting up with bleary eyes. "Wuh?" he murmured.

"It's your turn to watch the camp," Harris whispered, his dark eyes glittering in the shadows. The fire was low, enough that the darkness of the forest gave way to the moonlight and stars above. Only the embers remained, poking out of a warm blanket of ash against the cool frost. The boy shook the fallen leaves from his hair, sitting up.

"What do I have to do?" he asked with a yawn, rubbing his eyes.

The older man handed him his hunting knife. "Keep an eye out for predators or intruders. Wake us if anything comes along."

The boy nodded, tossing tangled ebony locks away from his face as he tightly gripped the sheath of the knife. Harris gave him a reassuring smile before stepping back to his resting place, laying against the wall, and covering himself in his dirty blanket. Vantis blinked, scanning him for a moment. He shifted his attention, emerald eyes glancing over to see his father fast asleep, laying flat on his stomach and resting his cheek against his forearm. With how gentle his expression was in slumber, Vantis could almost see the visage of the man in the portrait back home. A twinge of sorrow touched his chest.

The father I knew was never real. He wasn't a framed picture or a statue. Or some heroic knight. He was just another soldier. In the end, the same as the monsters he killed.

The boy frowned.

And yet... He never tried to hurt me... Even when he didn't know me...

'*...Van...tis... Yo..u... a..re... al...ive... th...at... wi..ll... al..ways... b..e... wo..rth... it...*'

He said those nice words to me before he knew he was my father... He said I was worth it. Does he still think that now?

He pondered this, wishing to see the gallant man he was told about. He wanted father to hug him and say those words again, say that after everything... he was worth all the pain and suffering. But all that resting face did was breathe softly in its slumber, leaving the boy to his own thoughts and worries. Vantis gripped his blanket and wrapped it tighter around him, stifling his welling tears.

After about thirty minutes of silence, the boy's eyes drooped. There had been nothing, save for the sounds of lively insects and owls. Their songs were enough to lull the child back into the warmth of his shroud and drop his head onto his propped arms.

After all, nothing has happened so far... What was there to worry about?

A horrible loud sound immediately jerked the boy awake, his hand lurching for the knife beside him. It sounded like the growls of a beast far too close to camp. He gripped the handle of the blade, refusing to pull it out just yet. Harris always warned him of exposed knives in tense situations. Better to be cautious than to hurt himself.

Wide, terrified eyes scanned the bushes, spotting nothing. Then, another growl rose beside him. Vantis snapped his head over to his left to see the drooling, gaping jaws of his father as he laid on his side.

Thank the gods... he's just snoring... like a bloody bear.

The boy gripped at his chest and sighed, shutting his eyes for a moment. Then, another roar rose to his right. Vantis ducked hearing the sound so close, only to see his uncle in a similar slack-jawed state, snoring just as loud as the troll.

One snoring bastard was already enough but two on either side...

Vantis pressed his fingers against the tragus of each ear, jamming them shut. Even after that, he could still hear the hellish noises, albeit far more muffled than before.

Suppose sleeping isn't an option, even if I wanted to...

Forced into attentiveness once more, the boy's eyes became more adjusted to the sights as his hearing dulled. As long as he focused on what was before him, he could drown out the terrible sounds... just like Harris taught him. And somehow... the gurgling roars of his family were breaking through, making his eye twitch with barely contained annoyance. Just before the thought of jamming a rock in his father's gaping maw became any more appealing to his tattered nerves, Vantis heard something shuffling in the bushes. The boy froze, willing his quivering hands to move away from his ears and reach down for his knife once more. Even though the raucous noise was enough to drive him mad, whatever was in those leaves scared him just a bit more. He slid his hand towards the handle, clutching it in a vice grip. More movement in the bushes. He raised the knife, half-tempted to wake the two men.

No, I can handle this.

The child clenched his teeth, steeling his resolve... only to leap back in terror as a rat scuttled out from the bushes and past the boy. It took all his will to not scream, instead falling on his backside as he watched the frantic creature scamper past the sleeping form of Adrian. Without any prior acknowledgment, a clawed hand lashed out, snatching the rodent firmly and pulling it close to his chest. The poor rat screamed, biting at the troll flesh helplessly as the man gripped it. Vantis couldn't help but be horrified for the creature. He shuffled a little closer, not noticing that the hunter behind him had long since ceased his snorings. The boy snatched a loose stick from the ground, trying to offer it out for the rat to hold onto. Either out of weakness or lack of understanding, the rat pulled away from the stick and wriggled uselessly. Vantis pouted.

That's a bust.

He tried tickling his father's fingers, only to see them lightly twitch in response as the poor creature continued struggling. Vantis sucked in a breath, watching his father suddenly move with wide eyes. He wiped the fuzzy writhing rodent across his drool-covered lip, coating it in an atrocious slime before settling back down. More sympathetic than ever, the boy began jabbing at the hand that held the prisoner. A low growl emerged from snarling lips and the fist clenched. In a panic, Vantis whacked his father's forehead with the stick.

"OW!" Adrian snarled, immediately loosening his grip to clutch at his head. The boy watched the rat quickly scuttle away to the safety of the bushes. A small smile split his lips until he came face to face with the enraged troll. "What on EARTH do you think you're doing?!" the man roared, getting up in his face.

"I-I'm sorry! There was a little rat and you were crushing him!" the boy exclaimed, shuffling back.

"A what?! Do you seriously take me for a fool? That a lousy excuse like that would hold any weight? That you struck me for a stupid rodent of all things?!" Those glowing rings narrowed, his talons lashing out to grab the hand that held the stick. The boy dropped it in fear as he cringed. Adrian, seeing his terrified expression, felt his rage melt away as he gently released the wrist, pulling away. He nervously beheld the claws, suddenly fearful that he hurt the child.

"You were hurting him..." Vantis whimpered. "I was just trying to help... I didn't want to see it die like that..."

Before Adrian could tentatively retort, a deeper voice resonated past them. "He's telling the truth, you know. You almost crushed a rat to death in your hand." One of Harris's eyes opened, giving the two a bemused smirk. "Before then, you used the fetid creature as a napkin..."

The troll scowled, tossing his gaze towards the dirt. "I... suppose it would have been a waste to simply kill and not eat the damn thing..." the fae sighed. He turned his attention towards his son, jabbing a finger lightly against Vantis's chest. "Next time, however... *Do* shake my shoulder. Don't strike me again," he snapped. "Am I understood?"

"Y-yes, sir," the boy nodded, watching those glowing rings scan his features.

The man sighed, lowering his hand and rubbing his forehead with the other. "Good. I'm tired of headaches at this point..." the troll muttered, turning his body away from the child to face the woods as he laid against soft furs.

Vantis released a held breath, letting his shoulders sag. He tossed a glance over to Harris, whose single eye finally shut. The hunter quickly fell asleep, leaving the child alone with his thoughts once more. The distant yips and howls of wolves kept Vantis alert for the rest of the early morning, leaving him in a state of exhaustion. Before he could fully gather his wits, he fell back asleep, too entranced by the song of slumber.

It was Adrian who awoke first, alerted by the first crows of dawn. The troll stretched his limbs, pulling his arms underneath his chest to sit up. His cerulean eyes scanned the clearing, noting nothing out of the ordinary... other than their supposed guardian fast asleep beside him. He gave the sight a fanged smirk before letting out a quiet yawn. The man pulled himself up to his feet, trudging over to the huntsman on the other side and gingerly kicking him.

At once, Harris's eyes snapped open, gazing up towards his friend. Adrian gave him a devious look, resting a finger against his lips and nodding over to the boy. Seemingly feeding off that devilish energy so early in the morning, a mischievous smile tugged at the older man's lip as his comrade helped him out of the dirt. The hunter grabbed his bow laid against the rock wall and a single dummy arrow, carefully maneuvering his way above the child's sleeping form. As he pulled back on the string, he ensured the sound of creaking wood was heard, loud enough for the boy to hear.

Vantis, suddenly aware of some unknown sound in the haze of sleep, blearily cracked open his eyelids to see his uncle standing above him. Green eyes rolled in his skull as he groggily blinked. The child sat up a little. "...wuh?" The huntsman fired, shooting the arrow against a tree ahead. The harsh sound was enough to make the boy yelp and duck for cover.

"Ah, and then an ambush came and killed the boy in our sleep. The enemy was already on top of him before he could call out a warning..." the huntsman sighed, shaking his head in mocking sorrow.

"Yes, and I had to explain to Wren why I was dragging a stuck pig behind me," Adrian hissed in an oozing tone, holding out his hands in a plaintive manner. The two men chuckled at each other while the boy poked his head out from under the blanket.

"You guys suck..." Vantis muttered.

"Not as much as you do as night watch," the troll jeered.

Harris just slapped his nephew's back playfully, giving him a hearty smile. "Don't take it too hard, everyone struggles with their first watch. You'll learn to keep more alert in due time," he nodded wisely. Vantis couldn't help but twitch an eye as the two men began to gather up their things around him. The child ran his hands through his black hair, tossing away any leaves or dirt that had made it their home. By the time he staggered to his feet and rubbed his eyes, his two guardians were already standing at the ready, checking their weapons.

"I only managed to create five bolts before my watch ended..." the beast grumbled.

"Ah, that's fine enough. We shouldn't run into anything worth shooting. Worse comes to worst, I'll hand you some of my arrows," the hunter explained, checking the sharpness of his knife against his arm hair.

"Aren't those iron-tipped?" Adrian snorted.

The hunter gave him a nod. "Yes, just don't rub them across your bleeding face and you'll be fine."

A handsome laugh erupted from the troll's jagged maw. "Very well then! I suppose I shouldn't miss the target in the first place!"

With that settled, they both turned towards the boy, who was just starting to stretch. "Well? Ready to go?" Harris asked.

"W-what? But we just woke up...?" Vantis blinked, confusion creasing his features.

The huntsman chuckled. "Yes, and we must check the traps. We told you as much yesterday. That is unless you *don't* want breakfast."

Vantis's eyes widened before he furiously shook his head. "N-No! I'm hungrier than a bear! Let's go!" The child snatched up his knife and bow before scampering beside the two as they began their trek.

The sky had yet to mature from the deep indigo of night, with only the most mild of blues streaking across the horizon. Upon the eastern edge emerged wispy clouds painted in the warm colors of sunrise, heralding the sun's jubilant return. The ancient forest around them gave the hunters plenty of space to trek between the thick trunks, with much of the underbrush burdened with the falling leaves of early autumn. It was easy to crush the tangled bushes beneath their boots and hooves, enough to not notice Vantis struggling to maneuver around or through them with his knife. The two men chatted freely as they hiked, only stopping briefly to let the boy catch up. "Sleep well?" the hunter asked.

"Oh, as much as I could with a lump on my head..." the beast snarled, moving a low-hanging branch away from his face.

Harris belted out a laugh as he skipped over some rotten trees. "Yes, unfortunate that was! Perhaps giving the boy the last watch wasn't the brightest idea!"

"Ugh, at least if one of *us* had the last watch, we would've had a decent snack..." the troll muttered, leaping over the pile in a flurry of scattered leaves. The realization that he had a delicious rat in his grasp the whole time made him seethe.

"Then what are you thinking? First or second?" The older man held his hands against the belt on his waist, turning towards his friend as the child desperately began crawling over the fallen logs.

"First," the man answered, casting his gaze over towards the struggling boy. "Let the runt stay up, then at least he won't wake up to bother us later in the night."

"Yes, but that seems needlessly cruel... making him stay up after taking the last watch..." Harris sighed, shaking his head as Vantis flopped unceremoniously into the dirt beside them.

"Why even bother with the illusion of choice, then?" Adrian spat, folding his arms over his chest.

"Hey!" The child waved a hand in the air. Both of the men turned, gazing down at the leaf-covered boy as he teetered to his feet. "Don't talk about me when I'm right here! Don't I get a say in any of this?" he whined.

The two gave each other a look before Harris nodded. "Very well, then. Which watch would you prefer?"

Vantis thought about this for a moment. Second would certainly let him get some rest... His green eyes glanced at his father, who beheld him with an unreadable expression. Was that a mocking smirk? The boy felt a fire spark in his heart. He would show that smug bastard that he could handle it. "First!" he loudly declared.

Harris frowned. "Are... you sure? You'd be up for far longer."

"I can do it!" the boy exclaimed.

"Very well then, it's settled!" Adrian raised his hands dramatically. "We will let the child kill us all in the *first* hours of dusk!"

The hunter jabbed an elbow playfully in his ribs. "Enough of that, you ass. If the boy says he can do it, then have faith." The troll laughed as he stepped back, waving him off before continuing ahead. Harris slowed, waiting until Vantis was standing beside him and matching his pace. "So, Vantis. I hear you're an accomplished hunter..."

"H-huh?! Who told you that?" the boy stuttered, an expression of alarm crossing his strained features.

"Hmm. Well, if I recall your father correctly... He said that you went out in the middle of the night over two months ago to hunt a deer and shot him in the process..." the hunter explained, his hand on his scruffy chin in faux-innocence.

"I-! Um... well, you see..." the child stumbled over his words, hastily racking his brain for any reasonable explanation.

"I find that rather odd, considering that Wren made it explicitly clear that you weren't to go outside at night..." he sighed, closing his hawkish eyes. They peeled open with a sinister smile.

"Unless... you snuck out *against* her wishes and went without telling anyone where you were..."

"L-look, uncle," the lad stopped, holding his hands out defensively. "I did it for a good reason!"

"Good enough to rationalize going out into the dark forest when you were well-aware there was a deadly troll in the area?" the hunter pressed, raising a sharp brow.

Vantis sucked in a breath before letting his shoulders fall limply at his sides. "I just wanted to get something special for Wren..."

Harris blinked, shaking his head with a chuckle. "Heavens' will, you are your father's son..."

The boy scowled. "What's that supposed to mean?!"

"It means," the man stopped, stooping down to his level. Vantis's back was straight, his expression set with indignant pride. "That you are an absolute fool... and you possess a good heart." The man tousled the lad's hair, making him grunt in outrage.

"H-hey! Stop that! I'm not ten anymore!" the boy snarled.

"Oh ho! I see! If that's the case, then I fully expect you to be ready for hunting and combat training," Those brown eyes squinted as the older man beamed, his joints struggling against creaking bone as he staggered up to full height.

Vantis's face went pale. "Right here? Right now?"

"Well, not *now* but you're not ten anymore, right? And you are participating in a *hunting* trip of all things," Harris shrugged, pulling up a low branch for both the boy and him to pass through. "Buuut, if you aren't interested..."

"N-no! I'm interested! I'm plenty interested! I'll learn! Just as long as we can get breakfast first!" Vantis stammered, hastily moving along as his uncle's long strides continued.

"Hah! Of course. Once we're done with our preparations, food will be on the way. You needn't worry about an empty stomach," the older man reassured, patting the boy's back gently.

The troll suddenly spoke up, his voice carrying on the wind with the first bird songs. He was perched on his knees against the slope, illuminated by the first direct rays of sunshine. The light against his silhouette was so bright Vantis had to shield his eyes with a hand. "Oy, Harris!"

"Yes?" the huntsman called out, his voice echoing.

"I'm going to check the traps further up the cliff. Can you handle the ones here on the slope?" the elegant man pressed, gesturing generally towards their location.

"Sure, meet up with us when you're done!" the hunter yelled.

The three split off, with Adrian heading farther up the mountain while Harris knelt down, waiting for Vantis to flop down beside him as he worked at the first snare. From the looks of it, the trap was set off but the animal had slipped free. A mild annoyance to be sure, but a common one. He tossed the cord aside, running his fingers over the track left behind. A hoofprint. The hunter sighed, shifting towards his exhausted companion beside him. "Well, master hunter," he began with a smile. "How much do you know about snares?"

Vantis, still covered in leaves and sweat, wiped at his brow. "Umm, I know a decent bit."

Harris nodded, pointing a finger towards the trap. "Why don't you show me how to reset it?" The boy hesitated, giving his uncle a nervous glance before getting to work. Vantis managed to dismantle, reassemble, and set the snare up with only a few complications. He focused so hard that he hadn't noticed Harris next to him until he shifted his hoof, making the boy jump. Before he knew it, a fresh snare laid before him. Emerald eyes tilted up against the dappled golden light and investigated the appraising look on his uncle's face.

The hunter solemnly nodded. "Good work, the only issue I see before us is the line being a bit loose here," he explained, reaching over to adjust the knotting on the cord. "There. That way, the line will be tight enough to hold against the thrashings of the animal."

Vantis nodded, letting a prideful smile tug at his lip. The two moved on, clearing and resetting traps. They managed to gather two squirrels, with only two traps failing. Vantis got to set up another, this time choosing the location for himself. Harris watched, a sparkle of pride in his eyes as he saw the lad rush up to a particularly mature tree and set the snare in a leafy nook between the roots. "Good positioning," he complimented.

"I thought that if any tree climber decides to hop up or down from here, the leaf litter could hide the trap enough to catch' em!"

the child explained, leaping over the raised roots with a spry elegance that almost made the older man jealous.

"Smart thinking. We'll check these later before dinner," Harris nodded in approval. He cast his eyes up the slope, spotting Adrian between the layers of old trees, crouched over something.

"What do you have over there?" the hunter called out, climbing up the gradual incline with some effort as Vantis rushed along.

"Not sure... Looks like a squirrel... I think," the troll grunted, jabbing at something on the ground with a stick. Harris stepped over to his friend's position, kneeling down to gaze upon the curiosity. The boy scampered over to them, spotting the thing in question before cringing away in disgust. Vantis decided to check Adrian's quarry left by a rock instead of looking upon the carcass any longer.

It did indeed appear to be a squirrel, though one drained of all fluid. Its dry skin was pulled taut over its bones, its eyes collapsed inward and mouth agape. "What on earth...?" the huntsman mumbled. If he hadn't known any better, he would have assumed it was mummified... but its leg was clearly snagged in the snare. And these were only set yesterday. Adrian scanned the nearby area.

"It appears some deer came by... Though whether they approached before or after the scrap I'm not sure..." The troll gestured out to the scattered hoof marks.

The hunter leaned over, resting a palm against the dirt as he investigated the impressions. "There's something off about these..."

"Hmm?" Adrian craned his neck forward, trying to get a better look.

The huntsman gestured to the prints with his gloved hand as he spoke, "Look, they're not in sets of four."

"Sets of two... maybe there was a herd that passed by and messed up the lay of the tracks?" the beast mused, biting at one of his black nails.

"Not sure..." the hunter grunted, rubbing at the wild stubble on his jawline. "In any case, we should burn the body. If it's diseased I would rather it not spread," Harris sighed, pulling out his flint.

"Here, allow me," Adrian began, pushing aside the hunter's hands. He pulled the creature free of the trap and set it upon open ground, clearing away leaf litter. The troll nicked his palm with his stone hunting knife, barely flinching. He squeezed his bleeding hand into a fist, letting the blood drop onto the body in a thin layer. The beast licked the wound with his long, acidic tongue before bandaging it. "There, it should catch more thoroughly now," he affirmed.

The hunter snorted. "Using your blood as oil, huh? Guess you never forgot that old trick."

The beautiful man gave him a smirk. "Old habits die hard, it seems..."

"That among other things," the huntsman chuckled, finally getting the blood to light. The furry body burst into flames, immolating the little rodent into charred bones within minutes.

While they seemed unperturbed at a passing glance, it was clear that those hoof marks had set them both on edge. Enough that when the two met each other's gaze they simply nodded, sharing a silent conversation in that single moment. The troll was already gathering his things as Harris turned his attention to Vantis, who was curiously gazing at the raccoon stuck in a cage trap. "I think we should head back and get breakfast ready. We've caught plenty for now."

Green eyes glanced up and gave him a grin. "Hell yeah! Let's go home and eat!"

Adrian and Harris were uncharacteristically quiet, enough so that the young boy had taken notice. Something was wrong, but what it was they wouldn't say. It made the young Lionel nervous, causing him to flinch when his uncle spoke up. "Are you going to sell the fur?" He pointed at the raccoon nervously pacing in its cage.

Adrian nodded, a solemn expression overtaking his fine features. "Yes, when we reach the river we can split off so I can set this creature to rest." He was oddly gentle with the animal, even when the raccoon tried to gnaw at his exposed fingers. It didn't seem to bother him in the slightest. It was bizarre, seeing the vicious and abrasive troll so respectful with regards to nature. Vantis supposed it had something to do with the fact he was fae, being amicable to the creatures of the forest but hateful towards humans.

Or at least me...

The boy frowned, holding his elbows tightly. He felt a heavy pat against his back. "And while I'm gone, you can deal with this squealing baby while you skin our breakfast!" Adrian laughed. The boy scowled, trying to hide his nervousness at the concept of skinning an animal.

They slid down the sandy slope of the bubbling Lansaugh River, stepping upon the smooth pebbles that framed the delicate brook. The handsome fae continued downstream while the other two remained where they were. Vantis took this moment to dunk his head into the cool water, spending a decent amount of time washing the sweat from his head and hair. While Vantis was off cleaning his face, Harris pulled out a large water skin sagging over his hip, resting the opening near the ledge of falling water. When he sufficiently filled the sack, the hunter slung the sloshing weight over his shoulder, gesturing for Vantis to come along. The young lord tossed his head back, scattering droplets behind him like a curtain of rain. With a quick shake, he jolted to his feet, splashing past the shallow river and up the sandy slope ahead.

"While I'm certain you are no 'squealer', I don't believe I ever taught you how to prep wild meat, have I?" Harris asked, setting the dangling creatures away from the central camp. Vantis shook his head, eyes wide like a deer in firelight. The hunter set down the water skin next to Adrian's cave before returning to the animals. He gently gestured for the child to sit down, setting a skinning knife down beside them. "Here then. Let me start with an example and you can follow along."

By the time the two had finished, Vantis had thrown up twice, once nearly on the meat he was skinning. Harris had to carefully move the heaving lord's head away, gently scolding him for getting so close to wasting good food. But with a shaky hand and diminished appetite, the boy finally succeeded at skinning a squirrel. The huntsman collected the furs and set them upon the drying rack next to the alcove. Presumably, Adrian would find some use for them. Then he began the dirty work of removing the organs, leaving the intestines and stomach in a bowl beside him as the queasy child squirmed. Watching the retching Vantis with a small smirk, he chuckled, "I suppose a hunter's life isn't for you. Not yet, anyways."

"Ugh..." the boy groaned, holding his stomach and turning away. He heard one of the organs slide free of the body Harris was cleaning, making him shudder.

Leaves crunched and twigs snapped under the weight of an approaching individual. The tall form of Adrian crested over the hillside, striding with a decapitated raccoon held by the tail in his claws. Vantis squeezed his eyes shut and shivered. The troll stopped beside the two, giving the boy a bemused glance before turning towards his old friend. "Did he squeal?" he asked, deadpan.

"Not one bit. He did throw up though... twice," the hunter replied with an amused shrug.

The elegant man sighed. "Well, I suppose he did better than expected... good job."

Good job.

That phrase made something in the child's heart swell with pride, enough to make a tiny smile tug at his lips. His father, as despicable as he was, said he did good. Some of the queasiness fell away. He sat up, eager to rejoin the group as they chatted.

"So, did you collect the firewood?" Harris asked, popping a squirrel heart in his mouth. Vantis began retching once more, enough to make the two men stare at him.

The fae shook his head to clear his mocking thoughts. "Yes, plenty." One of his claws slung over his shoulder pulled up a rope-tied bundle, setting it down beside the pit. He snapped the lines with his talons, letting the pile of wood tumble apart. Harris cleared out the old ash, exposing the dull embers to the open air. As Adrian stacked the wood around the slumbering coals, the huntsman pulled out a wad of dried grass from one of his bags. He reached over and gingerly set it inside, letting the flickering heat catch the fronds and begin to gnaw away at the yellow fibers. By the time Adrian finished setting up the pit, the fire was beginning to roar to life, ready to cook breakfast.

Harris only needed a cursory glance towards Vantis to confirm how he felt about meat. The man sighed and poured the large water skin into a pot, setting up a spit to prop the small cauldron above those licking flames. When the water came to a boil, he added a sack of oats and spices, stirring with care. Hawkish eyes spotted his fae companion beside him skinning the raccoon, setting the pelt on a drying rack. "Mind if I eat this?" Adrian grunted, gesturing to the wad of flesh remaining in his dripping hands.

Harris waved him on. "Sure, none of us have any interest in eating meat at the moment."

The troll shrugged, opening his jagged maw wide to begin chewing on his prize. Vantis glanced over at the snapping sound, horrified by what he saw. The juxtaposition of his father's statuesque beauty against the disgusting gnashing of his teeth upon the raw meat was enough to send a shiver racing up his spine. His immaculate face was covered in blood and viscera, a macabre scene of ghastly, feral magnificence. The child squeezed his eyes shut, choosing to lean against a tree to try drowning out the noises and the reality that the beast feasting away was his own father.

Before his mind could fully ease into slumber, Vantis awoke to a bowl being shoved against his shoulder. His green eyes blinked, spotting Harris in his hazy vision before realizing what he was holding. Oatmeal. While not exactly a favorite, it was far better than any other offering nearby. The young lord gave him an appreciative nod before clasping the warm wooden bowl in his hands, drawing it down to his lap. Harris smiled before striding away. The child ate quietly, eyeing the two men discussing something only a few yards out.

"I don't know why... but I smell something odd in the air..." Adrian mused, holding his body in a state of alertness.

"Mighty fine way of saying you smelled a fart," the older man snorted.

The troll gave him a glare. "I'm serious. I've never smelled anything like this. It's like a cold sweetness in the air. Like a flower made from the softest of dew resting on a rotting corpse..."

The hunter raised a brow. "That personally made no sense to me, but if you sense something is amok then I have no choice but to listen. I trust your instincts, even more so than my own," he replied, his gritty voice echoing down the hillside. The falling leaves of autumn rained beside them, framing the old warriors in a brushing of gold.

Something was freaking them out, something that Vantis couldn't quite understand. But knowing they were acting with such concern made him nervous. Knights don't say things like that without the presence of a genuine threat. The two simply stood there, assessing the area. They glanced at each other before turning back, meeting up with the boy at camp. They nary said a word.

Chapter 19

The older man finished his meal last, savoring his food unlike the impatient pre-teen. "Well, Vantis. I'd say now is a fine time for some archery lessons!" he began, slapping his hands on his knees as he stood.

Vantis' eyes jolted up, shimmering with a barely restrained excitement. "Really?! Sure!"

The lad helped the hunter set up a woven target about twenty yards out. Harris plucked a charcoal pencil from his bag and drew a circle with a centralized dot upon the center. When the two finally finished tying the mat of reeds to a tree trunk, Harris began to speak, "Now, hunting exploits aside, how well do you handle that bow?" He pointed a gloved finger at the weapon resting against the child's back.

Vantis pulled it off his shoulder and gripped it in his left hand. It was a simple thing, a basic recurve bow bound in leather wrappings and a sinew string. The wood was well worn with use, the leather grip being replaced at least three times since he got it. It was a gift for his tenth birthday, and one of his most cherished possessions. "I might be bold for saying it, but I think I'm pretty good!" The boy puffed up his chest and grinned.

"Well, good enough to hit that big lump over there," Harris smirked over to Adrian, who was replacing the string on his crossbow.

"Oh har har," the troll rolled his eyes, checking the security of the string. "I was larger than the average bear, it's not exactly a grand feat to strike a large target."

"Yes, but based on what *you* stated, it threw you off the chase and stopped you from claiming the deer." The hunter gave him a knowing look. Adrian scoffed. "Sometimes stopping the opponent or prey is just as important as getting the kill. Preparations can make a difficult situation far easier to handle," he explained, turning to the lad as he drew out a starting line in the dirt. "Regardless if you meant to or otherwise," he added with a wink. Vantis couldn't help but feel a swelling of pride in his chest, something that the hunter immediately noticed. "Well!" the older man exclaimed, backing up behind the line in the dirt. "Show me what you know."

Vantis nodded, plucking an arrow from the quiver laid beside him. He nocked the arrow against the string, adjusting his stance to keep his legs slightly apart and his back straight. As he pulled back on the string, the lad sucked in a breath, holding his body in a confident stance while he aimed down range. Harris nodded approvingly, only approaching to adjust the position of his feet and the height of his elbow. "You don't need to hyper-extend it like that. Keep your arms straight to help guide the arrow down the range." The boy nodded, repeating his instructions under his breath as he fixed his stance. After the huntsman was satisfied, he stepped back, letting the boy continue. With a soft exhale, Vantis slowly eased his grip on the string, letting the line slide free of his fingers and send the arrow on its way. With a sudden harsh sound, the shaft burrowed into the target and drove itself into the tree behind it. It was only a few inches away from the center.

Vantis gasped. "Wow! Did you see that?!"

The hunter chuckled, clapping a hand against the boy's shoulder. "Excellent work. Better shot than Wren."

Vantis scrunched his face. "Really?"

The older man belted out a laugh. "She could barely hit the target!"

Adrian snorted, grabbing some of the huntsman's steel arrows and beginning to disassemble them. "If my limited memory serves, I believe it took her well over an hour to hit the edge of the target once."

Harris confirmed this with a nod. The boy shook his head. "Why was she such a bad shot?"

"Well, Wren wasn't exactly a ranged fighter. She tended to take a frontmost position in the army. Led most of the infantrymen." The hunter gave the boy a sheepish grin. "If there ever was a reason for Wren to hold any ranged weapon, something was going dreadfully dower."

The boy couldn't help but giggle at the thought, an enraged Wren beating the enemy with a bow. He shook his amusing thoughts away before pulling another arrow from his quiver and drawing it back. "Huh, then I'm guessing all the archers were under you, uncle?"

Harris nodded, glancing over towards Adrian to make sure he didn't grab too many arrows from his stores. "Five, Lionel," he called over his shoulder.

"I know, I know! We discussed this earlier! Stars and bones, you're a wretched nag!" the troll spat, setting away the arrows he wouldn't use before tossing the quiver back at the hunter. The middle-aged man snatched it midair, equipping it and pulling out his newly-made bow. He carefully strung the weapon this time, ensuring his braced arm wasn't in too much contact with the force. He let out a labored wheeze, checking Vantis's work after he finished. The young lord had hit the target each time, landing within the charcoal circle three out of his five shots. The boy was about to go out onto the field to retrieve them before Harris snatched his shoulder. He gave his uncle a bewildered stare.

"Before you head down, it is good etiquette to call 'man down range'. It informs everyone to lower their weapons and wait for you to safely retrieve your arrows," the hunter explained.

Vantis repeated the phrase under his breath before shouting, "Man down range!" His uncle gave him a nod of approval and urged him on. The boy collected his arrows and scampered back, a proud smile on his face.

"Excellent. Now, if you don't mind, I would like to test out my bow as well," the older man exclaimed, holding up the weapon. This time, the hunter had his arms covered in leather guards.

"Sure! I haven't seen you use this one before!" Vantis stated excitedly.

"I just made this one yesterday, so this will be my first time using it," Harris admired his creation as he explained.

"I mean, barring your little 'accident'," Adrian called out, chuckling.

The huntsman scowled and waved him off. "Oh, hush up, you! I made sure to have proper protection this time."

"That's a first," the troll purred.

"Shut the hell up, jackass." The hunter rolled his eyes before turning his attention to the target. Instead of pulling the string all the way back like he did prior, he only extended it halfway. The arrow slammed into the center of the target and embedded itself deep into the wood, the force enough to make Vantis look on in awe.

"Could I... could I try using it?" The child jabbed a finger towards the weapon. Harris raised a brow as he fired again, striking dead center once more.

"If you can pull the string back, sure," he sighed, handing the bow off to the child. The young lord was ecstatic, eagerly plucking an arrow from his quiver. The hunter made a sharp sound that made the boy jump. "Pull it *without* the arrow please. I don't want you to hurt yourself."

Vantis gave him a perplexed look. "Huh? It can't be that hard." His fingers went to pull... only they didn't move an inch. His brow furrowed as he tried again, straining against the tension. No dice. "What the heck is this thing?! I. Can't. Move. It!!"

"And that," the huntsman chuckled, plucking the weapon free from the boy's hands. "Is why I didn't have you nock the arrow. You probably would've just hurt yourself."

"And you can just pull that back?!" he gasped, sweat beading at his brow.

"Yes, because I'm older. That, and more years of training than you've been alive," he smirked, setting three arrows between each of his fingers.

The child was about to protest before the voice of his father echoed out from the camp. "Leave specialized weaponry for us old men. You would probably just end up causing more problems by trying to force the matter." There was a serious expression upon his ethereal features as he reapplied the fletchings to the ends of his new bolts.

"What? Are you calling me weak?!" Vantis snapped. Harris glanced beside him to cast a glare the boy's way.

"No, I'm calling you underdeveloped. You aren't ready yet. Human children have twig-like bones. If you try to force yourself to handle such extremes you will only delay your growth further," the man sighed, finishing the last refurbished bolt. He collected his work and stood up, snagging his crossbow and resting it against his shoulder. He approached the two with a second target of his own.

"Underdeveloped?! Your brain is underdeveloped!" Vantis snarled, clenching his fists.

"Vantis!" Harris roared. The boy jolted in fear. "What your father is *trying* to say is that things like this take time and practice. You cannot suddenly expect everything to come naturally! He is telling you to focus on your strengths and limitations to work within them. Not everything is a slight against you," the huntsman explained in exasperation. The lad lowered his eyes, frustrated but yielding to his elders. He understood what his uncle was saying. Harris shook his head, turning back to the target. He sucked in a breath, glancing at the grouping of arrows in his hand. "Well now, let's see if I still got it."

He gave Adrian a side-eyed glance. The troll leaned against a tree, dropping his belongings to the ground before crossing his arms. He smirked and urged him on. The huntsman closed his eyes and drew up a deep breath. When he exhaled, Harris pulled up the bow, slid one of the arrows in place, and fired. He repeated this with each subsequent arrow in rapid succession. All three landed alarmingly close to the center, threatening to shatter the previous two left behind. The motion was regimented. Deadly.

Vantis was in awe. "Earthly Mother! That was amazing!"

The high-pitched sound of excitement made Adrian cringe, rubbing at his ear. Harris let out an exhausted chuckle, staring at his quaking hand. "Ah, it appears I'm a bit out of practice myself. I'm getting too old to do that without a warm up."

"Still a good shot though," the troll grunted. "Now, since you all are having such fun, mind if I try out my new toy?"

The hunter nodded. "I need to go collect my arrows anyways. I don't want to damage anymore if I can avoid it." Harris set the bow on top of a rock as he called out, "Man down range!" Adrian grabbed the target he brought with him as he joined his friend's side. While the fae tied the mat to a high-hanging branch, the huntsman pulled his arrows free, tutting at the loss of one of the tips. They retreated, Harris wandering towards camp to repair the broken arrowhead. Vantis nervously backed up as the troll snagged his crossbow, checking on the mechanisms before applying a bolt. The boy couldn't help but gaze in nervous excitement, eager to see his legendary father in action. Adrian pulled the weapon up to his face, gazing down the sight towards the target over twenty feet away. He barely hesitated before pulling the trigger. The bolt snapped free and jammed itself into the target, sending it swinging violently. In a motion too fast for Vantis to follow, he plucked another bolt from his quiver and loaded the crossbow, firing once more.

This bolt struck near the first, despite the vicious flailing. He repeated this two more times, accurate if not true. Adrian lowered the weapon with a sigh. "I'm getting sloppy. Didn't get nearly close to the center."

Vantis was slack-jawed, watching that pin-cushion of a mat swinging against the force. His father was only two inches from the center, and each hit was extremely close to the next. The young lord jumped when he heard his voice call out the warning before starting his approach towards the target. After pulling his ammo free, he retreated and began anew.

The boy stood beside him, determined to work on his own target practice. This time, he managed to stick within the target's circle with each hit. He was still far off from the center and exceedingly slow... but now... He had a goal. He wanted to be just as good as his father. And, in a way, being so close to him while they both practiced made him feel a little more at ease.

After a few hours of this, the boy and the troll collected their things. Once they tore down the targets, the two trudged back to camp. Adrian settled back into his furs, checking on his bolts while Vantis plopped down next to his uncle. "My father..." the boy whispered. "He's just as amazing as the stories..."

Harris chuckled. "Seems he never lost his aim, even after all these years..."

"Yeah," the young lord breathed, drawing up his knees to his chest. "Why is the rest of him gone...?"

The hunter gave him a tight frown, sighing as he set down his arrows. "It would be best not to discuss such things."

"But why? You said it yourself! Father has all his fighting skills! So, where is the rest of him?" the boy raised his voice, setting his hands hard against the ground behind him. Adrian raised a brow at this, not bothering to turn his attention away from his bolts.

"Vantis... I shall not discuss this in front of him," the hunter stated, irritation leeching into his voice.

"And why not?" the troll's elegant voice spoke up, running a whetstone against the iron bolt. He seemed incredibly nervous putting his hand so close to the metal, flinching every time a finger hissed in pain.

Harris blinked. "Won't it make your headaches worse?"

211

"With the brat here? I doubt that they could," the fae snorted. Vantis scowled. "No, let him hear what happened, I cannot help but be curious myself."

The hunter blinked rapidly at him for a moment before turning to look towards the eager boy. The older man sighed, casting his eyes towards the sky for a moment before setting down his tools. "Very well, then. Settle in, will you?" Vantis crossed his legs in front of him, light sparkling in his eyes as he forced himself to sit still.

"A little over thirteen years ago, your father was still leading us under the banner of the Black Lion Executioners. At that point, he and your mother decided that they wanted to retire from the battlefield, after the armistice between Golossia and Solania. Before that, however, we had one last loose end to deal with. One of the Golossian warlocks had managed to escape from a battle, and we tracked him down. It was a small-scale mission really, only Wren and I were there with him on that day..." the hunter paused, his eyes far away. Adrian felt a small prickle of pain against the back of his skull. Slowly, he reached into one of his bags and plucked out a piece of willow bark, setting it in his mouth. This would not bode well for him. Yet he needed to know. What happened all those years ago? "It should have been easy, he was alone and severed from the power of the aversary..."

The troll's mouth moved on its own. "But I was wrong. I fell into his trap."

Harris's eye darted towards the man briefly before continuing. "We were ambushed. Somehow, the warlock had found at least seven other compatriots to isolate and capture us. Wren and I were helpless as our leader was felled before us, on his knees with his arms rent through with iron."

It hurt... It hurt so much. He'd failed them. He should have listened to Tobias. He should have brought the whole unit... But now, it was too late. Wren... Harris... they were behind him, held with knives to their throats. The smiles on those hooded figures enraged him so. The worst was upon the visage of the gnarled creature before him. A wizened, decaying breath oozed on the wind.

"Well, Lord Lionel... It appears even you can be deceived... That makes this easy." The warlock drove a blade between his plated armor and into his abdomen, relishing his howling cry as the metal sizzled in his organs. "Shame that at the end of the day, you clung to your humanity. That merely ensured your downfall. You can't save your friends... and you certainly cannot save yourself."

Adrian growled, thrashing against the arms that held his speared limbs away from his body. He hated this wretch... but he was right.

There was nothing he could do... nothing but...

"We don't know what the bastard said to him, or what Adrian had done. But soon... he went silent, slumping against those who held him. I remember the warlock raising his knife high in the air, ready to strike when..."

He'd made a deal. Those voided feathers embraced him. He shed but a single tear.

"He... seemingly broke free... I-I couldn't really see what happened next. One of the assailants had dealt a heavy blow against my head, so I was... disoriented." Harris shook his head. There was a hollow fear in his eyes from reliving this dreaded nightmare. "But there was blood, screams, and then silence. Only the warlock remained."

His talons burned as they burst forth from his gauntlets, bending and breaking the metal. His claws were covered in cooling viscera, his mind a hazy weave of distant thoughts. The wretch laid before him, trying to desperately crawl away. No. He wouldn't let him get away. He would take his family home.

He couldn't process the warlock's words as he drove the last threads of his life away. All he felt was the thrill of the slaughter, of protecting his loved-ones.

"...H...ome... Go... Ho...me..." the troll muttered, falling into himself. Adrian was shaking, clutching his head in agony. Harris was gazing out in another direction, lost in the past, unable to hear his friend's gibbering whisper.

"They were slain. It was over. But there was something wrong with your father, something wrong with Adrian. He was so... quiet. So still. Wren tried to talk to him, to snap him out of it. He had incidents like this before, but we had always managed to get him back. This time, however, all he did was grab our wrists and start walking, deep into the woods. He drove us on and on, demanding that we 'go home'... We were marching for so long that I honestly lost track of time. I didn't even have the wherewithal to check our surroundings."

Intruders. Aggressors. More blood. More screams. Wren was carrying Harris. He dragged them. He needed them safe. He would make sure they were safe. Safe...

"Your father protected us. He saved us from everything we encountered... but then... we found a villager. He... he almost killed the man until Wren stopped him. After that, he became incredibly passive."

I don't eat humans. I will not hurt villagers.

His mantra boiled through his thoughts, past the agony. Adrian squeezed his eyes shut. He felt sick.

The hunter gave the boy a conflicted expression, his eyes laced with pain. "Eventually, we did make it home. We made it to Willowbend. But Adrian... he just drove us on towards his home. The manor. After he made sure we were safe, he continued on, walking into the woods..." Vantis shivered. His uncle appeared so frail, so weak at this moment. He only ever saw him like this during father's birthday. When his eyes drifted over to his father, all he saw was a quivering man gasping quietly to himself. The boy was horrified.

"Wren chased after him and I followed. She ran ahead so fast that by the time I caught up with her, I only saw what made her stop while I was still trying to catch my breath. I watched Adrian's armor peel away from his body, I watched his humanity completely fade... I... watched him die. What was left... ran away, leaving us alone in those woods, with nothing more than the metal shell he left behind..." the huntsman finished. He was silent, enough that he finally noticed the quaking man. Harris jolted to his feet and rushed over. "Adrian?" There was no response. The huntsman gingerly shifted his head, spotting a thin line of blood dripping from the troll's clenched jaw. "Heavens above... Adrian, I'm sorry. I shouldn't have gone that far. Gods... your lip." He quietly tended to him, coaxing him to open his jaw. Harris moved the bleeding lip away from his fangs and started patching it up. Vantis was deathly quiet,

215

just watching the two. After carefully wiping the ichor away, Harris laid the shivering man down into the blankets.

Before he moved to attend to Vantis, he heard the man whisper, "I... just... wanted you two... to be safe..."

The huntsman frowned. "I know, Adrian... Please, rest now." He turned towards the young lord, approaching him with a defeated look in his eye. "...How about we go collect some more firewood?" His smile was weak. Vantis appeared more worried than disturbed.

"Sure," the boy nodded, getting to his feet and walking alongside his uncle. He waited till they crested over the hillside to begin speaking once more. "It... really hurts him, doesn't it?"

Harris nodded, an expression of shame creasing his features. He leaned over and plucked a heavy log from the leaf litter. "Yes... I went too far. I got... lost for a moment," he breathed.

Vantis nodded, almost expecting this. "Makes sense," he began, rummaging through a pile of dead trees to throw out some dry logs into the open. When the lad started crawling back out, his uncle began collecting the firewood. "He did something similar in the woods when I saw him for the second time. He started... holding his head and hurting himself. I thought it was like Wren and her panic attacks..."

Harris gave him a soft expression. "Honestly, that's probably not far from the truth. He shouldn't be able to remember anything at all after he turned, and yet, here he is."

"Talking like he never left," Vantis added, casting a wistful glance towards the blue sky. A flock of birds crested overhead, chirping joyfully as they began their journey south for the winter. There was an emptiness in the boy's eyes.

"It's honestly a testament to his strength," Harris smiled, taking the stack of wood and binding it with a rope. "Even after all the times his life was ripped away from him, he always managed to get back up, to come back to us. He was able to do the impossible time and time again. And this time, as hard as it may be, this is him getting back up to his feet once more..."

"I guess I understand, at least, why you defend him so much," Vantis began, starting another pile beside the first bundle. "But... That doesn't mean that he suddenly isn't a jerk. He's still mean to me. But, I won't shame him for forgetting everything." Harris almost spoke up before the boy hastily continued once more. "And I'm sorry that I never saw how much you and Wren were hurting... My father meant so much to you. I should have been there instead of making everything about me."

"Vantis..." Harris began, reaching out to the boy.

"But the truth is, I think... *you* were always my real father, uncle." The lad turned to face him, his jaw set hard. The older man stepped back, one of his hands holding onto the tree behind him.

I'm taking this away from him. I'm taking Vantis away from Adrian...

Harris's nails dug into the bark. His eyes were like that of a terrified deer. "You and Wren took care of me, even when father was... gone, and mother abandoned me."

"Your mother never abandoned you, Vantis. We've told you this before," Harris stated, shaking his head. "She needed to hide you."

"Yeah, and I haven't seen her once my entire life. She left me at the end of the day. Father didn't have a choice. But you two always stayed. You both loved me when no one else would." Tears started welling in the corners of his vision. "And... and... that means everything to me..." The boy's arms gave out and he dropped the firewood. He began wiping at his eyes roughly, sobbing. Harris threw his hesitation away, choosing to kneel down and embrace the child. The man let his nephew cry into his shoulder, feeling his small hands dig into his coat. "I love you, uncle."

The huntsman smiled, a welling of pride filling his chest. "I love you too, Vantis..." The two sat there, with Harris consoling the child while Vantis collected his thoughts. After a few minutes of this he pulled away, laughing to himself. The ravens softly cried out in the distance.

"Sorry about that. I guess I just needed to get that off my chest." The boy wiped his eyes with a handkerchief.

The older man just snorted. "Honestly, I'm just glad you felt comfortable enough sharing this with me." He glanced down at the woodpile beside them. "Now, why don't I take this back while you finish up that pile."

Vantis nodded, passing his gaze over the logs. "There's plenty of big ol' logs around here for me to get, I won't go far!"

"Very good. Come back in thirty minutes. Dinner will be ready by then," Harris nodded, wrapping his fingers around the line and hoisting it over his shoulder.

"Sure thing!" Vantis beamed before investigating the surrounding area, kicking up leaves everywhere he went.

Chapter 20

As he made his way back to camp, Harris smiled. At least he could get the lad away before he started cooking up dinner.

Sssshik... Sssshik... Sssshik...

The huntsman lifted his gaze at the sound, spotting Adrian sitting upright, a whetstone in hand. He was sharpening the belt of knives that the hunter brought with him for the trip. Knives with steel blades. The older man blinked, dropping off his bundle before approaching his friend. "I sent our companion away so we wouldn't have to worry about him getting sick. We can skin our dinner in peace now," he joked.

"...Odd. It's unusual for Wren to be that squeamish over meat," the man sighed, almost breathless. "Hopefully she's not ill..."

Harris jolted, glancing down at him. A freezing dread ran through his veins. The tips of his fingers went numb. "Adrian?" he barely whispered.

The man's head tilted up to face him. A tired, solemn expression coated his elegant features. He blinked with half-lidded eyes. It was disturbingly nostalgic. "What is it, Harris?" The man's voice was soft, barely audible over the roar of the flames.

"Are you... Are you alright?" the huntsman asked.

The lord raised a brow. "Of course... Why do you ask?"

Harris heard a faint hissing sound from his friend's hands. His umber eyes slowly fell, spotting the steel directly touching the troll's exposed skin. The hunter knelt down before him. "You should... cover your hands. The metal is burning you."

Adrian's hazy expression drifted towards his hands. "Ah... I see. May I borrow one of your gloves?"

The huntsman struggled to clear his throat, as if choking on a rock. All he could do was nod. He pulled the glove free from his hand, passing it to the man who frowned at his claws. "The corruption... it has spread to my right hand as well, it seems."

"It has been like that for quite some time, my friend," Harris croaked.

A soft smile graced his features. "Yes... once again, you are correct. I can always count on you to help keep my thoughts clear." Adrian shifted his gaze out over the woodland. The lord seemed lost in thought, only for his smile to deepen. "Hopefully Wren will feel better soon... mayhaps we can all enjoy dinner together for once. Though... I suppose we should start cooking right away if we want to eat on time." His glazed eyes glittered with hope. Harris's jaw clenched hard as he nodded, trying not to cry.

Lord Lionel is right here... I am looking at a dead man.

"Of course..." the hunter bowed his head before marching over to the spit. He diligently worked away at the firepit, the soft gaze of his leader driving him on like a beast of burden. The sounds of sharpening blades continued once more. Harris turned his gaze as the initial setup was finished, now waiting for the water to boil. He opened his mouth, almost eager to probe further into his friend's fractured psyche before he turned away nervously. Instead, the older man stared into the heart of the flames. "... Adrian?"

"Hmm?" he answered gently. Heavenly Father, he had the voice of an angel. This couldn't be real.

"Why... are you sharpening those knives?" the hunter finally blurted out.

The young man blinked at him, almost innocently before turning to the blade in his gloved talons. "Why, I couldn't seem to recall the last time I sharpened my belt earlier... So, I figured it would be in my best interest to do so now before our next fight..."

He still believes we are on the front...

Harris grimaced. "I see. What year is it again?"

The lord turned towards him with an expression of alarm. "Good heavens, Harris. Are you already growing senile? You are only thirty-seven, you know. If you keep acting that way, I'll be accused of dragging the elderly into a war!" he said with a chuckle. He continued his craft, working at the knives with the skill of a trained expert.

Harris had to fight the urge to sob right there and then. "Ah, how foolish of me..."

"Not foolish. Unless you decide to continue with your devilish tricks, that is," the commander smirked, his eyes closed as he worked.

Harris silently continued to prepare the meal, fighting with his trembling lip. He so desperately needed to say something. Something that he wished he said all those years ago. He dumped the chunks of meat into the pot before turning once more. "I'm sorry," the hunter blurted.

Adrian shifted his attention towards the older man. "... For what?"

The huntsman paused, trying to hunt for the words in a sea of emotion. "... For talking about what happened that night. When we were ambushed by that warlock..."

The lord gave him a sympathetic frown. "You needn't apologize... It's good to remember. After all, I still don't regret my decision."

"There had to have been another way..." Harris pleaded.

"Not one that could be thought up and executed at the time," the ghost shook his head. "I did what was necessary, Harris. I did it for her and for you..." He set the final knife onto the belt, sliding the strip away to move towards the fire. He took a deep waft of the cauldron before tutting under his breath.

"It doesn't change the fact that I wished for better, Adrian. I wished that you didn't need to give up your humanity to get us out of there. I wished that you could have been there for your son. For your wife." Harris's eyes were laced with a deep agony, one that made the lord rest a palm on his shoulder.

"Yet in the end, they both got to live because I stopped that man. I saved you and Wren from an unceremonious execution. That's all that matters. Everyone is still alive because of what I did," he reasoned, patting his friend's back before reaching over to grab at a bag of spices. The man stuck his hand inside, pinching out some dried leaves and salt to sprinkle into the bubbling stock. He gave the stew another whiff with a satisfied nod. Harris couldn't help but smile.

"... I missed you..." the hunter managed to choke out.

Adrian's eyes squinted with a hazy joy. "And I missed you too, old friend."

Soon, the confused lord drifted over to his furs, falling asleep on his stomach with a contented expression. The overwhelming sense of fulfillment the hunter had from that conversation alone put him at ease. He finally had his closure. Now, no matter what happened, he would always care for the man Adrian had become. Even if the commander he knew was gone forever, this new person was just as precious. He had his final words. He had his peace.

Soon, Vantis returned and Adrian awoke once more, with little recollection of what he had said and done in that brief period of lucidity. The rest of the day was quiet, filled with the contentment of good family and food. The hunter hardly noticed the passage of time, instead enjoying the wonderful moment before him. Not a single snarky comment bubbled forth from the troll's lips, and the tired boy didn't yell at his father once.

Chapter 21

Vantis was flagging as the sun set over the horizon, enough that Harris didn't exactly trust his conviction when the boy said he would take the first watch. The way the child's shoulders sagged and his eyes drooped were enough for the older man to be on guard, even as he began to settle down for the night. The huntsman came to a rest against the cliffside, wrapping himself in his ratty blanket as he turned his attention towards his fae companion. Adrian was once again up on that hillside. He kept scanning over the silhouettes of gnarled trees, a concerned expression weathering at his confidence.

Something was wrong. For what reason, he was unsure. But there was something out there... something was stalking them.

His jaw hardened, glancing over towards the boy slumped against the wall. Vantis's emerald eyes were glazed over, blinking habitually to clear the haziness from his sight. This would not be enough. The fae man cast one final glance over the brush-covered hillside before retreating back to camp, back to his den. On a whim, he snagged one of Harris's steel hunting knives, tucking it into his shirt. It was dangerous to have such a repulsive metal so close to his fragile flesh, but the blade was certainly stronger than his own brittle stone knife. If there were any predators in the woods, he would be prepared. The troll nestled himself into the folds of his fur blanket, laying on his stomach as he eased himself into an unnerved slumber. Harris, initially concerned, contented himself by settling closer to the boy. At the very least, if anything happened, there was a solid chance he could shield him from harm.

With what little preparations could be made, the two huntsmen fell asleep, leaving the tired but determined Vantis to keep watch. Silence washed over the camp, only to be drowned under the soft sounds of bats and owls in the distance. The dense shadows beyond the roar of the fire were his only company. The boy pinched his arm, grimacing each time a jolt of pain broke through the brain fog. It was awful but necessary. The discomfort was enough to keep him alert, and honestly preferable compared to the alternative of removing his blanket and exposing himself to the frosted air. He sniffed, wiping at his chilled nose as he blearily gazed ahead.

Nothing is going to happen...

He thought to himself. His fogging breath swirled and danced in the air before him.

What animal would be dumb enough to brave the cold and try to hunt a bunch of armed men?

The boy frowned, readjusting his wool cloak.

If I was out at this time... I would just go home... Home...

Vantis' thoughts drifted, his small frame sliding against the wall and leaning against the remnants of a dead sapling ensnaring the weathered stone.

Home... with Wren... Harris... and father... and.... mother... Would mother hate me as much as father does? Would she even know who I was if she met me? Would she even care? Mother...

Warm tears drifted down his crimson cheeks, providing only the illusion of warmth as the chill settled into the droplets. "...Mother... I... miss you... I want to see you... to talk to you..." he whispered, his arms shaking with the cold. He stifled a hiccuping sound as he pulled his shroud tighter. "...I... wish you were here..."

A melody softly flew over the hoots and chitters in the night. The notes spun as they wove through the air, drifting gently over the camp. A delicate, fine song, as if from the voice of an angel. They seemed to pass harmlessly over the sleeping men and settle upon the shoulders of the distraught boy, who perked up at the sound. "...what?" he muttered, a sparkle of lucidity gaining foothold. Emerald eyes shifted about, trying to find the source of the ethereal singing. There was no fear in his heart, rather, a sense of weary comfort. It sounded so nice, after all. Vantis staggered to his feet, letting the blanket drift away from his shoulders. He stepped forward. The song began to make sense. There were words.

...Vantis... Vantis, my dear... Come to me...

The boy jolted, trying to find the source once more from where he stood. Something primal was trying to warn him, something begging him not to listen. But why heed such thoughts when he felt so warm... so... nostalgic?

228

Vantis... I'm here.... It's mummy... I'm here to take you home...

"Mo...ther?" Vantis muttered, barely feeling the cold. His eyes were glazing over, a sickly film coating his vision. The last fragment of sanity reached out, falling short. "Mother!" the boy cried.

It was Harris who awoke first. His umber eyes snapped open, sharply lifting his head as he heard the boy cry and shuffle forward. Vantis was at the far end of camp, past the fire, past his bed, past safety. "Vantis?" he called out, shaking the last vestiges of sleep away. The child moved into the bushes. "Vantis!" the huntsman yelled, staggering to his feet. "Vantis, what on earth are you doing?! Get back here!"

Now Adrian snapped awake, pulling himself up sharply. "What's all the racket?!" he snarled. Before he could cuss out the older man for shouting, the troll saw the boy rush off into the night, screaming for his mother. "Shit..." the beast hissed, throwing his blanket away and leaping to his feet. That was when he too heard the ethereal song. But instead of giving him comfort, it filled his stomach with the sickly bile of dread. "That singing..." the man muttered as he rushed towards the fire. He snatched up his crossbow and his quiver of bolts. Adrian had a terrible feeling that he knew exactly what was happening. "Harris!" he called, pulling the string back on the weapon and preparing a steel bolt.

"What?" The man was already halfway into the woods, alarm clear on his face.

Adrian rushed to his side. "Can you hear that?" he pressed.

"Hear what?!" the hunter snapped.

"The bloody song, you rotten goat!" the troll hissed. Harris paused, focusing for a moment.

"...Yeah... What the hell...?" The man's eyes hazed over for a second before he shuddered, covering one of his ears.

"It's fae, get some iron on hand," Adrian grunted, scanning the tracks left in the boy's wake. If Vantis was being enthralled right now, he would be easy to track.

The hunter gave him an affirmative look. "I'll grab my bow and catch up! Go find Vantis, I've got your back!" The troll nodded before holding his crossbow at the ready and dashing into the woods, following the tracks as fast as his legs could carry him.

Harris cursed under his breath, rushing back to his things to retrieve the bow and his quiver. As a final layer of security, he began to reach for the belt of knives before he heard something nearby. The snap of a twig. He nary moved a muscle, instead shifting his eyes upward towards the bushes west of camp. There, glistening in the pale light of the half-moon, was a woman. She was lithe, but not frail. Powerful, yet not intimidating. Her face was immaculate, a visage of beauty as if sculpted by the hands of a superior craftsman. Her eyes were the color of autumn, matching a mane of fiery hair that cascaded down her shoulders and framed her bosom favorably. She was covered from her shoulders to her feet in a black gown, decorated with images of embroidered oak leaves. The stitch work was superb, and not a single snag or tear marred the hem, even as it grazed against the tangled branches. She moved like a ghost, weaving through the bushes out into the open. Her scarlet lips were pulled into a delicate smile. In all honesty, she was the most beautiful creature he had laid eyes upon in well over thirteen years. It was enough for him to drop his guard for a moment... but only a moment.

Harris cleared his throat, adjusting his back. He expertly slid one of the knives into his right sleeve as he pulled away from the belt. "Good evening," he smiled.

"Evening," the woman replied, her voice ringing out like the song of a windchime.

"Now," he began, carefully adjusting his grip on the knife under his sleeve as he stood a few yards from the woman. "I believe... that this is no place for a lady..."

Her smile deepened. "Any place can be worthy of a woman."

The huntsman chuckled. "If that's the case, then I hope you wouldn't mind me asking as to why you're here at such a wee hour of the night?" The song was caressing him now, teasing at his mind in a way nothing short of euphoric.

She cocked her head, a stunningly innocent action as she almost seemed to glide forward. He could smell the sweet scent of sap and fertile dirt on her person. "I am here for the same reason as you, to find food."

"I see. Well, I don't believe my friend is as charitable as I, else I would have offered you food and drink from his stores," he gave her a dashing smile.

"That won't be necessary," the woman sighed, approaching the hunter. Her left hand pulled free of her long sleeve, brushing tantalizingly against his chest. He had to fight as the intoxicating song began to gently press in on him. "I think I have found myself something much better..."

"Ah, me? Surely a beautiful lady such as yourself can do far better than a withered old man?" He leaned into the freezing hand as it pressed against his cheek, breathing in her scent. A part of him wanted to fade away, fade into the precious beauty before him.

It wouldn't be too bad of a way to go, huh?

The hunter chuckled to himself as that frozen palm began to steal away at his warmth. "Ah, but older men such as yourself are rife with experience..." she giggled. "So, please, won't you dance with me under the stars?" Harris was on the precipice, all he had to do was—He jammed the edge of the knife against his wrist, dangerously close to his indigo vein. A twinge of pain and wet warmth jabbed at his senses, enough to chase away that blasted song.

His free hand ran against her delicate arm, gently dragging his nails along before softly taking her corpse-colored hand into his own. He felt the heat leave his fingertips. He readjusted his grip on the knife again and slid his fingers down her curves before settling at her waist. "It would be my pleasure," he purred as he led on. The two danced elegantly in the eerie moonlight, weaving and winding against their embraced hands. As he twirled his partner away from the fire, he glanced down beside him. Two sets of cloven prints. He saw the tips of her black hooves disappear under her gown as she sensually spun. The pieces locked in his hazy mind as he quietly jammed the knife against his throbbing skin, drawing another rivulet of blood.

I cannot die tonight.

He pulled her in, feeling her frozen form drain more of his life away. She wrapped her free arm against his back, the tips of her nails pressing against the thin fabric of his shirt. "I must ask, are you all alone in these woods?" the huntsman questioned, concern creasing his features as he pulled away to stare into those fiery eyes.

"Oh, no. My sisters are about. Though... they are not nearly as lucky as I," she exhaled, her breath stinging with the scent of rotten iron. "Though... you have asked so many questions of me but I have yet to hear about you..." she sang, brushing a strand of roguish hair away from his face.

"Then ask away," he invited, sliding the blade against his frayed nerves once more.

She glanced down at his legs and smiled. "How does such a... *handsome* man such as yourself come to be? You smell of beasts, hold the stance of the forest, and yet are no kindred..."

Harris smirked. "It's a matter of poor circumstances, I'm afraid."

"To the contrary... I find that I quite like it..." the woman sighed, pulling the man further from the fire. Further from safety.

"Is that so? Well, I am truly glad to be graced by your eyes then," he stated. His arm was throbbing, his grip waning. He needed to find a way out *now*.

She let out a chiming laugh. "Oh, and so well mannered too, I see!" She paused before speaking once more. "Now, for my next question..."

"I can do something better," the huntsman leaned in, caressing her cheek with a scarred hand. She shivered under his touch.

"Oh?" She breathed, her pale flesh almost flushing.

"I can tell you a secret," he smiled. His hawkish eyes narrowed with an enchanting expression. "Though, it is for your ears only..."

The woman giggled, "My sisters shall hear none of it." The ethereal beauty came in close, holding his back gently as she rested her angular head against the man's shoulder.

He brushed a wavy strand away from her ear, tucking it back gently as he leaned in close. The huntsman let out a soft, fogged breath as his lips curled into a vicious snarl. "*You and your sisters are going to die tonight.*" With a single fluid motion, Harris flicked the blood-stained steel knife forward and drove it hard into the woman's back. The fae shrieked in agony and outrage as she wrenched away roughly, but not before the man scored a deep gash into the area where her kidney would be. Yellow blood splattered across the dirt as she lurched away, clutching her side.

"You... wretched bastard!!! You dare strike me?!" The woman's face contorted into a vicious roar, her sharpened fangs clear to see. That immaculate beauty was shattered under the oppressive feral rage that consumed the fae, revealing a hideous beast beneath. Her nails lengthened into long claws as she lunged forward, slashing at his chest. The huntsman only barely dodged in time, the knife-like talons scoring his shirt wide open and grazing at his freezing flesh. He staggered back over to the fire, putting the roaring flames between him and the monster. She stalked forward, her tongue lashing at her lips. "You are going nowhere, huntsman. I was going to treat you to a beautiful death at my loving hands... That was until you dishonored me with that terrible blade!"

"Shame, and here I was hoping a harlot like you would be into such a thing," he smirked, shifting around the fire as the two circled one another. The fae hissed, holding her claws at her sides.

Those flames in her eyes were wildfires, gleaming against his only source of safety. But that too would fade. As sure as the growing shadows upon her carved features. He had to strike before she had a chance to retaliate, lest those talons slice him to ribbons. Adrian and Vantis needed him, and he certainly wasn't going to leave them alone with these monsters. Based on what she said, "sisters" implied at least two more of these creatures. Taking one out here and now was the least he could do. "I'm going to enjoy draining every last drop of your beastly blood. And when I'm done, I'll exsanguinate that stupid boy next, the deal never stated that he had to be alive when we captured him..."

Deal?

Harris gritted his teeth. They were after Vantis this whole time, waiting for the boy to be alone and weak. The drained carcasses, the odd footprints... He should have made him rest. He should have listened to Adrian's concerns. He should have sent the child home. But it was too late for regrets now. As the two predators circled, looking for an opening, he found his as she aligned her back towards the wall of the cliff.

Now.

The huntsman lunged, stepping a hoof into the licking flames of the fire to catapult himself into her chest. He jammed the knife into the fae's sternum with both hands as she roared, tearing her claws through his back. He howled in pain as he tightened his grip on the knife and continued his rush forward, throwing all of his weight into the attack. The force slammed their bodies against the cliffside, scattering rocks all around them. He was on the war front once more. He was fighting for his life. Harris managed to pull an arm free and press it against her throat to stop those gnashing teeth from sinking into his flesh, coldly twisting the knife before ramming its blade deeper into her bosom. Even as she tore deep gashes into his back, the white-hot pain only drew him deeper into focus, deeper into a wild fury. Blood the color of golden sap smattered against his face as her screams melted into the night and melded with the song of the forest, yet another target to be eliminated. He was a trained killer after all. He was Lord Lionel's prized assassin, his right hand. And he would be damned if he'd let this bitch win.

Before he knew it, the vicious thrashings faded, replaced with drained gasps. When all of the fae's struggles ceased, he drew his blood-soaked face up to hers. There was a primal fury and terror in those eyes, once so full of pride. Her crimson lips shuddered with her final gasps, some breathless words upon those fangs. But no air would come to greet them. The fire in those piercing eyes faded, and the body slumped dead to the ground.

Harris staggered back, finally noticing the burning agony in his right leg. He smelled the grotesque scent of burning hair wafting from below and shifted his gaze. His right leg up to his knee was badly burned, covered in rapidly-forming blisters and charred flesh. The only force keeping him standing was his adrenaline, a force that made him ignore the dripping ichor against his back and wrist. It was the same force that would make him grab his weapons and rush off into the brush, chasing after his best friend and his nephew.

Chapter 22

Adrian barreled through the brush with the force of an avalanche, smashing through the vines and branches with ease. The world was nothing but a blur, streaks of dull color that faded at the corners of his vision. His breath was a flood of fog that poured forth from his jaws, like smoke from the mouth of an enraged dragon. His crossbow was held tightly in his talons as he flew ahead. The boy's distinct scent of fineries and parchment guided him on, past that horrid singing. Such songs were meant for mortal ears, sung to draw them in like moths to a flame. Like a spider weaving an artistic crystalline web, it was created for one sole purpose: to hunt. To kill. When the prey was too entangled in the call of beauty, they were slaughtered, every last drop of life blood sapped away until only husks remained. The squirrel was just a precursor of what was to come. If only he had taken it more seriously...

Adrian hissed, driving away the remorseful hindsight with a snarl. What did it matter? He was getting the boy back. And now that the intruders had revealed their hand, they would meet the full enraged force of a powerful mountain troll.

But I'm not a mountain troll...

He flinched, darting past a grouping of tangled brambles. His legs propelled him with a force great enough to scatter the leaf litter around him in an autumn flurry.

I'm just a man. Albeit one with great strength and speed... but still just a human.

"Shut it," he cursed his thoughts, letting a branch scratch his cheek as he flung himself past it. Crimson dripped away from the slash, staining his smooth skin. He was still a troll, even with this accursed form and dower thoughts. His fury was just as mighty as the rest of his kin. These beings slighted him. They invaded *his* territory. His lands. He would make them pay for their intrusion, with or without his monstrous form. He caught the scent before he could spot the forms in the dark. The troll dug his sandaled heels into the dirt as he skidded to a halt, raising the crossbow to eye level with uncanny precision. Hellish hate blazed in those sapphire rings.

Several yards away, illuminated by a shaft of pristine moonlight, stood a beautiful woman with the slumped form of Vantis held within her knife-like talons. Her hair was a straight ebony waterfall that ran all the way down to the small of her back, glossy under that silver glow. Her narrow features were cast in a luscious expression of success, smiling down at her prize. Those deep grey eyes only shifted when she heard the clicking of the weapon in his hands. The wind tossed the hem of her long blue dress from the dirt into the air, revealing the embroidered shapes of branches and vines in the light. The child was barely standing, his eyes glazed over with a milky haze. He was softly mumbling under his breath, all the color wrenched away from his fragile form. This ignited a flame in the beast. "Put. Him. Down," he ordered, barely containing the lines of saliva exiting between his sharpened fangs.

The woman gave him a faux look of shock. "Now, why would I do that? It was he who came to me," her slimy voice curled.

The troll growled. "You tricked him."

"I gave him what he wanted. He wanted to hear the voice of his mother... and I sang it to him," she smirked, her crimson lips spreading that ghastly smile wider.

"A rotten bitch such as yourself is the furthest from his mother!" he spat. How dare this monster compare herself to her?! Her smiles were genuine, her hands strong yet delicate, her mind and eyes as sharp as blades. She was the most beautiful creature he laid his eyes upon and...

...*who was she?*

He threw the doubt away. The fae woman gave him a hearty laugh. "Oh?! And since when has a dreaded mountain troll ever cared about lineage?" Her black hair fell over her shoulders, covering some of Vantis's limp face. "This one smells of you... Is he yours?" Her glassy grey eyes flickered up towards the beast, her expression held with a deadly ease. The troll's jaw clenched. "Ah, that appears to be the case... All the more curious as to why you care in the first place..."

"Does it matter?! He's mine so put him down!" Adrian retorted, swiping a claw towards the ground.

"You are in no position to give *me* orders, beast. After all, troll spawn are worthless to their fathers... That is..." She gave him a wide, glittering grin that revealed those sharpened fangs. "Unless..." She turned, her stark white hands caressing the child's cheek. "This boy is a long-term meal of yours?"

Adrian roared in fury, his fingers tightening over the trigger. The woman's ebony talons stroked at the child's neck, dangerously close to piercing his tanned flesh. The troll's rage faltered. "Oh no, you don't. You wouldn't want me to strike him, now would you? If you hit me, my finger might just..." she slid it softly against the boy's throat, making Vantis gasp as a thin trickle of blood beaded to the surface. "Slip..."

Adrian snarled. "Stop! Don't touch him!"

"Oh, what did I just say, troll? You are in no position to be giving orders. This is a matter of ancient deals, between us and the mortal," the woman stated, stepping back. Her blue gown flourished wide in the soft breeze, revealing her deer-like legs underneath.

"Who made a deal with you?" he barked.

She gave him a dainty shrug. "Why does it matter? They certainly didn't extend their wishes to a lowly monster like yourself."

"That's my son, you whore. And these are my lands. I have all the authority here, and as intruders you damn well better give me a good reason not to cut you down and devour you all." Adrian stepped forward. The woman flinched, stepping back.

"*Whore...?*" she hissed, her ghastly beauty marred by an outraged growl. "You, a fucking bone-headed imbecile, dare call *me* a whore?!"

His angelic face curled into a sinister grin. Time to twist the knife. "Well, I *can* smell the foul stench of your loins from here, wretch."

"YOU DARE?!" the fae howled, pulling her claws away from the boy. That was all he needed. His hands snapped the crossbow up to his eye, his breath steadying for a split second as he pressed down on the trigger. The iron bolt launched free with a soft hiss. It sailed true and jammed right into the area between the monster's right collarbone and the base of her neck. A gasp exited her lips as the beast lunged forward, tossing aside the weapon and moving at a breakneck speed. He wrenched the knife from underneath his shirt, pulling it free from the sheath. In an agonized panic, the woman released Vantis and staggered back, trying to pull out the iron bolt from her sizzling flesh. Adrian's free hand reached out, snatching the boy before he could fall. He pulled him close to his chest for a moment before smoothly sliding him into leaf litter and throwing himself forward. The intruder screamed in rage as he slammed into her, tossing the woman down the hill with himself tailing close behind.

She rolled roughly, smashing her head against a rock that scattered a thin line of golden ichor across the detritus-covered forest floor. The troll could only be seen for a moment as the echoes of blue light left behind by his glowing eyes darted forward. He threw his body on top of the dazed fae, straddling her between his thighs. The woman roared in fury and slashed, driving her talons across his belly. Adrian grunted, stifling the tears of pain as he held up the knife with both of his hands before driving it down. With an inhuman roar, he jammed the blade deep into her sternum, cracking clean through bone and piercing her tender organs underneath. A pained howl exited the woman's jaws as she raked at the troll's face, cutting three clean lines across his beautiful features. He pulled the knife free from the boiling flesh and drove it down once more. Another gout of ichor splattered on his chest, another rush of euphoria filling his mind.

Yes, finally. A real fight. This was what my kind were made for. To kill. To slaughter. This witch is on my lands. She is my prey. She is meat. She is dead.

Adrian belted out a horrifying roar, the sound alien to a being of his shape and size. He was so distracted by his fury that he failed to notice that the fae had pulled the bolt free. She drove it deep into his side with a hiss, right where one of her claws had pierced his abdomen. A hot burning sensation filled his organs, forcing him to drop the knife and catapult back, away from the woman. He writhed in agony, pulling the horrid metal from his body and flinging it away. By then, the heavily injured monster was upon him, pinning him down with one arm while raising the other high into the air.

Deadly talons glittered in the moonlight, ready to put an end to her opponent. With a low snarl and all of his strength, the troll thrusted his head forward, peeling open his jaws to wrap around the cold flesh of the fae's throat. She gasped, missing her target and instead slashing weakly against his back. Adrian clamped down, feeling an explosion of ichor fill his maw and meat pulverize between his teeth. His claws grabbed at her shoulders and shoved away, tearing the trachea cleanly away from her body. Not a sound exited that elegant mouth, and nothing but fear filled her vision as those eyes fluttered shut. She was dead before the body hit the ground. Adrian spat out the hunk of flesh in his mouth, gasping for breath.

At first, all he felt was a self-satisfied joy as he fell back into the dried leaves.

I won.

He couldn't help but chuckle. This was the first good fight he had since... well... ever. Only the hazy human memories had anything to compare, fighting to the death in such a regard. With talons for fingers and speed to match his own, she truly was inches away from cleaving his head clean off. Yet he won.

Stupid bitch. You're not even worthy to eat.

He laughed again, letting a line of ichor-soaked spittle jettison from his fangs. Oh, how fun! He could feel the flesh of his belly already beginning to seal shut, filaments of tissue reaching out and snapping the wound closed. His face was in a similar state, albeit failing against the man's twisted expression, forcing the gashes to open once more. Only the stab wound in his side failed to close at all, leaving a burning sensation deep in his organs. His left eye was glued shut by blood and the cut dangerously close to the lid, leaving only his right to gaze out towards the stars. The song was still there, just far more subdued than before.

That song... That alluring song... The boy!

The troll's smile suddenly fell. He grimaced as he hastily shoved himself up from the dirt. Adrian crawled forward, past the limp fae's body to grasp the hilt of the hunting knife. It was still coated in the sizzling yellowed flesh of his opponent. "V-Vantis?!" he gasped, desperately stumbling to his feet. "Vantis!" Adrian began to climb the hill, stopping at various points to clutch his stomach and hurl bloody mucus from his maw. He wheezed, grimacing in pain as he struggled his way up the slippery slope. Just as he staggered to the top and reached the boy's side, he saw a shape exit the bushes a few yards away. With one hand holding his abdomen shut, he brandished the knife with a snarl.

The person reeled back. "Adrian?!"

Relief washed over the troll as he relaxed his stance, lowering the knife. "Harris? Are you alright?"

The deer-legged man rushed over, falling to his knees to check on the catatonic child. "I could be better, but I'm alive. And you? You don't seem to be in the best shape yourself," he responded. The hunter held the boy gently in his arms, checking his body for injuries.

Adrian smirked, the act tearing open one of the cuts. "The witch gave me a hell of a fight, but I managed to bring her down with minimal injury to the child."

Harris frowned at the thin scratch upon the lad's neck, producing a roll of bandages to gingerly wrap it up. Adrian pulled his hand away from his abdomen, the wound now closed enough to hold itself, at least as long as he didn't overexert it. He knelt beside the two. "What on earth is happening...? What are these things?" the hunter questioned with a growl, turning to face the unseen shadows.

"They are baobhan sith," the troll stated plainly. Harris raised a brow in response. "Vampiric fae that prey upon huntsmen during moments of self-indulgent weakness," Adrian explained, wiping his hand on the leaves before gingerly peeling open Vantis's eye. It still had a faint glaze, but the color was returning to the iris and his skin. A sigh of relief exited his ichor-stained lips. He shifted his attention, smelling the blood of his companion. "You're injured. Terribly so based on the scent," Adrian stated evenly.

Harris grunted, wheezing as a wave of agony rushed up his spine. He was beginning to recall the wounds once more. "It's... nasty but I'll be fine. We need to get out of the woods. There's at least one more of these... baobhan sith creatures."

The troll's eyes narrowed as he nodded. "We have to tend to those injuries first or you'll bleed out... or worse. Infection will take root."

The hunter hissed as he struggled to pull away. "It's not a concern at the moment. We need to get Vantis to safety. They are after him specifically."

Adrian sighed, snatching the roll of bandages from the hunter's hand and circling around to his friend's crimson back. The beast cringed at the sight, taking a moment to cut away the tattered shirt with his claws. Harris didn't bother to protest at this point. Hells, he doubted the man could stop him even if he wanted to. The troll glared at the injuries, quiet assessments muttered under his breath. He sighed, letting the scent of blood make his mouth water. "I'm sorry, my friend. But I need to clean these wounds."

"With what?" the older man snapped, casting a glance over his shoulder. His eyes widened. He saw the palm of Adrian's monstrous claws cupped, filling with a yellowed slime pouring from his mouth. "No. No way in hell!" Before he could protest further, Adrian braced his free arm around the hunter's front and gently washed his back in the acidic sludge. Harris howled in agony as the bubbling liquid sanitized the slices and cauterized the open cuts. It was a burning, hellish pain, enough to make the man see stars as he mindlessly wailed. Adrian's grimace held firm, determined not to lose his friend on this night. He was going to get both of them home. As the older man slumped forward into the troll's forearm, he began to wrap up the cuts, murmuring quiet assurances. When his back was fully bandaged, he cut the roll free with a clean knife from Harris's belt and tucked the loose strap into the weave, turning to wrap up the severely burnt leg. Just as he finished tending to the man and helped him to his feet, the song abruptly stopped. Both men gave each other a nervous glance. Silence overwhelmed the night, not even the owls and bats daring to cut through the sickly dread. The next moment, an agonized shriek shattered the veil, making both of them jump and turn their attention towards the camp. Someone found something. All it took was one small exchange of knowing glances before Adrian scooped up his crossbow and the resting child. Time was short.

"The village is over an hour's walk away... Once she finds the second body, we will be sitting ducks," Harris explained, trudging through the brush with a pained wince. He held a knife at the ready, shifting at the slightest disturbance.

"Not if we can keep up the pace. As long as we can get close to the village itself, she won't be willing to make a mad dash for us," the troll explained, leaping over some logs. Harris was deathly quiet after that remark. He didn't need to wonder if he could make it in the first place. Adrian held the child close to his chest, oddly frustrated with seeing the blood stain his fine clothes. This was a life-or-death situation and he was concerned about laundry? Since when had he ever cared about the state of clothing, anyways? Or maybe... he was just worried about the boy getting sick?

More human thoughts. I'm becoming less of a troll each day.

He hissed, lowering his head as he cleared the way for the older man. They ran for only half a mile before Harris began to quickly fall behind. The second howl of rage echoed over the forest as Adrian heard the collapse of a body behind him. He whipped his head around, seeing the huntsman on his hands and knees gasping for breath. The fae man quickly scanned the hazy fog of the night before rushing to his side. "Harris, we need to keep moving."

"I..." the older man gasped, clutching at his injured leg. "I'm afraid I cannot follow you any further, old friend. It appears my wounds have finally caught up with me..."

"Nonsense!" the beast hissed, hooking an arm under his right shoulder and hoisting him up to his shaking hooves. "You've been through far worse!"

"Ah, but..." The man teetered against a tree, weakly grasping his bow. His head was lowered, only tilted to an angle to give the fae a soft smile. "I'm not as young as I once was... Go on. Go without me."

"Bullshit!" Adrian roared, gripping the collar of his shirt and yanking the huntsman towards his face. The man felt so fragile in his grasp. "I'm not going to let you sacrifice yourself for some stupid sense of honor!"

A gloved hand grasped the troll's wrist. "It's not about honor, you fool. It's about keeping Vantis alive. Please, just go."

Adrian's head jolted back in outrage. "And what?! I just let my best friend die like a lamb to the slaughter?"

Harris's mouth opened for a moment in shock before chuckling to himself. "Ah... well, I'll just have to catch up to you."

The troll was silent, glaring at his stupid smile and his stupid bravery. All of this was so idiotic. And he wasn't having any of it. He lowered his head, letting his black hair cover his face. "I'm sorry... old friend."

Before Harris could retort, Adrian drove a fist into his stomach, making him double over with a gasp. His wide eyes could only beg the question before fluttering shut. With a loud grunt, the beast threw the limp huntsman over his right shoulder, holding him still with one hand as he desperately clutched the child with the other. "No one is dying in my woods," he hissed, spittle exiting his jaws.

Wren is going to sever my head from my shoulders when she sees what I've brought back with me...

His face twisted into a devilish smirk. That was when the laughing began. A soft, delicate thing that chilled at his very bones. Adrian cast a quick glance over his shoulder before throwing himself forward, following the scent of the village.

~~~~~~

Brambles slashed at his legs and tore at his flesh, scattering fine droplets of blood as he flew ahead. He wasn't concerned about the spreading of his scent. No matter what he did, no matter how hard he could try hiding himself, she would find him. Harris was too heavily injured and Vantis was the target. He could not hide. He had to run, even if the forest desperately clawed at his hide and begged him to stay. Adrian refused to lose his family. "Not again," he muttered as he launched himself over a small cliff. The troll landed hard three yards below, feeling his muscles snap and shriek in agony. He winced, gritting his teeth before willing those frayed nerves onward. He could hear the song grow stronger, and the sound of something crawling fast behind him. The noise was too loud. Too close. Adrian adjusted his grip on the boy cradled to his chest and the man against his shoulder. His instincts fired before his reason would. He swung around, lashing out a foot and letting his exposed talons within his sandals score across something. In the dense shadows, he saw a disturbingly long claw retreat back into the darkness, back towards those glowing golden eyes that faded away. The troll snarled before continuing his race.

It would've been so easy to repel the baobhan sith. That was, if he was a human. All he would need to do is pray to the Heavenly Father and beg for safety and forgiveness, as so many wretches often did. Their belief and devotion to their god would be enough to repulse any fae, himself included. It was disgusting, seeing such a petition while blind to reality. Such weakness tasted of bile. Adrian could not do so. He could not give prayers to the wretched gods. Doing so would be in direct violation to his very nature as a wild spirit. It would tear him apart from the inside.

Instead, he spat a curse, feeling a talon rake across his thigh as those scramblings behind him continued. He heard a soft giggle echo through the brush, spotting the edge of a green dress flowing through like water. Adrian hissed, taking a knee as his muscles snapped and failed. "Wretched bitch..." he spat, biding his body time to mend itself. Thankfully, the slice did not go too deep, making it easy to recover. He set the boy down, taking this moment to snag a throwing knife from Harris's belt. With a sharp hiss, the troll flung the weapon out into the brush. He heard a frightened cry before the shuffling changed direction. His claws pulled another blade free, throwing it towards the direction she ran. This time, the scream was laced with a terrible agony, a sharp sound that interrupted the song and made the man's ears ring. He cringed, feeling his leg recover enough to move before scooping up Vantis and rushing on.

Adrian could see the faint lanterns of the village ahead. He was getting close, and she was getting persistent. He slammed his heels in to stop as a blur flashed in front of him, sailing back into the brush just inches from the boy clutched in his grasp. Adrian cursed before launching himself over some tangled brambles, letting adrenaline guide his screaming body. It begged for rest, it cried for food but he would not listen. He wouldn't admit it outright, but he was more terrified than he had ever been before in his life. For once, he was getting answers. For once, he was beginning to embrace his wretched human side. For once, he found friends. Family. One wrong step, one slip, one fuck up... was all the fae woman needed to get the upper hand and take it all away.

He thought about Vantis and his annoying smile. He remembered his excited joy when they did target practice together. And honestly, the troll enjoyed it as well. He always figured the child was useless, but the boy proved he was willing to learn and grow. He was stubborn, that was for sure. But he was also abandoned. Scared. Adrian knew how that felt. He knew what it was like to lose his family. He would not let this happen again. He would not let this poor child suffer for his stupid mistakes. One way or another, he was responsible for him. He was Vantis's father. He needed to step up and protect the family he had been separated from for so long.

You are alive, Vantis. That will always be worth it.

That was the final conclusion he made before bursting out of the woods. He staggered out onto the grass, still trying to move even as more of his precious blood fled from his skin. At around four yards in, he heard a harsh sound. Adrian whipped around, determined to defend his family once more before meeting those emotionless glowing eyes. One elongated hand poked out from the brush, only to slowly lift and sink back into the foliage. The eyes blinked slowly before receding into the dark, leaving the man alone in the open. The chirping of crickets slowly came back into focus, an eerie calm filling the crisp air. His breath came in ragged gasps, his brow thick with sweat. The troll turned his gaze from the undergrowth towards the manor up on the shallow hill. His body let out one more cursing shock of pain before letting him continue his trek towards safety.

Adrian trudged up to the front door, wearily casting his gaze over towards the buildings. Thankfully, no villagers appeared to be out at this time. The troll couldn't help but breathe a sigh of relief. Carrying the bloodied bodies of two of the most well-known individuals in this town would have sounded every alarm. His shining blue eyes gazed at the boy curled in his left arm and the old huntsman hung above his right shoulder. Then he turned his attention to the door ahead of him. Gingerly, he laid Vantis down beside the doorway before slamming his fist against the hardwood. It shuddered with a low thud. Only the briefest of silence precluded the muffled sound of a woman loudly cursing. His keen ears picked up the sound of someone rushing down the stairs, hesitation before the individual swore once more. The door was flung inward, revealing an exhausted woman in a nightgown bearing a gruesome axe. The aggressive look on her face and the weapon made him flinch, reeling back as the homeowner lowered her weapon. "...Adrian?" Wren whispered softly, now more shocked than enraged.

"Wren," the troll bowed his head, hastily picking up the boy. "Please! Let me in! Harris and Vantis are in danger!"

251

A series of rapid blinks greeted him. She gazed upon the two limp figures in his arms for a moment. "Earthly Mother, what the hell happened?! Get in!" she urged, gesturing wildly for him to get inside.

The heavy air around the threshold lifted, and the troll let out a held breath, throwing himself inside and kicking the door shut with the back of his heel. He carefully set the boy and the hunter down, falling away from them with a ragged gasp. Wren tossed her axe aside and rushed over towards Vantis, checking his pulse and his bloodied clothes. She quickly realized that the blood wasn't his own and moved onto Harris, hastily removing his coat. The woman grimaced at the gruesome display that was his flayed back, with rivulets of blood leaking from the soiled bandages. "What happened, Adrian," she glared, said more as a statement than a question. Only the flickering light of a nearby oil lamp illuminated her face, making Wren appear far more menacing than she probably meant to.

"Baobhan sith," Adrian gasped, examining his injured leg. When her confused expression deepened he elaborated further. "Vampiric fae women that feast on the life force of emotionally weak hunters. They were trying to take Vantis... and Harris got injured slaying one. Based on what we could gather, at least one remains outside right now."

Her umber eyes were dark pools of concern, lowering the man in her hands gently onto the ground. She stood to her feet. "Very well then. Are you hurt as well?" she asked, an edge of softness to her stern tone.

Adrian shook his head. "Nothing I can't heal. I need to go back out there."

"What?! You just got done telling me that there is some dangerous blood-sucking bitch outside and you want to go back? No way in hell!" Wren snarled, drawing herself closer. "You're not going out there alone."

"But someone needs to tend to these two now. And even though she can't get in through direct means, it doesn't mean she won't find other ways to get what she wants. I can handle a fight outside," Adrian reasoned, holding his thigh as he stumbled back to his feet. As the warrior opened her mouth to further protest, he interjected, "But close quarters, there's only one person I can trust to protect these two. And that's you." Wren took a small step back, looking into his sincere and desperate eyes. The fear inside was evident, not for himself but for the two unconscious individuals slumped over on the floor. Conflict warred in her eyes as her lip drew up in a snarl. She squeezed her eyes shut and clenched her fists for a moment. "Wren... I know I ask for much, but please, trust me..." Adrian whispered, leaning back against the front wall of the foyer. His legs were shrieking in protest. He wanted to collapse here and fall asleep. He wanted to stay inside with the rest of his family, but he knew that he would be useless here. That, and the troll was still enraged by the audacity of those wretched fae. They needed to pay for hurting his kin. He had to fight.

Wren looked away, starting to kneel down beside the child. She gingerly moved a stray hair from his face, her face twisted up with an all-consuming emotional agony. She lowered her head. "Fine. But get back here alive when you are done. I'm not burying you again, you hear me?"

Adrian felt a smile tug at his dirtied face. He missed her so much. "Understood," the troll responded before approaching the fallen hunter. He carefully stripped him of his belt of knives and threw the strap over his shoulder. With a deep breath, he turned around and stepped outside, closing the door behind him roughly. He could hear the woman inside rushing towards one of the side rooms, presumably to grab medical supplies. The fae man closed his eyes, reaching for the crossbow dangling at his side and pulling it up to his chest. The song began, alarmingly close this time. By the time he loaded a bolt and held it at the ready, he opened his eyes.

Standing before him, on the far end of the dirt pathway, thirty yards from the rows of villager homes, stood the baobhan sith. She was tall and lanky, like a leafless young tree in autumn. Her deep scarlet hair billowed in the breeze, a tattered flag clawing at the air. Piercing golden eyes shone under the shadows of that hair, spying him with the gaze of a calculated predator. Disturbingly long, thin arms were held at her sides, skeletal claws twitching in anticipation. Her emerald green dress drifted in the breeze like a ghostly apparition, revealing elegant deer legs held in a dominant stance. An air of eager tension surrounded the fae's body, feeding off of Adrian's own instinctual savagery. His hand was steady, aiming true towards her chest.

"Oh, great mountain troll, why dost thou greet thee with such malice? Thee has't taken much, after all..." her voice sang on the breeze, weaving through the tense air.

"You attacked my family," the troll growled, his lip curled into a sneer as his fangs glittered in the moonlight.

"'Family'? Such terms art foreign to thee... Unless, thy nature is unraveled?" Her thin scarlet lips tightened into a smile, her head cocked in a mocking manner.

Adrian hissed, his grip tightening against the wooden stock. "I am a troll, if I decide I want something, even a family, I can have it if I so wish," he snarled.

"Is that so? Pirthee tell, dost thou hold faith in thy tongue?" The fae woman sneered. Adrian's eye twitched. He was gripped by hesitation. Her amber eyes flashed with a joyous zeal. "I think not. Thee has't no faith, no value in thy own words. Not as a human, nor as a fae..."

"These are my lands, wretch!" the troll roared, feeling the hairs on the back of his neck rise with rage.

The woman cackled, lifting an emaciated claw up to her mouth as she laughed. Her eye fell towards the man, an intense expression washing over her features. "I'm afraid that those words has't no bearing. Without faith in thy humanity or thy heritage as a troll, thou art simply... nothing," she explained with a smile. As if to prove her point, she swiped her hand across the air in front of her sharply, sending out needles of ice towards the man. Adrian cursed, rolling off to the side just moments before one of them could pierce his flesh. A few stray daggers sliced through his shirt, leaving exposed flesh in their wake. He quickly aimed and fired, sending the bolt toward the woman's chest. The baobhan sith darted away, like a puppet on a string as she let out a giddy cackle. "Thou has't taken mine sisters, O' great nothing. Thee has't slighted me. Before I pay mine dues, I shalt reap vengeance. Mine sisters shall collect retribution!" the fae hissed, swinging her talons around and dragging up towards the sky.

Adrian felt the air rapidly cool around him, his fogging breath the last warning before he dodged again. This time, a talon of ice reached up and slashed against his shin, making the troll cry out in pain. His trigger hand reached up to the belt of knives and threw one, striking at her thigh. She almost seemed to blur with how fast she advanced, slashing at the man's left forearm. The troll was forced to drop his crossbow, gripping at his limp arm as he rolled away, back towards the door. There was a prickling of fear racing up his spine.

The woman drew her blood-covered fingers up to her mouth, licking at the crimson ichor with a rapturous shiver. She moaned in ecstasy, savoring the flavor. "Ah, an exotic aroma. Thou art truly interesting. Art thee sure thee mind falling to mine embrace? I couldst maketh it delightful for the both of us..." she enticed, strutting over with the grace of a specter.

"Mayhaps, only if I get to shove this inside you first," the troll smirked, pulling out the larger hunting knife from under his shirt.

The fae giggled, pulling her legs apart sensually and running her claws down her thighs. "Very tempting. Runneth me through, most wondrous Nothing. I desire to taste thy blade deep inside me..." she purred.

An outraged growl exited his gritted teeth. He lunged, slashing the blade towards her chest. The fae woman dodged, raking her claws across his belly. Adrian snarled in pain, whipping around to slash behind him. The iron clipped her shoulder, making the woman hiss. She kicked a hoof against the inside of his knee, throwing him off balance as she slashed up his back. The troll roared in agony, throwing himself onto his hands and knees before tackling her legs. The baobhan sith let out a harrowing cry as they fell, the man landing on top and jamming the knife towards her chest. She managed to twist away just in time, the blade only piercing the area just below her right collarbone. She flicked out a talon, a wave of energy sweeping behind the two.

A thick, thorny vine wrapped around Adrian's neck and yanked him and his foul weapon off the woman, giving her a moment to rush to her hooves. The troll ripped the knife through the plant, the severed pieces shriveling as the magic peeled away. His icy blue eyes were pinpricks now, his bloodied mouth foaming in a frenzy. He let out a feral roar, slashing wildly as the woman danced around him. She laughed all the while, weaving around him like a ribbon as the hunched beast threw his weight around. In a moment of instinctual clarity, he extended his claws, slashing against her abdomen as she darted past. The woman cried out, jumping away from the moonlit monster. She held her stomach, watching that sap-colored ichor leak from under her dress. The mad troll lifted his fingers towards his maw, letting his black tongue lap up the blood. He shivered with excitement.

"Thy claws art sharp. And thy scent is wild," the woman gasped. She hid her face, almost ashamed. "Couldst I has't madeth an error? Couldst a disgusting half troll be an alluring partner?"

"Shut up!" he snarled, his slavering maw sending a line of saliva across the grass. "Stop playing around and die already!"

He charged, throwing himself with a speed that she did not expect. The fae barely dodged the stabbing motion, feeling the blade make a thin slice across her side. The woman winced, her glowing golden eyes too fixated on the knife to notice the claws extended towards her. They raked hard across her cheek, drawing blood and snapping tendons. The fae woman howled in agony, jumping away from the man to hold her face. "Very well," she hissed, watching the troll lunge once more. "No more games..." She pulled one of the throwing knives she collected from within the folds of her dress, flinging it towards his left collarbone. It struck him with a force strong enough to throw him against the wall of the manor.

Adrian tried to pull away, only to see the fae approach and pull out a silver blade as long as her forearm. The baobhan sith ripped the iron dagger out of him, only to drive the other into his left shoulder, impaling him and locking him against the wooden wall. The jagged blade effortlessly ripped apart muscle and sinew, making him cry out. His free arm dropped his weapon, weakly reaching up in an attempt to pull it free. She threw the iron knife away and drove a nail of ice through his grasping hand, pinning it to the wall as well. Adrian gasped, tears blurring his vision as icy fingers wrapped around his jaw. The fae tugged him up towards her face, gazing down upon the bleeding troll. She leaned in and snarled, "At first, I considered sparing thee. Such a uniquely handsome troll such as thyself shouldn't be so carelessly wasted. But alas, thee has't forced mine hand. The deal hath said to bringeth the Lionel or proof of his death. Thee desire thy family so much? Then thou can expire with them!"

With that, her left hand curled in, cradling a blue flame. Adrian's eyes widened in terror. The next second, she drove her flaming palm into his side, the fire catching against his skin like oil. His flesh boiled rapidly, blood hissing against the pressed heat. The troll howled, thrashing against the blades that held him in place. Blood poured from the agitated wounds as he desperately attempted to flee, to get away from that terrible flame. Unfortunately, the stronger fae had him pinned, both with her forearm against his throat and by the very hand that was immolating him. The fire quickly spread against his abdomen, boring a hole deep into his side. The blaze greedily supped upon his blood as it feasted upon his flesh. The shrieks were finally awakening the townsfolk, lamplight emanating from the faraway homes as their occupants stirred. The baobhan sith smiled, relishing his cries. "Thoust should consider thee blessed. If not by mine own hand, other kindred wouldst merely slaughter thee by their own means. Expire with thy beauty pure."

Wait? Others?

A loud thud resonated from the left. From the now-open doorway, Wren stepped through, holding Adrian's arbalest at the ready. The fae woman pulled away with a hiss. "Get the fuck off my property," Wren commanded before pulling the trigger. An iron great bolt flew free, ramming into the fae's chest and flinging her backwards. Wren reloaded the weapon as the writhing creature attempted to pull the metal shaft free. Her lanky hands boiled as she yanked it away, staggering to her feet. Before she could react, another bolt impaled her, this time pinning the fae woman against a tree in the front yard. The baobhan sith cried out, holding her shaking hands in front of her as she gazed down at her festering body. Wren dropped the crossbow and pulled out her axe, marching towards the intruder with a hateful shimmer in her eye.

"Thou dare?! Thoust dare strike me with thy boarish implements?! I am ancient, foolish wench!" the fae gasped, reaching out with her claws. Her perfect marble skin began to crack, revealing a rough scaled texture broken up by pin feathers. Her fangs were bared, her glowing eyes boring holes into the knight before her.

Wren merely scowled. "Quit gibbering, you filthy hag," she spat as she swung that mighty axe, severing the fae's head clean from her shoulders. The monster's face froze in agony as it fell, landing with a sickening splat; leaving the limp, twitching body impaled against the tree. The knight drove the weapon through its skull, ensuring the creature's demise before turning towards the house. Her battle-hardened expression immediately softened at the sight of the burning man. "Adrian!" she cried, rushing to the troll's side. His head hung limply to his chest, his breath shallow. She grabbed his cloak and patted out the fire before it could catch against the house. Wren grimaced before yanking the silver needle out from his shoulder, the ice dagger having faded the moment the fae's life exited her body. The troll fell limply into her arms, driving the two of them to the ground. She held him still for a moment, just trying to process holding her beloved leader for the first time in well over a decade.

A clawed hand reached up and held her shoulder. "Wren..." Adrian wheezed.

"Adrian?! Oh, thank the stars you're alive!" Wren gasped, holding him tight.

"There... might be more fae... looking for Vantis..." he warned. He tried to struggle to his feet, but she held him fast.

"That doesn't matter. You are injured. Bad. You need to get inside," she argued, pulling the both of them to their feet.

"But I... I can see in the dark, far better than you... I can... sense them before they arrive... I can... protect you all..." he breathed, trying to pull away.

"Adrian..."

"Please, Wren. At least let me stay as a lookout. I won't... I won't fight anything. I'll just send out a warning. I can heal... Please... let me stay out until dawn..." he pleaded. He could barely stand. The rest of his strength was devoted to keeping him conscious, to fight on in spite of the burnt chasm on his side. The pain was more than he had ever felt before...

At least not since Terminahill...

Wren was terrified to let go. To let him leave her arms. She was scared of what would happen if she did. Would he disappear again? Would all of this just be another awful nightmare? But more than all of that, she just couldn't bear to say no to him. She grimaced, pulling her shaking hands away to let the man stand on his own.

Adrian staggered, hunched over as he held onto his side. He was certain she never saw how bad the burn was. If she did, Wren would have never let him go. It was better for it to stay that way. "Fine," the dame grunted, plucking the arbalest from the ground. Her eyes were downcast as she spoke. "Dawn, right? I'll come collect you at the first sight of sunrise. Don't engage any of the intruders. If you do, I'll kill you myself."

"Of course, Wren. I promise." The troll dipped his head, feeling a pulse of energy shackle him to his word. He trudged over to the tree with the impaled, headless carcass and climbed up to the first low-hanging branch he could find. There, he braced his back against the trunk and gazed out over the village.

Ah, how nostalgic... I used to rest here in this tree every time I needed to sit down and think...

A soft smile cracked his dry lips. What a pleasant memory.

Wren reassured the emerging villagers as they left their homes, urging them to head back inside where it was warm. Some had questions about the noises they heard, with the honored Lady explaining that they came from some wild animals that attempted to break into their backyard. While this clearly did not explain everything, most of the villagers were too exhausted to press further, choosing to leave their inquiries for the following day. Wren cast a single glance over to the slumped man in the tree before going back inside.

Adrian laid there, for what seemed an eternity. The only sounds to keep him company were the hoots of owls and chirps of resilient insects. His side was screaming in pain, enough to cripple him. He failed. He failed to kill the intruder. If Wren had not stepped in, he would have burned to ash along with the rest of the house. He couldn't defeat the fae. His sunken eyes gazed out over to the forest he called home.

Without faith in thy humanity or thy heritage as a troll, thou art simply... nothing...

Those words rang clear in his mind. She was right. Adrian had no certainty in what he truly was. He was not human, as ancient bindings still held him fast. But his desires, his memories, his actions... None were that of a mountain troll. He was something else entirely. Something between bound and unbound. His eyes slowly flickered, only jolting open when the chasm in his side was compressed under his dead weight. He hissed, readjusting his position.

Was he truly void from existence? What was he? Was he the ghost of a man animating a fae corpse? He did not know. Outside of his existential crisis lay something else. He thought about Vantis and his pained expression as the life was sapped from him. He saw the betrayal and sadness in his eyes. He saw the hope flicker away into a deep numbness when the boy closed his eyes. That child shouldn't have had to bear witness to such terrors. No one should find it in their interest to torture such a weak creature. And more would be coming. The baobhan sith said as much. More would come to feast upon his light and life. A child, who barely had a chance to grow and change... would fall to the onslaught of a mysterious deal.

No. I won't let that happen. Who gives a damn what I am? None of that matters. I am Adrian Lionel, and nothing any wretch dare say will hold any value against that fact. I will protect my lands. I will protect my family. I will...

Adrian's thoughts began to fade as the horizon shone with the first rays of sunlight. His eyes, dry and weary, fluttered against his failing will. He smelled the burning of the fae corpse below him, the pure light searing its foulness to ash. His left shoulder had healed, letting him rest weight against it as he slumped over. The troll couldn't lift a finger, couldn't move a muscle. All he could do was bear witness to the coming morning, the last vestiges of ash fluttering in the breeze, and the sounds of fast footsteps beside him. His neck burned with an incredible soreness that made him wince, but he just barely managed to turn to face the approaching person. It wasn't Wren, like he was expecting... It was Vantis. The boy was covered in his night attire, fresh and far away from the bloodied fine clothes he wore prior. As weak and pale as he was, he ran. Deep worry settled upon his brow as he called out. "Father?"

"Hush, child. You will disturb the others," the troll gently chided, a playful, dull smirk upon his dirtied face. "Don't make me reveal myself yet... I cannot..." He attempted to move only to wither against the agony at his side. At first, the boy scowled. It was only when he saw how weak the troll was that he returned to his previous concern. He hardly knew what to say. All he could do was clench his fists. Vantis was tricked. Drawn away and almost slaughtered. He put everyone in danger. Tears welled in his eyes. He opened his mouth, preparing to apologize- "I'm sorry," the troll said, forcing the boy to shut his mouth. Vantis tilted his head in confusion. "I'm sorry I couldn't stop all of them. You shouldn't have had to deal with this so young. Human children... deserve peace. It's what I fought for... for so long." The man turned his head, revealing the gashes across his brow.

Vantis couldn't help but gasp. "F...father..."

"Apologies hold little value in the customs of my kind... Only action can rectify my mistakes... So I promise you this: I will do *everything* in my power, *everything* within my grasp, to ensure your happiness and protection. I will make sure that not another nefarious fae touches you... I promise you this, Vantis..." His left eye completely failed, the lid sagging uselessly. He wanted to readjust his position, he was getting so terribly uncomfortable here... before he fell away completely. The air rushed past, the sense of falling.

Oh. That's a familiar feeling. Not again...

As the ground rushed to meet him, he uttered one last time, "I promise, Vantis..." He wasn't even awake to hear the boy's cries for help.

Chapter 23

Adrian was covered in something warm and soft. It was lighter than his furs but heavier than his clothes. What was this? And why did it feel so... familiar?

His eyes flickered open, blinking blearily at the opposite wall. The dark wood glittered back at him, with its elegant trim and various deep score marks. His eyes rolled in his head for a moment, trying to clear the heavy fog that held his mind and limbs fast. He couldn't move, not yet. He felt heavy and bound, covered in wrappings. Not quite dissimilar to the time he found himself in Harris's cabin.

Yes... I'm in a bed... My bed...

Thick mud-brown blankets covered his body, embracing him in a cozy warmth that made him advise against moving for once. His dark eyes shifted towards the right, spotting what he hazily knew was something called a 'nightstand'. An unused oil lamp stood at the ready, resting firmly at the center of the table. On the floor beside the mattress sat a bundle of furs and bones, all collected from his cave. He even managed to spot some of the other trinkets; greeting him with their gentle glinting surfaces against the thin beams of sunlight breaking through the velvety curtains.

Adrian's eyes slowly drew themselves over, spotting a figure resting in a plush chair at his bedside. He smelled her long before he saw her. That sweet scent of wildflowers and parchment. Wren was sitting back, her arms crossed as her head sagged against her right shoulder. Tresses of auburn hair lightly covered her face, with a thick, messy braid draped over her left shoulder. Her expression could only be described as stern exhaustion, something someone would get after many hours of active duty.

Here I go disturbing her home again...

Adrian frowned. He turned fully to the left, seeing another nightstand, upon which sat a stack of familiar books. He felt some of his strength return to his limbs, enough to want to move. The troll willed himself to sit upright, against the protesting of his joints. The shuffling of the sheets was loud enough to make Wren's eyes softly open, turning her attention towards the wounded man. He touched the bandages covering his left eye, feeling it open and close with little issue. His gaze drifted down, spotting a loose-fitting blouse covering his chest. When did he get this? "You alright?" Her voice made him jump. Wren's face subtly flinched. "Sorry, I... didn't mean to scare you... I just wanted to make sure you were recovering."

Adrian shook his head. "N-no, you're fine. What happened?"

"You fell out of a tree," she stated plainly.

"Ah," he breathed, resting his hands gingerly in his lap. "I suppose my exhaustion finally caught up with me..."

Seconds of pained silence followed. The awkward air between them was thick enough to gag him. It was Wren who spoke up. "...Thank you."

"For what?" he asked, looking at the woman. Her face was lowered, her hands clasped as her arms rested on her knees.

"For protecting him. Both of them. For bringing them home safe," she elaborated, her hands fidgeting.

He was honestly unsure what to do with that statement. So much so, he felt driven to divert the conversation elsewhere. "... It would be advised to keep the boy inside from here on out. The fae said there would be others searching for him," Adrian explained, casting his gaze towards the thin lights reaching into the room.

Wren grimaced, clearly disturbed by the thought. "Did they say why they were looking for him?"

"They said that there was a debt to pay."

This just seemed to darken her features with worry. "I don't know who would even be aware of his existence... let alone someone in league with monsters... After all, there's a reason Vantis is here without his mother." She paused. Her knuckles clenched white. Wren's lip quivered. "What do you remember?"

The elegant man cast his gaze towards the ceiling, rummaging through his muddled memories. "Many things... Little things... I... remember this house," he gestured to the walls. "I remember you, I remember Harris... and many more faces I cannot attach to names..." The troll shook his head, straining against the dull ache settling against the back of his skull. "It is as if I am a book torn in half. I have the first half, but someone absconded with the latter pages."

Wren shifted uneasily in her seat, her eyes boring into his. "Then I take it you don't recall the boy's mother."

"N-no. I cannot," Adrian started, staring off towards the far wall in shame. An indescribable pain filled his eyes. Wren only nodded in response, almost expecting this answer. She folded her arms and sat back. "All I know is... whoever she is, I loved her dearly. I loved her so much that it hurts to think of her... My very body burns at the sight of fragments of her face... " he trailed off, wiping a tear from his right eye. "I'm sorry."

"Don't apologize," Wren demanded, shaking her head. The act tossed some of the loose strands of hair in front of her face.

Adrian adjusted his seat in the bed, grimacing against the chasm in his side. "Thank you... for caring for the boy when I could not."

She gave him a soft smile, only a twitch at the edge of her lip. "It's the least I could do for a friend." Her umber eyes glittered against the filtered light, casting her face in deep shadow. "Hells, compared to what you did for me, it's more than worth it."

"I- I'm afraid I don't understand," the man blinked, shaking his head.

She chuckled. "It would take too long to explain..."

The smell of smoke behind him. She was covered in blood...

Adrian's mouth opened. "I hardly think that picking you up from burnt-down ruins qualifies as a reason to be stuck with an insufferable, annoying, demanding little shit for thirteen years."

Wren's smile deepened as she turned away. She had to stifle a laugh. "How do I explain...? For lack of a better term... you taught me how to be human again."

"Ironic," the troll grunted, a mild scowl decorating his fine features.

Her eyes drifted back towards the injured man. "I suppose it is."

Adrian's finger twitched with energy, sweat beading at his brow. He gazed at his hands. He needed to say something. Something important. This was his chance. "I'm sorry... for scaring you..."

"It's... it's fine. Harris is an idiot and you got dragged into his mess," Wren frowned, curling in a little.

He snorted deeply. "Understandable, all things considered. He attempted to convince me that he knew how to make pottery," the troll snarled.

Her eyes lit up a little, a sparkle of excitement lurking underneath those dark pools. "Yes, I believe he told me about that. Sometimes Harris gets it in his head that he can do anything..." she added with a chuckle.

"Yes, like firing an untested bow without a guard..." he turned towards her with a smirk.

"He explained that to me as well," the woman sighed, looking back down towards the hall. "It's from my understanding that he didn't even know what the hell he was doing. He just saw someone make the bow one time when he was a child and just declared that he could do it himself. Who the fuck thinks like that?"

"Him, apparently!" Adrian laughed.

"It's no wonder Vantis is so foolhardy, so headstrong. If *that's* his role model?" She gestured wildly with her hand towards the boy's room.

The troll lowered his head and sneered. "His *other* role model is arguably far worse. And well, he doesn't particularly like him. Hells, he said he hated me."

"He's just frustrated," the woman argued, shaking her head. "He loved the idea of who and what his father should be. He created an image in his head, one everyone spouted and told tale of. The one the politicians decided was the best to slap on statues. They never showed... who you really were. And that means he *never* knew who his father was. Only what they said you were. And obviously, we *tried* to curb that behavior... But well... you saw how that went," Wren sighed, her eyes distant and frustrated.

"And what does that make me?" Adrian pressed, his eyes hollow.

Her hands reflexively twitched. "I... don't know," she shook her head. "But, what's your plan?"

Adrian's neck pulled back, his body receding into himself a little. "Well, if more beings like the ones prior arrive, I suppose it would be in my best interest to keep an eye out." She raised a brow. "While I struggled with the... creatures before, not all of the intruders will be baobhan sith..."

"No, it will probably be worse, knowing our luck," the woman grunted, scowling towards the window.

"In any case, I should probably remain close by. But I... I don't want to hurt anyone anymore... I'm tired of hurting people... If you so desire, I can make sure that you never see my face again..." Adrian clasped his talons tightly together, the nails dangerously close to his green flesh. He refused to look at her.

"That's not what I want," she argued.

"Even if... the sight of me upsets you?" the man pressed.

Wren hesitated for only a moment. "Yeah," she affirmed with a nod. "Even if it upsets me. I can't argue anymore that you aren't Adrian... But you must understand. I'm talking to someone who barely knows who they are... When they mean so much to us..."

"I'm sorry..." he apologized softly.

"It's like watching an old man with dementia living a new life. They're experiencing whole events differently, seeing the world through foreign eyes... It's confusing and it hurts them, but at the same time it hurts others because they knew who they once were..."

she paused when she finally saw the pained expression on Adrian's face. He so desperately wanted to know, to understand what he left behind. His life as a wild troll felt so distant now. He could barely recall the scent of his cave anymore. "I'm sorry..." she whispered, folding into herself. Her hands were digging into each other now.

The troll reached out and set one of his green palms over them. To let her know that she wasn't alone. The troll sighed as he slowly blinked. "I'm glad you are able to talk to me. As hard as it may be."

She gritted her teeth. "It would have been easier if you were dead, I'm not going to lie. I truly don't mean to be cruel about that either..."

His eyes darkened as his hand slipped away. "You don't think I haven't tried...?" One of her hands lashed out and gripped his, shaking.

"Don't say that... Please don't..." she whispered. Her lips quivered for a moment. "I'm sorry we weren't there. I'm sorry we didn't try harder to find you."

"Funnily enough, that was actually the first time I woke up..." he recalled, his eyes lost in a faraway place. Her head jolted up to meet his gaze. His eyes flicked over to her with a delicate smile. "Two years ago. I was being chased. Constantly being chased. Faces yelling, crying... I was chased back to my cave. I wasn't allowed to go near that village anymore. Something... something in my mind couldn't handle that... not seeing it ever again. So I... thought about flying," he recalled, lifting his head up as if to feel the wind. He remembered those fluffy clouds, flying so serenely past. Past his anguish. "I had feathers, I had wing arms... so I figured..." Wren was shaking hard now, her eyes welling with tears. "Maybe I could... Maybe I could fly above," Adrian stated, nodding his head. "But when I fell... I woke up."

"I'm so... so sorry..." she mumbled, unable to speak past her trembling.

He wasn't paying any attention to her words. He was too far away now. "There were suddenly so many things in my mind that weren't there before... so many memories... feelings... And I... have been piecing it together ever since," he finished, a certainty in his expression as he gazed upon her.

"We... had no choice. You kept forcing your way in. Trying to get to him, to us. There was some recognition there but... you have to understand," she pleaded, her watering eyes staring into his solemn expression. "We thought you would *hurt* him." She almost choked out the words. "You were twice the size of a man and four times as strong..."

He smiled, resting his other hand on top of hers. There was a loving energy in those eyes. They were burning her alive. "You made the right call."

These words hurt more than anything ever had. More than losing her home, her innocence, her leader. It was like stepping into a wild blaze. "I... I didn't want to..."

"In any case, you did the right thing," he reassured. His voice was soft, gentle. More gentle than anything she had ever heard before.

"It couldn't have been right if it killed my friend..." she choked, letting the tears run down her face.

"I can't die," the man stated.

"Everyone dies, Adrian," she whispered. "Aladarr died... and Old Dusk, he came pretty close one time..." The woman held on tighter to his hand. Afraid to let him fall again.

"Then perhaps I just had the will to get back up again," he sighed with a shrug. "Perhaps my wretched humanity decided to rear its ugly head. After years and years of torture, it woke up."

"And all that needed to be done was knock some sense into you? Literally?" Wren tilted her head, trying to hide her horror. She was digging her left hand into her arm, hard. Adrian spotted this and reached out with his own free hand, resting it softly upon her's. Her fingers twitched for a moment before relaxing, letting him hold on. She let out a held breath.

"Now now... none of that," he reassured. His smile was as stunning as starlight.

"I know..." she said quietly, feeling his fingers gingerly wrap around hers. Her lip was trembling once more. He could plainly see how much she was hurting. It was enough to make him cry.

"I'll be honest with you, I don't know where to go," Adrian began, moving the rest of his body to the edge of the bed. He was so close to her. "I'm... not a troll... not completely... and I'm most certainly not human..." His eyes drifted down to his talons holding her scarred hands, delicate and deadly.

I always admired those hands...

"So while I'm... Well, for a lack of a better term, stuck like this... I suppose I have nowhere to go," he chuckled, fighting against his own emotions. He wanted to run away, flee to the lonely safety of the woods. But that life wasn't for him anymore. It never was.

"You can always come home," Wren replied with a shaking tone. "Come back to us, if you want."

Adrian's gaze shifted towards the violet book beside him. He slid his hands away from hers and reached over, plucking it gingerly from the pile before resting it in his lap. He opened the tome and ran his fingers across the weathered pages with a smile. At this point, Wren wrapped her arms around her stomach and sank into herself. "But if I do that, I will hurt you," he sighed. "So, I suppose I cannot do that. I don't hurt people. Not anymore." He closed the book and set it away, moving deeper into the bed. Her hand reached out and snagged at his sleeve, holding it in place. His sapphire gaze drifted down towards that quivering hand.

"Please... don't leave... not yet..." she breathed, just barely audible. He could not see her eyes. "Just for tonight... please... stay here." He nodded softly. "I-I can go," she started, a hint of panic in her tone. As if her presence was hurting him.

"Wren, it's not me that I'm worried about, it's you," he explained, his brow furrowed with gentle concern.

That's just how Adrian always was, always worried. She started laughing, her shoulders shaking as she hid her head. "I should probably be worrying about me too... but I can't help but think how Vantis must feel about all of this..." Wren shook her head, almost in

275

disbelief. "For me, you are someone who came back. Different, but still more than I ever could have hoped." She lifted her head, her cheeks flushed red with tears. Her smile was crumbling. "But for him, you never existed. It was something he thought up, a dream he had. And now reality is nothing like he expected. As the saying goes, 'never meet your heroes'..." Adrian snorted. "And there's other things he doesn't know about. Some of the horrible things we did... Things that I *never* want him to know about... For gods' sake, he thinks we're heroes!" she laughed. "Sure, the Golossian sorcerers were no saints. They were monsters, through and through. But not everyone we killed was a monster. What would he do if he found out? Would he hate us? Reject us?"

"Wren," he called. He held onto her grasping hand with his own. He let her soothing warmth bleed into his skin as he held on. "I think, with what little memory I have, that we did what we must to survive."

"I know, it's war," she hissed, more to herself than him.

Adrian's eyes softened. "I gave orders so that you could be standing here right now. If he's not willing to understand that, then I suggest that the battlefield be not for him. Honestly, scaring him away from it seems like an excellent idea," he added with a snort.

"You must think us fools... for shielding him from the truths of the world. But I... He's going to inherit so many problems from your and his mother's life." Wren pulled away, wrapping her arms around herself. She glared, seemingly at some unseen image.

"I wish I could protect him-," Adrian began, but she cut him off before he could continue.

"Just don't run away," she said, this time with more conviction. "I know it's going to hurt, and it's going to be messy, and that nothing is ever going to be perfect. But I don't want to give up because it's difficult."

His lip curled over his sharp fangs. "Sounds more like you are trying to convince yourself than me."

"Heh, I might be," she said with a laugh. "I never wanted this... No, that's not true. More so, I wasn't ready for this. It wasn't the plan."

"Plans never seem to follow through... I just wish I was there for you," the troll sighed, leaning against the headboard of the bed. Her eyes twitched, as if she was stabbed in the heart. "Perhaps I can make it up to you. I left so much behind, in a state of disgrace, honestly. It is in my best interest to do so, right?" He turned, one of his wavy strands of hair falling onto his shoulder. His smile was wonderful and genuine.

"Right..." she gave him a weak twitch of her lips. She reached out for him once more and he took the hand, cradling it like a pane of glass. The woman stood up and leaned over, resting against his shoulder. Adrian pulled his free hand out and wrapped it around her, pulling her close. "I... really missed you... Adrian. Even this much... I'm so glad you're back..."

He rested his head against hers, breathing in her familiar scent. It felt like home. "I missed you too, Wren."

"All I ask," she started, her hand reaching up and holding the arm that held her tight. "Is that you try to get to know your son."

"I've been getting to know him *well enough*," he breathed, giving her a tight smile. "He stabbed me in the face fifteen times the first time we met." Wren pulled away in shock. "With a steel knife no less!" Adrian exclaimed, gesturing towards his nose. "I was simply trying to scare him off. He wandered into *my* cave, trying to hunt for a troll!" He threw his hands up in the air, exasperated.

"That little idiot..." she turned her loving gaze towards the hallway.

"I tried to threaten him, and what do I get?! Fifteen bloody stab wounds to the face!" he laughed. "I had to escort him out at that point!" He shifted in the bed, his eyes shining with a hint of pride. "He did... decent damage, I'll admit."

"Hell of a first impression," she laughed. Her eyes were glimmering in the thin light.

She's so beautiful...

"Ever since then, he *begged* to be my friend! That was..." he trailed off, his smile falling.

"Until he found out you were his father..." A grimace creased her face.

"Yes, and since then he has been doing well to remind me of how moody teenagers can be. I've been told they are little bastards, but seeing it first hand is something else!" That grin returned, bright as ever.

She paused. "I'm not sure if you would have approved of it, but we wanted to wait on giving him fighting lessons until he turned thirteen. We could have started sooner, I know, but most children shouldn't have to learn. But we knew..." Wren sighed, leaning back in her chair. It creaked slightly in response.

"We know what kind of world we live in," he agreed, looking away.

"And you know what he is going to be getting himself into after this..." Her gaze was cast to the ceiling.

"I've been told that I am a lord of some kind," Adrian sniffed.

"You are," she said with a nod.

"Yes, and if he is the sole heir; unless the progenitor returns before he comes of age... He will be forced to take up the duties..." the troll sighed. He snapped his eyes to her. "I will do everything in my power to protect him when that time comes."

"Thank you," she whispered, dipping her head. Wren shook the residual tears from her eyes. "I'm... sorry, I should let you get some rest..." The lady of the house stood, marching towards the door. Adrian followed her with a concerned look. "Help yourself to anything you need. If you can't find it, ask." The troll nodded. "...Have a good night, Adrian." Wren said, her expression buried under the regiment. Being emotional outside of the room would only give Vantis more excuses to be insufferable.

"Wren?" Adrian called just as her feet left the threshold. She whipped around, confused. He gave her a wondrous smile. "Thank you for not chopping my head off."

"And thank you for not ripping Vantis in half. It would have made the last thirteen years rather pointless," she replied.

"Well, if he *is* my son, he should grow a new half pretty quick," he snorted.

Her face fell to pure terror. "Oh, I hope he's not that bad... "

"Well, let's hope for the best then, shall we?" the troll laughed. Wren only nodded in response before pulling her hand away from the threshold, closing the door behind her. Adrian was left in the darkness. He let out a sigh, realizing how well that conversation went despite everything.

I didn't get throttled and I didn't want to throttle myself... A success in my book.

The beast chuckled, receding into the dense blankets to enjoy that ever-present warmth. He fell into a deep slumber not that long after.

Chapter 24

Adrian awoke some time later that evening, his crusted eyes peeling open into the amber-colored light leaking through the curtains of his right window. Drifting particles were the only interruption to the piercing rays, the disruption enough to make the man shift towards the left. The scent of dust was more prominent since Wren left, making the troll cough.

When was the last time anyone cleaned in here?

Irritated and desperate for fresh air, Adrian sat up, drawing himself towards the edge of the bed. He tossed away the blankets, spotting a fresh pair of trousers covering his legs, more refined than his huntsman garb. While the bandages and sore wounds protested, he managed to settle his feet onto the hardwood floor. With a deep breath, the troll heaved himself upright, tottering as the blood rushed in his ears. His talons lashed out and gripped one of the bed posts, grinding shallow cuts into the wood. He couldn't help but curse, clutching at his aching head with the other hand.

The sensation of his fingers touching the wrappings made him scowl, as his face had most certainly healed at this point. He ripped the bandages off with little effort, tossing them onto the nightstand beside him. Adrian then unwound the wraps on his arms; being greeted with fresh, unmarred skin. He rubbed at the flesh, sighing in relief before moving on to his other injuries. The troll hesitated as his talons touched the ones on his abdomen, fearful of what he would find below. Burns took much longer to heal, and based on the throbbing pit that resonated there, he could only imagine the carnage. The man let out a painful shiver before turning his gaze towards the window in front of him.

He shuffled forward, pulling the velvet curtains with only the tiniest bit of force. A tall, narrow window greeted him, held shut by a single latch at the top of the pane. He unlocked the mechanism and shoved the window open with much more gusto, feeling the stuck sill finally give away with a loud snap. Adrian had a sneaking suspicion that it would give him trouble, it always had when he was younger. He often had to call upon his father, much to the merchant's chagrin. Now, as a full grown troll, he had all the might he needed to lift it himself. After securing the panel to its zenith, he rested his palms against the sill and leaned out.

A cool, fresh breeze flooded the room, chasing away the dusty, stale air. His wavy ebony hair fluttered past him, following the current of the wind. The village unfolded before him, the view allowing him to see the farms, residences, and the mercantile district all the way in the distance. People milled about like ants, living their lives with no awareness of the horrifying creatures that were on their doorstep the night prior. Against the painting of the sunset sky behind him, Willowbend was breathtaking.

How many times did I get to see this as a boy?

He smiled softly. It was wonderful to wake up to the village once more. The troll breathed deep, cherishing the fresh scent in the air. Adrian let out a contented sigh, releasing his grip on the sill to trudge back inside towards the other window.

After the man had sufficiently aerated his bedroom, he began to investigate. After all, he never got to see this place the last time he visited the manor. As expected, all his treasures from the cave were collected in a haphazard pile. All things considered, the fae couldn't help but be impressed. This must have taken innumerable trips up and down the mountain. A tiny smirk tugged at his face as he plucked the silver-bordered mirror from within, taking a moment to examine his features. While the cuts on his face had healed, there was a slight weakness to his left eyelid, causing it to drift lower than the right. The rest of him however, was unmarred. Beautiful even. And as foreign as the sight was, he couldn't help but begin to appreciate it. His pointed ears framed his face well, giving him an ethereal air that sharpened at his eyes. His troll eyes made him look deadly, a feature that melded nicely with his vicious fangs poking past his parted lips. He was an elegant beast. No shame in that.

Adrian chuckled, setting the mirror on the nightstand holding his books. He found the violet book where he had left it, gingerly peeling it open and running the pads of his fingers across the yellowed pages. His smile deepened.

How long have I wished to touch these pages once more? All that is left is to learn what they say. What wonderful story did mother wish to share with the world?

283

Carefully, the fae closed the tome, setting it neatly on top of his other treasured books. He gazed upon the walls, spotting odd... claw marks? The man strode over, running his fingers across the cuts. He cocked his head, his hand mimicking the motion required to score such deep wounds. Troll claws. His claws. He *had* been here before.

The twinge of a headache made his lip curl up into a snarl. He shook his head, pulling away from the marks before continuing his tour. Dressers lay abandoned and empty, scarred with more tooth and claw marks. A chest sat in the far left corner, drawing his gaze away from the mangled furniture. The man got down to his knees and pried it open, spying stacks of parchment and trinkets. A claw reached in and pulled out the loose sheets, flipping through them with a flippant curiosity. More jumbled symbols, more headaches. The beast hissed and set them down roughly, turning his attention to the miscellaneous items. There were rocks and twigs intermixed with high-class goods. One of these was a small tube.

Curious, he pulled it out to take a closer look. There was glass at both ends, with one side smaller than the other. He thumbed around it before pulling at the smaller band of brass, extending the tube three times its size. The troll blinked, deciding to gaze into the glass. What greeted him was the wall, albeit far closer and more detailed than he was expecting. The sight confused him enough that he pulled away, trying to sniff for any magic. Nothing.

A spyglass...

Ah, yes, he remembered. Father gave him this for his fourteenth birthday. Something to get the boy out of his hair and out of the house. Adrian recalled moments when he clambered up tall oaks and gazed out using the glass, seemingly seeing the edges of reality. He retracted the instrument and set it aside before continuing his search. There were other things his mind recognized; a compass, a sextant, several charcoal pencils, a fine quill, multiple different spools of ribbon, a stamp with some lion-shaped seal. All mild curiosities.

He was about to retreat from the chest before spotting a book at the bottom of the pile. Adrian narrowed his eyes, his talons reaching in and scooping up the tome. It was covered in flecks of dirt and debris, enough that the troll had to swipe a palm across the leather-bound surface. There were stems sticking out from the pages. Intrigued, he cracked it open, almost letting something flat and dry flutter away from the paper. Thankfully his claws managed to safely catch the item before taking a good look at it. It was... a flower. A pressed white flower with five wide petals. It was dry and yellowed with age, but by all accounts, it was intact. As if frozen in time. He set the flower back and flipped through more pages, finding more plants pressed against the paper. Why on earth had he done this? What was the point? There were small scribblings here, much fewer symbols here than on the other paper. They were so short and compressed... Were these names? Before he could investigate further, Adrian heard the sound of rushing footsteps. He quickly and quietly set the book away, tossing the other trinkets on top before he heard the footsteps recede down the stairs in the distance. The troll couldn't help but sigh.

Dodged a bolt with that one...

With one more furtive glance at the objects, Adrian closed the chest and made his way back towards the bed. He considered laying back down again before a horrid sound emanated from his stomach. On que, a dull, disconcerting pain followed, making him grimace. How long had it been since he last ate? The troll sighed, gazing down at the flesh on his arms.

Healing so much is not exactly conservative towards resources...

Even at the risk of encountering Vantis, he had to abide. A hungry troll was something to be feared after all. Silently, he opened the door and closed it behind him, unconsciously taking the time to readjust his clothes. Walking from toe-to-heel to soften his footsteps, he gracefully made his way down the stairs and turned the corner towards the dining area. The man hesitated at the door frame, keeping his ears open to possible disturbances. Based on what few noises he could hear, it appeared the child was outside in the backyard.

Stars and bones... luck is on my side.

Adrian smirked and confidently strode into the kitchen, scanning the area. A long, large oaken table sat in the center of the room, surrounded by three walls-worth of cabinets and counter space. The overhang between the cupboards and the counters was decorated in garlands of drying herbs and spices, well stocked for the coming winter months. He spied some garlic swaying above the wash bin facing the front of the house; the shutters open and letting a fresh breeze roll in. He smiled at the sight, good memories overriding his headache. He reached out and plucked one of the bulbs, examining the cloves carefully. Fresh and fine, with a smell pungent enough to make his mouth water. Even before the plague of his human memories, he found a particular liking to the plant. It was one of the few foods outside of flesh and bones that he actively sought out, digging up bulbs with a feral excitement. Funnily enough, the Green Man often placated him by growing the plants by his cave. His face fell.

I haven't seen the Green Man in so long. He must be awfully worried.

The troll sighed, hooking the cracked bulb back on the line with the rest of the garlic. He didn't fancy rancid breath today. Instead, he made his way towards the pantry, one of the few walls not covered in counter space. His talons scraped along the wooden floor as he entered, gazing about. He spied some bread and cured meats towards his right and endless jarred substances to his left. In front of him were various ingredients: flour, powders, barm, nuts, dried fruits, and casks of unidentified liquids. As overwhelming as these options were, the troll settled on the bread and dried meat.

Even if his palette expanded due to his human form and Harris's meddling, he couldn't bear to prepare anything outside his comfort. He was about to snatch some rolls when his mind scolded him.

Don't be daft! Get a plate, you heathen!

He frowned. Why on earth would he do such a thing? He was a troll after all.

And yet you are a guest in a high-class home, have some manners!

Adrian snarled, unwilling to fight the nonsensical reasoning further. Probably more stupid human habits. He already seemed to know where to look, as he confidently opened the cupboard next to the wash bin and plucked a clay plate free from the stack. He stomped his way back to the pantry and loaded it up with food. While the reason of a starving beast is limited, he at least made sure not to completely deplete the stores of all breads and meats. He would make it up to them later with a deer after he left.

Adrian eagerly pulled a chair from the corner of the kitchen and set it beside the table, plopping the plate down to begin his wonderful meal. Savoring wasn't exactly on his mind as he wolfed the food down. Taste had no place in the burning agony of hunger. Some of the troll's saliva fell free from his maw, sizzling against the table slightly as the acidic sludge burnt in. He immediately wiped it off with a napkin he grabbed from behind him, ignoring the passing damage to the fabric. The table was far more valuable anyways. Adrian almost cleared the plate when he heard the sound of the door leading to the backyard slam shut. "Piss it all," he hissed, swiping his sharp tongue across his lips. He finished his food and dabbed at his lip with the burnt napkin just as he heard a knock on the dining room door. Adrian stood to his feet, clearing his throat as he called, "Come in."

A small hand pushed the creaking door in, revealing Vantis on the other side. "Father?" he called, nervous.

Adrian sighed and straightened his back, "Yes? What about me?"

"You're..." the boy gasped. "You're okay!" He rushed around the table, slamming into his legs. The troll grunted and latched onto the counter before snarling.

"Stars and bones, child! You almost threw me to the floorboards! Get off of me!" the troll growled.

Vantis pulled away, rubbing his eyes. "I thought you died! You had a hole in your side, you weren't breathing right, and you were cold to the touch! Wren spent days trying to fix you up!"

Days? That at least explains why she seemed as tired as she was... and my appetite.

"Yes, yes, and as you can see, I am just fine now," he said with a dismissive wave. This seemed to be the last snarky comment required to set the lad off. He backed away with a fire in his eyes.

Vantis scowled. "Are you kidding me? After everything, you still can't help but be a jackass, can you?"

Adrian began to retort before clamping his mouth shut. Why *was* he being so aggressive?

You are afraid...

Those words sang in his mind, forcing him to shake his head. "I'm... I apologize. It was rude of me," he bowed his head slightly, punching down that indignant troll pride. "I suppose... I'm still new to this... this whole 'father' situation. I'm going to need some time, Vantis," he explained.

Vantis squinted at the man, folding his arms. Seemed honest enough. "...That's fine. Just try to be nicer. You don't need to act like someone shoved a rock up your ass all the time," the boy advised snidely.

The troll had to fight the urge to growl. Unfortunately, this brat did appear to be related to him after all. After taking a deep breath and settling his temper, he replied with a tilted nod, "I'm glad we could come to an agreement, then."

Vantis turned away, dusting himself off as if he just won a major battle. The boy glanced over towards the area where the troll's room would be. He spun with a sly smile. "Well, I bet'cha glad that I grabbed all of your stuff now, huh?"

The troll's eye twitched. "Yes, but next time," Adrian snarled, approaching the child calmly with his hands folded behind his back. He lowered his head just inches from the boy's, piercing rings boring into the adolescent's soul. "*Ask* before you take someone's things. Otherwise, you are just a thief." Vantis glared in response, following him with his gaze. The fae stopped by the doorway, eager to get out of the small room. "Now then, would you be so kind as to show me to your caretaker?" the troll requested, turning slightly towards the boy.

He sighed. "Fine, follow me," the child mumbled. As Vantis shoved past and went ahead, his father stepped through the threshold, realizing a split-second later that he forgot something.

How rude. This isn't a bloody cave. I shouldn't leave evidence of my meals everywhere I go!

The man diverted towards the kitchen to set his plate away. His sharp nails clicking on the floorboards seemed to alert Vantis that the troll was not following. Vantis scowled in response. "Really?! You tell me to lead you and you run off somewhere else?" The irritation in the boy's voice was evident.

What an impatient little sh-

Suddenly, he felt a powerful yanking sensation, as if he was grabbed by the throat. The troll gasped, clutching at his neck as he fell backward. Vantis stopped inside the doorway and groaned, moving to scold his wayward father before seeing him on the floor gasping for breath. "Father?!" the boy cried, rushing to his side. As soon as the child was within three feet of the troll, he felt the pulling sensation cease. Adrian sucked in a breath, wheezing as he desperately flipped onto his stomach. He drooled ceaselessly, watching the acid burn at the floorboards. Vantis fell to his knees and held out his hands, hesitating to touch the man. Instead, the boy folded his arms fearfully. "Do I need to go get Wren? Are you sure you're okay? Maybe you need to stay in bed..." Vantis muttered nervously, quickly casting his gaze towards the doorway.

"N-no... I just... I have no clue what just happened... It felt like someone tied a rope around my throat..." the fae gasped, rubbing at his skin.

"A rope? Is there another monster here?! Did they climb through the window to get you?!" The boy leapt back, pulling out his knife as he eyed the sink window with a primal terror. Adrian flinched at the foul scent of cleaned iron. Why on earth did he carry that thing around the house?!

"No, no... nothing of the sort. It wasn't fae..." the man gave him a dismissive wave. A stray thought crossed his mind. "In fact, it felt more like... like the violation of a pact..." Adrian grunted, stumbling to his feet.

"A pact? With who? Argh, it doesn't matter now! You go back to bed! At least if you're there, I won't need to worry about you falling onto the hard floor! I'll go grab Wren and she can tell us what's going on! She's smarter than anyone else in the whole village!"

...Other than Ms. Merri.... or Mrs. Feliana..." the boy explained, suddenly distracted by all the seemingly smart people he knew. But as the boy went on, something stirred in the troll's head.

Go back to bed.

Adrian staggered to his feet and made his way to the door, following Vantis out. As he climbed the stairs and watched Vantis rush down the left hallway, he frowned.

Why on earth am I going to bed when I can just follow the boy to Wren? It's not far...

The man turned on his heel to follow the child before a bolt of pain raced up his spine. It was enough to make him jerk and cry out in agony. Vantis whipped around, fear in his eyes. "See?! You're not okay, I'm gonna to go get help. Lay down, father!" the child pleaded.

Lay down.

Adrian's body moved on its own, trudging back towards the bed despite his protests. Before he could try to fight back, his knees buckled, tossing himself onto the mattress. As he flipped over and gasped for breath, the pain ceased. "What... on earth...?" he wheezed, clutching at his forehead. It only took a second to realize what happened.

I... was forced to follow orders... and got injured if I failed.

He trailed that line of thought. His face went pale.

*I promise you this: I will do **everything** in my power, **everything** within my grasp, to ensure your happiness and protection...*

Adrian made a deal with his son, to ensure his contentment. The statement was incredibly vague, the worst thing he could do as a fae. He pledged himself to the boy, to abide by every whim and wish to ensure his 'happiness and protection'. He would have to follow every order to keep Vantis happy. Any signs to the contrary would spell his doom. Adrian threw himself into a trap of his own making. The troll wanted to vomit right then and there. Moments later, Vantis rushed back into the room with Wren in tow.

I cannot let the boy know.

"What the hell happened? Vantis told me you fell over and said something about a rope around your neck?!" Wren gasped, scanning him with concern. Just the tiniest fragment of annoyance marred her gaze. Though he couldn't be sure if it was for him.

He sat up, giving her a reassuring smile. "Don't worry, Wren. It was just a brief spell. I'm fine now."

"No, you're not! Please tell her what happened! Wren, it was really freaky!" the boy yelped.

"Vantis, please. I'm fine," he held up his hands, trying to placate him.

Somehow, this made it worse. The child's frown deepened. "You're lying! Stop lying to me!"

293

Adrian shuddered, feeling his will pull away. His tongue squirmed on its own. "When Vantis came into the kitchen and told me to follow him, I tried to put away my plate. As the boy went ahead, I felt an intense choking sensation around my neck. I suspect it has something to do with the deal I made with him." As soon as the monotone speech stopped, he immediately went pale.

"'Deal'?" Wren cocked her head, folding her arms.

Vantis rushed over to his bedside. "What do you mean, father? What deal?"

Shit shit shit. Don't say anything. Stay silent. Just be quiet for once or bite off your tongue!

"Please, father. Tell me," the boy pressed, concern lacing his features.

The sorrow in his eyes forced him to oblige. "I promised to do anything in my power to protect you and ensure your happiness. That includes-" This time, he did bite his tongue, hard. The troll cried out, writhing in pain as blood flooded his mouth. Some leaked past his lip.

Wren rushed over, gesturing towards the door. "Oh, for fuck's sake! Vantis, go grab the bandages from downstairs!" The boy just blinked in shock. It took another scolding before he threw himself downstairs as fast as he could. The woman turned towards the troll, rubbing her temples. "Is that true?" she spoke, barely above a whisper. Adrian gave her a tear-filled nod. "Son of a bitch, Adrian. You couldn't have picked a worse thing to say, huh?" She gave him a pained, empathetic frown. The troll whimpered, rolling onto his side away from her. Vantis stumbled up the stairs, tripping once before slamming into the room.

"I got them! I got them!" he declared, wildly waving a roll of bandages. Wren snatched and unraveled them, fighting with Adrian to make him sit still. Vantis saw the struggle and made a split-second decision. "Father, sit still for a minute! Please, I'll cry!" A threat. A jolt of electricity made the troll's back arch, paralyzing him. The woman blinked, honestly unnerved by the frozen terror in his eyes. She struggled to open his locked jaw. The child ran over to the other side of the bed and saw what was happening. "Open your mouth so Wren can fix your injury," he ordered. Adrian's maw snapped open, crimson-laced saliva pouring down the sides of his mouth. Wren cursed and shoved the wad of gauze into his mouth, careful not to touch any of that acidic slime. After his tongue was sufficiently wrapped and the blood absorbed, the woman gingerly coaxed him to close his jaw. Adrian was horrified. His mind was racing a mile a minute.

This is it. It's over for me. A child has complete control over me.

"Vantis, don't do that," Wren scolded the boy.

"What? I just got him to do what you needed to help him! It's not my fault he made a stupid fae deal!" Vantis argued.

"Yes, and you shouldn't take advantage of him!" she snapped.

"And I'm not! I didn't do anything of the sort!" he huffed.

"Ugh, just leave, Vantis. Please? Give your father some rest," she sighed. The boy glared at the shivering man.

What a pathetic asshole, getting me in trouble... The boy thought with a scowl. He stomped out of the room, leaving the two alone. *There's no way he made a stinking deal with him!*

The minute is up. I am free.

Adrian gasped, lashing up onto his hands and knees. He was shaking hard. The sheer amount of linen jammed into his mouth stopped him from saying anything, but Wren seemed to know exactly what was on his mind. She held out a hand.

"Come on, let's get you out of this room. You... always seemed to feel better after giving yourself a moment to breathe," she added with a smile. Her stance was awkward, seemingly unsure how to feel. Adrian just numbly sat up and followed her down the stairs, wrapping himself tightly in the cloak gathered from the foot of his bed.

As she crossed the steps down to the foyer, the troll dutifully trailed behind, leaning against the wall that bordered the side of the steps as she hung a left at the ground level. She led him down a hallway, every so often casting her worried gaze over to him as she carefully made her way forward. Eventually, they stopped at a weathered oaken door. Wren twisted the knob with a furtive click. "I... did some renovating since you last left... I hope you don't mind." she whispered.

Adrian's weak gaze shifted up towards her, a flash of annoyance as he pulled the half-melted cloth out of his mouth and threw it in a wastebin by the door. His tongue was healed enough. "This place was always meant for you. I told you to do as you wish, did I not?"

She gave him a pained smile. "Yes... Yes you did."

The light flooded in as the painted sunset sky shone above. The troll squinted and covered his face with his forearm before readjusting to the brightness. Wren led on into that cool evening, moving through a grassy clearing. She turned to face him with one of her hands resting on her forearm. The light glittered against her frame.

Ah, the rays of dusk make her hair appear as incandescent flames...

Adrian resisted the urge to gawk as he crossed the threshold. His toes sank into the soft grass, the coolness of the coming night soothing his burning joints. He let out a soft breath as he scanned the clearing. The yard was bordered by a tall wooden fence, a patchwork of different panels revealing the various attempts at something's intrusion... or perhaps escape? Within the borders were a mix of both raised and ground-level flower beds, all containing a kaleidoscope of colors and features. Strawberries next to turnips, garlic next to green onions, chrysanthemum next to asters; everything was an expression of agricultural artistry. He held onto his cloak tightly as he wandered over to one of the beds, kneeling down before gingerly holding out a hand to cup a scarlet celosia. He admired the flame-like shape of its petals. Others billowed gently in the breeze, brushing past his fingers and tickling his skin.

"It's... breathtaking..." he muttered, gazing out over the weaving foliage. He even spotted a small apple tree in the center of the yard, with a few green apples still clinging to the laden branches. He turned to face the woman awkwardly standing behind him. "Did you do all of this?" he implored. Wren gave him a curt nod. The troll rested an arm on his knee. "It's beautiful, Wren. All of this." Between waving strands of black and stark-white hair, laid a serene expression upon his face. It was a peace that she had yet to see in many years. Wren held her breath for a moment.

A loud bang caught both of their attention; Adrian dropping to a crouch in a panic. When his companion did not follow suit, he followed Wren's less-than-concerned expression towards the right of the high fence; where a large wooden building, not too dissimilar to a shed, stood. A harsh slam rattled the wooden door, making it shudder dangerously against the metal latch. "Earthly Mother, she heard your voice," Wren whispered under her breath.

"Who?" the troll pressed before hearing a shrieking neigh. Some kind of horse, by the sounds of it. Instead of moving away, Wren rushed towards the latch.

"Son of a bitch, not again! Don't break the damn door!" she hissed, unhooking it and jumping away to the side. Without a moment's hesitation, the door swung open roughly and a gigantic beast threw itself forward, galloping out onto the grass. The creature tossed its jet black mane in irritation, trying to clear its vision. A mottled dark grey draft horse stood between them, muscle-bound and hellishly savage. Its sharp, almost rusted red hooves dragged at the earth, the feathering around its ankles trailing sickly ebony fur behind it. Its face was scarred, like the rest of its body, endless battles written across the exposed pinkish skin. Dark crimson slitted eyes stared at the troll and seemed to flicker with a feral recognition. The snout opened, revealing a row of vicious, jagged fangs. This combined with the sharp spikes running along the horse's neck made it clear that this was some unearthly beast. It wasn't fae, whatever it was... and it was barreling straight for him.

Adrian quickly stood to his feet and stepped back, watching the beast skid to a halt in front of him and start tossing its head. It let out a loud whinny before lowering its snout and exhaling in the troll's face. He blinked. "Ah... I remember you..." he said with a smile. The man reached out and gingerly rested his palms on the underside of the monstrous horse's jaw. The creature leaned in and snorted, nuzzling at his face. Adrian chuckled. "Did you miss me, dear Whisper? You've probably never seen me like this, have you?"

The mare nipped at his clothes gently, trying to tug him towards the center of the yard. "Ha! Whisper!" the man protested playfully, turning his attention to the tree in front of them. The apples were low enough for the horse to easily snag but she seemed determined to drag him there. He laughed. "Do you want me to hand you an apple? You lazy beast..."

He gingerly removed her fangs from his blouse before waltzing over to the tree, the shade casting the two in a dappled lighting. Wren could only watch, her eyes glittering as she watched the troll talk to his beloved behemoth of a steed. His talons reached up, plucking an emerald fruit cleanly from the dewy branch and handing it over to the fussy creature. Whisper peeled back her lips and gripped the apple's edge with those terrifying fangs before tossing her head back and crunching down on the delicious treat. Adrian chuckled again and delicately ran his talons down her mane, detangling some of the worst knots. This wasn't saying much, as it seemed she was well cared for. Her fur was freshly washed and brushed, her mane sparkling and only lightly tousled, her hooves clean and shaved. Whisper nuzzled him again, gesturing for another apple. Even after his decade of absence, even after three years of battle, even after all the corruption she faced during the war, she was still just as excited to see him as the first time they met.

Adrian tended to her quietly before turning to face Wren leaning against the stable. Her eyes were distant, a quiet agony behind them. "I assume you've been treating her well?" he called, his elegant voice trailing on the wind.

She gave the horse a frustrated smile. "Despite her best efforts, yeah," the woman responded. She sighed, approaching the hulking beast. Wren ran her hand down Whisper's side, smiling softly. "She always got so fussy when you weren't around... It took forever for us just to keep her here in the yard..."

A flash of grey. The scent of a dirtied beast. He was feasting on a deer. She laid beside him, unperturbed.

"Ah... so she tried to seek me out," Adrian breathed. "I suppose you just missed me..." he whispered, resting his head against the horse's forehead. Wren had to strain to hear what he said next. "I missed you too."

A flicker of movement caught the woman's eye, drawing her gaze towards a second story window. One of the curtains to Vantis's room swayed forcefully. Her expression darkened. Vantis had a wonderful gift, given by his father during a dire time. A pact to shield and keep him happy... a dangerous gift. One of her hands dug into her sleeve while she watched the horse urge the man to walk her along the fence. Adrian laughed before leading her on. The troll's face was creased in a grin, simply enjoying the presence of a beloved companion.

Vantis could have killed him if he wasn't careful with his words...

Sit still for a minute...

That vague statement could have made him stop breathing...
or worse... stilled his heart.

Her grimace held fast, staring at the weathered walls of the manor. No child should have that much power, least of all a boy like Vantis. He was too eager... too wounded by the lack of blood-related parents. What would happen if he felt entitled to them? Could she even stop him?

These dark thoughts consumed her mind, even as Adrian spoke up from behind. "Wren!" she jolted, pivoting sharply with a concerned expression. She saw Adrian staring at the horse in shock. Whisper had lowered her head, gnawing on something. Crimson feathers fell to the grass. Her eye twitched. She had never seen *that* before...

Wren's mouth opened and closed, new strings of bewildered thoughts tangling with her words. Adrian spoke up. "Is that... normal? Last I recall, Whisper ate grass and other green vegetation... am I... missing something?" The troll stepped back towards Wren, jabbing a talon towards the lazy-eyed beast.

She finally found something to say. "Well, that explains all the dead animals near the stable. Guess it really wasn't a cat like Harris was saying..." Adrian slowly turned his head towards the woman, dumbfounded.

"Are you telling me that this has been an ongoing issue?" he muttered.

Wren's smile was tight, almost afraid that the horse might spot her suspicious discomfort. "...Yeah. At first, I thought it had something to do with the stray cat Vantis brought home... or maybe an owl?"

"An owl?!" the troll hissed.

She shrugged, her smile shifting. "There were blood and bones everywhere! Maybe a particularly vindictive owl!?" Adrian was stunned. His face made her irritation boil over. "What?! I never considered the fucking *horse!* Perhaps you should've said something about it!"

"Whisper's never done anything of the sort!" the troll held up his hands as he shouted. "She only ever ate green things!"

"Well, look who's the fool now?!" Wren roared.

"Both of us?!" he yelped. The heated woman paused. Connections were being made. Silence. Then came a loud laugh.

"Ha! I guess you're right!" She wiped a tear from her eye. "Suppose she played us all for fools..." Whisper merely lifted her head to stare at the two of them before exaggeratingly crunching on the feathery carcass. Adrian chuckled.

"Always was good at making people uncomfortable. Must've gotten worse with age," he mused. He reached over and led the hellish beast towards the stables. Wren followed along, only hesitating to cast a final look towards the window. Still as death. She shook her head with a sigh, crossing her arms. As the light faded underneath the weathered wooden awning, she became acutely aware of the echoing footsteps of both Adrian and his steed. Uncharacteristically, Whisper went inside with little protest, only lingering by the gate after he closed it. The troll scratched at her mane one last time before turning towards Wren, who was leaning against one of the outside support posts. The fading light behind her made her smile glow, those umber eyes glittering in the shadows. Adrian felt a shiver run up his spine. It was as if he was staring directly into a flame.

"I remember when we made this thing, y'know? After you changed, Whisper wouldn't let anyone ride her. She refused to be stabled with any of the other village horses. Hell, she fought with most of them. Time and time again, she just ended up back here, waiting for you in the garden." She pushed away from the post and turned around, gazing out into the yard. Her eyes were distant. "Whenever you would show, she would try to follow... But Harris always seemed to bring her back... He was afraid you would hurt her..." Adrian approached the woman, stopping at her side to gaze upon her shadowed face. She ran her nails lightly down the wood grain. "Eventually, we decided that sending her away would only hurt her... and more than likely lead to someone putting her down. So we built this," she slapped the oak post. "Well, some of the craftsmen helped."

Wren turned to look at the troll. The light in her eyes was entrancing, like fireflies dancing across the evening sky. "You were right, y'know." Adrian blinked in confusion. She smiled. "There's some really good people here, Adrian. You weren't kidding when you said a place like this was worth fighting for. We couldn't have survived here without their help." She turned, keeping her face from view. All the man could see was the loose hair outside of her braid fluttering freely in the wind, like tongues of fire lashing at the cold air.

His eyes slowly blinked, shifting towards the house, towards his past. The troll would have to leave tomorrow. The promise was only for tonight. And now that he knew the boy had access to a vague deal, he was more eager to leave than ever. For now, he would avoid him. If he was lucky, Adrian would be able to prevent Vantis from seeing him before he left. And Wren... she would finally be free of him-

"Thank you," she said suddenly, her weathered voice soft and kind.

The troll blinked, drawing his attention forward. "F-for what?"

She shifted, the last golden rays crowning the top of her head. "For bringing me here."

A bizarre stabbing sensation hit his stomach. Like he ate a bad squirrel. "I... of course," he bowed his head slightly. "That was always the plan, was it not?"

There was some other emotion behind those eyes, one he couldn't quite place. "Yeah, I guess it was..." The two stood there quietly for a moment, enjoying the soft sounds of night rising in a gentle lullaby. Only the gentle scrapings of Whisper lowering herself into the hay pierced that hallowed night. It was the fogging of Wren's breath that caught his attention.

"It's getting cold. We should head inside," he suggested, starting to make his way forward. The lady of the house nodded, joining him as they made their way inside. She shut the door behind them and locked it with a key in her pocket. As they reached the foyer, Wren spoke up.

"You're leaving tomorrow, right?"

"Feh, as if I would suffer the boy's power trip any more than I have to!" he scoffed.

There was a sad look on her face. "I'm going to talk to him about that, probably after I cart Harris's old ass home."

"Is he still in the infirmary?" the troll asked.

"Yeah. He'll be patched up enough for us to take him in and help him recover. He's not going to go back to his cabin for a bit," she sighed, gazing towards the front door. "I'll probably be out getting him ready to go by the time you leave..."

Adrian's hard stare softened. "I won't be far. I'll need to be within range of the village to look out for more intruders."

One of Wren's fists clenched. "Just... don't be a stranger. You will always be welcome here. Anytime. This may be Vantis's and my home... but it's also yours. Don't forget that, okay?" Her pleading eyes met his, and he felt another jab at his stomach.

He smiled, bowing his head. "Of course." Adrian turned and began his ascent up the stairs, stopping at the ledge of the second floor. He rested a palm against the rail as he gazed down upon her. "Good night, Wren."

"Good night, Adrian."

Chapter 25

The night came and went without incident, without a single pesky memory or horrible nightmare. All was silent, all was still. Adrian never slept better. He was awoken by the thin rays of morning sunlight assaulting his eyes. It appeared that the blasted curtains in both the east and west-facing windows were in a perfect position to let the light rest upon his face. A fantastic motivator, he had to admit. The man lifted the edge of his lip in a snarl and shifted over to his side, away from the window. Unfortunately, he could only enjoy such mundane frustrations for a moment before the reality of his situation sank in.

It's time to go.

The troll frowned. As much as his bed made him feel safe, as much as being surrounded by his family brought him joy, he was useless here. He couldn't smell the creatures hunting his son from inside a building, much less fight them. He had to go.

Adrian heaved himself up into a sitting position, taking in the room one last time. He soaked in all the details; every color, scent, scratch in the walls, and the way the light bounced off of everything. A wistful smile tugged at his lip, hoping he wouldn't forget this memory. The fae pulled himself off of the mattress and grabbed one of the bolts of fabric in the pile of trinkets by the bedside. He unfurled it onto the bed, setting those items with the highest value to him inside. Adrian was willing to part with a few things for now, they were safer here anyhow. The troll had to pause to make sure delicate items like his mother's book and his mirror were well padded by furs and other soft materials before tying the ends of the sheet together to create a rough bag. He sighed, grabbing it by the ends and heaving it over his shoulder with a soft exhale. The items jostled in protest before settling against his back as the man walked out.

Adrian crossed the hallway and ran his hand gingerly against the banister as he strode down those beautiful stairs. He smiled at the pleasant memories of rushing up these stairs to show his mother something, most likely alive and certainly not allowed to be in the house. As he made his way over to the foyer and towards the bench with the shoe pile nearby, footsteps rapidly approached from upstairs. Adrian was already sitting down and wrestling with his sandals by the time Vantis made it to him. "G-good morning!" The boy gasped, clearly mentally recovering from a near tumble while rushing down the steps.

The troll flicked his gaze up to face him. "Morning."

Vantis glanced at the linen bag laid beside him. "Um, what's that?"

"My stuff," Adrian grunted, managing to shove a foot into the shoe.

Vantis's emerald eyes widened. "Y-you're... you're leaving?!"

The fae sighed, resting his elbows on his knees as he halted his work. "Yes, I am. Someone needs to protect you from the outside. Since your uncle is out of action for the time being, it appears that duty falls to me."

"'Duty'? That's not necessary! I don't need protection outside!" the teenager protested.

Adrian scowled. "After what those monsters said and did, I believe it's more than necessary. More will be coming."

"Then why don't you stay here? You can protect me better!" the boy pressed, clenching his fists.

Blue rings slowly eased shut with a sigh. "Because, Vantis, I work better outside, and I needn't bother your caregiver further."

"'Bother her'? If anything, she seems happier now that you're back! I haven't heard Wren cry out in her sleep once!" Vantis argued, gesturing towards her room. "Don't go!"

The man belted out a laugh, making his son flinch. He gave the child a malicious smile. "Oh? But I thought you hated me?"

Vantis turned away sheepishly, lowering his gaze to the floorboards. "Yeah, I did but... I... That doesn't mean I wanted to see you get hurt like you did a few days ago! It was... awful..." His words were barely a whisper.

The troll raised a brow as he settled into the remaining sandal. "Regardless of what you may think, I have already made my decision. I am leaving." With that, he stood up, plucking his bag from the ground and throwing it over his shoulder before starting to move towards the doorway. Vantis glared at him.

Why is he always like this? Why does he always have to try so hard to stay away? Does he hate me?

The child was about to accept this, to turn away without a single word before flashes of terror electrocuted his body. Images of blood, freezing cold knives, monstrous teeth, red eyes, and his father's rotting bloody body. The song... that horrible, awful song that put sickly thoughts in his brain. Those images rocked him to his core, making him shake in place.

More will be coming.

More flashes. Terrible scenarios of his father severed into pieces, his head lying on the grass in front of him. Finding him riddled with arrows and impaled to a tree. Imagining him burning to ash and reaching out to him. Losing his father again. Losing Lion. Losing his family.

Adrian twisted the doorknob and pulled in, letting the morning breeze ruffle his hair. He took a deep breath and started towards the threshold. "No," Vantis spoke up.

The troll stopped, tilting his head with a perplexed glare. "What?" he grunted.

The boy's head was down. He was still shaking, his fists white-knuckled as they trembled at his sides. Adrian smelled salt. Something glistened against the rays of dawn and fell from the boy's face. Vantis lifted his gaze. An emerald fire burned at their core, a level of determination that made the fae's expression twitch. "No. I'm not letting you leave."

The audacity of such a statement! Such insolence was enough to make him forget he was supposed to fear those words. The troll bared his fangs, taking a step closer to the door. "You wouldn't dare, you little shit."

Vantis's eyes narrowed. The young lord suddenly sounded much older, much more refined than he ever did. "If you leave this house without my permission, the distress it would cause me will put you in violation of our contract. And I *don't* give you permission. I *order* you to stay here in the manor and protect me. Only by my words alone can you come and go," he declared.

Adrian felt that rope begin to tighten around his neck. "No! Let me go, you runt! I will not be trapped here!" He turned, determined to fight the deal before it could fully grasp him. The troll barely crossed the doorway when a burning pain forced him to his knees, making him cry out. He dropped his sack beside him, gripping at his throat. Adrian gasped, spotting small burning marks rising like a pox around his exposed skin, the scent of searing troll flesh making him wince. He reached out, trying to touch the pathway ahead of him as his nails slammed into an invisible barrier. "No!" he roared, attempting to slash it away. The troll watched as his nails shattered at the tips, falling painfully beside him as he clutched his bleeding hand. Vantis kept his gaze down, squeezing his eyes shut while trying to drown his father's anguished yells. Those screams were replaced with the image of his father's clawed face half-eaten by wild wolves.

I don't want to lose you again... Please, don't make me lose you again...

Eventually, the pain was too much to bear. Adrian threw himself back into the house, still holding his quaking talons. The nails and skin grew back effortlessly, leaving him alone with his quiet whimpers. His hate-filled glare snapped up to the boy. "You... little shit!" he snarled, lunging towards him. Vantis only took one frightened step back as the man faltered, realizing how close he was to hurting his son. Those quivering hands fell to his sides as the troll backed away, defeated. It was deathly quiet. The beast stood up to full-height, an intimidating monolith that cast the child in a deep shadow. "...Yes, my lord," the fae bowed graciously. The sight made Vantis sick. "Your wish is my command. Until your next request, I shall roam these halls like the foul *pet* you wish for me to be," the man spat with barely contained malice. Adrian snatched his belongings from the floor and slammed the door shut before stomping past the child and up the stairs. Vantis's lip quivered. He saw how his father looked. That expression.

Now he hates me.

~~~~~~

Adrian slammed his bag onto the bed and raked his claws across the wall in a fury. His eyes were nothing but tiny pinpricks, his fangs frothing with a hellish rage.

How dare he?! That little shit dared to use my gift to trap me?! A mighty mountain troll?! I should have devoured him when I had the chance! Like all my kin before me!!

Adrian glanced at his claws, noticing the slivers of wood stuck under the nails. Beyond the skin that gave him purpose, hope of his station in life, was the lightly tanned flesh of a human. His rage melted away like his expression, falling to a defeated stare.

*You are not a troll. Stop lying to yourself. You are a filthy human. And now... nothing more than the pet of a child. You are **his** lion now...*

The man sank to his knees, holding his arms tightly. He felt the nails dig into his flesh. His face was lax with emptiness, eyes dull. Going outside was a faint dream now. Wren would always see his accursed face. She would suffer for a child's selfishness. His talons pulled free of the bloodied blouse, rising up to rest his palms against his cheeks. His left hand twitched, clenching against his skin. His fingertips tilted ever so slightly, softly pressing his nails against that fragile flesh.

Is my true face underneath this? Is this just a...

Pain stopped him before he could go further. The man let out a gasp, realizing what he was about to do before crawling back into a corner, terrified. He had done this before... so long ago...

He was in a bed with fresh linens. His head and his left arm were heavy. Everything hurt so bad. Adrian reached up with that weighted arm, trying to block his eyes from the terrible light of the window beside him. Instead of seeing his soft, rounded nails and tanned skin, he saw a monster.

Disgusting, long, mutated black talons stretched out before him, covered in lumpy green and grey flesh that bubbled like a pox. Bits of shiny bone stuck out from various points between the bandages, like teeth budding from gums. The man let out a hellish scream. He wanted to flee the arm, to get it away, but no matter how hard he tried, his other human hand couldn't wrench it free.

His voice... It sounded so wrong. Like a wild beast. Adrian reached up with both of his hands to feel at his jaw, only to wail louder. He was touching the mangled mess of his lipless mouth and textured flesh, teeth growing out of every available space on his gums. More bones grew out of patchy spots, more teeth. His hand thumbed up to his nose, feeling nothing but a sunken cavity in his face. Nurses rushed into the room, trying to restrain the panicking man. He wanted to scream, but all that came out was a disgusting roar.

My face! What happened to my face!? I'm in hell! I died and went to hell!

The physicians were useless against his overwhelming strength, the man able to throw them off with ease. They looked on in terror, horrified by the hunched over hideous man. That left claw covered half of his monstrous face, casting one of his feral eyes in shadow. He couldn't hear their voices as they called for aid.

Enemies! Monsters!

Adrian growled and crawled into a corner by the door, shoving himself hard against the stone wall. When did he get here? Where even was here?! He glanced around, finding nothing to indicate a location. He was a wild animal, watching the shivering doctors with a predatory glare. Their bodies were pressed against the wall, overwhelmed at the sight of such a terrifying beast.

The enemy... They did this to me...

He growled and rose to his feet, his now black-clawed toes grinding into the stone. That mutated arm extended its fingers into a clenched claw. Adrian parted his jaws and snarled, horrified by his own noises. A flash of a memory. Blood. Death. His friends. A sickening smile full of teeth like glass shards. Beady eyes boring into his soul. He was overwhelmed in shadow.

They would pay. They would all pay.

Before he could lunge towards the helpless yelling doctors, an individual confidently strode in. He was older and well-trimmed, his reddish grey hair indicating a man well into his fifties. He was dressed in black leathers, the attire of a traveling doctor. Adrian barely had a chance to recognize those tired eyes as the man pulled something free from his coat and brandished it in front of him while the doctors cowered behind him. Adrian snarled and charged, only stopping the instant he noticed what the object was: a hand mirror. Staring back at him was a disgusting face coated in green and gangrenous black flesh. Sunken eyes that were nothing more than seas of black with blue glowing rings gazed back with a horrified expression into the glass. The monster in the mirror opened its mouth into a bloodcurdling scream, clutching its face and hiding it from view as he staggered back to his corner.

My face! Heavenly Father! Save me! My face!

He roared, letting lines of his saliva scatter as he shook his head. He felt a flap of flesh slap against the fingers pressed in on his cheeks.

Yes! It's a mask! Take it off! Get it off!

Adrian's claws reached over and dug into his skin, the pain enough to make him cry out. The traveling doctor got closer, a deathly calm painted over his features.

It hurts! But it will come off! I just need to fight the pain! Fight the pain and my face will be fine!

A sickly smile curled his jaw as he wailed, dragging his black nails through sinew.

So close! I can do this! I can do this! I can-

He never saw the doctor approaching. Those soulless eyes bore into Adrian as the man reached out with a gloved hand. He barely heard the voice over his own shrieks. "Enough of that." A finger touched his head. A wave of calm overwhelmed him, forcing his hands to go lax and fall from his face. His eyes fluttered for just a moment before fading into the depths of sleep.

Adrian rocked back and forth, sobbing quietly as he came to. Yes, this had happened before. Back when he had first become kin. When he had chosen to take on the curse of troll's blood. The doctor had saved him from death's cold embrace. Both from Terminahill and from himself in the hospital. And now he was doing it once again, falling backwards into despair. The man hung his beautiful face in his arms, letting his sorrow lull him to sleep.

Chapter 26

Adrian awoke on the floor, his cheek and back throbbing from the hard wood. There was something soft covering him, a blanket. He weakly pulled himself to his knees, breathing heavily. A brief glance towards the window told him it was likely the afternoon. He touched the fabric lightly, recognizing it as the one that often sat at the foot of his bed, hanging from the base board. He held the blanket tight, frowning. Adrian worried that Wren might have seen him in such a horrid state. He certainly hoped not. Maybe the brat did this just to lord it over him. For a moment, he considered whether or not the boy truly cared for his comfort... that was until he remembered the extreme violation of his freedom.

Probably wants his stupid pet alive and healthy so he can bark more selfish orders.

He scowled, tossing it away onto the bed. The man teetered to his feet, dusting himself off with rough hands. He cast a glance towards the bed, considering just giving up and sleeping until he was requested, but pride snagged at his shoulder.

No point in moping. If I cannot leave, I can at least attempt to occupy my time.

He considered all his past-times, his favorite activities. Taking a walk was out of the question, hunting was impossible, and sharpening his weapons would require him to bother Wren. He couldn't even preen or decorate his feathers... He ran through all the possibilities before spotting a violet shape on the bed. Adrian approached the object, pulling it towards his face. His mother's book.

I suppose I could try to re-learn how to read...

The troll held onto the leather-bound tome as he left the room, descending the stairs towards the reading room. He kept his eyes away from that horrid portrait and instead found a chair resting in a corner by a bookshelf, facing the opposite wall. A window stood beside it, covered in dense velvety curtains like the ones upstairs. Noticing that this one wasn't facing the front where other villagers could see him, the man felt comfortable enough to try to open it. He gripped the silk cord and tugged, pulling one of the side drapes away to let him see outside. Adrian smiled, happy to see the beautiful autumn colors once more. The trees swayed jovially in the breeze, the muffled rustling putting his mind at ease. He pulled the chair closer to the window and browsed a few of the tomes resting upon old wooden shelves. He frowned at the amount of dust, running a finger through the grey filaments. Adrian sighed, realizing that not many came down here, most likely due to this shrine dedicated to his past self. The man huffed, watching a puff of dust sprinkle to the floor.

That's it.

The troll scowled and marched towards a broom closet, stealing some rags and making his way over to the shelves. Then, he began to dust, covering his face with his blouse as he swiped the cloth over each book and each exposed slab of wood. Inevitably, he finished cleaning the entire bookshelf, stepping back to admire his handiwork. Then his eyes peeled over towards another on the other side of the fireplace. After dusting that, he figured he might as well clean the tea table and wipe down some of the couches. Soon, the mantle and all of his old weapons were dusted, with Adrian stepping into the kitchen to grab a whetstone to begin carefully sharpening them. He made sure that each of the deadly blades had been honed to a razor's edge before returning them to their respective homes, all the while avoiding the largest piece on display. The weapon that he had relied on throughout the Golossian War. The weapon forged from the blades of his fallen friends. Terminus.

The dust-covered, sweaty man pulled away from the fireplace, glancing down at the egregious amounts of soot left upon the hearth. That wouldn't do. Before he knew it, he was sweeping the floors and grumbling about the state of things like a maid, angrily swiping at cobwebs above him. After several hours of frustrating but rewarding housework, the reading room was finally clean. Adrian admired his labor as he rested his hands against his hips.

"Certainly a sad state of affairs... Though I suppose it's nothing new!" he chuckled. The man stopped mid laugh.

What on earth am I doing? I'm a mountain troll, not an obsessive brownie!

Adrian scowled. "Well, I've always kept my cave clean and well-stocked. I refuse to live in lesser conditions!" he hissed, arguing with himself. If he couldn't have his way outside, then by the stars above he would make sure this place was perfect for him. Now, if only he could decorate these gaudy curtains with some bones or shiny rocks...

Adrian shook his head. "None of that. As soon as the brat lowers his guard and makes a single mistake, I'm out of here and depositing an enraged raccoon in my stead!" he declared, amused at the thought of an angry beast frightening the boy. Not harm. Just scare him a little and shred his bedding.

Great. Now he really was thinking like a brownie.

With an exhausted huff, he threw his cleaning supplies in the closet and plopped his backside into the chair, cracking open one of the books he gathered. This one appeared elementary enough, with words alongside pictures. Fantastic. Something that can make his life easier for once.

C. A. T.... Cat. I've seen those. Pleasant little scoundrels.

D. O. G... Dog. Awfully loud and bothersome for hunts. Rather nippy as well.

F. A. E... Fae. Us spiritfolk...

This went on for a little while, his mouth moving with the words written on the page. Every so often, his hand would flick out, moving in a familiar, yet foreign way.

Ah, yes. This was how I said these words when I could not speak...

He smiled, mimicking the words in the book with his mouth and his hand. After a few hours of this, another sound drew his attention. The sound of the foyer opening. Thankfully, he was partially hidden behind the bookcase, letting him lean back and avoid direct line of sight as the strangers came in.

"Oh for fuck's sake, Wren! I can get up a bloody lip on my own!" Harris snapped.

"Shut the hell up, will ya? I'll spill you onto the floor if I hear one more complaint!" Wren snarled.

Good heavens... that sounds amusing.

The troll shifted his head forward, resting an elbow on the chair arm and laying his chin upon the palm. He set the book aside on the sill, eager to see his two companions. Harris grumbled but said nothing intelligible as the frustrated grunts of Wren echoed in the halls. The loud clacking sounds of something hitting the threshold filled his ears as he imagined the comical sight. Eventually, the woman let out a loud growl and shoved whatever she was pushing hard, making Harris yelp in pain. He saw a wheelchair roll forward, the huntsman resting in it and gasping as he held his bandaged back.

Oh. Shoving the chair pressed the backing into his wounds. Agonizing.

Adrian snorted and decided that enough was enough, getting up from the chair to go and greet the two. The shift in movement made the ex-soldier's eyes dart towards him, alarm soon overridden with reason. "Adrian?" he called.

The troll gave him a warm smile as he approached, his hands on his hips. "Harris. You are looking well," he greeted.

"Feh, as well as I can be while smothered by gauze and busybodies!" The middle-aged man gave him a playful scowl.

"Well, as inconvenient as it was for you, I'm glad you are well," Adrian gave him a tilting nod with his hands folded behind his back. There was a regal essence to the action, something the huntsman found nostalgic.

"As to you, old friend," Harris smiled, wincing as he gingerly leaned into the well-cushioned backing.

Wren shut the door behind her with a frustrated huff, grumbling about the doorway before facing Adrian. There was an expression of pleasant surprise on her face. "Adrian? I thought you would have left by now..."

The troll's dark eyes glittered with malice. "Yes, that was until the young lord decided to tighten the *leash*..."

The woman's face went pale. "Vantis, no..." A flash of fury graced her features for a brief moment before she shook her head. Harris seemed perplexed to say the very least, shifting his gaze between the two of them. "What was the order?" she asked flatly.

"That I did not have permission to leave the house. That I came and went only by his words alone," the fae explained with a snarl.

She lowered her head. "I see." He could almost smell her righteous fury. When she lifted her face, however, no such thoughts could be found. "Well, as much as I wish I didn't have to bother you, I might need help hauling this scrawny jackass onto the couch. That's going to be his permanent home for the next few weeks."

Harris opened his mouth. "Oh for pity's sake! I'm right here!"

"Yes. And you've done well bitching about it the whole way here. So shut the hell up, and let the big man toss you onto the fainting couch, you fucking pansy," Wren snarled as she pressed a few fingers against her forehead. The flame in her eyes grew brighter.

Adrian raised his brow. "Hmph. Good thing I cleaned the reading room when I did, huh?"

This seemed to placate the rage for a moment, a calm clarity washing over her. "You... you did?"

"Mhmm," the troll nodded, delicately scooping the protesting older man into his arms. He did his best to avoid the padded injuries on his back.

"Argh! Adrian, you bastard! Put me down!" the hunter growled.

"You heard the woman," Adrian shrugged. "It's either this or she tosses you into a closet." Wren cracked a genuine smile at that jab. The troll dutifully marched over to the couch, effortlessly pushing it with his foot so that its occupant would at least be facing a window, before carefully setting the deer-legged man down.

Meanwhile, Wren had taken it upon herself to hunt down some pillows and a blanket as the huntsman swatted the fussy fae's hands away. Once the two finished making the couch as comfortable as possible for their friend, Adrian eased Harris down upon his plush throne. And, as a final touch to their pampering of the old hunter, Wren draped a heavy wool blanket over him, backing off so that he could have a chance to settle in.

After a series of grunts and curses, the huntsman snuggled in with a huff and gave Adrian a scowl. All the fae could do was cross his arms and give him a sly grin. Harris sighed, shifting uncomfortably. "This must be how a king feels, huh?" He didn't even bother waiting for a response. "It's terrible. Off with his bloody head." Adrian's smile deepened, shaking his head before following Wren towards the main hall.

"Thank you, Adrian. You saved me a ton of time," she sighed, running a hand through her unkempt hair. Her braid was far messier than usual, likely having been done in haste. The troll only waved his hand in such a way that conveyed, 'my pleasure'. Wren snorted. "There's still much to do. Everyone's home now. That's reason enough to celebrate." As she strode on into the dining hall, her companion gave her a perplexed look. He followed along, sensing that she needed the aid. Wren made her way into the kitchen, roughly tossing the door open before making a sharp turn towards the pantry. The veteran woman scanned the shelves for what she needed, half turning her head to the troll as she began to gather up ingredients. "Mind giving me a hand?"

"Literally or...?" Adrian replied with a smirk.

"Smartass," Wren snorted, starting to pile things into his outstretched arms. After a few back and forth trips, they had everything they needed. The woman lit the fire under the water-filled cauldron on the other side of the room, making sure the pit wasn't too overloaded with soot. By the time Adrian realized what was happening, she had already shifted her attention to the counter. The lady of the house was hard at work, combining some fresh eggs she'd gathered earlier that morning to a mixture of various powders, quickly whipping it into a dough. She spooned out some of the water from the cauldron before it boiled, pouring the laddle's-worth of warm liquid in a small bowl. Then she grabbed the jar of barm and tapped some in, lightly stirring before setting it aside. She turned towards Adrian, who was already busying himself cutting up vegetables. Carrots, turnips, onions, garlic, all shoved into a pile by his blade. She didn't seem too surprised, taking the loaded board when he was done and pouring it into the remaining water in the cauldron. Just as he finished rinsing his hands in the wash basin, she called out. "You know how to apply barm to the bread, right?"

Adrian snorted, already taking the bowl and gradually mixing the contents with the dense dough. "Of course, you are the one who taught me after all."

A soft smile graced her face as Wren worked away at shaving down some of the dried meat. She set the bits aside and lit the oven, working it up to the right temperature. Adrian set the loaf inside the bowl and covered it, letting the dough proof as he danced around his cooking partner to wash his hands once more. He turned his attention to the quickly forming vegetable broth, stirring it occasionally before adding chopped chives to the mixture. The aroma was extravagant. Before he knew it, the dough had risen, and Wren was setting the loaf into the center of the stone oven before closing the door, letting the heat take care of the rest. She paused, watching Adrian spend some time cleaning up the powders left on the counters while she rinsed her hands. He gave her a passing glance. Wren had turned her attention towards that picturesque window, listening to the cheerful sounds of robins and thrushes. She nodded thoughtfully. "That thing I ordered should be ready to be picked up by now..."

"That 'thing'?" The troll raised a brow as he weaved over to the stew and lifted the ladle over a small tasting bowl, pouring some out before setting the utensil down. He put the bowl to his lips and blew before having a taste.

Hmm... needs more salt.

Adrian held it out to her. "Yeah..." she said absentmindedly, reaching over and grabbing the bowl. She took a brief sip before handing it over. She frowned. "Needs more salt." With that, she walked out of the room. He heard the front door close in the foyer, leaving him alone to deal with the discrepancy.

The troll sighed and went over to the pantry, snagging a large block of salt. Using a file from the drawer beside him, he began grinding down the rock, reducing it to a fine powder. He scooped up a thumb-sized mound into his palm, tossing it in and stirring it into the stew. Adrian gave it another taste-test before finally declaring it fit for consumption. He shifted his attention to the oven, opening the door to check on the bread. Still pale as a babe. The troll sighed and latched it shut, instead making his way back out into the reading room to snag his book. Harris only gave him a passing glance before returning to his own tome. Based on his brisk pace, he seemed busy enough.

Adrian sat down at the kitchen table and flipped the book open to where he last left off. He studied for about twenty minutes before checking on the bread once more. Now pleasantly golden, he took the large spatula hanging by the wash bin and gingerly slid it under the loaf, careful not to burn himself as he pulled it out and set it onto the counter. While the bread smelled fantastic on its own, he couldn't help but add some black pepper and garlic to the top, mixed with a light, buttery glaze. He smiled at his work, just about to sit down before hearing the front door open again. Wren marched her way in, carrying a large package wrapped in parchment paper towards the counter. Whatever it was, it smelled divine. She noted the loaf standing proudly with a satisfied nod. "Adrian? Could you grab the large stone dish from under that cabinet?"

"Of course," he nodded, turning towards the far side of the kitchen to extract the pan. It was huge, to say the very least. He had never seen such an imposing dish before. Wren gestured for him to set it beside her as she unwrapped the package. Before his wanting eyes laid an uncooked venison rump roast, the scent teasing at his senses. The troll had to let out a deep, almost euphoric sigh before backing away, combating the urge to pounce and devour it himself. Instead, he set his butt in a chair, watching Wren prepare the meat with hungry eyes. She had a loose smile, no doubt acutely aware of the torture he was going through. After ensuring the roast was properly seasoned in the pan, she fished some of the thicker vegetables out of the stew and scattered them around the meat. With a loose pouring of some of the stock around the edges of the pan, she heaved it up and into the oven.

Wren flopped into the chair opposite of the man with a sigh. Adrian let out a breath of his own, relieved to not have the sight of that tantalizing flesh taunting him anymore. Instead, he turned to his book, tracing a nail along some of the words. The woman tilted her head, noticing his studies. "What book do you have there?"

The troll gave her a sheepish grin. "I'm... not entirely sure. I... well... It appears I have forgotten how to read."

Wren blinked, not an ounce of judgment upon her sweaty features. "Hmm... Well, you taught me how to read all those years ago... Perhaps I could teach you this time?"

A stab in his gut, a slight flinch. But he was honestly happy to hear this. Outside of Harris, she was the one person he trusted not to ridicule him. "Yes, I would quite like that," he answered. Adrian couldn't stop the genuine smile as she waltzed over, resting a hand against the table as she leaned down. Her sweet scent filled his nose and set his mind at ease for the task ahead; gesturing to the first confusing word.

Chapter 27

The two continued to work on Adrian's vocabulary together, with Wren informing him that the book he had been studying from was called an "encyclopedia". She helped him through the letters and how they sounded, gesturing and speaking at the same time. It was pleasant, learning with her. As impatient as she seemed with the others, Wren led him on with a gentle hand. She seemed acutely aware that yelling achieved nothing, especially with him. The troll supposed it had, in some part, something to do with Vantis's behavior. They ran through a legion of words for the next few hours until the time came for the roast to be taken from the oven. While Wren worked on extinguishing the flames of both the oven and cauldron, Adrian got up and sliced up the bread into knuckle-thick slices before arranging them on a platter. The two resumed their dance as they finished dinner, weaving and moving effortlessly alongside each other as they set the table. When everything was ready, Wren dusted herself off. "Alright, all that's left to do is call the boy and wheel in the old fart."

Adrian chuckled. "I'll handle Harris. I'll leave the brat to you."

Wren gave him a playful smirk before making her way upstairs, leaving the troll to deal with the man clearly giving him the side-eye in the other room. It would have been comical if Adrian hadn't any clue with whom he was dealing with. Adrian placed the wheelchair by the couch and made a motion to scoop up the huntsman. The huntsman batted at his arms with a disgruntled hiss. "I can get there myself, Adrian!"

"Nonsense, your foot smells like a roast and your back is made of shredded lettuce, let me help you," the man sighed.

"Earthly Mother, I said I could do it mysel-" Harris's protests were silenced as the fae suddenly scooped him up and set him unceremoniously into the chair. The huntsman was unleashing a torrent of all sorts of wondrous curses, all things that brought a smile to the troll's face. Harris huffed and readjusted his uncomfortable position as he was led into the dining room, greeted with the most exquisite of smells. It was enough to silence the man as he quietly examined the food with gawking eyes. Wren entered shortly after with the downcast boy following behind. Vantis dared not meet his glaring father's eyes as he settled into his chair. The teenager was uncharacteristically silent, politely folding his hands on top of each other in his lap. Harris cast his gaze between the boy and the troll, eyeing Adrian with an expression that screamed, '*We'll talk about this later.*'

As soon as Adrian and Wren sat down, they all began to eat. Harris sampled a bit of everything, eager to try some decent food outside of the gruel they gave him at the infirmary. Adrian cut

329

himself a slice of the roast, making a mental map of the utensils around him as his body instinctively used them. Forks, knives, spoons, feh. All so incredibly superfluous when he had perfectly useful hands! But despite what he thought about this, he knew he wouldn't neglect them. They went through the effort of setting them up, might as well use them. So Adrian silently cut up the slice with the knife and fork while observing the others. Wren seemed to have a similar expression on her face, seemingly only using her utensils to set a good example for Vantis. If she failed at her etiquette, then what was the point for the boy to follow? Her frustrated glare continued as she fought with her particularly juicy cut, trying to shovel some vegetables on top for a fuller experience.

Vantis, Adrian noted, was the only one not eagerly making their way through the platters. In fact, it appeared he had only grabbed a slice of bread and a small ladle-worth of stew. He was absentmindedly stirring it with a vacant gaze. Wren seemed to notice this as well, finishing her cut of venison before setting down her fork. She quietly cleared her voice. "Vantis? You've been stirring that bowl for several minutes now, I think it's probably cool enough," she stated.

The teenager's eyes widened. "Oh, right. Sorry..."

His caretaker frowned. But before she could press further, Harris spoke up. "Heavenly Father, some good fucking food for once..." He was leaning over his bowl of stew, gingerly sipping at it while clearly fighting the urge to wolf it down. "Which one of you sorcerers made this?" He jabbed a finger at the bowl. Adrian nodded towards Wren. Wren nodded towards Adrian. The huntsman blinked, watching the two. "Either way, it beats the months of oats and dried meat I was living on."

Adrian snorted. "Honestly, I prefer the roast in this case."

Wren gave him a smirk. "Adrian, you would prefer meat in any situation," she retorted as she dipped some of her bread in the bowl of stew.

"And the fact that someone managed to make it taste good even after all the superfluous additions? It's positively admirable!" His fangs opened wide as he chomped down on another slice.

The woman snorted, looking away as she tended to her meal. "Well, I appreciate the compliment, even if it does come from someone whose main diet mainly consists of bones and raw flesh."

Adrian puffed out his chest a little. "A perfect diet for a healthy troll such as I!"

"A diet I'm glad you expanded. The fact that I more often than not *smelled* your camp before I saw it was nauseating enough," Harris chuckled.

"Hey now, you didn't exactly smell like a fresh rose yourself!" the troll shot back.

Harris sneered. "Well, I didn't exactly have time to consider rolling around in fragrances while trying to keep your dumbass alive!"

"Try a dirt bath at this point, you old goat," the man waved a hand dismissively.

"I'm not a bloody quail, Adrian!" the huntsman laughed.

The troll gave him an expression of faux-apology, glancing at his deer legs under the table. "Ah, and here I go forgetting your condition. Well, in that case, perhaps a fine licking would do you some good!"

"Oh, you motherfucker," the hunter hissed, his lip curled in a playful snarl. Adrian was grinning ear to ear.

"If you two are gonna be jackasses at the table, the least you can do is not make me spit up my dinner," Wren sneered, trying not to laugh. Adrian let out a chuckle before leveling his gaze upon his son's reaction. The child's face remained downward, unchanged by the foul-mouthed jovial chat between the adults in his life. There was no emotion. Nothing. In fact, the man was certain the young lord heard none of it.

Vantis kept his gaze down, focusing on the food. It was good. Wren's cooking was always good, definitely better than Harris's but... guilt gnawed deeper. For every bite he took, that vicious feeling burrowed deeper. He recalled what Wren said to him before she called him down to dinner.

The candlelight beside him flickered and danced in the inky blackness that threatened it. Vantis was sitting at his desk, running his fingernail across the map of Solania, along the Grey Swallow Road. This trade route would be the easiest way to reach the capital of Alavantis. A week-long journey by the fastest horse, a three week-long trek by foot. He frowned, tapping his quill against the table. There was only one issue. The main roads were patrolled by knights, especially after the Golossian War. His other hand moved from the map to touch the letter beside him, staring at the lion-crested wax seal.

If what mother said was true, the knights might know who I am... and with father...

He mused, setting the paper on top of a weathered tome bookmarked to a page littered with government symbols. Vantis sighed. It would be complicated. But it didn't matter now. No rush. The young lord had yet to navigate the hellish situation he put his father in first. It was the sound of approaching footsteps that drew his hand over the book holding the letter, smoothly shutting it. The boy twisted in his chair just as his caretaker entered. Wren's mouth was set in a hard line, clearly upset.

Earthly Mother, help me. She knows!

"Vantis," she began, her voice firm but neutral.

"W-Wren?" Vantis mumbled, faltering under her gaze. Was that disappointment he saw?

Please... Please don't look at me like that...

Before his mind could run through its endless tangled strings of excuses, the woman made her way over to the chest at the foot of the bed and sat down. "I know what you did," she stated plainly. Vantis winced. "Do you understand what you've just done?"

Gods, her quiet tone made the child want to run away into the woods, the oozing disappointment more agonizing than any wound. Even more so than the freezing cut across his neck.

Vantis gulped before he began. All the words, all the excuses, all fell away as his lips began to move. "I didn't want to lose him..."

Her dark brown eyes softened, even if her stoic expression remained. "You could've hurt him incredibly easily, you know that?"

The boy nodded. "He was hurt so badly, Wren... He... I thought I lost my father... I... I don't want him to go. I don't want him to get hurt for my sake..."

"And yet you chain him, hurting him for your own sake."

The teenager clenched his fists, feeling his nails dig into his palms. "I know. I feel awful. I... feel like I want to throw up... But... he's alive. He won't be out there alone. Everyone is home now, Wren. Everyone but her." He paused for a second, choosing his words very carefully. "You said you lost father once before, right?"

Wren's eyes darkened under the shadows of the firelight, almost as terrifying as the monsters he encountered in those woods. She closed those intimidating eyes and sighed. "Yeah."

"And now I can stop that from happening again!" the boy exclaimed.

"But that doesn't mean you can just take away his freedom," Wren stated evenly.

He clenched his fists in his lap. "But he's in danger, right?"

"It's complicated, Vantis... You cannot just force someone to stay without consequences. He may come to resent you for this, if he hasn't already. You have to be careful, or you risk driving him away forever..." she explained, giving him a sympathetic expression. "You have an amazing gift. An incredibly dangerous gift. Honestly, just as terrifying as giving a toddler a crossbow..." Vantis frowned, opening his mouth to retort before he was promptly shut down with his caregiver's raised hand. *"That wasn't meant to be a jab. I meant to say that you have something that you cannot completely understand at your fingertips, something that can spell the end for your father, you, and anyone caught in the crossfire. The only difference between the wielder outside of age-related circumstances is..."* The woman leaned in, her face creasing into a knowing smile. Vantis gulped. *"Is that you are aware of who you hurt."* The boy glanced at his hands, that sense of dread and guilt creeping upon his shoulders. He could... no... he did hurt father with his demands. He saw the burning of his flesh, the tearing of his nails against the threshold. The screams made him thrash his head violently.

"I won't hurt him. I won't take advantage of this! I just want everyone home! And even if mother isn't here, the rest of my family is. I'm not the only one in danger. Uncle is really hurt and father almost died. This is the only way I can stop them from killing themselves for my sake. I'm not losing anyone again! I'm not going to sit by as everyone dies for me!" the young lord explained, his voice rising. He was so enraged, so frustrated seeing his father's mangled body in the bed. Seeing Harris in such a dire condition made him want to throw up. And watching Wren take all of it while still working as the leader of a trading company was enough to make him hang his head in shame. No more. Vantis was small and weak, that was for sure. But Wren was right, he did have a gift. It was dangerous. And he would do what he must to make sure that gift went to good use. He refused to see his loathsome father die in such a horrifying way.

All Wren could do was hang her head and sigh. *"I just hope you will find the strength to do the right thing... Whether that is now or the next coming days. Please, consider my words..."*

Vantis's eyes scrunched as he forced away shameful tears. Instead, he got up from his desk chair and approached his caregiver *with his arms outstretched. Wren sadly smiled and embraced the boy, gingerly rubbing his back. "It will be okay, Vantis. He may not be the man I knew all those years ago, but he is still worth fighting for. Just keep an open mind, alright?"*

Vantis frowned at his plate. Keep an open mind, huh? The boy sighed and grabbed the slice of bread, a hint of frustration in his exaggerated chewing. As he did, he suddenly became aware of how... odd it tasted. It wasn't like Wren's other loaves, it was lightly spiced with just a hint of butter soaking into the crust. It was good. Very good. Enough to drag him away from the mental turmoil and open his mouth to speak. "Wren, this tastes delicious! What did you do to make it so buttery?"

Wren shifted away from Harris and Adrian's current argument on the ethics of Harris eating venison. It was clear that the troll was trying to rile up the huntsman, and appeared to be succeeding wholesale. She smiled at the boy. "I don't know. I didn't make this one. Your father did. You should go ask him."

Vantis blinked, his eyes darting over towards his father's smirking visage. He finally tuned into the conversation. "Adrian, having hooves does not make me a goddamn cannibal!" the huntsman growled.

"No, the way you chew does! I've only seen deer chew on grass like you do oats!" Adrian laughed.

"Oh? And what does that make you? A bloody bear?!" The older man's face curled into a smirk.

"Ah! In reference to such a clever and beautiful beast?! Why, I don't mind that at all! But for you," the troll proudly gestured to himself before pointing a finger at Harris, who was glaring daggers at him. "We might need to consider attaching some antlers to that massive forehead of yours if you want any sort of visual cohesion," he added with a sneer.

"Oh, you are *so* lucky I'm stuck in this bloody chair..." the huntsman hissed, gripping the armrests. While Vantis was visibly perturbed about the conversation before him, Wren seemed less than concerned. In fact, she appeared to be enjoying the moment, a gentle smile resting upon her features as the two men argued. In truth, it was completely playful, not dissimilar to the way they used to act in the war. Even in his irritation, Harris's snarl was cracked into a smile. They played this song and dance before, even if the troll had long since forgotten.

"F-father?" the boy piped up. Adrian turned to face him. That slimy smirk faded as his face hardened into a stone cold frown. Vantis winced. "Umm, you made this bread, right?" The man merely dipped his head in a nod. "It's really good... "

His dark eyes slowly blinked. "I'm glad you can appreciate my work." It was empty, like an endless void threatening to swallow him whole. The young lord shuddered. Harris glanced between the two, his playful smile quickly evaporating into a concerned frown. There was that familiar look shot towards the troll.

We are going to talk.

Adrian couldn't care less. If the child wanted to fight here and now about his cooking he wouldn't budge. He would just take the insult and compartmentalize it later. It would only be more fuel for his vengeance. Vantis's next words made that stern glare crack only a bit. "Mother, Wren, and uncle all said you were a good cook...

I'm... I'm glad that wasn't a lie. It's all really good. Wren and you did awesome... Really..." the child mumbled.

Adrian could only blink in response. For once, the wild, stalking thoughts that roamed his mind's halls fell to silence. His sapphire rings glanced over towards Wren, who was giving Vantis an encouraging nod. The troll sighed. "Thank you, I truly wished for this to be special."

"As did I," the lady of the house chimed in. "Having everyone home at last is worth celebrating..."

Vantis's gaze cast towards the plate with a sad smile. "Everyone but mother..." The room withered in silence, a tense shroud over all faces but Adrian. Upon his was a mix of conflict that made his expression borderline emotionless. The boy spoke up. "But that doesn't matter. Uncle and father survived horrible monsters and saved me! Wren got everyone safe and sound and now we can all be here! I think that's enough for me."

Harris let out a soft sigh, nursing at his bowl of stew while Wren gave the boy a sympathetic expression. "I know she would want to be here. I genuinely do."

The teenager shrugged, digging into his food. "It doesn't matter. My family is here. That's all I care about." This seemed to placate his caretaker, as she shifted the topic to something more mundane. And while the others continued on in small conversation, Vantis's mind was affirmed.

He would search for his mother. He would bring her home. Now all that was left to be done was to locate her.

Chapter 28

Adrian watched the table disband, first with Vantis going to bed and then Wren starting to pick up the dishes and put away the leftovers. Based on what he could hear, most of it was being set in the cool larder below the pantry. All that was left was the troll and huntsman, who was still nibbling away at his stew. This was his third helping. Adrian had never seen him eat so much. The troll promptly started gathering the remaining dishes.

"So, what the hell was that about?" Harris grunted, pointing towards the direction the boy went. "I knew he was a brat but I didn't expect everything to be so tense... and the way Wren reacted earlier... something clearly happened."

The troll sighed, setting the used utensils down on top of his plate. His eyes were dark, frustrated. "The boy and I got into a bit of an argument... and he got the better of me."

The huntsman raised a brow. "That's rather curious. I didn't think he could ever get the drop on you. I always assumed he went in swinging at the start."

Adrian chuckled, "Well, I suppose it didn't help that I handed him the blade that led to this."

The huntsman furrowed his brow, taking another sip from the bowl. "Care to explain that in words an old man can understand?"

The fae sniffed, continuing to reach across the table towards Vantis's plate and adding it to the top of his. "During the night those fae attacked... I stayed out as a guard until dawn. I was rather injured and had poor mental facilities at the time..." he began, snagging the boy's fork and knife. "Then I made a mistake," the man hissed, setting Wren's plate roughly onto the stack. "I made a promise to the boy." At this point, the troll paused and turned to face the hunter. His eyes were empty pools, enough to unnerve the weathered warrior. "That I would do *everything* in my power to protect him and ensure his happiness."

Harris was silent for a moment before the wheels in his head began to turn, and his face fell into a horrified stare. "No..." he breathed.

"Yes, old friend. I just gave my son, who hates me, a loaded crossbow to level at me everytime I piss him off," he gave him a sickly sweet smile.

The huntsman set down the spoon. "Then... what happened today?"

"I tried to leave, to go out and separate us from each other the moment he realized what he could do and... Well... he found me and wasn't too happy with my decision..." the fae explained with a growl. His talons were digging into the tablecloth lightly, his eyes glowing with malice.

"He trapped you here. Fuck... Is there anything we can do?" the older man cussed, trying to gesture for an opportunity.

Adrian shook his head. "No dice. I can only come and go by his words alone. I'm stuck here as his little pet until I can find a way out."

A grim expression held the hunter's sullen features, his umber eyes trained on the surface of the stock rippling in his bowl. He spoke up. "Bludgeoning him won't work, it would only make him more steadfast than he already is... There's nothing we can do now. We can only hope the boy comes to his senses to see how wrong and dangerous this is..."

"Exactly," Adrian grunted, gathering up the rest of the dishes. "And now... Wren will have to suffer seeing my wretched face for that boy's selfishness."

"Well, I wouldn't say she's suffering," the hunter argued, gesturing towards the kitchen where she was gathering up the remaining bread to add to the pantry. Wren was humming softly to herself as she worked. "In fact, since you came here, Wren has been smiling more than ever before. No one is unhappy with you being here." Adrian was silent for a moment, gazing upon Wren's back as she packed things up. That sick feeling in his stomach appeared, causing him to flinch. Harris continued, drawing the troll's thoughts away. "But I know that *you* are suffering. There must be a way to circumnavigate this. You are fae, there must be some tricky way to override the child's power trip."

The fae man shook his head, moving towards the empty goblets and balancing them on the stack. "Unfortunately, I'm a mountain troll. We aren't exactly known for our great genius in most cases..."

The veteran puffed his chest a little as he gazed towards his old friend with pride. "But Adrian Lionel was. I have faith you will figure something out."

Adrian laughed. "Yes... I suppose in the meantime I could always use the method all others use for children: just sick his mother on his hide!" Harris almost dropped his spoon as he coughed. The troll's face fell as he turned away. "Though I suppose that wouldn't exactly work now... He doesn't have much respect for the woman, probably less so than me..." His mind faded away to her featureless beauty, the fragments of memory stabbing into his mind like daggers. He desperately wished to see her lovely face once more. Anything to make his horrid pain go away and have her in his arms. All Harris could do was frown and look away.

Was that... shame upon his face?

He wouldn't deign to think upon it anymore. "So, I suppose you and Wren will have to do it in the interim. If I call upon you, it's sure to be for backup!" Adrian added with a laugh.

Harris was trying not to shake, starting to drink directly from the bowl as he finished his food. "B-But of course, old friend. I'll see what I can do to stop him from being a wretched brat about it!" The huntsman gave him a weak smile as he handed the bowl off to the fae, who took it up and added it to the pile. Once he was sufficiently loaded up, Adrian turned towards Wren, who was by the wash bin cleaning their cooking implements.

"Ah. Well, I had better go help Wren clean up. I would rather not leave her to pick up the mess we made alone," Adrian sighed, hoisting up the precarious stack before moving towards the kitchen.

Harris merely nodded, lost in thought. All he could do was grip his drink and stare into the distance, conflict riding his features. Adrian waltzed in with the wobbling dishes, adding them to the pile on the side and snagging a towel hanging next to the wash basin. He began drying the washed implements and setting them away in their respective homes. As he caught up with Wren's pace, it began to appear as another well-rehearsed dance; him reaching over to grab the dishes she held by her side before turning and smoothly setting them away. Umber eyes glanced up, spotting them as they worked. Each motion was fluid, neither person messing up or stepping upon the other. It was as if they already knew which step they would take and how they would respond. They were both smiling as they worked.

It was beautiful.

The huntsman fought against the conflict in his heart, against the wishes of his dear friends. His grip tightened upon his drink, and his eyes squeezed shut. It took all his will to stave off his tears. To not cry in the face of such sweet serenity in a drought of happiness.

Chapter 29

The next few days were a grand test of the troll's patience. Time and time again, without fail, Vantis would approach him and ask to accompany him. Fearing the embarrassing consequences otherwise, the fae would relent and proceed to be bombarded with many more ridiculous requests. It was little things, starting with being shown the young lord's room and all his "fantastic" trinkets and books. Next, it was him lending an ear as Vantis vented about the constant inflow of academic requests by his caretaker and tutors. Soon, he was helping him clean up the room and tidy the papers. In fact, five days after his torturous imprisonment, he found himself doing just that.

Vantis was beaming ear-to-ear, cleaning and collecting papers just as his father was. It was wonderful, spending time with Adrian. As soon as his initial hatred had fallen away, the teenager was eager to learn more about the man. Despite his frequent complaints, rude commentary, and tendency to be a bit of a wet napkin, his father was still kind to him. A part of Vantis figured it had something to do with the nature of their pact... But a hopeful fragment thought it nothing more than good will. He was fae after all. He most certainly had a way to get out of this. Hells, after Vantis poured his heart out about his wretched reading assignments, instead of brushing it off and letting him deal with it alone, the troll offered to *help*! How awesome was that?!

The teenager coughed as he cleared an untouched part of his desk, wheezing against the cloud of dust billowing up his vulnerable nose. He waved a hand in front of his face, turning towards the window. The lad rushed over and tried his hand at the sill, only for it to remain firmly stuck in place. No matter how hard he pushed or pulled, no matter what angle he tried, the window wouldn't even let out a squeak. The huff and puffs of the boy made the fae roll his eyes.

How pathetic...

His mind flashed to an early point in time.

Little Adrian was still struggling with the sill. His father sighed, hatred baited for but a moment. The well-dressed merchant gripped the sill and shoved upward, prying it free and letting the boy rejoice. As the blonde-haired man turned around and left his child, Adrian could only follow his exit with happy eyes. Father helped me! He loves me!

Adrian snarled, shaking the memory away. He remembered how cruel his father was, how little he cared for him after mother's death. It was enough to make the troll set down his stack of papers and march over, gingerly moving the boy aside. Vantis grunted and glanced up at his father as he watched the troll effortlessly push it open, letting the fresh breeze steal away the stagnant air. The boy gave him a deep smile. "Thank you, father." The troll almost scowled before stopping himself.

Father loves me!

The beautiful man sighed and bowed his head slightly. "But of course. The dust was quite irritating to me as well." As Vantis went back to his chores and hummed away, Adrian strode over to a stack of papers and set them at the front of the desk. "I will not go through these. I don't understand your method of organization well enough to sift through them."

The boy, eager to discuss his machinations, jumped at the chance. "Oh, it's super simple! You just go by date. All the papers with the same month on the top right corners will go together. Then you just go in order through a standard year. That's how Wren taught me to do it!"

Adrian's eye twitched.

Damn it.

With a sigh, the troll sat down and began to cross reference the scribblings in the corners. With the various lessons Wren gave him while they prepared the past few dinners, he could at least identify what the months looked like on paper and how they were arranged. It was mindless, terrible work, but work that would most certainly stop the boy from getting upset. Whenever he was made aware of his son's discontent, the troll would feel a dull ache spread from his shoulders up his neck; a general discomfort he would come in contact with regularly now that he was spending time with the lad.

"Honestly, before you came here, we never paid too much mind to cleaning up." The boy spotted the troll's raised brow as he swept past. "Not that we were gross or dirty or anything! Wren was always super busy and I was swamped with stupid assignments. Both of us were too tired to bother focusing on anything outside the public spots," he explained with a sheepish grin. Adrian merely gave him an affirming grunt as he set aside the spring stack. His talons brushed the cover of a leather-bound book under another of the haphazard piles, catching his attention. His claws pulled the tome free and beheld the worn cover.

"History"

That was the only word he could recognize. In the center, a rather familiar symbol was embossed on the front. The stylized image of a snarling lion surrounded by the arcing rays of the sun. The symbol of Solania. Memories of this sigil emblazoned in stone architecture and scarlet flags frayed at his thoughts, making him wince.

Vantis piped up. "Then you came along and started fixing stuff. Wren has been able to work without so much stress and Harris doesn't need to worry about bothering us. You just take care of everything! Makes me realize that my family needs a ton of help, and that I have to try to help too."

Adrian flipped open the book as he gave the back of the child a sideways glance. "Ah, so you make me help you clean your room instead?"

The teenager flipped around, an indignant expression painting his features. "I never asked for you to help me! I just

347

complained about the work and *you* started doing stuff!" he retorted with a hiss.

A slight twinge of pain jabbed at the fae's shoulder. Adrian sighed. "Yes, because your misfortune causes *me* pain. And I would prefer to make the agony short and sweet as opposed to watching you flail about."

The boy was about to retort until he watched the man grip his own shoulder and massage it with a grimace. Vantis closed his mouth slowly and sighed. "Sorry, father. I forgot that this whole deal thing hurts you. I'll try to keep that in mind."

Adrian snorted. He was certain he picked up that apology from Wren. Though whether he would follow through as she was oft to do remained to be seen. The troll turned back to the book and flipped through, reading what he could as he gazed at the pictures. Most of the images were bordered by a crest shield, each symbol lovingly sketched within that smooth pentagon structure. Each had a caption he couldn't discern. But based on everything he could gather, these were...

Emblems of the state.

He frowned. Why was one underlined? None of the other books were written on. But this particular image, of a feather laced in rose thorns, was distinctly marked. Those rings of blue narrowed, continuing his investigation. Vantis was mumbling quietly to himself as he swept by the bed, not bothering to watch the troll work. Sometimes his father could really come off as an asshole.

Adrian flipped a few more pages before something fell free from the binding. In a panic, he snatched the loose paper from the air, worried he had somehow damaged the book. Upon closer inspection though, he realized that the color of the parchment was off. It was far too cream-colored when compared to the yellowed pages of the tome. The page had been folded over, sealed shut with a lumpy red blob pasted to one of the edges. The troll curiously flipped it in his grasp, analyzing the blob. Based on the way it felt... It appeared to be wax, pressed via a stamp. Right into the shape of a feather wrapped in rose thorns. Before he could peel it open to look further he heard the boy cry out before snatching the curious thing from his hand.

"Hey! Don't snoop around!" the boy gasped, hugging the letter tight to his chest.

The fae growled, exposing his sharp fangs. "I'm organizing your bloody desk. 'Snooping' is but a small part of that task."

Vantis scowled. "Yeah, well, I don't need this one organized." His eyes passed over to the book in the troll's black talons. The teenager carefully reached over and snatched it from him. "It's for a project."

"A project for what?" Adrian pressed.

"Ugh, what does it matter? It's a personal thing, okay? I'm not comfortable talking about it..." The boy set the paper back into the book and closed it, hugging it tight to his chest. The troll sighed, shaking his head.

"Very well, then. Couldn't read anything anyways," the man grunted before going back to his work.

"... you can't read?" Vantis asked, genuinely confused.

"Not anymore," the troll answered blandly, slapping more assignments into the summer pile neglected in front of him. "Only just learning now."

The boy shivered in horror.

He forgot how to read? That can happen?

Vantis gripped the book tightly in his hands before gingerly setting it into the chest at the foot of his bed. Even the idea of such a thing terrified him.

If I'm like him and I turn into a monster... will I forget everything too? Will I forget how to read? Write? How much would I forget until it stopped? Father supposedly became a feral beast...

He shivered once more as he gazed at his father's back. The boy could sense the frustration in his motions, cussing as he struggled to remember what month he was looking at. Vantis sighed. "Father?"

"What," the troll growled.

"You said you wanted to go visit your campsite, right?"

The chair groaned as Adrian shifted towards the lad. Those intimidating rings bore into his eyes. "Yes?"

"Why not do that instead of doing stuff here? I can finish all of this by myself, no problem. Just take Wren with you so you both can stay safe from more monsters!" the boy reasoned. At the sight of the troll's widening eyes he added, "Just be home before nightfall."

The troll slowly stood from the chair, his back creaking in pain as he arched up to full height before giving the child a low bow. "Of course, my lord." Vantis had to fight the urge to gag again. He hated being called 'lord'. It made his skin crawl. And he was certain his father did it on purpose, a small jab to spite him for his shackles. It was enough to make the boy look away as the man retreated towards the door before closing it with a dull thud.

Now left alone in the dark hallway, Adrian let out a hissing sigh. Finally, a chance for fresh air. He had been itching for this chance for a while now. As if he would argue against such an order! A sly smile pressed against his fangs as he shook his head and walked on, eager to locate Wren as requested and get out of this cushy prison. The man halted at the oaken door, hearing the disgruntled mumbling of the merchant woman as she sifted through documents. Wren had been like this since Adrian had recovered enough to care for Harris. It seemed she had dropped all her work just to care for the two of them. Honestly, it was enough to make the troll feel a twinge of guilt. His fist only hesitated for a second before knocking firmly against the wood. The noises inside halted for a moment as the woman sighed.

"Come in," she called out. Adrian politely let himself in, standing near the door as the tired veteran gazed up at him. Instantly, her expression softened. "Oh, Adrian. Have a seat, I just need to finish up one last thing."

The fae gave her a bow of the head before settling down in a chair next to the door. With his talons delicately wrapped together, he waited patiently for her to finish with her work. She flipped through ledgers and letters, scribbling furiously. A few minutes later, she slapped the paper aside and roughly plopped her quill in an ink pot, rubbing her temples. She cleared her throat before saying, "I'm sorry about that, what can I help you with?"

"Well, I had been meaning to go back to my campsite and collect a few things. Unfortunately," he added with a hiss. "The boy decided that I could not be trusted to do so alone. It's either you or the cripple downstairs."

"Harris isn't going anywhere," she responded, nodding thoughtfully. "And heavens forbid you take a wheelchair through those woods."

"I'd have to carry him," the troll sneered.

"Exactly. More a hindrance than help. Is there any particular reason you need to be tailed?" Wren asked, her voice edged with concern as she rested her elbows on the desk.

"According to the brat, to keep us 'both safe from monsters' or some other nonsense," he added with a dismissive hand wave.

"Probably for the best, but why do I have a feeling that there's a little more to it than that?" The woman raised a brow, shifting some of her work aside.

"There could be," the troll sighed, sagging in the chair a little. "He could be ensuring that I don't try to escape, even though the rules by which he had set for me wouldn't permit me to stay out past nightfall..." He paused for a moment, letting out a sigh. "Regardless, it appears he cares for our safety or some such. Though I cannot imagine why he would want me to pester his guardian of all people."

"Probably because I'm the only one he trusts with you right now," she grunted, a small smile set upon her cheeks. "I mean, think about it. If we were to run into something like that bitch you encountered a week ago, there's not a single person in the village that can do more than piss themselves."

Adrian shook his head. "No no, that wouldn't do. I would have to wander those woods with a blindfold, which I'm not entirely keen on."

"If anything, you'll stand out far less if I'm there with you," she gave him a deeper smile, a hint of mischievousness on her brow. The merchant pulled back from the table and glanced through the unfinished papers. She sighed. "Well, if you give me about an hour, I should be able to finish up this letter..." she rubbed at her temples, frustration clear. "Running a business is not easy, especially during the fall months..." she added with a chuckle.

"If memory and the recollection of others serves, I did so from afar," Adrian mused, trying to strain his memory. Only images of frustration and paperwork showed up, nothing to read amongst the jumble of symbols.

"Yes, now imagine that on top of taking care of a child," Wren grunted between her fingers.

"Exactly, I don't envy you for a moment." A brief pause of silence. "I'll just leave you to it and get changed. Don't want anyone seeing me in these fancy clothes, lest they think I've been licking the boots of the Willowbend lords," the fae sighed. Adrian stood to his feet and bowed, a solemn expression upon his beautiful features. He made his way to the door, turning his back on the woman before she called out.

"Adrian?" She said, hesitation in her tone. He shifted his gaze to look at her. Her lip moved uselessly before she shook her head. "Ah, nothing. Sorry about that. See you in a couple hours," Wren responded, shuffling through her papers. The fae man merely nodded before exiting the office, closing the door softly behind him. While most men wouldn't be able to hear past the hollow echo of the door closing, his ears pricked at a sound. The sound of Wren settling in her chair, sighing. A muttering. He couldn't quite tell what she was saying. All he could sense was frustration, like she wanted to say something but just couldn't. No matter.

Time to get ready.

The troll made his way to his room, tossing on the huntsman garb he had recently re-sewn with the help of Harris and Wren. It felt nice to be back in his first set of clothes since turning into a human, like stepping into a warm cave to rest. He sighed, adjusting the gloves on his hands as he strode out the door, making his way downstairs. There Adrian sat, patiently resting upon the bench near the front door. He flipped open his encyclopedia and ran through a few vocabulary words, trying to keep himself busy.

As the sun crested over its zenith, the lounging troll perked up at the sound of a door shutting and a person moving over to another room. Adrian stood up and set his book back into the reading room, passing by a snoozing Harris. Just as he heard that door shut as well, the man made his way back out into the foyer, patiently awaiting the woman stepping down the stairs.

Wren sighed as she approached the threshold of the reading room beside the troll. "Alright, Harris. You'll be in charge, if anything goes wrong-" she paused, realizing the huntsman was dead asleep. "Damn," she grunted, crossing her arms. "And here I was thinking I was being funny putting the injured man in charge."

"No, if you wanted to be funny you would slap a piece of paper upon his brow reading 'captain'," Adrian sniffed.

Wren pondered this for a moment. A small smile stretched across her lips. "Actually, I have the next best thing." With that, she grabbed one of the smaller crossbows perched from one of the shelves and set it upon the table next to the sleeping hunter. She pulled a scrap of paper from a tea table and scribbled 'in case of emergency' in charcoal next to the weapon.

Adrian nodded approvingly. "Surely that will be enough to unnerve him." He pulled away from the wall, approaching the door and grasping the handle. "Shall we?" The elegant troll gestured to the open doorway as he pulled a linen blindfold over his eyes.

The autumn leaves fell all around them like a delicate rain of color, casting the world in a fiery hue. It was just after midday at this point, around what humans declared was "three o' clock". Villagers still milled about, running through their work and lives unperturbed. Thanks to the lighter and looser material, Adrian could see shadows of movement past the blindfold, watching Wren guide him onward while people passed around them. His back stiffened. One of the villagers, a lithe, thin man, was approaching the two. "Ah, Lady Wren!" he called.

The woman in front of him turned, facing the stranger with a friendly tone. "Hello, Terris. Lovely afternoon, is it not?"

"Why yes it is!" Terris exclaimed. Adrian's skin prickled with discomfort. Based on how his shadow moved, it was clear he was watching him. The troll turned his face away towards the woods, something to soothe his fraying nerves. "I know you must be busy, Miss, but if I may have but a moment of your time?"

The dame seemed to shift her gaze worryingly towards her companion before stating, "Of course, but do be quick. Lion here was about to show me where the attack occurred."

The villager perked up at this statement. "Ah, and that's just the thing! I know Harris was horribly injured after that dreadful altercation upon him and the young lord... but will he be present at the Autumn Festival this year? The children do love his stories, and I'm certain it would put everyone in bright spirits after the horrible news."

"We'll have to see how well he's doing by then. Right now, he is in bed recovering, but perhaps by then he will be in better condition. More than likely he will still be in a wheelchair."

"Oh, good, good! We shall have to make appropriate accommodations then!" Terris exclaimed, clapping his hands together. Adrian fought the urge to flinch. "You are welcome as well, dear Lion!" he gestured towards the blind man.

"Oh, uh, thank you," Adrian muttered, bowing his head before turning away. With that, the man left them to their own devices, carrying on with a wide smile upon his face. Wren merely sighed and continued on into the Willowbend Forest.

Chapter 30

They were several yards into the undergrowth before Wren spoke up. "It appears you made a bit of a name for yourself," she remarked.

"Not on purpose," the troll hissed, yanking the blindfold off his face, letting it fall upon his collar.

"Hmm, well, it's better than them thinking their hero has come back from the dead, right?" she questioned, a smirk lacing her lips.

"Anything would be better than *that*," he growled.

"It would certainly complicate things, that's for sure," Wren commented, leaping over a log.

Eager to change the topic, Adrian spoke up. "When was the last time you journeyed into these woods?"

"Hmm, every now and then with Vantis... Maybe over a year ago? Just little trips with him and Harris when I had the chance," she replied, resting her hands upon her hips as she pondered this.

"I never saw you, though that's probably a good thing." The troll crushed some dead twigs underfoot as he continued ahead.

"We tended to travel pretty close to the town, maybe a mile out," Wren explained.

"People made sure to chase me a mile out from the village, so I suppose that checks out," Adrian reasoned.

The woman grimaced, pain gripping her features. "I... really wish we didn't have to... I'm sorry..."

The fae merely shrugged in response. "What does it matter? I was a wild beast, right?"

"Clearly not," the merchant hissed.

"It matters not. That's not who I am anymore. Now I'm stuck like this," Adrian glared, gesturing towards himself.

A tiny smile tugged at the edge of her lips. "You seem to be taking it well enough."

"Not that I had much of a choice," the troll sighed.

"You're making the best of it, at least in my eyes," she reassured.

"Either way, as long as I can escape the annoying brat on an occasion, this form isn't too terrible," the troll waved dismissively, raising his head to look upon the woman.

"I know you two haven't had the best of reunions but... I promise the boy isn't always like that." Wren turned, facing him. Her brown eyes glittered in the soft golden light. Auburn hair fluttered delicately in the breeze, a curtain of fire over her soft face. Adrian's stomach flipped, making his face twitch.

The fae sighed, looking away as he clambered over a cliffside. "Oh, he's just excited to have a new toy. He'll get bored soon enough and discard me."

"That's not how he is," the knight shook her head, climbing beside him. "I know him. He's not like that." The troll merely sniffed and continued forward. "If anything, I would describe it as overprotective. And... albeit in a twisted way, he's trying to make sure he doesn't lose his family. What little bit of it he's found," she explained.

"Yes, yes, and it's driving me to madness. Though, I suppose you've already told him that, didn't you?" Adrian grunted, slicing a vine free from their path with his talons.

"More or less," she replied with a sigh, pushing away the loose vegetation. The troll leapt over some fallen logs, holding out a hand for her to grab. Wren took it and jumped beside him. Her axe clacked against her hip as she did, the metal shining dangerously to the fae's eyes. "How far out is your camp?"

"About another mile. Though that doesn't account for vertical movement," Adrian explained, climbing a series of exposed roots to head over towards the ravine.

"Shouldn't be that much longer now," the veteran reasoned.

"No, but the bloody deer seriously cannot consider the wellbeing of the travelers trying to get here," he snarled.

She chuckled, climbing up to the top beside him. "Well, we aren't exactly on the main paths, huh? I suppose Vantis would've had a hard time getting here." The troll grunted in response. It made for a good hiding spot, that was for sure.

"The goat also reasoned it had the best firewood, materials, and prey in all the forest! Blah blah blah. Excuses. I believe he just wanted to torture me..." the troll hissed playfully, scrambling down the sandy shelf with a frightened grimace.

"He was probably just trying to hide you away," she laughed, following close behind. Her boots fell upon the roots gracefully as they traveled down. "Perhaps to keep you all to himself," she teased.

The troll shivered with a scowl. "Repulsive. He truly would be a greedy bastard then."

Wren let out a powerful laugh. "Either way, it seems it all worked out in the end."

"Everyone all cuddled up in the manor as one big happy family?" Adrian turned back with a mocking eye flutter.

Wren's smile faltered a little. "Something like that..." Her boot crushed one of the roots a little harder than he expected. Thankfully, it appeared she didn't slip.

Adrian shifted his head, letting a lock of wavy black hair cover his features. "Who knows, perhaps you'll awaken to a giant troll in your home, completely unable to fit through a doorway," he mused.

Wren let out a small laugh. "Well, if we have to, we'll say we need to do some renovations and bust down one of the walls."

"And then what?" he paused at the river, kneeling down to wash his face with the icy water. It felt fantastic against his sweaty brow. "We go back to how things used to be?"

"Depends if you go crazy again," she shrugged, settling beside him on the crushed shale shore. "Or if you're just as sane as you are now." She dipped her hands into the water and took a drink, seemingly admiring the crisp taste. "Although, knowing what I know now, I doubt I would let up regardless." She turned to face him.

"What? Will you lead me along like a lost puppy?" Adrian sneered.

"No, I'd hunt your ass down and start bludgeoning you."

A look of alarm crossed his features. "Literally?"

"If it came to it," Wren replied simply, shrugging.

"Well shit," he breathed. "For now, that won't be necessary. I'm feeling perfectly fine at the moment."

"Then the big stick won't be needed... for now," she added with a wink.

~~~~~~

They were quiet for the rest of the trip, only the sounds of their weapons filling the void outside the soothing songs of nature. Crunching leaves fell away as they finally approached the camp. Adrian sighed. "Well, at least the baobhan sith carcasses burnt away in the sunlight. It could have been worse."

Before them laid a ransacked clearing, the fire pit scattered and leaves covering the remaining areas not consumed by mud. Footprints of all sorts were scattered throughout, clearly in opposition to the deep hoof prints that danced across the floor. Wren knelt down, examining the tracks and noticing droplets of blood near the fire. She followed the trail over to the cliff face, smatterings of dull rusted-brown decorating the cool rocky surface.

Adrian was examining the hole that once contained his food stores, now completely dug up and destroyed. With a frustrated frown, he kicked at the stone covering the hole free with the pad of his foot. While he was marching about, he collected some loose knives scattered around the clearing, tucking them away on his belt. Next, he gathered his fur bedding, thankfully untouched by the ire of wild beasts. He rolled the mats up and tied them together, hoisting them up and over his back. He turned to see Wren kneeling down, picking up a shiny silver object by the bloodied wall.

"A needle?" she muttered, twisting the narrow silver blade in her hand. It was engraved with winding markings and odd writings. Adrian came over, instantly recognizing it as the same kind of weapon that had pinned him against the house during that dreadful night. He shook his head.

"Well, there goes home number two," the fae sighed, turning towards the clearing.

"At least it was just a campsite," she reassured, still gazing upon the object in her hand.

"It was the closest to a home I had since I lost my cave," he replied flatly.

She furrowed her brow. "I'm... sorry. That was rude of me. I'm just happy you three made it out of here alive, honestly." The knight dragged her hand across the bloodied wall, pain in her dark eyes. "The old bastard's lucky he didn't get his throat slit. Seems he was cutting it pretty close..."

"He's smarter than that," the troll stated, standing beside his friend as she looked on at the carnage. "This isn't the stickiest situation I've seen him get out of."

"No, I suppose not. Certainly was a close call though," Wren argued. The troll nodded.

"Either way, I got what I wanted from here," he gestured to his laden back with the bundles of furs. Wren's fingers were still rolling the needle, enough that it drew his attention. He flicked out a finger towards the hand, curling it in a silent invitation.

She handed the piece of metal over to him, watching those green fingers wrap around the cold metal and pull it up towards his face. "Is it a weapon they used?" she asked.

The troll frowned. "Looks similar to the one the eldest used... But this..." he paused as he gazed upon the markings with a furrowed brow. He shook his head. "Unfortunately, despite being fae, I'm afraid I cannot read the tongue of my kin."

"Either way, if it's got inscriptions, it could prove to be useful," the woman remarked. She held out her hand, awaiting the metal. Adrian gingerly set it back into her palm as he turned away. "Maybe there's something in the library to decode it. Or someone I can flag down from my contacts."

"At least to find out where they came from," he sighed, gazing out over the woods. "It's neither here nor there..."

"According to Harris, he called for Old Dusk about two months ago. Perhaps he'll know something," she reasoned, setting the blade into a knife sheath. "Though we don't exactly know when he'll get here."

"With what limited memory I have of him, he comes and goes as he wishes. Could be sooner. Could be later. No reason to dwell upon it further," he shrugged, starting to move towards the edge of the camp.

"While a good friend to have, he's a cryptic asshole," she spat with a smile.

"Hate to be the bearer of bad news, Wren... But he's not the only one of us like that," the troll teased, revealing his sharp teeth.

The knight gave him an amused snort, following alongside him. "Oh, I know."

"The only reason I'm more straightforward is because my kin tend to value action over a silver tongue," Adrian explained, his face set with a prideful elegance.

"Ain't that the truth. Of the few that I've met, you certainly weren't a big fan of speaking," she smirked, her shoulder bumping his as they walked together through the loose undergrowth.

Adrian turned to face her, a tender smile upon his features. "Wren, I was a bit of an extreme example."

"I suppose so," she sighed, casting a final glance behind her. She surveyed all the two hunters had built and how they had lived. Her face softened. "It was a good home, Adrian."

"It was, but only as long as family was there. Now that they've gone away, it means nothing," Adrian explained plainly, looking ahead. Wren turned towards him, astonished before giving him a soft smile. "Come along, I'm done here."

"Yes, commander," Wren replied mischievously, only her eyes showing her true feelings. The man scoffed and turned away, making his way back over to the river. "What's the plan now?"

"Add these things to my 'horde', as the boy calls it," he replied, grunting as he slid down.

"So all of this was just an excuse to get out, stretch your legs, get some fresh air?" Wren pressed. The troll simply nodded. "I just hope nothing tries to ambush us on our way back. I would much rather this be a simple retrieval mission," the woman sighed, looking up at the canopy above them. "Though knowing our luck..."

"No need to dwell upon it further. If something happens, we will merely deal with it as we always have," Adrian reassured.

"Oh, but what if it's a mighty dragon?" She teased.

The fae sniffed, puffing out his chest. "Wyrms haven't been sighted since the time of King Alavantus."

"There are rumors of some seen south of Dragon's Rest," she added, jabbing at his arm with her elbow.

"Nonsense!" The troll spat. "I have been there countless times, and not a single dragon was in sight. Nothing but a few Golossian war parties last I checked!"

A flash of blood. He was unarmed. Or so they thought.

The merchant woman let out an amused snort. "I suppose there are some who think the name is in reference to a different threat. Some unholy beast. Either way, I heard the place is haunted as hell."

"Bullshit. Even if that was the case, demons mean nothing."

"Not true," she retorted calmly. "They meant plenty of things in the war."

"Yes, they meant payday. And if not that, a damn good fight," the beastly man licked his lips, still remembering the foul taste of demonic blood upon his fangs.

All fell before his blade, before his might. All unholy scum would be devoured by his army. None would be free from his wrath.

"But that is in the past," he sighed, shaking the confusion from his mind. Wren frowned at his bizarre behavior but dared not press the issue.

"We should probably head over to Harris's cabin while we are out. Perhaps collect some of his things, considering he may not be back for a little while." Her hands gripped each other tightly, remembering the grievous wounds on his leg and back. Would he ever fire a bow again?

"Very well then, at least we can try to find something for him to work on," the troll nodded, shifting his pace eastward. He spotted the worry upon her brow. Wren noticed this and rubbed her forearms.

"If I didn't know any better, one would think the old man would be out of the game by now... Especially with injuries like his... That's enough to put down a normal man in the kindest of circumstances."

"Thankfully, he's no normal man," he reassured, resting a hand upon her shoulder with a comforting expression.

Wren seemed to lean into his warmth a little. "Yeah, I guess none of us really are anymore, huh..."

"Wren, you may have the least visible deformities out of all us, but you certainly were the most wild!" he chuckled. "I've never seen anyone come back from a battle and nearly devour half a deer flank!" Adrian let out a beautiful laugh.

"That was *one* time!" she groaned. "More normal than you!"

"Ha! I would've eaten the *whole* deer!"

"Yes, and be too impatient to cook it!" she pressed.

"Bah, what use would that be?! It's fine as is!" He gave her a dismissive wave.

"For you, perhaps. But we have parasites to contend with!" she snapped playfully.

"Well, boo hoo..." he bemoaned. The woman appeared to open her mouth for a moment before suddenly shutting her jaw. The troll appeared to notice this as he asked, "What? Another retracted scathing comment?"

"It's nothing. It was rude," she shook her head.

"Oh? Then tell me. I won't be mad. Such things are par for the course."

She bit her lip before sighing. "I was going to say that you left me with a bit of a parasite of your own... but that's terrible. It's a disgusting thing to say."

"No, you are correct. It's my fault. I left you, him, and his mother with all of this... I'll have to apologize to that poor woman as soon as I can..." he sighed, sorrow creasing his brow. The troll turned to look at her. Wren had a distant look in her eyes. There was so much to see... So much so he could hardly parse out one emotion from the other. All he could identify was pain, deep and agonizing. Yet as swiftly as it appeared she shook it away, facing him once more. He continued. "I'm sorry for taking your life away for this... I'm sorry you got involved in my family's hardship..."

"Stop apologizing, you big oaf," she snapped, that familiar frustration apparent once more. "Come on, let's hurry along. I want to be home in time to make an actual dinner instead of more sandwiches."

"I thought you liked the sandwiches we made," the man had a wounded expression.

"And I did! However... I would prefer a full meal after a long hike." She gave him a warm smile, one that set his stomach alight for a brief moment before he shook his head. "After all, those two will be hopeless cooking without us... Wait long enough and Vantus will be rifling through the cellar like a bloody rat."

"And knowing our luck, he will end up in the oven somehow..." the troll sighed.

"Which one?"

The fae paused. "Both, perhaps. Is there truly a difference?" The two laughed as they continued through those picturesque woods, not even bothering to notice the distant shadow watching them.

Chapter 31

The two managed to reach the cabin in record time, collecting some of Harris's books, trinkets, blankets, and his leather working tools set upon the desk. Adrian didn't miss a beat leaving the dark home as Wren lingered by the doorway. "Haven't had the chance to be here either... Too damn busy..." she breathed. "And with the festival coming up, I've been bombarded with even more orders for the party. They want to make a show of it."

"What for?" Adrian asked, scoffing.

She turned on the threshold, gazing upon him. "Well, there's a new guest in town. One that's made quite a name for himself lately." Adrian let out a loud groan of disgust, rolling his eyes as he turned away. She had never seen such a scathing look. "On top of that, the harvest's been good. Sales are up. Everyone is in good health. There's a lot to celebrate this year."

"I suppose. And I can't exactly get away with hiding within the house either..." he mused, flicking his claw along a loose vine wrapped around a mature oak. It fell uselessly in his grasp.

"You'd be driven mad by all the distant noise anyways. If you didn't go, everyone would likely just drag you out regardless," she shrugged, shutting the door behind her as she followed the man. "That's if Vantis doesn't get his grubby hands on you first." The troll merely nodded in response, meticulously shredding the vine in his hands. Wren paused before asking, "Why... did you give him that promise?"

He considered his response for a moment. "He's a child. He never had a chance to understand the weight of the situation. Hell, he almost died at the hands of monsters he couldn't possibly comprehend. We don't know who gave the order. We don't even know if more are coming. He could die from enemies my past life made." The troll paused, flopping onto a fallen log beside him. His eyes closed. "From the enemies I've made... I'm certain that's the only reason someone would target him for a deal."

"Worse comes to worst, we call in the calvary, right?" she reasoned, sitting beside the man. The troll sighed and hung his head. "Again. That's only if things get worse. But I won't hesitate if it comes to that for your sake."

"No, I'll just hide, if I'm a silent blind man, no one will think twice," he clasped his talons together.

"The only Adrian they'll see is a statue. You... remember Tobias, right?" she breathed.

An image of a regal man. His face was covered in scars. He was his shadow. His piercing blue eyes were enough to frighten those who defied him. A duelist of the highest caliber. A beast hidden beneath fineries. A monster.

Adrian struggled against the dagger of a headache before nodding. "He hates those things. There are more statues of you scattered around the countryside. All idealizations," Wren explained. The troll flinched at such a consideration. "His men have been going around and keeping the peace since the war. Stamping down cults and insurgents as efficiently as ever. Even if he never asked for the position of commander, I must say he is doing a mighty fine job."

"I... can't remember much of him..." Adrian whispered.

"Oh, and where to begin? He's a hot-headed psychopath who focuses on his chosen target like a falcon and doesn't let up. And the only person able to snap him out of his own madness... was you," she sighed, crossing her legs and leaning back against the log.

"Sounds like a mad dog," the fae muttered.

"He was... and soon he came to realize it. Now he focuses on tempering and controlling the frenzy. I'm certain he recognized you as his warden and keeper during the war... but you were more than that. Tobias looked up to you as a brother, blood or not."

"Blood is meaningless. Blood is meant to be spilled," the troll waved dismissively, reiterating an old adage of his kin.

She gave an amused snort. "Furthermore, he still holds on to your beliefs. Claims he serves the kingdom, not the crown. It has caused issues here and there, with him being a prince and all; but it's nothing he can't handle with Reigus's help." Adrian gave her a confused look. She blinked before explaining, "Our old commander. The one who brought you into the army. He's no longer in the military, but still serves as an advisor and politician."

"I see," the man mused. Other than a flash of blonde and stern eyes, nothing came to mind.

"He still plays the political game," she sighed.

"Humans love their games," the troll snarled.

"As do the fae."

"They get bored all the same," he shrugged. "Never cared for meddling in other's affairs myself. I just enjoyed my nice cave and its wide territory."

Wren shook her head. "I don't believe that's entirely true. Harris had to chase you away plenty of times. You were spotted constantly near the village. And there's your collection of books and trinkets. I don't think you ever let go of it all."

"Ah, so even you were made aware of the boy's little project?" he purred.

"Well, children are never as clever as they seem to think they are. I could smell it long before I saw it. Quite terrible, if you ask me," she sniffed, recalling that stale troll smell.

"I'm fragrant," he replied blandly. Wren's eyes suddenly widened before belting out a loud laugh. Adrian couldn't help but frown.

"That's a hell of a way of putting it!" the warrior exclaimed, wiping a tear from her eye. "It's been awhile since I've shared a camp with a troll, so I can't quite recall if that's always been the case!"

The troll let out a snort. He stood up briskly and strode forward with a soft smile. Wren was still trying to stifle her laugh as she raced after him, her face as radiant as the sun.

~~~~~~

They traveled along at a solid pace, only stopping occasionally to hear the birds chirping overhead. They were about half way home when the troll felt the hairs on the back of his neck stand on end. He suddenly stopped, holding his hand up in a signal. Wren immediately noticed and halted, her eyes darting about. One of her scarred hands laid upon the axe as she searched for the enemy. She raised her other hand and gave him a signal.

'Where's the enemy'

Adrian clenched his jaw subtly as he responded.

'Standby'

The two stood at each other's backs, scanning the forlorn forest around them. It was Adrian who saw them first. The beady little eyes of many small animals surrounded them. They softly chittered and chirped as if deep in gossip. Predators and prey both stood side by side without aggression, watching on. At the center of this congregation was a soft hum of power, one that stole the troll's breath. Magic weaved into his gut. He knew who this was. The moment he understood, Adrian raised a hand.

'Stand down'

The veteran woman peeled her fingers from the axe head, moving closer towards her commander. "What's going on?"

"It's him," the troll breathed. He stepped forward, an eager tension settling upon his shoulders. "Old friend?" he called out. His voice rang through the forest like a bell, echoing all around them. Silence met his call. Only the animals shifted their gaze, all eyes on a singular point. Adrian followed them until he saw it.

Those familiar pink pinpricks, his hunched form, the cloak of moss draped over his shoulders, his crown of antlers. The Green Man was standing before them, a nine-foot-tall sentinel casting a long shadow. Those eyes darted between the two, an impossible expression covering his fanged face. For Adrian, it read as tension. A nervous beast. The mountain troll merely grinned, excited to see him after all this time. "My friend, we've finally found each other once more," he extended his hands out in an inviting gesture, approaching the forest troll slowly. "It has been awhile, has it not?"

The Green Man's brow twitched, first in confusion, then surprise, before ending in a relieved smile. The fae guardian lowered himself upon one knee, letting some of the yellowed leaves attached to his head fall around him as he held out his arms. The two met, the larger being enveloping the man in a firm, yet gentle hug. Those tangled, branch-like fingers held onto his back as he let out a detritus-scented breath. "I was... worried... about you... I could not... find you...You were gone..."

"I apologize. It wasn't my intention to worry you..." Adrian whispered.

Those cherry blossom-colored eyes met his sapphire rings. "The trees could not... find you... nor the birds... I was afraid you left... or perhaps... worse..." Adrian shook his head, glad to prove him wrong. The forest troll pulled away, standing to full height. His eyes finally met the awestruck woman standing in the leafy clearing, a twinge of embarrassment tugging at his features. "How rude of me..." The massive fae gave Wren a gentle bow. "I... did not expect to be... entertaining guests... this evening..." The Green Man turned his weathered visage towards the man standing in his shadow. Adrian backed away a few paces as the troll scanned him with his gaze. "You appear... to be doing... well... Have you... faced much hardship...?"

"Not too much," the man responded clearly. "Before I moved into my current... arrangements... I found shelter here in the woods. The huntsman aided me."

His bark-like skin creaked as the Green Man nodded slowly. "So it would seem... Explains the... offerings... I am... surprised we did not cross paths... though I am certain... I would have been unable to... recognize you..."

"I can hardly recognize myself as well," the fae man frowned, gazing down at his clawed hands. "I... do not know what has happened to me. I just awoke like this one night..." The forest troll gave him a solemn grunt of acknowledgment. "Someone is being summoned here to help with just that. A supposed old friend of mine..."

"...The old one... from the south..." the creature breathed, his voice the crackling of bare twigs. The mountain troll nodded. "We have met... And while we do not... meet each other's gaze in... most regards... There should be no conflict... You needn't worry..." the guardian elaborated.

Adrian could only give a deep bow of respect before the mighty being. "It was not my wish to worry you so..."

The Green Man merely shook his head, casting more leaves from his brow and shoulders. "Please... worry not of such things... It is a fine development... to hear you are well..."

As his friend said this, Adrian recalled what he needed to say. "Have you noticed any odd occurrences in these woods?"

"Many things... yes..." the being replied, turning his head up towards the hills in the distance. "At first... it was the boy... taking your treasures away... Further still, nature has become disquiet... Animals taken... drained, yet not devoured..."

"It was a coven of baobhan sith. They made their way here a few weeks ago," the man explained.

The forest troll furrowed his brow. "That is... unusual. They prowl the winter wood... not the autumn..."

"They had an elder sister with them as well," Adrian stated.

Once again, the mighty troll shook his head, scattering more leaves. "That makes little sense... and yet... it does explain... the *foul* stench of death..." he added with a wrinkled sniff.

"I know not if others shall arrive, though there is reasonable evidence there will be," the man sighed, crossing his arms. The sheer difference in size was almost comical, considering how they were speaking.

"... I... shall be sure to warn you..." the troll reassured before turning his attention towards a flock of birds behind him. He lumbered away a few paces, breathing softly as he interacted with the sunset-colored birds weaving about his antlers and his outstretched fingers. Wren and Adrian looked on, the man with an expectant stare and the merchant woman mystified. The forest guardian checked their feathers before urging them on into the sky, watching them dart through the air until they finally turned south. The Green **Man** spent a moment analyzing the ground fauna before letting out an exhausted breath. Those pink pinpricks shut before his jagged maw opened, "...What... Do you remember?"

"Mainly my younger years as a human," Adrian responded clearly.

"I... see..." the Green Man sighed, turning to exchange a wordless glance towards Wren. Their eyes met briefly, long enough for Adrian to notice. Before he could question it, the fae was facing him once more. "And what of... the boy...? Is he... safe...?"

"For now, yes," the man nodded, staring out over the hilltops and ravines.

"Are... the baobhan sith... still ailing you...?"

"All three are dead," Adrian answered, his eyes laced with frustrated malice. He could still see the elder sister's leering visage in his mind's eye.

"Quite the feat... especially if... you are unaccustomed to humanity..." the Green Man smiled.

The fae man shook his head, letting his black and white hair sway over his face briefly. "It was not by my hand alone. It was the huntsman... and this woman here..." he gestured with a talon towards Wren, who was standing awkwardly in the clearing.

"Ah... I forgot... How capable you all were... Not that much... had been seen by these... very eyes..." the troll blinked.

"All stories now," the man sighed, silently admonishing himself.

"Even stories... hail from fragments of truth..." the guardian sighed before resting a claw upon an ancient maple. "And I am certain... the woods shall not forget this... Whether it be a mighty battle... or the claws of a territorial mountain troll marring them... and making a fool of himself..." he added with a chuckle. It rang with the sound of fallen leaves.

"Have I yet to appease them?" Adrian let out a playful snort.

Amusement glittered in the Green Man's dark eyes. "Oh, they know you meant no ill will... But... " he sighed, turning towards the south. He was silent for a minute "Unfortunately... with regards to your condition... Such magic is out of my... realm of expertise..."

"The old one shall give us answers," Adrian reassured, dipping his head. "In the meantime... it is best we get moving..."

The forest troll nodded. "It is good... to see you once more... both of you... I'm sorry I could not find you sooner..." the Green

Man smiled. "It is not as if... the mushrooms root themselves... or the lichens climb high in the rotten wood of an ailing giant... And it is... not uncommon for the birds to lose their way..."

"Then I must apologize for asking for a final favor..." Adrian sighed.

The hunched guardian raised a gnarled claw. "...You needn't bother with formalities... What is... your wish...?"

Adrian cast a single look towards Wren, who was starting to turn away and collect the things they had dropped before the encounter. The man briskly approached the troll and gestured to him to whisper. The Green Man blinked before nodding, slowly kneeling until his face was next to the human's ear. "I need to make a gift for my friend here. I know she likes wildflowers... If I could have some seeds, mayhaps I can present them to her in bloom for the fall festival..." the mountain troll explained, nervousness in his voice.

The forest guardian's expression did not shift. He spoke in a low tone. "...You pick a less than ideal... season for growth... but I may be able... to accommodate... Though I wish to know... To what end...?"

Adrian paused, thinking hard on this. He spoke softly, "In gratitude. And in penitence for hurting her so..."

With that, the Green Man reached into his cloak, rummaging briefly before pulling his claws free. The troll raised the hand to his face before blowing softly onto his palm. Then, he lowered it, revealing several dried seeds, no larger than wheat grains. Adrian pulled one of the side bags off his hip, gingerly corralling the seeds inside before setting it back onto his belt. "Simply water

them... once in the morning... once in the evening... If you do so...
they shall sprout within a few days... Days after... they shall bloom...
I hope they are to your liking..." he instructed.

"Thank you, my friend," Adrian bowed his head.

Once again, the forest troll held him in a hug, whispering,
"Before you go... I wish peace upon you... In mind... and body...
Please... give yourself rest..."

The man could only nod in response as he was released, the
troll stepping back to watch him go. Wren was standing at the ready,
patiently awaiting Adrian's return. She called out, "Do take care...
And may the winds blow in your favor..."

The Green Man seemed shocked, his eyes widening at such
an old adage. A smile crept upon his lip as he responded, "...And to
you as well... Wren... May you and your kin find peace..." With that,
the ancient being turned, shuffling into the woods before a whirling
breeze passed by, enshrouding his back before revealing nothing in
its wake. The animals began to slowly disperse, leaving a single pair
of mourning doves perched upon a branch above the travelers' heads.
They preened at each other briefly before fluttering off.

Adrian approached Wren with a resolute sigh. The woman
let out a shaking exhale, as if from an impossibly held breath. "That's
the first time I've ever talked to him... It's... incredible."

"You're definitely not the first human to say that," the troll
smiled. "He can even steal the breath away from the younger fae such
as myself."

"How the hell do you go about your day after seeing something like that?" she asked, gesturing out over the woods.

"Wren, you spend every day with a mountain troll," the man laughed, continuing deeper down the worn trail. The dame followed along.

"Yeah, but I've done that for over three years before everything went tits up! It's different. Hell, even after meeting Old Dusk I was still surprised!" Wren exclaimed, the leaves fluttering past as she scattered the piles between their feet. She let out a snort. "Perhaps it is no different to Vantis when he first met you. Like meeting something from a folktale."

"For me, the Green Man is just another old friend, nothing more, nothing less..." he sighed. Wren could only see his wavy hair tousled by the breeze like a silk curtain.

She smiled. "Then I'm glad you got to catch up."

~~~~~~

Harris awoke suddenly, turning his bleary eyes towards the front of the couch. He grunted groggily. There was something on the table. Something that wasn't there before. The huntsman made a small grimace as he pushed himself up into a half-sitting position. He snatched the letter and read it over. It took a moment for his bloodshot eyes to recognize the symbols in front of him.

in case of emergency

The huntsman glanced above the paper, finally noticing a small crossbow set upon the table. An ounce of worry dripped down his sore spine. "...Wren...? Adrian...?" he called. No answer. Before the man could lurch to his hooves and begin to act, the hunter heard the front door open and a set of footsteps enter. Grogginess blinded reason; panic ruling his next actions as he quickly snatched up the weapon and snarled, "Hey! Who is it?! You can't just go barging into people's houses!"

"Oh hush up, you old goat!" Adrian snapped.

That wave of tension quickly receded. The older man's shoulders sagged as the troll came into view. "Oh, it's you two... What the hell was all this about?! 'In case of emergency...'" he snapped.

"Oh, he seems properly offended. I believe you did quite well, Wren," the fae man sneered as he set his hands upon his hips. Wren followed closely behind, tossing her muddied boots in the pile by the door.

"Glad you managed to sleep the entire time we were gone," she smirked. "Means you actually did something I told you to do."

"Yes, leave a child completely unattended..." The troll let out a playful hiss, exposing his fangs.

Harris scowled. "I'm sure he would've said something if he needed something..."

"At the very least make an unholy racket..." the fae sniffed, snagging the weapon from Harris's hands and setting the crossbow back on the shelf.

"Eh, if I didn't hear 'em, I must've been fucking tired," the huntsman shrugged. He cleared his gravelly voice. "VANTIS!"

Soon, an annoyed call echoed over the distant banister. "What?!"

"You dead?"

A pause. "No! Why?!"

"Good!" Harris grunted.

"...You're so terribly weird, uncle!" Vantis groaned before stomping back to his room.

Adrian pulled the pack containing all of the huntsman's things and plopped it roughly in his lap, making the old man let out a grunting wheeze. He scowled at the fae as he walked on past, taking a moment to examine the contents before giving a frustrated nod. "Thanks. I take it you two went out to my cabin?"

Adrian nodded. "Took care of my last affairs at the campsite before moving on..." the troll sighed, plucking his book from the window sill.

"That bad?"

"Bad enough that it's not worth salvaging," the beautiful man sighed.

"Damn, did you at least find the pot by the campfire?" Harris followed him with his head as he made his way over to the threshold.

"That and the bloody stone..." Adrian sniffed, tucking the book under his armpit.

"Wait, why on earth did you grab that? I know it's a hell of a good cooking stone but that's an excessive amount of weight to be lugging around!" the hunter chuckled.

Adrian stopped at the doorway, resting a hand on the side. "It weighs like a feather, Harris." On cue, he reached over to the last pack on the ground and pulled out the stone, flipping it effortlessly in his hand.

"I'll just say I'm glad I wasn't the one carrying it," Wren snorted, casting a sideways glance towards the troll.

"It's not that heavy. You're all just pathetic," he sneered, a playful smile gracing his features.

"Oh buggar off!" Harris snapped, waving him on. Adrian set the stone onto a nearby table before waltzing out.

"Why don't you rest?" the troll pressed.

"I've rested plenty! Wasted a whole damn day, by the looks of it," the huntsman sniffed, already rummaging through his collected things.

"Well, *I* need rest. Do make sure the boy is occupied, I would rather my sleep be uninterrupted," the fae responded.

"Do you want me to wake you up for dinner?" Wren asked, turning to watch the man make his way up the stairs.

"No, I'll be fine without it, good night," he called, leaving the two below.

Wren sighed, watching him disappear around the corner upstairs. "Good night, Adrian."

Chapter 32

Adrian found himself surrounded by the sleeping bodies of his soldiers. His grotesque visage was only lit by the dull flickering of firelight as he stared deep into the coals, paying little heed to the ghosts of moving shapes around him.

A young man sat beside him, binding up his arm with a roll of bandages. His striking blue eyes cast a brief glance over towards him, his mouth moving but making no sound. Adrian seemed to understand the nothingness as he responded, "Ta..ke... bet...ter... ca...re... of... you...r...sel..f..." His words were painful, a struggle against the mangled cage of teeth locked to his exposed gums. The man gave him a sheepish grin before turning back to his injuries, cutting the fabric free with a knife. His ear-length brown hair cast his handsome face in shadow, calling forth the shaded pits of scars that ran across his smooth skin.

This was one of his friends... one of his lieutenants... No... He was more than that. He was his brother.

The commander turned his mutated face from the flame, gazing across the camp. He hated the standard structure of leadership tents being in the center of camp, it called too much attention and value to them. All his best knights were tangled together like a roving band of nomads in their own personal tents, no different than the others.

Many soldiers had claws or mutated patches of skin, pieces of their humanity taken from them during this costly war. All were cast out, whether they be touched by demons, fae, disease, or poor reputation. All banded together as family. Be they leper or accursed, all but the worst had a place under his banner. Adrian supposed that was why they were all so very loyal, bound by brotherhood and circumstance. He watched a shield maiden approach a man covered in bandages and hand him a waterskin, wrapping him in a blanket as they quietly chatted. An amputee was helping a mutated soldier pluck some stray feathers away from his back, keeping the comb clean and maintained. Two men with bird-like talons ran the kitchen and gave out late night meals to the unit that just returned home.

Home.

Yes, that's what this was. These people, his Executioners, they were his home. He couldn't help but smile seeing all the contented faces in the distance, all the joy in this brief reprieve they all shared.

That was when he heard her muffled cries. Adrian turned his gaze, eyeing one of the tents encircling his flame. The shuffling of sheets, a whimper of terror, a gasp of pain. Ah, she was having another one. The commander stood to full height, the loud clanking of

his ebony armor drawing the eyes of his blood brother beside him.
There was nothing but sympathy in his icy gaze, uncomfortably
rubbing his shoulder with beastly claws as he turned away. Even he
knew the knight commander was the only one who could reach her.

So he moved along, stepping over blankets and bed rolls until
he reached the edge of her tent. His armored hand pulled free from
under his cloak, reaching out to knock at one of the support posts.
There was no answer, just more cries. He frowned, readjusting his
gauntlet before trying again. No response. Determined to aid in any
way he could, the lord reached for one of the flaps and pulled it aside.

Terrifyingly enough, there was no one there. Only a neatly set
bed roll and an axe laying beside it. Yet those whimpers remained,
driving his anxiety onward. "Wr...en...?" he whispered, glancing
around in a panic.

"Wr...en?"

"Wren!" he called out, lurching forward. The troll was sitting
up in his bed, enshrouded by darkness. His eyes quickly adjusted to
the night, realizing where he was. Back in his room. Just a dream.
Despite this, he could still hear her cries.

Wren was having a nightmare. The fae man stood free from
his bed, exiting his room to wander down the halls. The few
windows not covered by curtains let in rays of gloomy moonlight,
silver bars illuminating his frame as he strode past. His mind shook
away the final vestiges of sleep, leaving nothing but an instinctual
desire to ensure his friend's safety. This wasn't the first time she cried
out like this. Nor would it be the last.

Eventually, he reached her room. With a deep exhale, he knocked on the door, firm but not startling. The noises abruptly stopped. It was hauntingly quiet in those uneasy halls; only the distant groans of the manor filling his pointed ears. Before long, he heard a sound from within the tiny room. "...Come in..."

Adrian carefully twisted the handle and peered into the dark room, spotting the shadowed form of Wren sitting up in bed. Her glittering eyes were downcast, hands tightly clasping her forearms. The troll couldn't help but give her a concerned frown. "Wren? Are you alright?"

The veteran's eyes darted up towards his, pain lacing her vision. "I'm... I'm fine. Just a bad dream."

Hesitation gripped him. A part of him wanted to leave knowing she was okay; the troll that wanted to crawl back to its cave. His humanity told him to stay. His mouth opened before he could consider this any further. "Do you want me to go?"

Conflict washed over her face before she looked away. "N-no. You can stay... Come in."

Adrian tentatively approached, stepping inside the tiny room before shutting the door behind him. Wren pulled her legs in, letting the man settle down at the foot of her bed. It let out a tiny creak, making the man flinch as he settled down. He felt awkward, being in her room. He felt like he was violating her territory, invading her den. Every instinct told him to flee... and yet he remained. They sat in silence, the hoots of owls outside their only accompaniment inside the cramped space. Eventually, Wren spoke up, "I'm sorry for waking you... The dreams never really went away. Less frequent, I suppose... but still... well..." She went quiet, unable to articulate what to say next. Her scarred arms tightened around her legs, her shaded eyes hidden from view.

Adrian gave her a reassuring nod. "I figured as much. Vantis mentioned it some time ago..." He paused. "Have they changed at all?"

She gave a tiny shrug, shuffling deeper into her blankets. The cold was less biting than it had been prior to his arrival, but her fingers and toes still quaked against the cool air. "A little. Depends on the night. It's not very often that I dream of Redhollow."

He remembered the flames still flickering against the scorched wood. His talons tracing the marks where tongues of fire bit into the building. Skeletal frames of bodies attempting to flee. The remains of her monsters. Blood soaked the ground, only interrupted by a trail of bare footprints, footprints he would follow. The perpetrator was still out there. He never expected it would be her. There was a deep-seated terror in her eyes.

Adrian grimaced, clasping his hands tightly. "Is it wrong... to be happy about that?"

Wren's fading expression creased. Was it a grimace or a smile? He couldn't tell. And that terrified him. "No, it's not. I'm glad too."

"At least... Now you can finally move on from that point in time... You were trapped there for so long," he whispered. His voice was softer, delicate compared to the power that often held his tongue. His eyes seemed to dull in the darkness. "Though I... suppose the war wasn't much better, was it?"

"No, of course not. And I thought things were terrible before the Executioners..." she chuckled, leaning against the wall behind her. "The world quickly became madder than a hatter afterwards."

"And later I fell to my curse... Whatever happened was so terrible it made me forget everything." The troll rubbed his left shoulder, expecting to feel one of those bone plates arcing off like a pauldron. He couldn't even tell what time he was in. Not anymore. It was all so much. And he couldn't even say it.

"What do you think I'm having nightmares about?" She asked, her fiery eyes boring into his. A ball of guilt settled in his stomach, making him ill. He gritted his fangs in shame. "It's not your fault. It never was." She crept forward, touching his shoulder.

"... I am truly sorry," he muttered, his head enshrouded by his hair.

Wren frowned and punched him lightly on that very same shoulder. He couldn't help but smile. "I told you, stop blaming yourself. You did what you must to keep us alive."

His eyes drew up to the blackened wall ahead, his eyes darting about to read its surface. "It was the only idea I had."

"And if it weren't for that, we'd all be in a hole," she added.

"Who knows where that madman would have struck next," he growled, a deep sense of disgust welling up at the sight of those gnarled teeth.

"Exactly," Wren nodded, pulling away slowly as she settled back down. "Once again, you saved the kingdom."

Adrian abruptly shook his head. Time fell away.

He was at camp once more. Harris was telling a raunchy tale from his days in Laurend. Wren was laughing hard enough to choke on her mouthful of skewered squirrel. Adrian was smiling, fighting against the tightness in his mutated jaw. Firelight illuminated them all, deep in those dark trees. Home.

"Nonsense. I never gave a damn about any of that. All I ever cared about was you two. I just needed to get you two through another day."

Wren let out a small exhale. "I'm just glad that in the end... you came back to us. Seeing you trapped in limbo, so far from death and even further from life. It drove us crazy for a while. It's why I... took so long to let you go."

Adrian smiled. "I'm just glad that I got a chance to see you again. That I got to see you move on, just a little further. I was always terrified, y'know. That you would remain in that village forever."

She laughed. "I'll tell you one thing, I certainly wasn't ready to be a normal person again. The only reason I survived at all was thanks to Harris. If he hadn't passed the torch of commander to Tobias and instead remained as your replacement... Well, I'm not so certain I would be here."

Adrian frowned, terrible ideas invading his mind. The thought of her giving up. Of leaving.

No, she wouldn't. She would never give in. She would always try to move ahead, no matter what... Right?

His lips moved. "I was there too, wasn't I?"

"Sometimes," she nodded. "You'd try to get into the house. A few times you did. I think... the scariest time was when Vantis was young and playing in the yard. We left him alone for maybe... two minutes?"

He wanted to see them again. He wanted to go home. His claws trudged through the undergrowth, deceptively quiet compared to his frame. His head was down, his muzzle partially open to suck in the air. A new smell filled his nose. It was like that of the woman... and that huntsman... but different. Curious, the beast lumbered forward, spotting a tiny figure from between the fronds.

"Next thing I know, I come out onto the back porch and see you looming over him. The two of you were just feet apart, looking at each other... I froze in place... I don't know... just waiting to see what would happen..."

He slowly heaved a large claw, reaching out to the tiny pair of eyes looking up at him. The toddler was clutching a stuffed lion toy. There was no fear in his eyes, just curiosity mirroring the troll's own. His black talon was so close, delicately extending to touch the boy.

"Then Harris bolted out, screaming like a madman. He chased you off before you could hurt the boy. And thinking about it now, I don't think you would have..." she finished, her eyes far away.

"Actually," the troll began, letting out an amused snort. "I believe I can recall what I was thinking at that moment." Adrian turned towards her, a look of embarrassment darkening his features. "I had never seen a human so small."

"It is a bit astounding, I'll admit. How those sticky little goblins end up becoming people," she chuckled, thinking about the boy. Her smile fell almost instantly. "Unfortunately, I do believe that incident was when Harris became more... *aggressive* when chasing you off. I'm sorry about that."

"You've already said that," the troll grunted. "And yet you dare to yell at me for apologizing?"

"I know," the woman sighed, turning away. "I guess I am a bit of a hypocrite. I don't know, I still think we should have tried harder. Maybe get you back faster..." She shook her head. "But thinking about it now changes nothing."

"No, I'm here now. That's what matters," the fae nodded, giving her a warm smile. He leaned his head against the wall beside him.

The dame glanced over to the small window beside her nightstand, spotting the faint glittering lights beyond the faded glass. She began to shuffle a little. "It's late... I should be getting some rest." Adrian began to nod, moving to stand up before she continued. "But... could you do me a favor?" Her dark eyes awkwardly gazed at her hands, picking at a small scab on her knuckle. "Could you... stay here? At least until I fall asleep?"

"Of course," he bowed his head, settling back down onto the bed. "I'll keep watch tonight."

"Thank you," Wren whispered, lowering herself into the sheets. Adrian pressed himself against the wall, trying not to take up too much space as he gazed ahead. Slowly, he raised his right leg, pressing it against his body while the remaining one dangled below. He wrapped his arm around it, using the weight to keep it there as he curled in.

Before long, he heard her quiet breaths ease into a soft rhythm, her mind drifting off into sleep. Adrian glanced over, almost habitually checking on her before letting his head fall slack in front of him. He should leave. But the thought of Wren waking up alone from another nightmare stayed his hand. And sitting in such a way felt nostalgic. He slept so many nights like this, sitting upright with his sword to brace him. Anything to chase away the nightmares of choking on his own blood. Soon after, his eyes flickered closed and Adrian too fell asleep; at the ready to fight any monsters that dare crawl up from the abyss around them.

~~~~~~

It was the chirps of the first songbirds that drew Wren away from slumber. She rubbed her eyes, moving her legs to push herself from her side onto her back. As one of her feet bumped into something, the dame blinked. Blearily rubbing at her eyes, she slowly sat up; spotting the upright, but clearly slumbering form of Adrian. His eyes were shut, a serene expression set upon his features. She couldn't help but smile at the familiar sight. A small snort exited her nose before she reached out and gently flicked his forehead. The troll cringed away with a soft grunt. "Some night guard you are, falling asleep at your post. You could have gone back to your bed, idiot," she jeered.

The troll rubbed at his head in annoyance, before glancing over with a wry grin. "What? This is a remarkably comfortable wall." Adrian tapped the wood with his talons. He pulled away slowly, feeling a soreness fill his shoulders as he rolled them. "And to be honest, I was concerned that the moment I shifted position on this creaky-ass bed, you'd awaken once more." The fae stood up, stretching his limbs. They protested with a rock-like grinding sound.

"After I went back to bed again, I slept like a rock," she laughed.

"I certainly feel like one," Adrain sniffed.

"And that's what happens when you sleep against the wall!" she chided. There was a wonderful playfulness to her tone, enough to make the man smile.

"Well, you kicked me plenty during the night," he countered with a smirk.

"Probably deserved it," Wren added gently. She stood beside him and stretched, watching him for a moment. "If it's really that bad, we can draw a bath."

"Oh, you needn't coddle me like a child... or Harris," he added with a chuckle.

Wren belted out a genuine laugh, shoving him. "It's not 'coddling', it's caring! You couldn't have enjoyed being so crooked!"

"Actually," he breathed, moving towards the door. "It felt nostalgic." Wren stared at his back for a moment, a thought crossing her mind. She shook her head. Adrian spoke up. "Now, I'll get out of your hair so you can go eat."

"Oh, no you don't! You're going to be giving me a hand," The woman gently tapped his shoulder as he opened the door, letting the first light of dawn flood the chambers. He turned, gazing into her eyes. They dazzled like firelight.

He tisked under his breath and made a motion of disappointment as he snapped his fingers. "Well shit... I suppose I will if I must," he playfully bemoaned. Wren just laughed and shoved him along, ready to start the morning.

Chapter 33

Adrian was eager to finish his present in the coming days. While those precious seeds laid within that pouch, he took one of his beloved sleeping furs and cleaned it, rolling it up before heading to Vantis's room. He managed to convince the boy to go to the market, accompanying him to gaze at the various goods. He sold the fur in exchange for those shiny rocks, using them to purchase a decently-sized clay pot. Based on how it felt in his hands, he was certain it would be large enough to grow the plants safely, at least until next spring. He bought some fertilized field soil afterwards, stuffing the pot to the brim with the dirt before sneaking it back into the house with a distracted child lugging around a few new books. Thankfully, all the festivities had Wren working overtime to arrange things, keeping the merchant in her office as the eager fae separated from the child and sequestered himself in his room.

He placed the seeds inside the soil and gingerly sprinkled water upon them as per the Green Man's instruction. The troll smiled at his work, hiding the pot behind one of the curtains to absorb what little heat the coming autumn had to offer. And there it would sit, only occasionally disturbed as the man poured more water into the pot and checked on the budding stems. Before he knew it, he had some healthy sprouts with sharp, pointed leaves plastered against the window. A week after that, the buds were fit to burst upon bouncing stems. It was upon the dawn of the festival that he would give it one last look. There, upon evergreen stems, were a cluster of wild blossoms in sharp, starry shapes.

He knew not their name, what meaning humans ascribed them, nor their location of origin, but he knew this would satisfy as a gift. His talons brushed against those sapphire stars, gazing upon the deep blue edges fading into a shadowed violet center. The petals encircled a white pistel, shining like an evening star. It was entracing, those shapes, those colors. Enough to tug at the selfish edge of his instincts, to keep this beauty for himself. And yet Adrian gave a soft smile, eager to give his wonderful gift away to the person who deserved it most. He hid the pot behind the curtain, striding out of his room and down the stairs. Harris was hard at work, tying two pieces of leather together with a thick twine. The old man only gave the troll a cursory glance as he skipped down those steps. He let out a snort. "You look like a doe-eyed boy frolicking about."

"Oh, hush up! I'm in a good mood today," the fae snapped, approaching the couch-bound man to avoid shouting.

"Is that so? I suppose it has been awhile since you've last been to one of these festivals," the hunter mused, glancing down at his work as he tugged the thread through another set of holes in the leather pieces.

"More or less. I've always heard and seen them from afar, but never up close. And what memories I do have of such events are hazy at best. Mostly sights and smells," Adrian recalled, folding his arms as he gazed outside the north-facing window.

"Ah, but that's not what's on your mind, is it, old friend?" the huntsman smirked, pulling the pieces tightly together.

Adrian scowled. "Mayhaps it is. Mayhaps not. It's none of your business!"

"Oh ho ho! Touched a nerve, did I? Well, don't let me spoil that wondrous mood before Vantis does, shall we?" Harris belted out a loud laugh.

The troll let out an irritated hiss before moving past, flopping hard into the chair beside that window and picking up his mother's book. He could read a little more now, enough to gather basic information from a page. It was a struggle, but one well worth the effort. Anything to read the sacred words left by his beloved mother. As he dragged his pointer finger across the page, he muttered the words under his breath, pausing every time he spotted a series of letters that confounded him.

He could hear Wren outside barking orders to the townsfolk as they finished their preparations. She probably wouldn't be back until the evening. Vantis was busy with his final assignment, spending an excessive amount of time getting it done and off of his desk. Harris was the only one relaxing, focusing on a personal project as opposed to worrying about the festival. Adrian had yet to box up his beloved gift, worried for the plants' safety. All he could do to steel his nerves was read and distract himself until the time came. Then he would have to suffer through many hours wearing a blindfold and avoiding conversation, all the while battling a rising tide of feelings and memories that filled his heart with excitement.

The fall festival was always his favorite.

~~~~~~

As the sun began its descent over the western mountains, the first songs of the Willowbend Autumn Festival began. And Wren was already drilling Vantis on the arrangements. "Okay. This year, since your uncle is still recovering, you will need to help guide him around and get things as he needs them."

"O-okay! So uncle is going to tell his stories again?" Vantis asked, adjusting his blouse and trousers. He had to at least put a bit of effort into his appearance this time around.

Succeed with grace, right?

Wren was adjusting the cuffs on her sleeves, glancing out the open window to spy people beginning to gather in the center of town. "More than likely. He needs you this year. Please try not to kill him," she sighed.

"Of course! I'll do my very best, Wren! Uncle is going to have a great time this year, injuries or not!" the boy beamed, determination in his eyes. Sure, Vantis couldn't roam about freely like he usually did during these festivals, but he had a lot to think about, and helping uncle would surely cheer his spirits. After all, he finally knew what he wanted to say to his father... but had yet to articulate it. Uncle's wisdom might just be the final ingredient he needed.

"Very good," the lady of the house blinked, surprised at the lack of complaint. "Then I shall expect your best behavior!" She ruffled his hair before stepping out. The teenager let out an outraged grunt, meeting her devilish grin with a playful snarl as she closed the door behind her. Wren made her way over towards the dining room, spotting the troll hunched over something. She raised a brow. "What do you have there?"

Adrian jolted. "Ah! Er... Wren! Caught me at an odd time, you did."

She raised a brow, leaning against the threshold into the foyer. "Oh?"

"Just finished this," he grunted, turning around to present a large plain wooden box, held closed thanks to some ribbon tightly bound to the sides. His favorite ribbon.

Wren blinked. "A gift? For whom?"

"You," the troll answered, looking down at it nervously.

The woman blinked before letting out a small chuckle. "You didn't have to do that."

"But I wanted to. In thanks, for all the kindness you've shown me," the fae explained, his eyes tender as they gazed upon her.

Wren fought with an unknown emotion before stating, "Well, perhaps we can set it with the others before the gifting ceremony. That way you won't have to worry about lugging it around through the whole festival."

"Of course," the troll nodded, spotting the young lad rocketing down the steps behind Wren and accosting his uncle.

"Hey, uncle!" he greeted cheerily.

"Heavenly father!" The old man jumped, almost tripping on a rug as he traveled from his couchly throne towards the wheelchair. "You scared the daylights out of me!" he admonished.

"Sorry! But today's the big day, and we don't wanna miss it, do we?" The boy laughed, helping the man ease into the chair before the lad grabbed the back.

"Yes, yes, but there's no rush! We have a whole bloody night!" Harris yelped as the boy lurched forward, flinging the both of them out the door. "Vantis! You little shit! Careful! The road is full of gravel and dirt! Take it easy on my old ass!"

"You always said you were stronger than you looked!" the boy argued.

"Yes, but I still have stitches, you brat!" the huntsman cried, grunting loudly as the boy went faster. "VANTIS!!"

Wren chuckled as their voices disappeared down the hill, leaving the two of them alone in the house. "Ready?" she smiled.

"As much as I'll ever be," Adrian sighed, pulling up the blindfold and his hood. "Good?"

"Like a well-kept homeless man," she answered with a solemn nod.

"Very good," the troll remarked, taking up his gift and holding out his elbow. The dame led the blind man down the hill

with a gentle hand, being sure to warn him of oncoming obstacles.
She glanced at the flat grimace upon his face.

"Oh, come now. You could at least *try* to look excited," she
teased.

"I'm plenty excited. So excited I could spit," he hissed. Wren
just laughed as she continued on, deeper into the festivities.

The minstrels were hard at work with this celebration,
playing both original and classic arrangements, jaunty voices echoing
around the town square. Garlands full of dried herbs, garlic, leaves,
and small beaded baubles softly rustled against the buildings and
monuments, casting all edges in a sunset glow. Children ran with
baskets full of farm-fresh harvest, eagerly racing each other to see
who could fulfill the gentle cooks' wishes first. Lovers danced in the
dirt square, laughing gayly as their friends and family joined in.
People milled about, sharing stories of harvest, great projects, odd
happenstances, and the latest gossip with drinks in hand. It was
loud. And it only got louder as the blind man entered.

"Is that Lion?" a voice asked.

"The blind hero who fended off a bear?!" exclaimed another.

"It's Lion!"

"Hey, Lion! Here for our famous festival?"

Soon he was surrounded; people from throughout the village
eager to know more about this mysterious stranger and hero. The
troll shrank at the cacophony of voices. "I... um... uh..." the fae

mumbled, moving closer to Wren. Her warmth was his only comfort surrounded by so much.

"Everyone, please! Don't bombard him all at once!" the merchant demanded, a kind strength to her tone. She stood in front of her companion, trying to ward away the prying gazes.

"My apologies, my Lady! I didn't think we would find a hero out in these woods! I thought all laid within the village proper!" a male voice rumbled.

"Even if that's the case, he's just someone trying to enjoy a festival," she reasoned.

"And right you are! There are plenty of things to enjoy! Do you need a tour, kind Lion?" the voice came closer.

"I..." Adrian whispered, unable to finish his sentence as another overwhelming wave of sensations assaulted him.

"I will take care of that, Gerald. Please, go have fun!" The woman stepped in the way, a smile firm upon her face. The man merely nodded before moving along, noticing some mischief a few yards away.

"Oy! Ellis! Don't eat that!" Gerald yelled, frantically racing away to stop the child from biting down on a garland.

Wren smirked. "Keep an eye on your brat..." she muttered, a playful edge to her tone.

The others dispersed, eager to get back to the festivities. She turned back towards the blind man. "Are you alright?" Adrian only nodded, stretching out to full height. They moved along, quietly examined by the villagers as they circled towards the gift table. Adrian handed off the package to Wren, warning her it was delicate. She gazed upon it, noticing the child-like scrawlings engraved upon its surface.

WREN

The woman smiled. "Your writing is getting better. It's legible this time," she remarked. Adrian looked away sheepishly with a low growl. "Don't be upset about it, you are learning far faster than most. Hell, quicker than Vantis!" she added with a chuckle.

"He's a child... I'm supposed to be an adult and already know these things..." the troll sighed.

"Yes, and in two weeks," she began, gingerly setting the package upon the table, far from the edge as requested. "You have already learned as much as he did in two years."

The troll grimaced, turning over towards the roving shadows of people weaving through the games, stories, and food stalls. A wondrous smell wafted from that direction, a whirl of savory with just a hint of sweetness. "What's that I'm smelling?"

Wren stood beside him. "Well, it's either the roast, the maple glaze, or the spiced ale."

He shifted towards her shadow, holding out a hand. "Care to lead me on?"

"Of course, I'll show you around." He felt her hand clasp his gloved talons, pulling him along gently as she navigated the crowds.

Wren brought him towards the games where she described what the players were doing, then she moved to the craft stalls and told stories of each of the merchants. Afterwards, she led him towards the food table, where offerings of cinnamon-spiced ales and other sweet and salty goods were passed around. Based on what she said, the ox roast was still on the way, with the lovely smell of raw flesh slowly being supplanted by cooked meat.

She gingerly offered a cup of ale to him, his fingers reaching out and clasping the wooden sides firmly. The music echoed all around them, only dulled by the voices of passersby. He supped from the mug as he felt the woman shift position. "Ah, could you wait for a moment? There's someone I need to check on..." she trailed off, breathlessly moving away. Adrian merely nodded, standing awkwardly off to the side as people moved past to sample the fine foods. Some villagers seemed to notice his discomfort and offered a small plate of food to the blind man, of which he nervously accepted.

Wren walked out over to a porch, where a small old woman laid. Her eyes were cloudy, glazed with cataracts and malformations that made her gaze empty. She was beaming softly, her heavy smile lines betraying her years of joy and hard work. The elderly woman's face twitched, noticing the approaching footsteps long before the dame opened her mouth. She turned to face her with a wide smile. She seemed to be missing various teeth.

"Tabitha? Are you faring well?" Wren called. "It's Wren, by the way..."

"Oh, I know who you are, sweetheart. I doubt I could ever forget..." she creaked, leaning forwards on her cane clasped between her skeletal hands. "You are hard to miss with how often you yell at that silly boy..."

The merchant woman chuckled. "I'm sorry if I've caused any disturbances in the past!"

"Oh no," Tabitha waved. "It's been nothing short of entertaining hearing those lighthearted arguments at the odd hour!"

"Vantis can be quite the handful," Wren sat next to her by the stairs.

"Thankfully, it appears he has his own hands occupied dealing with the huntsman over there," she remarked, her curtain of grey hair falling over her face as she nodded. "The handsome one," she clarified.

"Ha! Are you talking about Harris?" the veteran woman questioned. Tabitha nodded. Wren's umber eyes glanced over towards the two in the distance, the man motioning for his nephew to watch out for the fire and help him get over a rock lodged in the wheels of his chair. The boy quickly rushed over and tried kicking the rock before attempting to pull the chair away. Loud yelling ensued as the chair tilted back and the older man yelped. The merchant smirked. "Yeah, now that Harris has the kid at his disposal, Vantis has plenty of assignments to keep himself busy."

As soon as he jolted the chair away, the teenager called out to a roving band of children wandering through the party. "Hey! Wanna see how fast I can make him go?" The children stopped and eagerly ran over, ready to watch the action.

"Oy! Quit that you little-" the huntsman snapped, only barely managing to halt a swear from exiting his gritted teeth.

"Come on, uncle! Let's give 'em a show!" Vantis laughed, feeding off the excited cheers of the kids.

"You're so strong, Vantis!"

"I know right?!" the boy beamed, holding his head high. "I can lug around uncle Harris like he's weightless!"

"You're almost as strong as your da!" a tiny voice squeaked from behind him.

"Nah! I'm already waaay stronger than him!" Vantis boasted.

"No you're not!"

"Yes I am!" the boy snapped. Harris just held his head in his hands, already too tired for all of this nonsense.

Wren shook her head, turning back to see the old woman beaming ear to ear as she listened in. "The little whirlwind aside... How have you been?"

"Oh me? It's been a good year. A very good year. It's lovely to hear everyone out and about again," Tabitha sighed, turning towards the open crowds. "Haven't heard this much positivity since Vantis was born..."

"That was ages ago at this point..." Wren sighed, rubbing her forearms. The first nips of the autumn frost were beginning to settle in.

Tabitha's clouded gaze fixated upon her companion. "How are you doing, dear?"

The merchant leaned back, resting her spine against the banister of the porch. The post creaked lightly under her weight. "There's... been a lot going on... Of course I'm worried about Harris's injuries, but he seems to be recovering well enough..."

"Men his age tend to believe they can do way more than is realistic..." she gave a solemn nod. "Things they haven't been able to accomplish in well over ten years..."

Wren smirked, scrunching her nose slightly as she saw the huntsman chew out the lad. "Usually, he's good at judging his abilities... but I suppose no one expected an angry bear during a camping trip."

"No one ever does! It's why you won't spot me camping!" the old woman laughed.

"I'm sure that's not the only reason, Tabitha," the dame gave her a wry grin.

"Oh, I can assure you, even without my eyes I could give those men a run for their coin!" Tabitha sneered, aggressively jabbing her cane out into the open air.

Wren couldn't help but belt out a laugh. "Glad you still got some fight left in you."

"Well, I still have to fight my grandson from time to time. Little brat," the old woman sniffed.

"And how is he?" Wren asked.

"Oh, good. His girlfriend is such a lovely lady. I wish he would grow some balls and ask to marry her someday! I would like to still be alive when they have their marriage dance!" Tabitha snapped, more playful than spiteful.

"Don't talk like that! I'm sure you got a few good years left in you!" the dame admonished.

"Who knows?" She shrugged, her shoulders popping. "The world is full of surprises."

"Then I guess we'll just have to light a fire under his ass, huh? Can't have you leaving with no regrets! Don't need your ghost scaring the daylights out of us!" Wren chuckled, tapping a boot on the ground.

"Most certainly not! The only ghost that haunts this wonderful place is that young man..." She creaked. Her eyes softened, gazing out towards the forest as she heard the squeaks of night creatures. "I used to hear him from time to time..." she sighed. "Though lately... I haven't heard anything at all. I wonder where he's off to? Perhaps he's at peace, seeing how well you raised his boy... Poor Adrian... that man was quite the whirlwind himself!"

Wren bit her tongue for a moment, shifting her gaze towards the blind man standing awkwardly as someone chatted with him. She grimaced. "Yeah, that... didn't disappear when we were in the war together."

"Obviously, the boy takes after his father! They're quite similar!" Tabitha chuckled, still hearing Vantis boasting in the distance. "Though I can't say he's nearly as charismatic..."

Wren snickered. "There's a lot of similarities, that's for certain. But it's clear he takes after his mother as well..."

"Brash as a goat," the crone remarked.

Wren glanced down at the dirt beneath her with a smirk. "About as stubborn as one too..."

"Though I believe that may have been from you, my dear." The old woman reached out and gingerly tapped the younger's hand. "It was you who raised him."

Wren sighed. "I suppose. The only other role model he has is Harris. And well..."

"He's an actual goat!" Tabitha chortled.

"I wouldn't say that to the old man! He prefers deer!" Wren retorted.

"Ah! I wouldn't dare! He's not that old anyways..." the grandmother remarked.

"Fifty ain't exactly young, Tabitha," the dame argued flatly.

"And what does that make me?" the old woman snapped.

"I don't know... You've been around ever since I came here... and you knew Adrian as a boy... that makes you... sixty-seven? Seventy?" Wren reasoned, staring up at the sky as she did some mental math.

"Sweetheart, I'm seventy-five!"

"Damn. Look at me being generous! You don't look a day over seventy!" Wren complimented.

Tabitha laughed once more. "Well aren't you just a doll?" She slapped her companion's leg lightly. "I could teach that man a thing or two..."

"Tabitha!"

"What? It's true! I'm allowed to dream! There's not a single older man in this bloody village and here comes this devilish bastard smelling like a peach!" the old woman exclaimed.

"I don't think you've smelled a peach!" the dame retorted.

"Ah..." Tabitha continued, ignoring Wren. "The first time my hands laid upon his face was the day I felt twenty years younger..."

"Tabitha! I don't want to hear about this!" Wren bemoaned playfully.

"Fine, fine," she grunted. "Never mind me! How's our newcomer, eh?"

Wren shrugged. "Fine. Rather overwhelmed. And it seems the townsfolk won't give him a break."

"It's not every day you hear of a blind man single-handedly taking on a bear," the old woman mused.

"He didn't 'take it on', he just led it off and guided the two back home..." Wren corrected.

414

"That's not what I heard. They say he wrestled it to the ground. That the wails in the night were him battling the beast," the elderly woman explained.

"Haven't known a single man who could wrestle a bear other than Adrian himself," Wren sniffed. "Even so, I would give a solid bet on the bear."

Tabitha chuckled. "Oh, I wouldn't know. I'm just an old woman."

"Yeah, well you're *our* old woman," Wren remarked. "So how about a drink? It's on me."

A giddy expression washed over the old woman's features. "Yes, yes... Do make haste. Before my grandson spots it! Hard ale!"

"I'll see what I can find," the merchant laughed, getting up and stretching her legs.

"Hurry! Before he comes back!" She shooed the woman on. Wren went over to the table, collecting a fresh glass of ale before returning, watching in shock as the old woman eagerly snatched the cup. She downed it in a smooth motion, letting out a sigh and a brief bow of gratitude.

"Good heavens, Tabitha! Pace yourself!" she admonished.

"Oy! Did you just give my grandmother alcohol?!" the grandson yelled, held back by his giggling girlfriend in the middle of the clearing.

"No, all I did was give her some apple cider. This is a party anyways, aren't we supposed to have fun?" Wren lied, giving the young man an innocent smile. Before the man could argue he was swept away into a dance, leaving his grandmother to her well-deserved treat. She turned towards Tabitha. "He's just jealous you could drink him under the table."

"I can out-drink anyone in this damn village..." she snapped.

"And let's not do that, huh? I'd rather you *didn't* die on such a fun night."

"We are here to celebrate the dead, not join them," Tabitha sighed, sipping at the remainder.

Noticing Adrian's discomfort in the distance, Wren began to move away. "Well, I need to go tend to our 'hero'. Will you be alright?"

The old woman nodded. "Run along now. Enjoy yourself, dear."

Chapter 34

The two bid each other farewell, the dame hastily making her way back to Adrian's side. The troll was relieved to sense her scent and familiar shadow. "Having fun, Lion?"

"I'm losing my fucking mind," the troll growled, trying to dodge past another couple.

"Well, here. This should take the edge off," Wren said, holding out something that smelled sweet and savory. Adrian tentatively reached out and plucked it from her hand, examining it. From the taste of it, it was some honeyed meat on a stick.

"Oh for fuck's sake, why must they put sugar on everything?" the fae grumbled, clearly enjoying the food.

"It's a party!" she remarked, twirling around him to dodge some children. "It's supposed to be grotesquely sweet!"

"Positively dreadful," he hissed, continuing to chomp down. He lashed his black tongue across his lips, lapping up every drop that ran down his chin. Thankfully, the other villagers were too distracted to notice the oddity. "But, I suppose I can understand. Finding a beehive was a treat much like this. The Green Man was oft to hide them from me," he recalled.

"Maybe he just didn't want a repeat of the mountain lion incident," she mused, leading him towards the center.

"It was a treat! Hardly a mainstay. I would save the hive long after I collected it..." Adrian explained. Wren stared as if he had bees crawling out of his ears. She sighed before shaking her head.

"What do you want to do next?" she asked.

"What do you usually do?" the troll grunted.

"Well," she began, stopping in her tracks. "I usually patrol around, checking in on vendors and villagers to make sure everyone is having fun... things of that sort. Otherwise, I suppose I just watch and listen to the others enjoy themselves."

"Feh, I can hear plenty already. Something about me wrestling a bear or some nonsense," the troll growled.

"Then how about we go somewhere you can't hear them?" Wren suggested. The blind man merely nodded and she led on, over towards the fountain. There were less people here; only the minstrels seemed to be present, playing their lilting melodies. The two rested on a bench nearby, gazing out towards the crowd as Wren began to nibble on her treats.

"What's it like out there? Can you describe it?" Adrian asked after some time.

Wren took a moment to swallow her food before explaining all that stood before them. The men drinking merrily at the tavern, the couples and children dancing in the town center, people milling about the food and game stalls, the traveling jester telling his ridiculous jokes to the kids, the staff hard at work setting up the bonfire, and the roast blazing over a massive open pit. She told him of the clear, colorful sky that was giving way to a starry night. The blossoms exploding with color, and the joy upon every face. Wren described it all. And Adrian couldn't help but wish to see it himself. "And there are the vendors hawking their wares. Competitors placed right next to each other to entice a little drama," she explained with a smirk.

Adrian chuckled. "Oh? Starting battles at a festival?"

Wren gestured towards the yapping salesman fighting over customers. "Well, they're here to work. This helps light a fire under their asses, and the competition drives down prices. In the end, it all comes back to benefit the Lionel Company and Willowbend proper..."

"Spoken like a true merchant," Adrian sighed. "And where did Wren, the honest baker, go?"

She laughed. "She's usually home trying to put food on the table. That's when she isn't battling an obstinate teenager and managing a business of course." Adrian let out an amused exhale and looked on, trying to give the shadows color and detail. Wren continued. "Oddly enough, I've been able to exercise that part of me far more since you've been around... It's a nice change of pace."

The fae dwelled upon that for a moment. "You needn't play any parts."

She shrugged. "I'm not hiding behind it. I like it. Anyways, what more can I describe...?" the woman picked at her teeth with the kabob stick, glancing about. "Well, I'm certain the smell of food is bombarding you, though, that's not all there is. There's perfumes too, extracted from the dried plants and concentrates we managed to procure from other companies..."

"Can't say I smell much of it. All I can smell right now is you," Adrian sniffed.

"And what does that smell like to you?"

"Like someone who's worked hard. Constantly sweating, yet putting effort into their hygiene," the troll explained. A trace of alarm washed over the woman. Adrian could see her silhouette lean down and take a whiff by her armpit without raising the limb. He continued on. "It also reminds me of dirt and wildflowers... the kind of scent I could smell far away from Willowbend; the scent of the rolling plains and fields of the outer world... A scent I truly cannot completely describe in the mortal tongue for its intricate nature..."

Wren blinked. "I've never heard that part of you..." she drew up her feet onto the bench and rested her arms against them, laying her head on her knees. The dame was smiling deeply, her eyes squinting in the evening starlight. "Even if I knew it was always something you had..." The man gave her a quizzical look, cocking his head slightly. "The stories you used to tell before you became a soldier... I always forget that you once aspired to be a storyteller... A poet? Bard, perhaps?"

"Well, I certainly prefer that term over minstrel," Adrian laughed.

"Based on how you acted in camp, I say you could perform a fine flyting!" she exclaimed, making the man laugh. "The way you could chew people out, spit insults to their face, and still get away with it without someone trying to cave your face in!"

"There's an artistry to it, my friend," he puffed out his chest in faux pride.

"And even then, even when you struggled to speak, you could put on one hell of a show. It's just different seeing it now. When it's... well... you." Her voice rang in his ears. He could imagine those beautiful eyes boring into him, her smile deep and wonderful. A spark of pain hit his gut, and he silently cursed himself.

"Me, huh?" Adrian reached up with a hand and touched at his throat, remembering the grotesque fleshy skin that sagged like a dewlap from his neck. What used to be a reminder of what he lost.

"Yeah, with your voice back, while all your strength and fervor remain," Wren began. "It's like meeting a new person. Even if I see some of the same... It's strange how many new things I learn about you."

"Is that a bad thing?" he asked, nervousness edging his tone.

"No, not at all. It just has me wondering how much of it has always been there and what is from these past thirteen years." Adrian saw her shadow turn towards the party, her hands clasped loosely together. "I'm starting to think that maybe... those years did not change nearly as much as I thought..." She readjusted her position on the bench. "It's a lot to think about. And as crazy as these past few months have been, it feels like things are finally settling down. Even with the threat of attackers on the horizon."

"We'll be ready," the troll reassured.

Wren nodded. "It's honestly nostalgic. Having to watch each other's backs. Being on guard. I wouldn't be surprised if I've gone soft these past few years."

"Based on how you dealt with the last incident, I'd point to the contrary," the troll sneered.

"Firing a big ass crossbow isn't exactly equivalent to driving an axe in someone's skull on the battlefield."

"And yet, there you were, cleaving a fae's head from her body with one smooth stroke..." he purred.

Wren merely grunted begrudgingly. "Maybe you're right. Definitely out of shape though."

"Well, if you need a sparring partner, I might be available. Since Harris is down, I have no one to practice with."

"Careful now, it's starting to sound like a date," she chuckled. Adrian raised his eyebrows under the blindfold.

"And yet I'm betrothed to another," he snorted.

Wren flinched. "It was a jest... my apologies." They both shifted at a sudden sound. It was Vantis, heard over the music and the distance.

"Uncle, uncle! Tell them about the bear! Tell them!" the boy pleaded.

"Ugh, fine!" Harris growled. He sighed, turning to face the horde of eager eyes before them. "So here I am, sleeping by the fire. This kid over here is keeping watch. Darkest night you've ever seen. I'm just on the edge of a dream when Vantis here runs off shrieking into the woods. Startled me half to death! I jump to my feet, looking around before I see this mad bear, charging after the lad through the trees!" He gestured above him with his hands, trying to give shape to the supposed mighty beast. "I wake Lion's rear end so he doesn't find himself alone at camp before racing on after the kid. Before I know it, I'm standing between a boy and a bear with finger-length, razor sharp claws!"

"Yeah! It was like nine feet tall!" Vantis flailed wildly with his hands, trying to leap into the air to show size. Some of the children gasped.

"Nonsense! It was no more than a yearling, hardly 'big' by any means!" the huntsman retorted.

"Oh yeah? If that wasn't the biggest thing then what is?!" Vantis snapped, trying to drag the story away from the faux tale. Even he feared the lie stretching too thin.

"Well, now if you want to talk big and dangerous, let me tell you about the inferno demon I fought with your father!" Harris laughed, taking another drink handed over by another villager. The rosy-cheeked man began to recall the tale of a massive possessed boar that nearly burnt down a quarter of the southern forests, and how the encounter had ended with his legs mutating. Both children and adults listened on with bated breath, eager to hear this treacherous tale.

Adrian couldn't help but smile. "Oh well, there he goes..."

"A little alcohol is all it takes for him to start telling stories..." Wren shook her head with a smirk. "That, and he's probably just excited to not be paraded around by the boy for once. Which reminds me of something..." At her companion's quizzical expression, she continued. "When he was little, Vantis used to climb into things and cause all sorts of trouble. One time, Harris had enough of him and threw him into a wheelbarrow before racing through town, bouncing the kid all around. They caused a terrible ruckus," she chuckled, her eyes sparkling.

Adrian smirked. "And let me guess, the boy enjoyed it?"

"He did! Oh! And then he insisted it was *his* turn to push, and Harris had to sit in it! He could barely get the thing to move a few feet and was so frustrated!" The woman went on, recalling this memory with a loving smile. "Then he came home crying to me that Harris was fat! All because he was too heavy to push. Vantis never even considered that he was too small to push around a fully grown man!" Adrian exploded with laughter, catching a few individuals off guard. Wren discussed other silly incidents in their lives, all with a level of enthusiasm that set his mind at ease. After a few hours of this, she spoke up once more. "Do you want anything? I'm going to be heading back up to the food tables for some seconds."

"Ah, if you could get me some of that apple cider, that would be wonderful," he graciously bowed his head.

Wren merely nodded and stood up, disappearing from his limited sight. As her footsteps faded into the general noise of the festival, he heard the music die down. The bards were taking a moment to breathe and drink some water, discussing amongst each other who would go next and what song they should play. The sounds of the villagers around him, the voices of both oddly familiar and new people alike, the vendors in the distance, laughter all around... it was enough to transport the man to a different time.

Adrian was young then, perhaps sixteen years old. Other young women about his age were attempting to court him on this night, even if all their comments were shallow. They loved his face, his grace, but the moment he brought up his writings he saw the light fade from their eyes, disinterested in his tales and poetry. The teenager sighed, sad that none shared his love for penmanship. Warriors were far more intriguing to the villager palette, what with grandiose tales of war, fortune, and terrifying scars. They bore no interest in his soft fairytales.

Either way, the festival was a time to celebrate, and what a better way for him to do so than to use the gorgeous voice he was given. He stepped in the middle of the square as people danced and fiddles played. He waited at just the right time, when the music stopped, to begin a tune.

A voice rang out across the village, strong and true. It was beautiful, enough to capture the hearts of the party-goers nearest to him.

"From the winter came the spring,
From the spring came the summer.
From her came the autumn,
With all its lovely color.

An artist and a songstress,
She drew me within her gaze,
She knew that I was hopeless,
Without her autumn haze.

I love you, my fall dear.
I love your cherished song.
I love you far and near dear,
I can never wait too long.

Please do not forsake me,
Please don't you ever fear.
Please come stay by my side,
My darling autumn dear."

Some couples stopped dancing. Children quieted down at their parents' urging. The minstrels gazed on. Wren was still chatting at the stand, unaware of what was occuring behind her.

"When the winter caresses my cheek,
I can't help but turn away.
Though the frost may make me weak,
My love shall never fray.

The spring shall come and dazzle,
With all her lovely lights.
I shall never be your vineyard vassal.
You cannot beat my love's sights.

I love you, my fall dear.
I love your cherished song.
I love you far and near dear,
I can never wait too long.

Please do not forsake me,
Please don't you ever fear.
Please come stay by my side,
My darling autumn dear."

At this point, more than half the festival had gone silent, enraptured by the blind man's voice. Harris noticed this before long and stopped mid-sentence at the crux of his story, his mouth slightly agape. Vantis glanced around. "What's going on? Why did you-" Then he heard it too. Adrian's voice belting out over Willowbend, echoing over the forest. One of the bards stepped up and pulled out his lute, softly providing instrumental accompaniment to the song.

"Summer, oh you gallant beast,
Your heat rages ever on,
But your might harbors no feast,
No not until you're gone.

One day she will wake up,
And paint the forest anew.
Then and there I'll see you,
Beneath that harvest moon.

I love you, my fall dear.
I love your cherished song.
I love you far and near dear,
I can never wait too long.

Please do not forsake me,
Please don't you ever fear.
Please come stay by my side,
My darling autumn dear..."

Adrian went silent, his accompaniment following soon after. Only the natural melody of the fall night purveyed the square. The troll quickly became aware of the unnatural quiet around him, nervously shifting in his seat to spot the villagers' shadows standing, only the children still running around. His lips fell, a creeping sense of fear racing up his spine. Did they know who he was? Did he give something away? Was he not supposed to sing that song? Before he could shrink away, he heard a clapping sound from the minstrels. From a single set of hands to many more. Some of the villagers snapped out of their confused nostalgia, either giving the blind man words of encouragement and cheers, or merely returning to their previous festivities. Either way, Lion had made his presence known, and that terrified him.

"Wow, how the hell did the stranger know Lord Adrian's song?" one villager beside Vantis whispered.

"I guess our little village is more popular than we thought!" another quipped.

"Lion's a natural!"

Harris was silent, a quiet mourning washing over him. A mourning he didn't think he would ever feel again. The huntsman lowered his gaze and held his scarred hands, lost in thought. "Uncle?" Vantis called, stepping by his side to check on him. The man's brown eyes were dark, darting about as if gazing upon a map. The teenager frowned, resting a hand on the arm of his chair.

"I just... need a moment..." he whispered, his gravelly voice gentle and pained.

His father's song was famous, and he was certain Harris had heard it plenty of times... But it never hurt his uncle the way it did now. All Vantis could do was try to shoo the protesting listeners, urging them to wait while Harris gathered his thoughts. The old veteran just furrowed his brow and closed his eyes.

Wren was at the bar, two drinks in hand as the people around her went back to their merriment. Her eyes locked on the fidgeting man, lost in some unknown sea of emotion. Before she could dwell upon it further, she shook her head and approached the sea of individuals bombarding him. "Alright, everyone! Give the man some space!" she yelled, parting the crowd with her shoulder. Most of the gawkers left with cheer, sending their congratulations as they ran off to more festivities. The band beside him patted Adrian's back as they started to play, inspired enough by the performance to play their own rendition of *Autumn Dear* themselves. The blind man grumbled and scooted away, desperately avoiding further interaction. Wren sat down beside him and held out a drink. As he sensed her presence nearby, the troll began to let out a held breath.

"Stars and bones, look at what I've gone and done now!" He gingerly reached out and grasped the cup, gulping down the honeyed ale with way too much gusto.

"Not only are you a poet, but you're also a singer? Definitely wasted your talents in the military, if you ask me!" she teased, nudging his shoulder. The troll scowled, shifting as he nursed at his cup.

"Yes, and look at what all that nonsense has done!" he hissed.

It was the sound of concerned villagers and a distinct shuffling that caught both of their attention. Wren saw Tabitha, shakily holding her cane as she drove herself onward against pained joints. Some onlookers offered their aid, only for the old woman to hold up a hand. She made her way over towards the troll, stopping but a few feet away. Her creaking voice whispered, "Adrian?" The fae man froze in terror. His talons scored deep marks into the wooden cup as his back pressed fearfully against the back of the bench. Wren clenched her jaw, sitting stock still. "Is that you?" she croaked. At the sound of the protesting wood, the woman recoiled her skeletal hand. "Please, please let me know if it's you..."

Adrian grimaced, leaning forward and allowing the elderly woman to run her hands across his face. Wren kept silent, just watching on. Tabitha's clouded eyes watered, her wrinkled lips quivering with emotion. At the sight of her unstable legs, the dame suddenly stood up and rested a hand against her back. "Please, Tabitha. Sit." The crone did not protest, settling down next to the man as Wren guided her.

"You were dead..." she whispered to him. Her hands clasped his with an unusual amount of strength. "You died... But you came back... You came home..." All Adrian could do was face the withered shadow, an overwhelming sense of familiarity shackling his limbs. "You smell different... And you feel different, but I'd recognize that voice anywhere," she stated warmly. "I remember the voice of that beautiful boy. I never forgot. I could never forget."

"...Please," the troll pleaded, curling his fingers around hers. "Don't tell anyone... I... I don't..."

Tabitha tapped his hand. "Telling them is not my decision. Even ghosts must have their reasons..." Wren let out a ragged sigh, loosening the tension in her shoulders. "None of that matters," the old woman shook her head. "You're home." She touched the side of his cheek, with all the love of a grandmother. Adrian was overwhelmed with memories of this woman.

She helped his mother give birth to him, and ended up being the one to save her life that day. She always encouraged him and taught him to appreciate the wilds around them. She always seemed to listen to his stories, gleefully clapping when he sang his little songs. She was the closest person he could call 'grandmother', and it seemed that she never lost her love for life, even as her eyes failed her.

"Welcome home, Adrian," she reached over and held the man in a hug, patting his back gently.

"...Tabitha... Thank you..." the troll whispered, embracing her in turn. They held each other for a moment before pulling away.

Wren rested a hand on the woman's shoulder. "It's getting a bit cold, is it not? Let's get you home."

Tabitha nodded slowly. "Yes, I do believe it is. I'm glad I got to hear you one last time..." She rubbed her weeping eyes with the back of her hand. "I'm making a scene..."

"No you're not," Wren consoled, rubbing her back as she helped the woman stand. As they both turned away, Wren called out. "Hey Lion? Can you go check on Harris?" Adrian could only nod, numbly getting to his feet to maneuver through the crowd.

Chapter 35

Harris appeared to have moved away from the crowd of children, now resting at the edge of the congregation while Vantis entertained the little ones. The lad was doing well, wildly moving his hands as he exaggerated his voice. It was enough to keep them off his back. Something the older man was appreciative of. His umber eyes moved from the eager listeners towards the hunched over blind man approaching him. "Lion? Are you faring well?"

Adrian stood beside him for a moment before crouching down. "I'm fine..."

"That's a hell of a set of pipes on you! Didn't expect that!" he exclaimed. His smile was strained, the tense edge to his tone enough for the troll to notice. Harris frowned. "Oy, Vantis!" The boy's head swiveled over mid-roar, his face twisted to a comical degree. "You got this handled, right?"

"Yeah! I'm just about to tell them how the boar exploded!" the teenager beamed.

The huntsman chuckled. "Don't disappoint!" He shifted his gaze towards the awkward fae beside him. "Hey, Lion. Could you do me a favor and push me out to the edge of town? I want to get some fresh air away from all the action." The troll nodded, getting up before walking the chair-bound man to the eastern edge of the village, far enough that the voices couldn't drown them out, yet close enough to hear them prep the bonfire for the dinner dance. Adrian plopped down in the cool grass next to his friend, both them facing the woods. "It's odd. I never knew much about that part of you. It's hard to explain but... that song felt like you," the huntsman remarked.

"I just got lost in thought, that's all," the fae sniffed. The fairies were dancing jovially in the trees, enjoying the music even from this distance.

"Where'd you learn a song like that? I never heard it outside Willowbend. Was it something you grew up with?" Harris pressed.

Adrian sighed, resting his elbows on his crossed legs. "No, it's an original work of mine."

"Really?"

"Yes, it's a song I made as a boy," the troll grunted.

"Heh, it certainly appears the town has taken it and ran!" the hunter chuckled. "I think they've done an excellent job preserving it." The fae scoffed. "Honestly, out of everything we did, that's probably my favorite of your legacies... It's something you made, not killed. Not some grand accomplishment either, just... a wonderful little tradition for a village festival. Regardless of intent. That's probably the way I'd want to be remembered."

"Oh, don't start..." Adrian gave him a wry grin.

"Well, now that you got your voice back, why don't you write a song about me before I die?" Harris smirked, nudging the fae's shoulder.

"I'd call it the 'Obstinate Goat'," the man sniffed.

"Ha! Make it a drinking song! Something everyone can get tipsy to, not mournful or any of that nonsense!" the huntsman laughed.

"Ugh, don't say that," the troll grumbled. "Sounds like you're already prepping for your funeral..."

"Well, I don't want everyone to be a sad sod during the ceremony! I want people to tell stupid jokes and stories! Make a real party of it," he explained.

Adrian scowled. "I'm not doing anything of the sort for a long time, you hear me?!"

Harris belted out a loud laugh. "Oh I know, I know. I'm not planning on dying yet!"

"I damn well know you aren't as weak as you say you are! I've seen you sneak off without your wheelchair!" the fae snapped.

"Gotta piss once in a while! And Heavens' forbid I go shit in a bed pan! You know how humiliating that is?" the hunter protested with a growl.

"I do," Adrian stated flatly.

"Ah, right. The doctor." Harris sighed, turning to face the forest. Even as the leaves laid heavily upon the tangled brush, they remained a steadfast guard against the outside elements. "Never did track that man down, even after all these years."

"I can barely recall much of anything beyond his face," the troll admitted, following his companion's gaze.

"I know you met him once or twice outside Terminahill, but I never got a chance to truly speak with him myself," the hunter explained, resting his hands on his blanketed lap. It was getting too cold for his aging bones, enough for his furred legs to tremble. "Packed up shop as you rose through the ranks. Suppose he didn't want to cause trouble for you..."

"Feh. He caused enough problems by keeping me alive," the fae joked dryly.

Harris snorted. "If anything, he did this land a service."

Adrian gave him a dubious look. "Are you honestly saying that you believe one man saved this whole bloody country?"

"Nothing of the sort. I'm saying that you were a major player. Without your words, your actions, no one would have believed it possible to beat back the Golossian Empire. Further still, you gave mutated freaks like me hope. Hope that we still had a place in this world, even when the powers that be were determined to snuff us out." he retorted, seriousness in his furrowed brow.

The troll scoffed, nestling deeper in his seat. "I did nothing. My men won those battles, not me."

"Under your leadership," Harris added with a smile. This was the first time since the change that Adrian ever referred to those soldiers as such. He turned to face his old friend, examining his amusingly frustrated expression. The two were silent for a moment, letting those old memories fade like the musicians behind them.

Harris thought back to the song he sung, the level of passion in his voice. He snorted. "If I didn't know any better, I'd say you wrote that song for a girl. What made you write it?"

The troll shrugged. "It's quite literal. I loved autumn above all other seasons. She was the most fiery and beautiful."

"Huh, and here I was expecting something more romantic," he snorted.

"Heh, you might be right. I believe the meaning changed... because at that moment, all I could think about was her..." Adrian breathed, massaging the pain above his intestines. The face unseen. A voice unheard. Yet there she remained, dancing in his eyes.

The huntsman pondered this for a moment. "Do you remember anything more about her?"

436

"No," the troll shook his head, clenching his fists. "It hurts too much."

"Don't hurt yourself over it. It'll come back... in due time," the hunter advised. "Old Dusk will be here soon enough. Perhaps you'll get your answers then?"

"That, or you'll find a massive troll in your midst once more..." Adrian curled in on himself.

"Eh, as long as you're still in there, I don't think I'll give a shit. And if you're not... Well, Wren ain't letting you get away that easily." Harris gave him a wry grin.

"She said she would chase me down and beat the sense back into me..." Adrian growled. Harris started laughing, his rosy cheeks clearly evident as he tossed his head back. "And why are you laughing?!" the troll snapped.

"Ah, don't mind me! Just dirty old man thoughts! I'm five drinks in and haven't had supper yet!"

Adrian puffed out his chest comically. "Oh, come off it! Will I have to bowl you over for fair Wren's honor?"

Harris only laughed harder. "I'm certain I'll fall out of this chair on my own! You needn't defend her! If I try to get up right now, a dinner of dirt will come to greet me!" The two men cackled together, scaring some of the nearby fairies away; fleeing deeper into the woods.

The troll paused. "Oh, no one is around, right? I suppose one little peek wouldn't hurt," Adrian mused, pulling the blindfold down to gaze into those woods. Even in the deep shadows, the colors of the fiery leaves dazzled him. A warm smile graced his features. "Ah, finally... There's the forest I love so dearly..." he breathed. "Though I'm not certain I could go back to it the way I used to..."

Harris shrugged. "You could always live on the outskirts like me."

"Oh? And what? Live together like two moody old men?" the beautiful man purred.

The huntsman snorted, "Well, you could set up your own hut somewhere out here, far from me if I stink that much." The troll laughed while shaking his head. They enjoyed the moment, hearing the sound of roaring cheers as the bonfire came to life, illuminating their backs and casting their faces in dull shadow. People were gayly dancing while others waited in line for their cut of the roast, the activity of the town coalescing towards the center.

"Beautiful night..." the old man breathed, easing his wounded back against the chair. The pain was dull, throbbing. His hooves pulled away from the edges and grazed the grass, his burnt flesh long since healed. Another quirk of his mutation. Harris couldn't wait to immerse himself in those comforting woods once more.

"Yeah," Adrian agreed, feeding off of that desire to disappear into nature's loving embrace. "But I suppose we better return..." he sighed, pulling his blindfold back over his face.

"Can't let them get all the good cuts, can we?" the hunter sighed. Harris grimaced while stretching his limbs, cussing as his back protested. The troll stood up and gripped the back of the chair, starting to make their way back to the party. "Who knows, maybe they'll let a cripple go first?"

"Well, if I move fast enough, I'm certain I could bowl over the opposition..." Adrian mused with a sneer.

"Heavenly Father, don't you dare! I'll throw up on you!" Harris growled.

"What? I'm blind! I might just trip!" the fae man gasped, coyly pressing a hand against his chest.

The huntsman growled as they approached the line. "Vantis!" he roared.

The teenager was in the middle of a story, holding a pair of branches above his head like antlers. He turned with an annoyed scowl. "What?!"

"Get me away from this blind idiot!" the hunter yelped.

"Oops! There's a rock in the road!" Adrian teased, lurching forward.

"You bastard!" the deer-legged man yelped, clasping the armrests for dear life.

The boy rushed up and moved Adrian aside, letting his devious father cackle and walk away into the line. "You alright?" Vantis asked.

"Outside of almost running over some poor sod, fine. Come along now, if we get some food now, I'll finish the story," his uncle sighed, urging the boy onwards.

"Ugh, fine... I was just telling them the story about the time I hunted a buck in the woods!" Vantis shoved him along, passing by some of the others in line. They graciously let the man pass to the front.

"Oh, and when did you do that?" the hunter goaded, smirking as he gazed behind the child.

"You remember!" Vantis cried. "When I snuck out that one night and met Li-" The teenager stopped, glancing behind himself to see where his uncle was looking. There, looming above the child, was Wren giving him a mighty glare. "Uh... nevermind. You know what? I'm full of fibs."

Adrian made it through the line relatively quickly, requesting a cut of the haunch. The cooks were generous in their portions, giving him two thick slices of juicy flesh that made his mouth water. He heard and saw the shadow of a bone get tossed into a bucket beside them, already tending to the next person. With a smooth motion, he plucked the bone free and tucked it away on his plate. His black tongue eagerly lapped up leaking saliva as he left, plopping down in a grassy corner next to a house, away from everyone else. Talons pulled the bone free from flesh, cracking it clean in half with his teeth as he guzzled the fresh marrow down. Powerful jaws crunched on the meal, swallowing eagerly before anyone else could see. The taste of fresh bone on his tongue was enough to make the troll shiver with delight, enjoying a normal meal for once as he gnashed his teeth through the cooked flesh. While he always preferred his food raw, something about the seasoned, roasted taste made it nostalgic, an old memory of him surrounded by friends as he dug into his dinner with glee. Lost in carnivorous ecstasy, he neglected to notice someone approaching, sitting down next to him. He lowered his plate before sniffing the air. Wren was beside him. Adrian released the tension in his shoulders, turning to meet her shadow as she ate. "I smell bones," he remarked.

She chuckled. "Yeah, want them? Managed to snag a rack of ribs." Wren held out some large, curved shapes. The troll eagerly held out his hands, accepting the bones as she placed them in his palms. She couldn't help but snort at the line of saliva oozing from his lip as he turned away and chowed down.

Harris, who settled beside them, chimed in, "When I'm done with my steaks, I'll hand over the bones as well."

"Thank the stars..." the fae muttered, chomping down on the warm meal.

Wren leaned back against the house wall. "Thank you for restraining yourself from eating the whole damn thing. How does it taste?"

"Divine," the beast grunted, protectively hunched over his food.

"We managed to procure it from down south, from one of the ranges by Lion's Rest," she explained, nibbling at a rib. "Cost us a fortune..."

"So, do you think it was worth it?" Harris grunted.

"Every penny," she beamed as she tossed another bone towards the famished troll.

She held out some of her vegetables towards Vantis. "Now come on, you. I know it's a festival but you need to eat some greens."

"Aww, come on, Wren! I ate some onion slices! Is that not enough?"

"No, at least have some peas," she held out a bowl. She wriggled it towards his scrunching face. "Come on! I know you like peas! They're buttered!" With an embarrassed sigh, the teenager snatched the bowl from her hand and began to nibble, looking around to see if any of his peers noticed the argument. "There, at least get some variety in you..."

"I've got plenty of variety!" the boy snapped.

"Says the lad who won't touch his spinach..." she muttered, mixing her plate of steamed roots together.

"They're repulsive! It's just leaves!" The child was aghast. Adrian, raising his blindfold a little, cast her a glance as the two argued. He moved his hand in a signal.

Jackass.

Wren snickered, pressing her fork against her plate as she held up a hand of her own.

Pain in the ass.

As the two laughed, Harris swallowed his mouthful and signaled.

Why not both?

All three were cackling, with the boy scowling at the center. "What's so funny?!"

It took a moment for Wren to catch her breath. "Sorry, it's a language we made up. It's a mix of military signals and a personalized sign language we made so Adrian could talk to us outside of his chalkboard. It made it easier to communicate when we normally couldn't," she explained, trying to stifle her laughing.

"Yeah? What did you say?" the child glowered.

"Nothing but wonderful things," the troll oozed, giving a gentle flourish of his hand.

"Oh yes," Harris agreed solemnly.

"Just strategizing a plan to make sure no one spoils the fun," Wren nodded, setting more food in her mouth. She chewed thoughtfully.

Vantis scowled. "Uh huh. You're lying."

"Maybe the truth is only for people who eat their greens..." Wren mused with a smirk.

The teenager paused. "Ick."

"Oh, it wouldn't kill you to eat some cabbage..." She pressed.

"Yeah? Then I'll end up part-deer like uncle!"

The older man set his fork, laden with chunks of roast, down on his plate before sitting up. He turned towards the boy with a flat expression. "I'm a hunter."

"Then why do you act like such a vegetable?" the boy teased.

The old man gingerly shoved the lad with his hoof. The child grunted. "Just because I'm in a wheelchair doesn't mean I can't fight back."

"You're cheating! You got hooves!" Vantis laughed, clearly not taking any of this seriously. The adults around him didn't seem to either, all their faces set in smiles and chuckles.

"Cease your tomfoolery or I'll throttle the both of you," Adrian sighed, pulling the blindfold back over his exposed eye.

"Yes, commander," Harris answered with a wry smile. The troll turned and sniffed in irritation.

Chapter 36

An hour later, after every plate and utensil was collected, the dancing started. The minstrels started playing their joyous tunes while adults and children alike pranced by the bonfire. Those remaining in the audience clapped in beat, laughing and urging the dancers on. Adrian was absentmindedly mumbling the words to the song under his breath. "Ah. I believe I know this one."

Wren yelled over the clapping. "It's a classic!"

"I used to dance to it quite often..." the troll mused, lost in rosy memories. "A part of me wishes to join them once more..."

"Oh?" The woman smiled, swiveling her head to face him. "Well, your wish is my command," she stated, standing before him with an outstretched hand.

"W-what?" The fae gasped, an uncharacteristic sense of embarrassment creeping up his spine. Even so, his quivering hand reached out and wrapped around her warm palm.

"Come along now! It's a good tune!" She laughed, pulling the blind man to his feet and leading him through the crowd. He turned away, feeling the eyes of the onlookers burrow into him as they cheered along. She dragged him to the center of the empty clearing, taking his hands into hers. While at first she led, skipping along to the song as they wheeled about, Adrian quickly found himself lost in the moment.

His feet glided across the dirt, soon guiding her along the floor with elegance. She was laughing, her shadow overwhelming his vision as he spun her around. And before he knew it, his smile opened wide, revealing his fangs as he began to laugh as well. The crowd was cheering the Lady of Willowbend and Lion on, watching in excitement as they dominated the scene with their joy and passion.

Vantis eyed the two, standing beside his laughing uncle as he clapped along. The boy's brow furrowed, watching them dance jovially. He saw Wren's face, the light sparkling in her eyes as she gazed up at him. He saw his father, with the most sincere smile he had ever seen plastered on his face, a beautiful laugh exiting his mouth. They were so happy...

Were he and mum that happy?

His heart skipped a beat. He clutched at his chest.

What if father no longer loves mother? What if he... What if he abandons her for Wren? He's... never that happy...

446

The blind man dipped her down, not noticing his wavy ebony hair sliding free from his hood. It wreathed his elegant face in statuesque beauty. She reached up, sliding the hair back into place smoothly with a single hand. Wren's smile deepened as Adrian pulled her up, skipping along in circles as they carried on, the two beginning to sing.

Father... won't care about mum anymore... He's losing her... because she's not here...

Vantis's face creased into a grimace.

If only she was here... or...

The boy froze, seeing their faces so close as they sang. The light of the bonfire cast them in a fairytale-esque glow, blinding them in the heat of passion. His mind was made up. He would say it tonight. He wouldn't let his mum be just a letter. He wouldn't let her disappear. He wouldn't let father and her love be just a faded memory-

"Oy! Go out there and have fun, will ya?" Harris snapped.

"What?! No!" he protested.

"Oh? Come on, surely there's someone you wanna dance with?" the huntsman urged, nudging his side. The boy teetered a little.

"No way! There's no passion out there!" the boy sniffed, crossing his arms and turning away. "No, my passion is the bow!" The huntsman blinked, taking a moment to process this before his snorting transformed into a howling laughter. Harris doubled over, unable to fight the absurdity of the statement as his eyes watered. "W-what are you laughing about?! Stop it!" Vantis hissed. The huntsman slammed a fist on his arm rest as he began to cough violently, a ridiculous smile creasing his face. The boy immediately became alarmed at the coughing, moving over to hold the man steady. "U-uncle!? Hey! Catch your breath!" The boy hastily reached for the hunter's water skin and handed it over. Eventually, Harris took a moment to breathe, accepting the drink before continuing to chuckle once more. "Look! Look! I'll go dance or whatever! Just stop dying!" Vantis yelled, starting to move away from his uncle.

"Go have fun, you little brat!" Harris coughed, leaning back in his seat. His wrinkled umber eyes turned towards Adrian and Wren, watching the troll accidentally step on her foot.

"Hey! And I thought you were supposed to be the graceful one!" she admonished.

"I'm blind, Wren!" Adrian laughed.

"No excuse!" she playfully snapped.

"Oh? Then let me stick this linen upon your brow and see how you fare!" his noble voice teased.

"Dear me, no!" Wren protested coyly. As the jaunty tune fell away, another took its place, this song more reserved as it told the story of a young maiden and a noble knight. They slowed in turn, with the troll gracefully bowing before her as he dramatically acted out the song. He too knew of this one, *Of Midnight's Calming Dew*. The ballad of a knight that would battle the winter's hells, all to give his love a beautiful mountain flower. Adrian spun around Wren with the experience of a practiced dancer, a playful smirk upon his lips. She gave him an exaggerated curtsy, following him as the story progressed. Before she knew it, he had dipped her down once more, the blindfold shifted just enough for the troll to gaze down upon her. The firelight made her skin softly shine, the darkness in her eyes reflecting that powerful flame. Her hair fell around her, her braid messy as they moved about.

She's beautiful...

Adrian's smile twitched.

"Oh, come on now! Now you're just showing off!" she laughed.

"What? I used to do this every year!"

Wren rolled her eyes as he pulled her up in a smooth motion. People were beginning to scatter, from the dance, from the crowd. The song was winding down, leaving them in that warm firelight. "I need to go back to my job now..." she sighed, pulling away from his warm hands. "There's still the gift-giving and cleanup to manage."

"Very well then," he bowed, readjusting the mask over his eyes. He had never appeared less like a troll. "Then I shall see you for the ceremony." Wren started to turn, making her way to the tables. Adrian's mouth opened on its own. "Wren?" She turned, her eyes trained upon him as the shadows moved around them. His lips quivered. "You... dance pretty well for someone with two left feet!"

"Ha!" she laughed. "And you dance well for a blind man!"

His smile drifted as she moved away, leaving him in that clearing. Adrian's talons fell to his sides, grimacing to himself. His mouth opened with the final line of the song.

"And I did it all for you,
Upon this midnight's calming dew..."

~~~~~~

Most people had gone away for the night, eager to continue with the harvest the following day. Some were drunk, others tired from all the action, even more amidst the stupor of a fine meal. But those who remained, the small children, their parents, and the lovers; they all gathered by a decorated table laden with gifts. Adrian was amongst them, sitting patiently in the crowd as the young children received their birthseason gifts. Painfully loud squeals of delight assaulted his ears, making his face crease with annoyance. They danced about with their new toys and dolls, slamming into their parents with gratitude before parading off with their prizes. The parents, most seemingly too exhausted to fight back, merely followed along, attempting to herd the little ones to bed.

The slightly older children were given tools and other trade implements, including little Corzan. Farin peered down from his puffed out chest, proudly patting the boy's back as he gave the lad his first set of professional tools. His stoic face was interrupted by his bushy mustache curling into an obvious smile, which only grew further as the boy slammed into his stomach for a hug. It was a tender moment that made the distant troll smile.

How long had the lad been waiting for those tools?

Next up, the young lovers' exchanged gifts, in honor of their birth season and their love. Jewelry and handcrafted goods graced their hands as they danced about their loves, the mushy tone enough to draw the remaining children away in disgust. Soon enough, it was Adrian's turn to present his gift. He stood up proudly and strode over to the table, thumbing about until he found the wooden box he had so carefully crafted. Some whispers rose up, watching this stranger engage in their tradition. The pads of his fingers trailed across the rough engravings as he pulled it free and pinpointed Wren's scent. He approached her beside the table, holding out the gift. The fae had never felt so ridiculously nervous, his hands quaking slightly as the woman took the box into her own. "Here, for everything," he muttered.

She smiled. "Thank you, Lion. You needn't get me anything, but I appreciate it nonetheless." With that, the troll bowed his head and sat back down in his seat, folding his arms carefully. He had moved his blindfold slightly to gauge her reaction. Wren turned towards the box, setting it down on the table before unwinding the ribbon. In one smooth motion, the ribbon pulled free and the lid of the box clattered loudly against the table cloth. Curious onlookers craned their necks forward, trying to see this mysterious gift.

Wren was motionless for a moment, before pulling the flower pot up and out of the wooden box towards her chest. That cluster of five starry blue blossoms bounced jovially in the crisp breeze, eager to breathe the fresh air. A soft exhale left her lips, touching the soft petals with the tips of her fingers. Her hand recoiled a little before pulling the pot into a hug. How often had she seen these beautiful little flowers sparkling in the hills of Redhollow? How often had she played amongst these very blossoms? Her umber eyes began to water at the edges. "Thank you, Lion... I... I hadn't seen these in quite some time..." she turned, approaching him slowly with her gift still in hand. Wren set the pot down on an empty chair next to him before giving the blind stranger a polite embrace. That beautiful grin graced her features once more as she turned towards the remaining staff at the table. "I need to run this up to the manor. Can you handle the rest of the party?" The others confidently assured her and urged her on, letting the woman take her gift and retreat back up the hill.

Some villagers whispered to themselves, poorly concealing their gossip as they prattled on. "Is that hill shine?" a merchant purred.

"Didn't expect a sight so far from the south! Musta' been a traveler of some sort..." another mused.

"How on earth did he grow them? This far out of their season? He must have been planning this for months..." the first pondered.

"Yeah, it seems like a lot of effort for a mere thank you," the second nodded.

"It certainly bodes interesting news for the Lady of Willowbend..." the man smirked, rubbing at his stubble.

"Oh? To what end?" The short man tilted his head.

The first sighed, resting a narrow hand on his hip. "Who knows? A random stranger comes by and saves one of the fabled heroes of the Golossian War along with Lord Lionel's heir. And then he proceeds to move in and make himself comfortable in the Lionel manor..."

"Knowing that woman, he's probably some strange fae trying to get on her good side rather than a man attempting to raid her bedchambers!" the second snapped, a nervous playfulness to his tone.

"Hmph, but hill shine has a unique meaning," the first argued.

"Oh?"

"They represent desire." The first's face coiled into a sly grin.

The second merchant sniffed, a lazy smile set upon his features. "Well, I know not of plants, that's your forte!"

Vantis listened in, his mouth creasing into a frown.

Hill shine, huh...

He'd never seen Wren act that way. While normal to most, Vantis knew when his caregiver was flustered or overwhelmed. It was enough to make his stomach leap in his chest.

Would he give a gift like that to mum?

Harris, who sat beside the disgruntled boy stared ahead, his hands gripping his blanket tighter. He too knew what those flowers meant. All he could do was glance over to the troll, who was sitting quietly by himself as the village murmured. The ceremony proceeded without incident, now with most of the villagers moving to their houses. Merchants settled into their caravans, the staff put out the fires, priests recited their nighttime prayers, and children were tucked into bed. Vantis approached the lone troll tentatively. "Uh, Lion?"

"What?" Adrian growled.

"I uh... just wanted to tell you I'm taking uncle back home to rest. Please just make it home safe. Whenever you can," the boy nervously looked away, tossing his gaze towards his uncle staring up at the stars.

The troll raised a brow but nodded nonetheless. "Very well then." The fae watched the boy struggle along with the wheelchair, Harris and him arguing all the while up that hill. Adrian turned, listening to Wren cleaning up with the rest of the staff before walking towards him. "Stubborn as a mule, is he not?" she smirked.

The fae sniffed. "Runs in the family."

She let out a small laugh. "Guess so... Harris isn't that heavy either. He should be fine."

"You know he's almost ready to walk now?" the troll grunted, listening to the boy call his thin uncle 'fat'.

"Really?" She tilted her head over towards him, hands on her hips.

"His leg is completely healed," he remarked.

"They might still give him crutches until his back heals."

"Don't tell him that I found a cane and set it in the back closet. Maybe he will lower his insurmountable pride enough to use it when he finds it," Adrian jeered.

Wren chuckled at that for a moment before shuffling in the dirt. "Would you walk with me? The party may be over, but I'm just now getting a moment to breathe!" The troll merely nodded before holding out a hand, letting the woman lead him on through the village towards the forest. They made their way over to a fallen log deeper in, settling down upon the rotting wood.

"Is anyone around?" the troll muttered.

"No, you should be fine," Wren answered, glancing about towards the empty center of town. The fae let out a sigh as he pulled down his blindfold, blinking away the blurriness before adjusting to the darkness. "So, did you have fun? Was it what you remembered?" she asked.

"More or less," the handsome man snorted. He turned towards her, watching the faint moonlight glitter in her eyes as she faced the village opposite of him. "Did you... enjoy the gift?"

"I did. It's been some time since I've seen those flowers... There used to be some near Redhollow," Wren sighed. Her eyes drifted away towards the unknowing distance. "...It may still share the same name and place, but with all its people gone... It's nothing more than a reminder." A pained smile creased her face. "Last I heard, they put up a memorial in the town square, and new people have moved onto the land..."

"It will make fine memories for someone else," Adrian reasoned, glancing back out over those forlorn woods. The celebrating fae had seemingly gone to rest, the fairy lights long-since dimmed.

"I just hope theirs will be better than mine..." the woman held her arms.

"The kingdom won't make the same mistakes it did during the war. I can assure you of that," he reassured.

"We can only hope," she sighed. Wren was quiet for a long while, letting the sounds of the night wash over them. Adrian could tell there was something on her mind, something she was struggling to say. Her lip quivered, searching for the words. "Do you think you'll stay? Regardless of the boy. Let's assume he breaks off the deal and grants you your freedom... If given the choice, would you stay?"

The troll considered this for a moment. His blue eyes drifted down towards his talons, pulling off a glove. He stared at the soft palm, in stark contrast to his old weathered claws. He considered his warm cave and the isolation, his friendship with the Green Man, how he enjoyed hunting and walking about as a free beast.

Wren, sensing his hesitation, piped up, "I wouldn't blame you if you didn't. Just know you will always have a place here."

"I will only stay as long as you are willing to have me," Adrian finally said.

"Well now, I'm not exactly considering chasing you away. I just got you back, damn it. I'm not throwing it all away," she said playfully. Her legs were tucked up to her chest, arms wrapped around them. Her eyes were glittering in amusement.

The troll let out a soft laugh before declaring, "Then I'll stay." Wren rested her shoulder against his, keeping her head away from his as she closed her eyes. "As annoying as the brat is, it's far more enticing to eat bones in a shiny house than a cave..."

The woman let out a tiny snort. "Can't imagine how boring it would be to patrol the woods looking for food. Never got why Harris did it."

"Oh, it can certainly be exciting but... after spending a month with that old man... I have found it far more interesting to hunt with a friend," he explained, breathing in her conflicting scent. "While there may be points where I desire seclusion, I don't believe I want to spend the rest of my days alone... Not anymore." The troll held his hand and rubbed it with his thumb. "No, that's not right... I don't think I ever did."

"Honestly, I've never seen Harris that excited about anything since you came back. He kept talking about how he wanted to try something, or how he wanted to get his hands on certain materials... All to help you out," she explained with a soft smile.

Adrian turned, his hair brushing against her cheek. He gave her a wry grin. "It would be a travesty to ruin that man's good mood now. And to be honest, I don't think I want this to end. I quite like it here. I like being around people."

"Then perhaps we should find a better story than 'heroic, mysterious blind man in the woods' if you stay long term. It will make things a tad complicated. They'll start asking questions... or worse. Make assumptions," Wren smirked.

Adrian chuckled, "Oh, as if imaginations haven't run rampant already? Talking of a twelve-foot tall bear!"

"Most certainly! The rumors are fairly tame now, but soon they will spiral into ideas of illicit love, or perhaps some supernatural force invading the village..."

"Stars and bones!" he gasped, rolling his eyes. "I wouldn't dream of it! All of these woods were mine in the first place!"

She snickered, covering her face. "Oh, are they now?"

"But of course!" he boasted, raising his chin playfully.

"Then what does that make the Green Man?" she smiled, resting her cheek on her arm.

A wide evil grin overtook his features. "A squatter."

Wren let out a snort. "Perhaps a lord in your case..."

Adrian laughed, resting his weight against her's. "Well, as long as he doesn't hear me, we will be in good standing. However, should you find me hanging upside down with vines tied to my ankles... then you know I've been heard!"

Nervousness glittered in her eyes. "Is he one to be so confrontational?"

"Not usually. But I have awoken to thorns in my nest!" the troll sneered. The tired woman let out a loud snort.

"Oh my. That's definitely more in line with the stories I heard! Paths swallowed by undergrowth, losing sight of game as you track them along; all relatively tame consequences of pissing off a fae if you ask me."

"Well now, I'd say he's better than a brownie," he gave a firm nod with faux seriousness.

"Oh yeah? And how does he size up to Old Dusk? I don't believe I ever saw him angry since the battles at the southern border," she mused.

Adrian pondered this. His memories of the ancient being were hazy, that was for sure. But he remembered his overwhelming presence. An ardent protector of the Duskhallow forest, even older than the kingdom of Solania itself. A being that could command a presence with a mere whisper. The thought of his gaze made the man shudder with an instinctual fear. "The Green Man is a gentle soul. He dislikes the undue harm of all living things. He let me live in these woods as one of them. Further back, he saved me as a boy. In his eyes, I have not changed," he began, pausing as he attempted to gather his words. "Old Dusk, on the other hand, by reputation alone, is less kind. A being like him would have seen me as a child and simply tossed me to the hungry wolves so that they may feast."

Wren snorted, the dark thought flattening her smile. "That... I can see. Makes me glad we have the Green Man instead of him in my backyard. Even if he was a valuable ally and a dear friend."

"Hmph... friend," the fae man echoed. The hairs on the back of his neck prickled. "Outside of what was told to me, I can't say I remember much."

"The two of you had closer ties than the rest of us did. Even so, we grew to have a mutual understanding. Friend of a friend, I suppose," she reasoned, drumming her fingers against her calves. "At least above tolerance."

"Ha! And most fae could hardly tolerate you!" he snickered.

Wren scowled. "Oh well, it comes with the territory."

"Need I remind you of the river spirits of Goldwater?" the troll nudged her side, giving her a devious look.

"Ugh!" The dame rolled her eyes, her feet resting on the grass below with a slight stomp. "Jealous whores. Somehow they took slight of me being a lone woman surrounded by so many handsome, strapping young men. Oh! And half of them wanted to swim up Harris's skirt," she growled, tossing a hand out in the air.

Adrian lost all composure, howling with laughter. He had to pause to wipe his eyes with a cold talon. "Ah, yes! To see if they could turn his hooves to fins!"

Wren gagged, shaking her head. "I don't even want to consider that! That's not even mentioning the kelpie. Harris didn't even think twice about seeing the horse in the river before considering it one of our own... Had to jump into that freezing ass river to drag the old man out of the water... stupid son of bitch."

"Well, I'm glad you fished him up! I wasn't exactly eager to get wet!" he laughed, bumping her shoulder with his.

"After we saw you sink like a rock with your stone bones?! No way in hell! Do you know how many times we had to haul your half-dead carcass out of the water?" She shifted on the log, directly facing him.

"Enough that it needs consideration?" Adrian gave her a sheepish glance.

"That's not even beginning to discuss the weight of your armor. You weren't exactly light, you know!" she admonished.

"So you're calling me fat?" he gasped, pressing a hand against his chest in faux surprise.

"No," she shook her head. "I'm calling you *dense*. In more ways than one."

"Oh... then I guess that makes it all okay then!" He cast a wry grin her way. They both got a sizable laugh from each other before Adrian turned his gaze back out into the woods. Those rings were just gently scanning the undergrowth before that prickle at the back of his neck rose up once more.

He froze. Something felt off. His eyes darted about, trying to seek the source of his concern. They suddenly stopped, finding a pair of glowing golden pinpricks staring back at him, only broken by a small blink. He raised a hand, signaling to his companion. Wren quickly saw it and tensed up, slowly following his alert gaze towards those eyes.

The lights seemed to notice their attention, as the shadows seemingly split before them to reveal an ancient, gnarled face. A gust of wind billowed around the two, shrouding the entity from them before falling away, revealing the creature no more than a few yards away. Those eyes bore into Adrian, an alien expression upon that weathered brow.

While the Green Man was large, this being was by far grander, about eleven feet tall. The creature was lanky, with gnarled tree trunks for limbs. His skin was as flaky as a river birch, fragments falling away like leaves from his form. Sharp, angular talons coiling like branches extended out, flexing as he unfurled his fists. He was hunched, much like the Green Man, but in a far more threatening manner. A covering of tangled leaves was draped around his body like a cloak, fragments of thorns and branches sticking through it as if threatening to impale anything that dared pounce. His vine-like tail lashed back and forth behind him, softly stirring the detritus.

Above all of this, rose his noble face. A long, tangled veil of lichen and fungus served as hair, only parted by a sharp, hooked nose. The jagged, bark-like fangs of his curled maw gnashed between lines of sap-like saliva, as if chewing on flesh.

Adrian knew what this entity was. This was the person he needed to meet. This was the great Duskhallow troll, Old Dusk.

Chapter 37

The ancient troll's piercing gaze rolled over the two, making Adrian's jaw clench. He slowly stood up, Wren following suit to rest a hand on his shoulder. "Easy. It's a friend," she whispered.

"I am well aware," he breathed, fighting his words as if the air was sucked from his lungs. The terrified man approached, keeping his head held high as he met those wizened pupils. Old Dusk lowered himself onto one knee, resting his massive claws on his thighs as he sized up the small fae.

His jaws parted with the sound of snapping branches. **"You Are Adrian, Are You Not?"**

The man shivered against the sound, his raging pride howling against his passive behavior. He pulled down his hood, letting his ebony hair fall to his sides like ribbons. "I am."

The beast let out an incredulous snort, his hair waving like wet mats of seaweed as he craned his neck about to see him. "**While You Are Very Different From The Man I Knew So Very Long Ago... And From That Beast I Saw Lurking This Wood... Your Eyes Are The Same. I Can Faintly Recall Your Scent.**" The crackling of wood made the man's eye twitch. All he could do was bow before the being, with a similar greeting given in return. The forest troll swung his head away from the humans, instead turning his gaze towards the village. A low groan resonated in his throat. "**Come. Let Us Get Out Of Sight. I Would Rather Not Invoke The Ire Of This Town.**"

Adrian nodded, moving deeper into the bracken with Wren close by. Old Dusk seemingly phased through the tangled mats with nary a sound, his feet padding against the leaves softly. His gaze was still locked on the man, the feeling making beads of sweat run down his back. After several yards of hiking, only the faintest glow of lamplight illuminated the way home, the thick trunks of weathered oaks and weaving vines blocking all sight of the massive being circling the clearing. After settling down into a crouched position, the ancient fae once again lowered his fanged maw towards the two humans.

Wren spoke up first. "It's good to see you. Harris is absent, despite being the one to call you here. He was heavily injured recently and is currently resting now," she explained, pausing before gesturing towards the man beside her. "But we were hoping you could help find some answers for Adrian here."

The sunset pinpricks narrowed, his face inching forward to scan the man. "**From A Glance, And From What I Have Observed These Past Few Days, It Is Complicated. I Have Some Ideas. But. Nothing Solid. What Do You Remember, Adrian?**"

464

Adrian shifted his legs, looking away to gather his thoughts. Finally, he cleared his throat and stepped forward. "Fragments. Pieces. My childhood is clear. But... my adulthood... my career in the military... I have shards of memory, but not all of them. I don't remember much of my allies... or even the face of my love..." His gloved hand gripped at his heart, a terrible burning infecting his chest.

The immortal creature lowered himself fully to his level, resting his forearms onto the ground. One gnarled hand lifted to his chin, rubbing it with thought. Scatterings of bark fell from the motion. "**Hmm... This Is To Be Expected. But. I Know Not Of Any Tales Of Kin Regaining Their Humanity. This Does Not Appear To Be The Case Upon Closer Observation. You Are Still, At The Very Least, Kin. Though, More Troll Than Man. Despite Your Appearance.**"

The smaller fae let out a comforted breath while Wren rested her hands on her hips. "Kind of ironic, considering how much of a troll he appeared before he turned into one. You could still say he was more man than fae then?"

Those alien eyes darted towards her. "**It Is More Than A Physical Condition, Wren. It Is... Ingrained In Him. One With Him. Not Just Flesh And Bone. Far Deeper Than That. What Some Call Soul, Essence, Anima...**" he paused to wave his hand about indifferently. "**Whatever You Desire To Call It, It Has Touched Him Entirely.**"

"... I can never go back," Adrian nodded, gazing at his own talons jabbing at the glove's fabric.

"**This Is True,**" the being nodded. "**And Yet. Here You Are.**" The man raised a brow in confusion, unable to read the troll's expression. "**Kin Cannot Retain More Than Basic Memories. Fragments. Hints. Perhaps An Errant Tick Or A Deep Fondness For A Favorite Food. Even Certain Scenery Or Locations. Never Entire Memories. Never A Full Childhood. This Is... Unprecedented.**"

A tiny jab of frustration stabbed at the man's thoughts. Only his brow twitched. "So I'm assuming a straight answer is out of the question?"

The forest troll's skin rustled against the wind like a rattlesnake. "**Like I Said, I Have Theories.**" The hand that held his chin pulled away, reaching out towards the handsome man. Adrian instinctively stepped back as those claws came dangerously close. "**May I See Your Hand?**" The man's left fist clenched for a moment before he took his glove off and settled it down upon Old Dusk's massive palm. The claws curled around it carefully, a surprising level of care as the being shifted it in his grasp. The forest troll moved the hand's palm upward, resting his sharp thumb above the soft skin. The motion was oddly familiar to the man. Adrian saw his eyes dart up to his, not moving his face an inch from its position. "**May I Draw Some Blood? In Order To Test It. I Promise, On My Honor As A Troll, I Will Not Use Such An Offering For Ill Will,**" he asked.

"As long as you do not carry it with you in any regard," the small fae declared.

The golden eyes closed. "**It Shall Be So.**" Then, with a seamster's precision, that claw dug into the mountain troll's palm, making the man flinch. Only a tiny drop of scarlet welled from the wound, beading on the claw. Old Dusk let go of his hand, pulling his claws towards his face to examine the drop. He rubbed it between the pads of his fingertips and breathed in the scent. His lichen-covered brow furrowed. "This Is Rather Peculiar. It Is Not Golden... That Should Not Be Possible With A Simple Glamour. Nor The Change In Size. But I Figured There Would Be Other Magics Afoot. Yet None Would Change Your Blood. Not So Thoroughly. There Is Magic. But No Illusion." Old Dusk brought the blood to his cracked lips and licked it, shuddering violently and shedding more bark around him. The hand fell to the dirt and wiped the remaining blood away. He raised his head high. "It Is No Human Blood. And. As I Have Said In The Past... There Is A Touch Of The Foul Taint Of Entropy."

Adrian's blood ran cold. What does that mean? Was he a demon?

"No More Than It Used To Be. It Would Not Produce Changes Like This. There Are Through, Powerful, Deep Magics That Bind You To This Form. I, Nor The Green Man, As You Call Him, Could Replicate Such A Feat. The One You Called Aladarr... He Could Take On A Humanoid Form. But Never One This Thorough. No More Than An Illusion. A Glamour," the being explained, nodding slowly. He gestured towards the man's chest. "This Magic, However, Is More Akin To Something That Could Change Its Form Entirely."

Adrian rubbed his palm as it sealed shut. He snorted and raised a brow. "A shapeshifter?" Old Dusk nodded. The man scoffed. "Such creatures don't exist! Not on this mortal plane!"

"Creatures With This Level Of Ability Rarely Show Themselves In This World. You Are Correct In That Regard.

Even You Only Crossed Paths With One Or Two, And Those Hailed From The Planes Of The Adversary. Not Of Our Ilk."

Blue rings dulled as they gazed upon those palms, a sinking feeling in his gut. "Does... that make me one of them?"

"**No,**" the troll asserted, shaking his head as lichen fell from his mats of hair. "**Far From It. Tell Me. What Other Changes Have Been Observed?**"

The man bit his lip, trying to think hard on the past months. "My healing... is not as strong as it used to be. Wounds close, yes... but the deeper the cut, the longer it takes. I don't weigh as much. I cannot break things as efficiently as I used to. But that does not mean I can't put force into something if I will it." He reached down to a palm-sized rock and held it in his hand briefly before crushing it to fragments. Wren watched as he tossed the dust away and that hand went limp to his side. Her gaze was far away, trying to figure out what was going on herself.

"**When You Awoke Like This, Were There Remains Of Your Prior Form?**" the ancient being rumbled.

Adrian pondered this. His brow furrowed. "I just woke up covered in dust."

"**Hmm. I Will Have To Locate Your Old Home. Perhaps Answers Lay There, Provided It Has Not Been Disturbed,**" the troll nodded, beginning to rise to his feet.

Adrian couldn't help but wince, "And therein lies a problem. My child has rummaged through everything."

Old Dusk tilted his head to the side, peering down at the man. **"The Little One Who Speaks Very Loud? The One Parading The Veteran Around?"** Adrian could only grimace and nod. A soft smile cracked the troll's lips. **"A Lively One. Like A Young Pup. Almost Endearing, If I May Say..."** Before a harsh slew of words regarding the boy could erupt from the man's mouth, the forest troll interrupted. **"In Any Case, I Shall Investigate The Remains."**

"...I can lead you there. I want my answers," the man spoke up, tossing a glance towards Wren.

She blinked, folding her arms. "I'll go back and explain the situation. You go on, just try to be back before dawn. If you can't... Well... don't keep us waiting." As she released her arms and shifted towards home, one of Adrian's talons wrapped around her hand delicately. The dame turned, looking into his glowing eyes.

"If anything happens, signal me. Anything. I'll try to get back to you all as fast as possible," he pleaded.

She squeezed that hand for a moment before sliding free. "I'll figure something out. But don't forget, we aren't helpless. We are far more prepared than last time. Get your answers, Adrian. And come home safe."

Something about the way she said "home" made his heart skip a beat, like it was the first time he found something right. *Home.* Yes, he had to come home. Adrian nodded with a smile. "As you wish."

With that, Wren picked her way over the logs and thicket, crossing over the barrier of nature before disappearing into the town proper. Old Dusk was already turning away and moving deeper into the forest as the man hesitated, watching her go. Adrian shook his head after a moment of conflict and began to lead on.

~~~~~~

The two beings hiked through the frosted woodland, both unnaturally silent. Adrian's breath fogged, sending a clouded trail behind him with each determined step. He almost jumped when the troll beside him spoke up. "**She Has Changed A Lot Since We Last Met.**"

"We all have," the man grunted, kicking away some thorns as he marched through.

Old Dusk shook his head. "**None More So Than Her.**"

The smaller fae couldn't help but raise a brow at such a statement. "Is that meant to be a joke?"

"**Had You Remembered More Of Me, You Would Know I Am Not One For Comedy. Just Because You Became A Troll And Then A Man Once Again... Does Not Mean You Have Gone Through As Much Growth.**"

"More of a regression..." Adrian hissed, his eyes narrowing. The dim moonlight from the waning crescent above cast his grim face in shadow.

The ancient being snorted. "**Perhaps.**" A hand slowly pulled away from his creaking side and swung forward, gently slapping the man's back. Adrian grunted and stumbled ahead, glaring at the wild guardian. "**Do Not Sulk, Adrian. You Have Performed What Some Humans Would Call A Miracle. You Retained Your Sense**

470

Of Self In The Face Of Magics Predating The Moment Your Species Rose To Two Legs..."

The smaller troll scowled. "Miracles don't exist. Those are the thoughts of foolish mortals, nothing more."

Old Dusk let out a slow, creaking chuckle. "**Perhaps. But As A Being Who Has Seen Many Centuries Pass, Watching Kingdoms Rise And Crumble, I Would Not Rule Out The Will Of Higher Beings And Their Whims.**"

Adrian's lips curled back from his fangs as he sniffed. "They hold no will over me."

"**And Neither For I. But That Does Not Mean Their Machinations Bare No Effect,**" the forest troll explained, snorting as the man beside him spat onto the ground. "**Their Agents Can Bare The Blade Instead.**"

"And they can bleed just like the rest of the mortals; die just as easily as a pig," he snarled. Even now, his pride as a trollkin was shining through. The man cleanly leapt past some fallen trees.

"**But With Enough Determination,**" the troll began, calmly stepping over the rotting trunks. "**Those Like You In Your Prime Can Rise Up And Stand With Even The Mightiest Of Troll, The Most Horrible Beings Of The Abyss, And The Wisest Of Old Spirits... Men Are Not To Be Underestimated, Adrian. None Should Know That More Than You.**"

"And yet I am no man," he sighed, shoving the bushes away.

"**And Yet You Are No Troll,**" the forest guardian purred. Adrian's hands clenched, wracked with frustration. "**This Is No Insult, Friend. Merely An Observation. You Are Adrian. No... Not Just That. You Are Adrian Lionel!**" His voice rose with pride. The smaller fae flinched at the sound of his name. "**Of The Black Lion Executioner Knights. You Are Adrian Lionel, The Mountain Troll Of Willowbend. You Are Adrian Lionel, The Merchant, The Bard, The Soldier, The Husband, The Father!**" The two stopped at the cliffside leading towards the mountain troll's old den; their gazes locked. Adrian's jaw was clenched, frustrated at hearing all of this. "**You Are Many Things, Adrian. That Defines You More Than What Blood Flows Through Your Veins. I Considered You Closer To Me Than Most Trolls I Knew... Well Before You Fell To What Lurked Within.**" The weathered beast lumbered towards him, lowering himself to the man's level. "**And If It Is Of Any Consolation... I Much Prefer You Like This Than A Mad Beast Roaming The Woods...**"

Adrian hissed under his breath and whipped around, marching along as his frustrated thoughts fought to untangle themselves. They continued in silence, hiking up the barren slope that led to the craggy cave in the mountain face. Adrian stopped at the entrance, gazing into that yawning mouth. His eyes trailed along, spotting the faint shining of bone amongst the gravel, the remains of his many meals. Score marks lined the ground and walls, markings of a beast well over three times his current size. The scent of decay and troll musk was replaced with a dusty haze, the last vestiges of his presence already faded. The tiny chirpings of bats echoed through the cave, the only form of life present inside. Adrian let out a sigh, his shoulders sagging.

He entered quietly, noticing his hoard absent by the scattered nesting material. While mostly intact, it appeared to be slowly falling apart as animals rifled through it. Interspersed between all the scatterings were the tracks of small boots: Vantis. The man just closed his eyes as a pit of wistfulness yawned wide in his gut.

"**A Fine Cave Indeed,**" Old Dusk remarked, crouching under the entrance before standing at full height inside. "**Though I Assume It Lacks Your Collection.**"

"It has been all safely deposited in my new home," Adrian answered, a hint of irritation in his tone.

"**Courtesy Of The Boy, I Presume? More So By Initiative Than Arrogance...**"

"Indeed," he grumbled, sitting on a rock by the wall. "He cares... far too much..."

Old Dusk wandered in, glancing past the man towards the rightmost wall. He reached forward and ran his hands along, feeling the grooves of the scattered scrawlings that decorated it. His brow furrowed, following the various words, phrases, and symbols; all before he found the most recent one.

A....D....R..I....A...N

Fragments of rock fell from his fingers as he traced those lines, sunset pupils snapping towards the somber man beside him. "**You Came A Long Way Before This Happened, Did You Not? You Were Already Remembering... Even In That Beastly Form...**"

Adrian snarled, gripping his arms tightly with his talons. "If we call it anything, call it my true form. And yes, I started to recall quite a bit..."

473

"Hmph, If You Insist. I Will Respect Your Terms. Even If I Disagree..." The ancient troll pulled his hands away, scattering more pebbles before moving towards the nest.

"I am fae, same as you. If you said this was magic, that means this form isn't real. Eventually it will fade," Adrian explained in a level tone.

"Perhaps. Though It Is Your Flesh Still. It Is No Artifice. It Bleeds, It Hurts, It Can Be Wounded. So Regardless Of Its Magic, It Is You," the forest troll argued. The man scoffed, kicking a small bone away from his feet. The being lowered his hand to the stone below, running the pads of his fingers along the dusty ground. "Where Did You Succumb When You Changed?"

Adrian stood up, moving towards the nest and jabbing a finger downward. The troll approached, kneeling to examine the bedding. A mix of sticks, leaves and parchment; all mashed together by a heavy weight, well used and loved. As he watched the forest guardian investigate, the man heard a bat attempt to fly past. Hungry even after the festival, he snatched it out of the air and bit its head off. A few others of the colony scattered, fluttering in a frenzy past him as the small fae munched on his meal.

Old Dusk finally lifted a dirtied scrap of cloth. "Ah, Here We Are. This One Still Has The Dust You Mentioned Upon It." Adrian swiped his black tongue over his bloodied lips before approaching. He took the cloth in and examined it, noting a fine layer of greenish-grey dust. He handed it back, watching the troll take in a deep sniff before shuddering against a sneeze. Only an irritated snort exited his nose, shaking his head. "The Smell Of Charred Flesh. Rancid And Foul," he remarked. "Ashes From A

Burnt Troll, If I Were To Guess. Which Gives Me Some More Ideas... But Also... Frustratingly... More Questions."

"I should preface that I was not set ablaze before this happened," the man flatly stated.

Those golden eyes snapped to his face. "I Figured, Considering You Stand Before Me Now."

Adrian smirked. "Well, someone tried, and I still survived."

Old Dusk nodded thoughtfully. "I Smelled It On You. Someone Burned You Terribly."

The smaller fae reached down and pulled up his shirt, revealing a disgustingly shiny hand-sized scar on his right side, above his hip. "Baobhan sith."

A repulsed grimace creased the ancient troll's features. "Foul Wretches. Bizarre To Pick You As A Target."

"I wasn't the target," he shook his head, letting the cloth fall over the wound. "It was the boy."

At that, Old Dusk frowned. "We Can Discuss That Matter Later. For Now, Let Us Focus." The being turned back to the cloth and the nest, picking up discarded teeth and feathers from previous preening sessions. Clearly noting that they were unrelated, he tossed them aside. The search continued.

After twenty minutes of this, the troll rose to his feet and tossed the evidence on the ground. **"Bah! I Believe We Have Learned What We Can From These Remains..."** Adrian merely kicked the twig he was shredding with his talons back over to a pile against the wall, where many preened teeth laid. **"My Best Guess As To What This New Form Is... It Is A Compression Of Your Old Body. You Have Burnt The Excess. I Do Not Know The Mechanism... Nor The Level Of Power Required For Such A Change... However It Is One Of The Few Theories I Have. There Are Cases Of Trolls That Lose Limbs... That Can Alter Them For New Purpose. Shape, Layout, Color, Even Precise Placement of Bone And Sinew. It Is A Rare Power Indeed,"** Old Dusk explained, gesturing towards the dusty cloth. **"This Would Be That, To An Incredible Extreme. Something Only Someone With Centuries Of Practice... MIGHT Be Able To Perform... Not That I Have Seen Such Things. However! That Does Not Explain The Blood..."**

"And even if that were the case, it would mean I couldn't change back. Not without the same level of effort anyways," Adrian shook his head, crossing his arms. It made no sense. He wasn't good at magic. He couldn't even wobble a rock, let alone change his body so drastically.

"It Would Take Quite A Large Sum Of Energy, Yes. Have You Noticed An Increase In Appetite? Or Is It Comparable To A Mortal?" the troll asked.

Adrian pondered this for a moment. "Slightly more than a human but less than a troll."

"Then It Is Likely... Not A Sustained Form... Rather A Current Constant. You Are Not Forcing This To Remain, You Are... Forcing Your Regrowth To This Shape. This Is Likely Why Your Healing Is Slower. It Needs To Be Directed, Given New Instruction."

The man lowered his gaze to his talons, the fingers starting to shake. That pit of helplessness grew. "So I *won't* be able to go back? I'm going to stay like this...?"

"Perhaps. But If This Is The Case, You Could, Theoretically, At Any Point, Revert. At A Great Cost. You Would Probably Be Driven By The Madness Of Hunger Afterwards. The Kind Of Which, Left Unchecked, Could Quite Heavily Damage An Environment. Let Alone A Village Full Of Easy Prey..." the old fae warned. Adrian's head jolted back towards the troll, horror all over his face. "But, Given Previous Information On Your Behavior As A Beast, You Might Be Able To Refrain From Such Barbarous Acts, Though You Would Likely Cause

Vast Damage To The Green Man's Domain..." Now the smaller fae was clenching his fists, a tiny spark of rage starting to light. "**Though That Is Not To Say It Could Not Be Done Incrementally... However, I Believe The Same Thing Keeping Your Memories From You Is Locking You Into This Form. A... Mental Block, I Should Say.**"

"So the more I learn, the closer I get to turning back?" the man asked, his voice quiet.

"**Perhaps Not. Perhaps A Better Awareness Of Your Body Instead. Though Obviously... This Is All Conjecture,**" Old Dusk corrected.

"I do remember one thing before this all happened," Adrian turned towards the back of the cave, where the inky blackness lay the strongest. He could almost imagine the entity emerging from the fog of night. "A man. It was me. It approached me and grabbed my face... It said it would show who it was..."

"**Did You Know It Was You At The Time?**" the troll pressed.

"No."

"**Then I Believe... He Has Upheld His Word,**" his gaze dared not meet his, only continuing to scan the cave. "**Would It Be Acceptable For Me To Rest Here During My Visit?**"

Adrian nodded. "That would be alright. But I don't believe I will be available to visit for some time."

"That Is Fine. There Is Much To Look Into. Eventually, I Would Like To Get More Information On What Has Been Assailing You And Your Family...But That Is Not Important Right Now..." Old Dusk bowed his head, resting on his knees. "I Have Much To Think On As Is. It Is Better To Take This One Step At A Time. I Will Likely Need To Speak To The Host Of This Forest..." he mused, rubbing his chin with a branch-like claw.

"And that is not a decision for me to make," Adrian grunted, following him with his gaze.

"I Will Seek Council If He Permits It. Thankfully, He Has Graced Me With Passage Through His Domain During My Stay, As Long As I Cause No Problems..." he sighed, a hint of begrudging acceptance in his rumbling tone.

Adrian clenched his jaw. Despite standing next to this creature, a competitor, another troll... he felt no territorial desires. Even knowing there were now three trolls crammed in the forest, he felt no aggression. Such a worrisome thought drew his mind away.

"Tell Me, Friend. What Worries You So? Why Do You Fear What You Are Now?"

Adrian's head snapped towards him. "Because it was easier then! Because I understood my place in the world! I had my cave, I had my territory, I had my food... I had everything I've wanted! And ever since these blasted memories came flooding back, ever since the fall... It's been getting far more complicated. I have been losing more of myself! I have been feeling things that I'm not supposed to! I've been dealing with a burning pain in my intestines every time I think about her!" The man waved his talons frantically, starting to pace

479

about. "I've been dealing with horrible emotions, terrible dreams, and a torrent of information that is seemingly never ending!"

"**Like An Entire Lifetime Being Poured Into Your Head...**" Old Dusk commented, following the man with his gaze.

Adrian whipped around, gesturing towards the fae. "Yes! And would that not frustrate you, *old friend*?"

"**I Would Not Know... However, I Believe I Can Understand Your Frustrations. But You Must Also Consider,**" the troll raised a claw towards the cave wall. "**When Have You Ever Been Content Just Being A Troll?**" Adrian's fiery eyes snapped towards the wall, glaring at those carvings. "**You Made Scrawlings...And Even If This Started After Your So-Called 'Fall', Whatever That Is, You Had A Collection Before Then, Am I Wrong?**"

"...no..."

"**You Had Correspondence With Another Troll... You Were Not Discontented Sharing A Territory With Him. You Bore No Hatred For Those Men At The Bottom Of The Valley, The Hunters Who Took Your Prey. You Sought No Lands Beyond, You Did Not Seek To Take Territory From The Trolls To The North Bordering The Green Man's Domain. You Did Not Seek Growth... You Sought Familiarity! A Home!**" Old Dusk explained, with far more energy in his voice. Adrian merely hissed and turned away, gazing outside the cave. The troll behind him rose to his feet once more. "**You Desired To Be With Them! You *Tried* To Be With Them Before You Found This Cave! You Fought To Be Amongst Them Again, Even If You Did Not Know Why!**"

The man shook his head, his body shaking with emotion. One of his hands reached up and held his forehead, fighting an oncoming headache.

"You Scared Your Wife! You Frightened Your Friends! You Almost Hurt Your Child-"

"I WOULD NEVER HURT HIM!" Adrian whipped around, scoring his free hand across the wall. Deep gouges marred the rock face as he roared.

"And I Believe You. They Would Want To As Well. But They Feared Enough To Call Upon My Aid In Those Trying Times. They Begged Me... To Leave My Home And See If I Could Help You! And Despite All. My. Efforts. All. My. Meditations. I found NOTHING To Help You! And It HURT To See My Friend Lose Himself!" The ancient beast loomed over the man, casting him in a shadow as he roared back. "Call Me Selfish, If You So Desire! Call Me Stubborn! Or Call Me Cruel If These Words Hurt You! But Even If You Felt Yourself A Troll, You Were Always There! Even When In Fragments! And It Is Nothing But A MIRACLE And A Testament To Your Boundless Strength As A *Man*, That You Found Yourself Again! Despite Giving In To Save Your Family!"

The two fae were but inches away from each other, Adrian's face locked in fury. Old Dusk remained steadfast, unblinking against the frothing beast below him. Eventually, the smaller fae snapped around, backing away towards the entrance with a growl. The old troll stepped back in turn and leaned against the wall, letting out a ragged sigh. He rested a hand against his cheek and rubbed it, an oddly mortal expression of weariness upon his alien features.

"I Am Sorry If My Words Hurt You, Adrian. But At The End Of The Day, It Is Good To See My Friend Once More... And I Will Do What I Can To Help, If You Will Allow It. But If You Do Not Want My Aid, I Will Go. It Is Your Choice," Old Dusk creaked, his back to the man.

Adrian flopped his shoulder against the wall, chuckling to himself before belting out a loud laugh. "Choice, eh!? That's one of the few afforded to me since my time in this wretched form! Since everything was ripped from me! But one of a few..." His laugh suddenly ceased. His back straightened and he turned to face the ancient being. "Fine. I want my answers. And I will do what it takes to get them. All of them. Even if I must tear through everything. I don't think I quite care anymore, because the individual who lived in this cave is *dead*!" he spat.

Old Dusk sighed. **"I Think You Are Wrong In That Regard As Well... You Think Too Much In Simple Dichotomies... That It Must Be One Or The Other..."** He turned his massive frame towards the man and approached, kneeling before him. **"You Have Proven To Me, Despite The Odds, And Despite The Last Thirteen Years... That Even When Everything Seems To Have Fallen Away, *Nothing* Must Be One Or The Other.... You Have Proven Everything I Know About Kin Wrong... You Have Defied *Every* Expectation And Persisted! I Believe That Beast Is No Different. And For Once In Your Life, I Think You Are Truly Whole... Even With Pieces Still Falling Into Place..."** he reached out with his gnarled hands and gently rested them on the man's shoulders. **"I Think That You Are *You*. You Are The Sum Of All Your Experiences. Be That As A Troll, As A Man, Or Anything Between..."** Adrian turned his head away, unwilling to face him. **"And Regardless Of Where You End Up, I Have Full Confidence. At The End Of The Day... Whoever You Chose To Be, Will. Be. YOU. And I'm Glad You Called Upon Me. I'm Glad**

You Chose To Let Me Help... Because I Would Never Force It Upon You."

"...It is late..." Adrian muttered, keeping his head low. "My family is expecting me."

"**Then I Shall Not Keep Them Waiting,**" Old Dusk smiled sadly and, in an act lacking any of the vague familiarity the man was used to, pulled him into a tight hug. Adrian could smell the scent of rotting sap on his breath, holding him there for a moment. It was frighteningly human. A moment later, the forest troll pulled away, almost embarrassed. "**Stay Safe, My Friend. And May The Winds Blow In Your Favor...**"

The small fae staggered back, trudging towards the yawning opening ahead of him. "Do take care..." he remarked before heading on his way. He left the massive troll to rest in his old cave, his old home.

~~~~~~

Adrian hiked through the woods, periodically stopping to lean against a tree. He could never turn back, not without harming his family and not without harming the Green Man. His beloved body, as strange as it was, was something he truly took pride in... And now it was gone, replaced completely by this weak, pathetic frame that grew no fur, no feather, no external teeth. He didn't even have a tail. He was a bald, useless ape... And that was what he would remain. Adrian sagged to his knees, holding his arms tightly.

Hopelessness dug into his flesh, biting at his vacant features. Would he ever hunt again? Feel the rush of the wind as he chased his prey and pounced? Or would he be forced to use human weapons forever? Could he pad about the forest and rest where he pleased, or would he be forced to set up camp and arm himself in fear of wolves and bears? This was all fine at the start, presuming his condition would resolve itself.

But now...

No one gave a shit. No one cared that he was suffering from all of this. Everyone was just so happy to have their friend back. Did his thoughts or wants even matter? Or should he just pretend he was happy? Adrian Lionel the human felt so far away... and yet close enough to invade his psyche. It felt like his thoughts and feelings were all overwritten by a person he barely knew. But of course this was all fine to everyone else.

He lifted a shaking claw up to his face, peering into that deep, dark green flesh. This patch of skin, these claws, were all he would ever see of his beloved past. The rest of him was gone, replaced with the mind of a man desperately attempting to crawl out of his skull. Adrian gritted his teeth and curled in, letting the cold embrace his sides as he fell down. But in his boundless sorrow... there was happiness, the joy of being around his friends. Harris was a wonderful hunting partner who always seemed to know what he was thinking, and Wren... She was the strongest human being he ever met. She worked with him, taught him how to read again, cooked with him, danced with him, and listened to him. She was so kind... He suddenly gripped his stomach, fighting the urge to vomit. But then there was that woman, the one from his dreams... his love. Would she ever love him now, or would she wait until he was completely overwritten and back to the man she wanted? Love... for a face he couldn't even imagine... or barely remember.

It was deplorable, and yet he reached out for it anyway. Just as he had for all these wretched memories. Memories that made the people around him laugh and cry, memories that made him learn new things every day. Would he truly be willing to give it all up? To give up all the joy and accomplishment he gained these past few months just for that fleeting sense of security?

No.

He winced.

I can't. I've come too far. Even if my body remains this small... this weak... This was always my wish from the start. I wanted to know who I was. Even if it hurt me. Even if I suffered for all eternity for the answer...

His sapphire rings ran up from his palms towards his scarred tanned skin. That soft flesh that hugged his frame so tightly. That was who he was. A weak man. A weak man who led armies. A weak man that took down a troll and avenged the deaths of his comrades. A weak man that made allies and friends from all walks of life. A weak man that fell in love. A weak man who sacrificed himself for others.

Adrian staggered to his feet, gripping the tree beside him tightly before moving along. His footsteps felt distant as his thoughts drifted over to his family. To his child.

He truly was nothing. And maybe, just maybe... he could tolerate that.

Chapter 39

Adrian found Vantis alone, sitting in the same tree he himself laid upon during that fateful night. The child's eyes were glazed over, fraught with worry. As rattled as he was, the troll refused to put the revelations he gained upon the child. The words between Old Dusk and him were theirs alone. Instead, he spoke up. "It's late, why are you still up? And outside no less?"

Vantis rested his head against the tree, those emerald eyes staring down at him. "I'm... trying to think about what I want."

The fae snorted. "You want a lot of things."

The boy closed his eyes and shook his head. "Not really. I have Wren and Harris. I have an amazing home full of amazing things. I never have to worry about eating. I have tutors. I'm learning about stuff that tons of kids don't know about... but I... I'm just missing one thing," he explained as his gaze shifted upwards. The horizon was still as dark as a pool of ink, the bright stars glittering coldly above.

Adrian sighed, approaching the tree and leaning against it. He folded his arms and looked up at his son. "This is about your mother, isn't it?" All he could see was the boy's head slowly nodding. The troll sighed. "We at least know she's at the capital, right? It's not a complete mystery."

The child pulled out a slip of paper and wiggled it loosely. "This is the envelope from her last letter. It's got a seal on it. Something I was looking into." The fae narrowed his eyes. The letter in that book. The child grasped the envelope in both hands, gazing down upon it. "It's got the seal of the political district's courier system..."

"Yes, and why did you need to know that information?" the troll asked, though he had a sinking suspicion of what the boy would say next.

The child sighed, setting the letter in his overcoat pocket. "Because I want to go find her."

Adrian scoffed. "You're not allowed outside the village. Especially now, considering the current situation."

"I know," the boy said plainly. "But that's just the thing..." Adrian saw him shift position, both of the lad's legs dangling from the side of the branch as he sat upon it, gazing down at his father. "I never considered that I could... die."

"Most children don't," the man grunted.

There was a deep agony in the teenager's eye. "And I almost *did* that night, over two weeks ago. You and Harris included!" The boy held his arms tightly, trying to jostle away the icy air settling in. "I almost died just after realizing my father was alive. I almost died after having an answer I dreamt about for so long..." His breath fogged as the boy lowered his head. "And I almost died having never seen my mum's face..." For once, Adrian was silent. He had no retort. Instead, he just gave the boy time to continue down his line of thought. "And I came to a conclusion... that I can't live with that. I can't live knowing that at any moment, some monster could snatch me away and no one would ever find me. That I would never have my answers." The child braced himself for a moment before jumping off the branch. He landed with a staggered stance as he fell forward. After dusting himself off, he turned towards his father. "So I've made a decision!" he declared.

"Oh? And what does the mighty lord desire?" Adrian's voice oozed.

"I'm going to go find her... and you're going to take me there," Vantis stated, keeping his voice level. There was a fierce determination in his eyes.

The troll blinked before letting out a loud, snorting laugh. "Stars and bones, child! Have you lost your mind?! And outside another ludicrous, vague order, how do you suppose I do this?"

The young lord frowned. "That's also what I wanted to talk about. I... don't like this... whole 'deal' thing. I hate it. I hate how it makes you feel. I hate how slimy it makes me feel. It's awful." He shook his head roughly, as if trying to shake off some corrupting force. "I don't want it anymore! But I don't want anyone thinking you whisked me away like those monsters tried to do! If I give you this order, people won't be able to blame you for my choice. The blame will lay solely on me!"

Honestly, that was surprising. Adrian always figured the child was power hungry and corrupted, just like any other human with a fragment of control. But here he was, admitting he hated that power and was trying to rid himself of it. Quite odd indeed. The troll shook his head with a growl. "Oh, yes, and what purpose would *I* serve, perchance?"

"You were the commander of the Black Lion Executioners, one of the greatest monster fighting forces in all of Solania. You might not be the person I heard everyone say you were, but you are way stronger than anyone I've ever met! If anyone can protect me from the monsters outside, it's you!" Vantis boasted, excitement glittering in his eye.

Adrian scoffed. "Despite your attempts at flattery, I feel you may have neglected to remember that I was almost killed the last time I tried to defend you. And, if I recall correctly, you made *quite* the stink about it."

The lad's eyes darted to the ground. "I know... but we weren't prepared then. We didn't know that... things... would chase after me. But now we do, and I've got this!" The child pulled out a large heavy tome covered in aged leather.

The troll held out a hand, and Vantis slapped it into his palm. The fae examined it, unfamiliar with this orientation of words. "And this is...?"

"It's an Executioners' copy of the Guide to Fairies! I read through as much as I could, especially on those baobhan sith creatures! There's even a section on mountain trolls like you!" Vantis explained as Adrian flipped through it. A clearly talented artist inked the ethereal images gracing each entry, including the vicious form of a terrible mountain troll. He couldn't help but snort.

"Cute," he grunted, not willing to admit that he couldn't read a lick of it. He slapped it shut with a single hand, giving it back to the boy.

Vantis held it with glittering eyes. "As long as I have this, we'll never be in the dark!" The troll scoffed, certainly not sold on such an idea. The boy frowned. "Come on, father! Don't you want to see mother too? Doesn't some part of you miss her?" Adrian grimaced. The burning queasy feeling in his gut made him wrap his hands around his stomach. "Plus, she's in the center of a city that has all sorts of protections against fae. Some legends say that King Alavantus planted it on top of a conquered fairy mound! I'll be safer there than out here in the open!"

The troll growled, "Oh really? So you just waltz straight through a fae-slaying city with a troll bodyguard? Brilliant. Truly awe-inspiring."

Vantis glared. "Look, I could be taken at any moment now, father. I at least want to *try* following my greatest dream..." Adrian stared at the boy, his face emotionless.

I went to war for a dream... I lost my life for a dream, twice... but I gained a new one from those dreams... I found my family again.

The man sighed, resting his talons on his hips as he turned away. His ebony hair billowed like a silken curtain in the late night breeze. "I cannot do anything unless it is by your word alone. What you decide, is for you to tell me," he declared, his elegant, powerful voice barely above a whisper. Vantis blinked, looking down at the book and the letter. The boy thought long and hard.

This is stupid... but I want this. I need to see her. I need to thank her... for giving me to Wren and Harris. To my true family. To the right place to find my father.

And maybe... father will love her again...

The young lord cleared his throat, setting the book away. On que, the troll shifted slightly, gazing upon him with those unnerving eyes as he awaited orders.

"I command you to travel with me and protect me on a journey to the gates of the great city of Alavantus. You will do what you believe is best for my survival, and ensure that I make it to the city alive. Nothing you do will be in opposition to this goal, including telling Wren and Harris. In exchange for this, I declare that any demands or terms of your promise to me after this request are rendered null and void. You will be free of this deal forever," the boy demanded evenly.

The troll felt a presence leave him as he let out a shaking breath, rubbing his neck. "Your final wish is my command, young lord." The fae deeply bowed, making the teenager flinch. "And now that's out of the way, how long have you been reciting that command within the depths of your chambers?" he asked with a smirk.

"Longer than I wanna admit..." Vantis sighed, letting his shoulders sag. He gazed out over the decorations for the Harvest Festival, savoring every last memory he had. It truly was an exciting one this year. "But we need to get to bed. I wanna leave before Wren and Harris find out. Wren's going to be helping some of the villagers take down the garlands in the center of town."

"Hmph. I suppose we will need to take Whisper as well?" the troll grunted, starting to turn towards the house. The child followed close behind.

"Yeah, she's fast and strong. I doubt anyone would want to mess with us when we have her. I'll just have to make sure I've got everything together before we leave," the boy explained, pausing at the door.

"Very well then, when Wren leaves... that is when we will act," Adrian said with a nod.

Vantis was shaking with energy now, endless thoughts running through his head as he opened the door into the main foyer. He raced up the stairs and launched himself into his room, already loading up a bag with supplies. This left Adrian alone in the pale moonlit hall. The man sighed, closing the door softly behind him.

He didn't like this. No, he hated this plan. He had just gotten Wren and Harris back, he'd just got his answers from Old Dusk, he'd just found his home... and now he would have to leave it all behind to chase after the ghost of a person that he seemed to love so dearly. The familiar burning pain filled his intestines, making him flinch. As he trudged past the reading room, he saw the slack-jawed form of Harris, loudly snoring on the couch. His cheeks were visibly flushed, even under so little light. The troll smiled for a moment before continuing.

"Adrian..."

Her unclear voice wove through his thoughts, making the beast clutch at his skull with a whimper. He staggered to the top of the steps and made his way towards his room, closing the door with his foot. A wave of desire filled his organs with a queasiness that made the man want to throw up.

"I love you, Adrian..."

The man wheezed, wiping at his drooling fangs as he tettered over to the bed. He sat down, holding his stomach.

Her body was so soft, so wonderful. He loved her so much. Her hands caressed his skin, sending shivers up his spine.

A low growl exited those jaws, his body flopping uselessly to the side. The tightness was unbearable. He knew what needed to happen next. He reached down, his hands shaking. Soon, the pain melted into euphoria and he saw her eyes, for only the briefest of moments.

"You're no monster..." she whispered softly, laying against his chest. His heartbeat was heavy, no doubt lingering in that hazy instance of joy between them. She was smiling. He, even with his grotesque features, was smiling as well. He was done with war. He wanted to go home.

This memory was pleasant, a reminder of everything he fought for. For that beautiful woman. The only woman to...

Wren's smiling face flashed in his mind, the moment she said 'thank you' in the backyard. The moment they cooked dinner, cleaned the kitchen, went to his camp, danced at the festival. Each moment, each memory... with her at the center.

He frowned. That wasn't right. He belonged to another... didn't he? It *had* been thirteen years... Did his love move on? Did she find someone else to share those tender moments, that feeling of joy? The troll winced, turning in the bed to crawl under the sheets and cover himself. How dare he think like that. He belonged to her. "I belong to her," he muttered, softly repeating to himself.

Even as Adrian said that, even as he fell deep into sleep; Wren's face lingered, never once fading from that radiant expression.

Chapter 40

In the wee hours of the morning, Adrian crept into the reading room. His darting eyes spotted the shadowed form of Harris, resting quietly. The huntsman's aged snoring was nowhere to be found, putting the troll on edge. For a human, it would be impossible to hide from this outrider's keen ears. But Adrian was no human. His feet trod carefully, avoiding the loose floorboards with the expertise of a skilled bandit. In minutes, the fae was at the fireplace and the old man remained still. He glanced at the wall of glittering iron, a prickling of fear arcing up his spine. The man needed a weapon, one capable of slaying fae. A knife was not enough. He needed to stop the monsters before they even got close to the boy. For a moment, his eyes drifted over to Terminus, the ghastly blade calling to his fragmented memories. His hands clenched.

No. I can't wield that. It would paint a massive target on my back, not just for the fae... but those Executioners as well.

Deeper still, another thought tickled at his mind.

I don't deserve it, anyways.

Instead, his sapphire rings scanned around the forbidden weapon. Other implements rested proudly, some javelins, knives, and an arbalest. Perfectly content with the rate of fire from his current crossbow, he instead plucked some knives and bolts from the wall, adding them to the belt strapped around his waist. While doing so, he saw a beckoning glare from a weapon above them. There, perched at the highest point, was a glaive, crafted with the finest dark wood. It was accented with verdigris copper feathers and engravings, all terminating at a curved steel tip that shone like a fang.

Ah, that will do.

His talons reached up and lifted the haft off of the hooks, gingerly drawing the heavy polearm down to his face. His skin prickled fearfully being so close to such a devilish edge, the scent of oil emanating from the blade's surface. The weight felt right in his claws, enough for him to settle it upon his back with a javelin sheath.

As he confidently made his way out, he cast a final wistful glance towards the sleeping man. He was going to betray Wren and Harris once more. The fae was going to whisk the boy away to lands far away, at the mercy of the elements. All for one stupid child's dream of satisfaction. He wanted to call out, to grasp that man by his shoulders, and tell him what Vantis was going to do. He didn't want to leave. He wanted to stay home.

But at the end of the day, Adrian had made a deal. And with this one, he could not inhibit his quest, even with a warning. It would only make things more complicated. Further still, this would be the last time Vantis could take his freedoms away. He could do as he wished. The troll would not sabotage that. So instead of saying anything, the sullen man turned and continued down the hall, letting the hunter rest easy. A part of him couldn't help but give everything one last look, as if he would never see it all again. Hell, that could very well be the case. He was going out of his element, into the heart of enemy territory.

An image of that scarred young man flashed before him, a horrifying snarl of fury upon his regal features.

Adrian didn't know where that man, Tobias, laid. And honestly, he didn't want to know. Solania was a big country, perhaps he was far away. Even so, his mind lingered upon that dreadful image, long enough to make the hair on the back of his neck rise.

Adrian ascended the stairs, gathering the last of his weapons from his bedroom before closing the door behind him. He would have to finish mother's book later. The troll's fur cloak drifted behind him heavily like a chain, pulling him the further he went. The fae's eyes laid upon Wren's door as he passed, fully aware she wasn't in it. She was down in the village, helping the others clean up the fall festival. He would not get a chance to say goodbye, even if he wanted to. His frown deepened. The shadows grew deeper as he continued down that forlorn hall. Vantis opened the door to greet him, laden with a bulging side bag and his bow slung behind his back. He appeared to have changed his fanciful clothes for more modest hunting garb, matching his father. There was a sparkle in his eye as he approached. "Ready!" he whispered.

"Are you certain?"

"Yup! Got the book, mum's letter, my journal, some pens, and plenty of rations!" the boy exclaimed.

"Very good," the man nodded, glancing over his shoulder down the hall. The first rays of dawn were peeking through the windows, leaving the forlorn shadows to fill the hall. Hesitation gripped him.

"What's wrong?" the boy inquired.

The troll blinked slowly. "Nothing, just considering logistics."

Vantis blinked. "O-oh. Okay then! We should probably hurry though, before uncle wakes up!" The lad began to tiptoe down the hall, his excitement barely stifled. Somber, the troll followed behind, dragging his feet all the while as they made their way to the back door. The young lord produced a key, inserting it into the lock gingerly before opening the door, cringing as the rusted hinges groaned. The troll merely sighed and shoved past, making his way out into the garden. Adrian couldn't help but wonder...

Where will she plant her gift next spring?

He frowned, turning towards the stables as the boy was already across the threshold. Whisper made a delighted whinny, nuzzling up to the boy as he cheerfully hugged her massive head. "D'aww! I missed you too, girl! We're going on an adventure! Aren't you excited?" Vantis explained.

Her inky, red-tinged eyes blinked slowly, seemingly not understanding the words, but instead feeding off of the excitement. Her rusted hooves dug at the earth below her, impatiently awaiting the door to open. Vantis did so, taking the time to attach some side bags as his father strapped a saddle upon her back proper. The monstrous steed only seemed more pleased now that her beloved rider had come with her favorite child, nuzzling him lovingly. Adrian cast a worried smile her way, scratching at her cheek before giving the straps a final check. "How long?" he asked plainly.

"Huh? What do you mean?" the teenager piped up, securing his satchel to his side.

"How long will it take to get to the capital?" the fae man grunted, applying the reins. Whisper's sharp fangs nibbled at the bridle briefly before letting the man finish his preparations.

"Hmm... well... according to this map..." the boy began, pulling a roll of parchment from his bag and unfurling it. His brow furrowed as he gazed upon the route scrawled onto it. "About two weeks. That's if we follow the main routes and don't have any detours."

Adrian grimaced before glancing back at the house. "Very well then. We shall keep the distractions and stops to a minimum." Vantis eagerly moved past his father, snagging the reins and gingerly pulling Whisper along. It only took a brief tug for her to understand what was happening, beginning to pick up the pace to the point she was dragging the lad along.

"Oy! Whisper! Haha! Relax!" the lad giggled. Adrian trailed behind, absentmindedly closing the gate behind him and locking up the stables. His eyes were distant, pained. Vantis was already unlocking the gate to the village proper, Whisper stomping at the ground in annoyance.

The troll approached his side. This was his last chance. "Are you sure about this?" he questioned.

The boy gave him a quizzical look. "Yeah? Of course I am! You want answers too, don't you?"

The fae man hesitated, almost biting his tongue before answering. "I suppose so..."

After three years of mental torture, meeting his son, turning into this amalgamation of man and fae, living with his friends, and bearing witness to so many painful and wonderful memories... He couldn't deny the satisfaction of finality. Knowing who he made this child with would be the last major piece. Hell, it could unlock the rest of his sheltered memories.

Or kill me.

He shuddered. At the end of the day, he would never know unless he followed this boy. He was no troll... and yet... no man. He was *nothing*. But as long as he kept this witless worm alive, he could perhaps learn to be *something*. With all these memories, all of his thoughts, then he could decide who he wanted to be. He could decide what the name Adrian Lionel meant.

The fae sighed, helping the lad up onto the gargantuan beast. Whisper shuffled uneasily, awaiting her second rider. While nervous at first, he leapt onto the saddle with ease, the motion as routine as sharpening a blade. He gripped the reins in his gloved talons, tossing away his final screaming thoughts of doubt. This was it. No turning back.